JUMP PAY

RICK SHELLEY

ACE BOOKS, NEW YORK

This book is an Ace original edition,
and has never been previously published.

JUMP PAY

An Ace Book / published by arrangement with
Bill Fawcett & Associates

Ace edition / August 1995

All rights reserved.
Copyright © 1995 by Bill Fawcett & Associates.
Cover art by Stephen Gardner.
This book may not be reproduced in whole or in part,
by mimeograph or any other means, without permission.
For information address: The Berkley Publishing Group,
200 Madison Avenue, New York, NY 10016.

ISBN: 0-441-00230-7

ACE®
Ace Books are published by The Berkley Publishing Group,
200 Madison Avenue, New York, NY 10016.
ACE and the "A" design are trademarks
belonging to Charter Communications, Inc.

PRINTED IN THE UNITED STATES OF AMERICA

10 9 8 7 6 5 4 3 2 1

MEET THE FIGHTERS
OF
THE LUCKY 13TH

COLONEL STOSSEN is the only commanding officer the Lucky 13th has ever had. He doesn't always like what he has to ask his men to do, but he always knows they'll do it—or die trying.

LIEUTENANT COLONEL DEZO PARKS has been the executive officer of the 13th ever since his predecessor was killed by an enemy tank. He is next in line for command of the unit—if the invasion leaves him anything to take command of.

SERGEANT JOE BAERCLAU has been a soldier for a quarter of his life, in some of the heaviest action of the war. He is unsurpassed at hand-to-hand combat despite his small stature. And when his eyes begin to "smolder," his men will follow him anywhere.

CORPORAL MORT JAIFFER, the "old man" of his squad, always wears a cap to cover his growing bald spot. He doesn't trust the new antigrav jump belts, but if they take him into the action, he'll take his chances with them.

PRIVATE MAL UNDERWOOD is the only rookie in his squad, big and young and untested in combat. He is about to find out what the rest of the unit knows all too well—the truth about war.

Ace Books by Rick Shelley

UNTIL RELIEVED
SIDE SHOW
JUMP PAY

PROLOGUE

There was nothing to distinguish this room from more than a dozen identical rooms on worlds scattered around the star systems of the Terran Cluster controlled by the Accord of Free Worlds. As always, even the name of the planet on which the room was located was classified.

The circular chamber and its furnishings were a uniform pearl-gray, giving the place a nebulous quality in soft lighting. The junctions of walls, ceiling, and floor were hard to distinguish. In the center of the room there was a large circular conference table, with each place having its own compsole and monitor. The space above the center of the table normally displayed a spherical star-field projection, three meters in diameter. Now, however, it displayed a planetary globe. The half-dozen men in the room were standing together on one side of the globe.

Only one of those men could have identified the world on display at a glance prior to the start of this briefing. There was nothing particularly remarkable about the world that could be seen on a projection of this scale. There were two continental landmasses, remarkably similar in outline (rather like a pair of lima beans) on opposite sides of the world. Each continent had one end extending just across the equator, one from the northern hemisphere, the other from the southern. The "convex" side of each "bean" was to the northwest. The other extremes of the continents were both near 80 degrees of latitude, north and south respectively. A "bridge" of islands seemed to connect the tropical ends of the two continents, a loose chain extending across the 2900 kilometers separating their nearest points— more than 1200 small islands in three main archipelagoes. The distances between islands varied from less than one kilometer to more than 300. The islands varied in size from less than a single square kilometer to areas slightly over 8000 square kilometers.

"The world is Tamkailo," Encho Mizatle, the Accord's minister for defense, started. He took a couple of steps away from the other men in the room, to the side and slightly closer to the globe. The projection was rotating so that Tamkailo went through a complete "day" in four minutes. Encho stared at the world for a moment, until a whisper behind him caught his attention. He half turned toward the others again.

"Yes," he said, "a Schlinal world." He paused long enough for two deliberate blinks. In between, his eyes ranged across the faces of the other five men. "An *important* Schlinal world." He took a deep breath and turned to stare at the image of Tamkailo again.

"A fair approximation of Hell, in human terms," he said. "To put it in terms some of you might be able to relate to, think of it as Venus about twelve hundred years into the terraforming project there." That would have been about two thousand years before this meeting. Mizatle had been an academic before gravitating toward politics. His field had been the history of mankind's expansion away from Earth, primarily the esoterica of the earliest period. It tickled his vanity to know things that perhaps no more than a hundred people in all the settled reaches of the galaxy might

even guess ... or care about. "The chain of islands between the two continents gives a misleading impression.
The tropical zone is, to date, virtually impossible for humans. At least without extensive protective gear and support services that are beyond the reach of a field army on
campaign." He stopped the globe's rotation so that the
chain of islands was in the center of the side facing the
group.

"The *average* daily high temperature in the tropic zone
is forty-seven degrees Celsius, with extremes of fifty-eight
known. The actual record is almost certainly several degrees above that. Combined with Tamkailo's atmosphere,
it makes the tropics off limits to humans without special
gear except at night, when the temperatures do occasionally
drop near normal human body temperature. Briefly."

"Too much carbon dioxide and too little oxygen, isn't
it?" Major General Kleffer Dacik asked.

Mizatle nodded. "The nitrogen component of Tamkailo's atmosphere is almost identical with Earth's, but the
percentage of oxygen is one point three percent less, and
most of that is carbon dioxide. Additionally, the normal
surface air pressure is moderately high in comparison to
most settled worlds. In the more temperate zones of
Tamkailo the atmospheric differences are ... marginally
acceptable. But not in what are, for humans, superheated
conditions. Especially if those humans must be active. Even
the Hegemony has, mostly, left the tropics and subtropics
alone, doing no more than establishing minimal communications relay facilities there."

Mizatle's cough was affectation.

"Obviously, Tamkailo would not be a very inviting
world for most settlers. The native life forms are of no use
to humans, and the plants and animals we are accustomed
to do not, as a rule, thrive on the world. Tamkailo does
have an abundance of certain metal ores which lend themselves to industrial exploitation. The Hegemony has always
used Tamkailo for that, and for some minor industrial
purposes. A minimal population, drawn from penal exiles
and their families, provides a continuing labor pool. Now,

however, the Schlinal warlords have found another use for the habitable zones of the northern and southern extremities. They have turned the world into an arsenal. In fact, certain Schlinal communiqués have taken to referring to the world as Arsenal, capital A. Intelligence has taken six months to confirm that Arsenal and Tamkailo are, indeed, the same world." He did not say anything about *how* military intelligence had managed to intercept and decode enough Schlinal communications to analyze, and none of the men in the room were incautious enough to ask.

"It has become a collection point for military matériel, munitions, and other equipment. There has always been a military garrison on the world, but that has been dramatically increased of late. We suspect that the new troops are staging on Tamkailo for another offensive against the Accord." Mizatle permitted himself a sour chuckle. "Even before the recent arrivals, the number of Hegemony troops outnumbered the, ah, civilian population by a factor of three to two."

"We're going after this world?" General Dacik asked when Mizatle did not continue immediately. It seemed a safe guess.

Mizatle nodded absentmindedly. "The buildup has been slow," he said. "We *think* that is because they are having difficulties putting together the men and matériel for a new push into Accord space. Fighting both us and the Dogel Worlds has proved trying for the Hegemony." None of the others saw Mizatle's thin smile. He was staring at the projection of Tamkailo again. "I think they have always made the mistake of dismissing our potential. And now the Schlinal industrial sector is having great difficulty avoiding shortages. If we can take Tamkailo, or at least destroy the bulk of the munitions there, we will buy the Accord a lot of time. It might even be enough to make the Hegemons seek peace with us, so that they can concentrate on what they see as the greater threat to their security; the Dogel Worlds. That would give us a chance to liberate the Accord worlds that the Doges have taken."

While Mizatle was talking, General Dacik had taken out

a pocket compsole and entered a request for data on Tamkailo. He scanned the first screens quickly, with growing dismay. When he looked up from his compsole, he found that the defense minister had turned around again and was staring at him.

"A difficult objective, Minister," Dacik said.

Mizatle nodded again. "P and I have been working on this for several months, General." P and I: Planning and Intelligence. "They have come up with several possibilities. You will be commander in chief for this mission. The final selection will be left to you. We're not so much interested in capturing the world as we are in destroying munitions and military assets. Tamkailo is too far inside Schlinal space, and far too marginal a world, for us to covet the real estate."

"We have a military briefing set up for you, Kleffer," General Hobarth, the chief of Accord P&I, said. "My staff is at your disposal."

Dacik looked around. Everyone was staring at him now. "We'll give it our best," he said. He had very little choice.

CHAPTER 1

"Hey, Sarge. We really gotta use these things?" Corporal Mort Jaiffer held up the antigrav belt as Joe Baerclau walked into the troop compartment. Even sitting on his bunk on the transport ship, Mort wore a soft cap. Of late, he had been doing everything he could to conceal the growing bald spot on his crown. Some of the other men in the platoon joked that the only time they saw Mort without a hat or helmet on was in the shower. Hair regeneration therapy was not a standard military treatment . . . unless the hair loss was the result of a wound suffered in the line of duty.

"Unless you've learned to flap your arms fast enough to fly on your own," the platoon sergeant replied.

"Damned things are dangerous," Mort said.

"That's our business, Professor," Baerclau reminded him.

"We did too good a job on Jordan, I guess," Mort said. "If we hadn't brought those scientists out of that place, we wouldn't be in this position."

This would be the first time that the new, improved antigrav belts would be used in an actual combat situation. And since the 13th Spaceborne Assault Team had been responsible for rescuing the researchers who had made the new belts possible, the 13th had the somewhat dubious honor of being the first Accord combat unit to be fully equipped with the new devices. Better batteries, built-in thermal rechargers (human body heat could give the batteries a full charge in four hours), and more reliable controls distinguished the new model from the old. The changes were so radical that the new system was identified as the Mark I Corey antigravity belt, rather than as the second iteration of the older Desperes belt.

"The alternatives weren't very appealing, as I recall," Joe said. He liked to egg "the Professor" on. Jaiffer wore the title with some legitimacy. He had been an associate professor before he joined the Accord Defense Force. He was an intellectual, but he was also an excellent soldier—a rare combination.

In a very quiet voice, so soft that Baerclau almost missed it, Mort said, "Sometimes, I think that the lucky ones were the guys who bought it early, first time out."

Joe pretended that he didn't hear. "You got your fire team squared away?" he asked.

"As squared away as we're going to get before we jump." Mort looked up from his bunk and met the sergeant's eyes. "Just philosophy," he said, lowering his voice again, "not foreboding."

"I hope so," Joe replied.

The entire twenty-nine-man second platoon of Echo Company was billeted in one compartment of the transport, stacked three high in the rows of bunks. There should have been thirty men, but the platoon still lacked an officer, a platoon leader. More than half of the platoons in the 13th's eight infantry companies were short platoon leaders.

Echo's 2nd platoon was much like any other. The line platoons were organized in four 7-man squads, with the platoon sergeant bringing the count to twenty-nine. Each squad was divided into two fire teams, the first with a sergeant and three privates, the second with a corporal (the assistant squad leader) and two privates.

Second platoon's first squad was also rather typical; the only difference between it and many of the other squads in the 13th was that, this time, it was going into combat with only one rookie, one man who had not seen combat before. The new man was Mal Underwood, from Bancroft. Mal was big and young—105 kilos big and 18 years young. The demand for replacements in the Accord's fifteen SATs had become such that Mal did not meet the SATs' original requirements. He was neither a combat veteran nor a veteran of at least a year in uniform before coming to the 13th. In the last nine months, since the Jordan campaign, most of the replacements coming into the SATs did not meet either of those criteria. But Mal Underwood had lived and worked with the squad for nearly seven months now, assigned to its second fire team. He had been one of the first replacements to reach the 13th after its return from the previous campaign.

Sergeant Ezra Frain was the squad leader, Mort Jaiffer his assistant. Al Bergon, squad medic; Phil "Pit" Tymphe, and Olly Wytten completed the first fire team. Wiz Mackey was the remaining man in the second fire team. Tymphe and Wytten had joined the unit before its last campaign, the liberation of Jordan. The rest had been together even longer, since before the liberation of Porter—part of the first Accord counteroffensive of the war.

Joe Baerclau walked on through the compartment, stopping occasionally to speak with various men. In another few hours, they would be going into combat. For most of them, it would be "again." The waiting never got easy. The rookies had fears of the unknown. The veterans had other fears. They knew what to expect. Knowledge could be worse than imagination.

Before he left the troop bay, Joe rapped on the bulkhead to get everyone's attention. In his "drill field" voice, he announced, "Breakfast is at oh-three-forty-five hours ship's time. Final briefing will be forty-five minutes later. You get to sleep in the next thirty seconds, you can still catch eight hours. Get it while you can.''

It was not the largest invasion fleet that the Accord of Free Worlds had assembled in this its first war. In the two years since the Accord had started its attempts to liberate the worlds captured by the Schlinal Hegemony, there had been too many fleets assembled, too many ships—and men—lost. There were also other missions in progress at present, scattered across a million cubic light-years of space. Men and matériel had been brought together from wherever they could be found. Some of the units were significantly short in manpower. Critical supplies—primarily munitions and food—were deemed adequate, but there were no abundances, not enough of anything to make any commander or quartermaster content.

But the Hegemons had taken severe losses as well, and they had been fighting for more than a generation, first only against the Dogel Worlds, but more recently also against the Accord. The Schlinal warlords were having increasing difficulty meeting the demands of carrying on simultaneous wars—separate wars, because the Accord and the Doges were not allies. The Doges had also taken Accord planets. The day of reckoning for that had not yet come.

The fleet dispatched to take the Schlinal arsenal world of Tamkailo was still not insignificant. The ships carried three of the Accord's fifteen spaceborne assault teams, elite troops. The 5th, 8th, and 13th SATs had all seen hard combat before. If only the 13th was near full strength now, the other two were still significant units. Each of the SATs had combat engineering units assigned to them for this mission—one battalion split three ways. An entire Wasp air wing was also part of this invasion force, in addition to the Wasp squadrons assigned to each of the SATs. Two light infantry regiments and a half dozen Special Intelligence teams rounded out the strike force.

Ten thousand three hundred men to capture a world.

•   •   •

Drop Day had already begun for Colonel Van Stossen and his senior staff officers. Although each would make a pretense of retiring for a few hours before the jump, none would succeed in sleeping.

Van Stossen had commanded the 13th since its inception, the first man slotted in its table of organization. It was, however, unlikely that he would remain in command much longer. One of the most senior colonels in the ADF, he was due for promotion to brigadier . . . if he survived this campaign. If and when that promotion came, he would be bumped up, out of the 13th, unless the TO was changed to make the top slot a flag command.

Lieutenant Colonel Dezo Parks was the executive officer. His promotion to light colonel had come several months before, but he had been the 13th's exec since Porter, when his predecessor was crushed under the treads of a Schlinal Nova tank. That loss had also catapulted Major Teu Ingels from command of Echo Company into the slot Parks had vacated, as operations officer.

Major Bal Kenneck, intelligence; Major Goz (Goose) Tarkel, air wing commander; and Major Henry (Hank) Norwich, Havoc self-propelled artillery commander, completed the colonel's staff. As most of the 13th prepared to get what sleep it could during their last ''night'' aboard ship, Stossen and his staff went over battle plans for what might have been the hundredth time since embarking above Albion, the 13th's garrison world.

A 3-D display above the conference table in the room adjoining Colonel Stossen's cabin stepped through the plans. The war-gaming computers had run hundreds of thousands of simulations, using every conceivable variation of possibilities. Even under ''ideal'' (for the Accord) conditions, the battle plan worked only one time in seven. None of the men sitting around this table expected anything near the ideal once they finally reached Tamkailo.

''I'd bet that no army in history has ever pulled off a plan one-tenth as harebrained as this one,'' Bal Kenneck said.

''The other options were worse,'' Stossen said. General

Dacik had explained the main variants of those other options to his commanders before hitting them with the plan that he had finally chosen.

"Within an hour after we hit air, the whole thing's going to be wrecked," Teu Ingels said. "We'll be playing it by ear from then on."

"And deaf," Kenneck mumbled. Louder, he said, "The first small deviation will throw everything off schedule. There's simply no way to run a campaign this size on split-second timing."

"Making one unit do the work of three," Dezo Parks said. "It's not the first time we've had to do more than our share of the work."

"The 13th isn't what it was a year ago," Kenneck shot back. "And it's not just us. It's all of the units. We're trying to take Tamkailo with far too few assets. We've got no business staging this invasion without sufficient forces to do the job."

"Regardless," Stossen said. "If we let the Hegemons make whatever invasion they're staging for, it'll be worse. That's the important thing this time, to inflict maximum damage on the enemy, no matter what the cost to us. We don't have to capture and *hold* Tamkailo. We only have to wreck their offensive capability to give the Accord time to get back to full strength. And if we do pull this off, it might be enough to end the fighting with Schline."

The playback of the battle plan ended and cycled back to start over, showing the initial deployment.

"So we improvise," Stossen said as the computer representations of landing craft started to descend into the atmosphere of the planet. "That's why we've been over all of this so many times, so we'll recognize where the trouble is and have a leg up on meeting whatever happens."

Whatever happens. Stossen closed his eyes for a moment. He held few illusions. It wouldn't be pretty. Twice in the past eighteen months he had led his men back from the brink of total destruction. He couldn't help thinking that it was too much to hope for to be able to do it a third time.

●   ●   ●

The dawn line was approaching the eastern shore of Tamkailo's southern continent when the invasion fleet disgorged the first landers and the Wasp fighters of the three SATs. The separate Wasp wing (the 17th Independent Air Wing) was held back for the moment. The SAT Wasps would have a vulnerable period. They might have to ground before their support vans could land to provide them with fresh batteries and replenish their munitions. During that critical phase, the rest of the Wasps would have to provide all of the air cover, over two continents.

On the far side of Tamkailo, the simultaneous landings on the other continent would take place as night was falling. Roughly a third of the invasion force would fight for a foothold there while the rest attempted to quickly overpower the defenses of the main Schlinal base on the southern continent.

Navy chaplains stood by in the passageways leading to the shuttle hangars. There had been services just minutes before, during breakfast, but there were always last-minute words of comfort to give. Once inside the landers, the men had only their own thoughts, and few found comfort there.

The shuttles carrying the 13th's infantry companies were the first to leave the transports. The 13th's mudders would be first down. Their immediate job would be to secure landing zones for the rest of the initial drop team at Site Alpha—the 8th SAT, the 97th Light Infantry Regiment, the 17th Independent Air Wing, the Wasp support vans, and the Havoc artillery and their support units. The 5th SAT and the 34th LIR would be attacking on the other side of the world.

"Remember who you're supposed to key on," Joe Baerclau said over his platoon channel. Once in the shuttles, the men had all pulled down the visors of their combat helmets. The helmets' radio links were more dependable than any other sort of communication, even with the squads all bunched together on the lander's benches.

It wasn't just because of the crowded conditions that no one moved much. Weighted down with forty kilograms of gear, no one *wanted* to move. Any movement took energy while the shuttles were attached to the transport—still within its artificial gravity field. Once the shuttles separated and the men were treated to near-zero gravity, they still wouldn't move around much. Each man had private thoughts to think.

Joe took several deep breaths and closed his eyes as the lander moved away from the ship. The seat belt pulled at his middle as the shuttle accelerated toward Tamkailo and the drop zone. Joe could feel his nerves tightening up. His stomach cramped. He had to struggle to keep from clenching his teeth. Nerves, not fear: it never got easy. His arms rested on his knees; he clutched his Armanoc wire carbine—too tightly—in both hands.

Just like a drill, he told himself. Sometimes that worked. This wasn't one of those times. Joe and his men had made three practice drops using the new antigrav belts. They had attended classes and watched demonstrations first. Proper use of the controls had been drilled into everyone as fully as everything else was. The belts were just another piece of equipment. Joe was still nervous about them. As was Mort and, probably, every other man about to drop into combat on nothing but a web belt, leg straps, shoulder straps, two small AG motors, and two equally small batteries. If the motors, batteries, or gyroscopic stabilizers failed. . . . No one had been *killed* on any of the practice jumps, but there had been plenty of minor injuries, ankles or knees strained or sprained, a couple of broken bones.

And there had been no enemy fire to complicate the practice jumps.

Joe opened his eyes and looked around. Most of the men were looking at the deck between their feet. Joe wasn't monitoring any of the squad channels, but he could imagine squad leaders talking to their men. He had given enough of those talks himself in the past. Pep talks.

Platoon sergeants weren't supposed to need pep talks, but Joe wouldn't have minded one at the moment, anything to keep him from thinking about what the next minutes and hours might bring. He had seen more than his share of combat, he thought. So far, he had been lucky. He had never been seriously injured—nothing that couldn't be repaired quickly, in the field, without a long stint in a trauma tube.

But he had seen too many comrades killed.

"Five minutes until drop," Joe announced over his platoon channel, relaying the information that First Sergeant Izzy Walker had just given him. "Check the gauges on your drop belts." Joe looked around, mostly to the squad leaders, making certain that they were checking themselves as well as their men. Then he checked his own gear.

"Three minutes. Check weapons." For most of the platoon, that meant an Armanoc wire carbine that fired small lengths of collapsed uranium wire from a twenty-meter spool. A spool of wire was good for twenty seconds of continuous fire—a meter per second in centimeter-long snips. The rifle's power pack would last for two hours of use. Against body armor, the zipper was reliably lethal only at ranges up to about 80 meters, sufficient for most combat requirements. At ranges greater than that, up to about 150 meters, wire could only be effective if it hit the places where soldiers weren't armored, or where the net armor had become weakened by use. Beyond 150 meters, the Armanoc was no more useful than an office stapler. One man each in second and fourth squads had sniper rifles, Dupuy rocket-assisted slug throwers. The Dupuy was known as the cough gun from the sound it made. The RA rifle had a flat trajectory and an accurate range of seven kilometers—for what little use *that* was in any practical circumstances.

Joe glanced around the troop bay again. In every previous combat landing, the shuttles had grounded. This time they wouldn't. The assault plan called for the landers to go no lower than three hundred meters. At that height, the four doors would be opened and the men would jump. The 13th's infantry was jumping in on antigrav belts. The rest of the invasion force would ride their shuttles all of the way in.

"On your feet!" the jumpmaster called. "Stand in the doors."

Each squad knew which door it would jump from. Joe moved with first squad. He would be the first man out the rear left exit of the shuttle.

"Forty-five seconds," the jumpmaster warned. The shuttle was braking rapidly. The men braced against one another and hung on to rails placed head-high along the aisles.

"Thirty seconds." To men carrying forty kilos of gear the extra gee-load of braking was almost intolerable. Joe's legs felt as if they had suddenly swollen to the size of elephant legs, and as if the muscles had turned to slack rubber bands. He blinked as his vision started to dim.

Then the load was gone. The shuttle eased off and the gee-load dropped to no more than 1.5. Joe took a deep breath.

"Ten seconds . . . nine . . . "

Joe's attention shifted to the hatch in front of him, the droning countdown fading from his hearing. For those few seconds, Joe forgot all about the other men in the shuttle with him. He felt encapsulated in a pocket universe that consisted only of himself and that gray door no more than twenty centimeters in front of his eyes.

As the hatch sprang open and the wind passing by created a partial vacuum, Joe leapt outward before the jumpmaster's final word—"Jump!"—was fully spoken. The wind caught Joe and pulled him away from the shuttle and the other men hurtling through the hatch.

Tamkailo lay below.

CHAPTER 2

Captain Zel Paitcher was more than a little nervous about this combat mission as commander of the 13th's Blue Flight. It was his third campaign, but he was going in with nothing but rookies behind him, seven pilots who had never seen combat, none with more than thirteen months in uniform or two hundred hours in the cockpit of a Wasp. The other three pilots of Blue Flight who had survived the liberation of Jordan had all been transferred to serve as part of the cadre for a new fighter wing—still in training.

Gerry Easton was Zel's wingman, Blue two. Ewell "Pitcher" Marmon and Tod Corbel were Blue three and four. Frank Verannen and "Halfmoon" Sawyer were five and six. The flight's final pairing consisted of Ilsen Kwillen and Will Tarkel—Kwill and Will to the rest of the squadron. Tarkel was the nephew of the 13th's air wing commander, Goz Tarkel. The Goose made no demands, showed no undue preference for his brother's son. Will had to get by on his own talents. There was no real alternative for a fighter pilot. The enemy would give no latitude to nepotism.

"Just keep your heads," Zel said over the flight's radio channel. "Keep the formation tight and don't panic." Command had made Zel feel at least a decade older than his twenty-one years. Combat had ended his youth. Command had seemingly propelled him to a premature middle age. The promotion to captain that had followed the Jordan campaign (and the death of Slee Reston, his best friend and the former commander of Blue Flight) had been a hollow achievement. Zel would have turned it down if he could have. He couldn't look at the silver insignia without remembering Slee and the way his Wasp had exploded.

Blue Flight was in a power dive, accelerating toward the ground. They had been launched from their transports 180 kilometers up. But they were in air now. The Schlinal satellite network had been knocked out minutes before in a coordinated attack around Tamkailo. The inevitable confusion to the enemy's command, control, and intelligence gave the invaders a slight edge during the early minutes—or even hours—of an attack.

Zel's eyes flicked across his head-up display and the two monitors below it. There were no enemy fighters in the air yet, and the Wasp's target acquisition systems had detected no enemy radar. That meant that there were no major defensive systems tracking the fighters. Yet. The Wasps were virtually invisible to any radar. And in the dark they were invisible to almost anything that might be looking at them, even highly trained human eyes.

The Wasps were too high for them to see pilots racing toward their Boem fighters on the ground. The sudden loss of communications with all of their orbiting satellites would demand a Schlinal fighter scramble, if only until some nonmalignant reason could be found for the sudden silence. Arsenal. The Schlinal warlords knew that they had to defend the stockpiles of munitions and the regiments of troops being marshaled there. Even though it was—relatively—far from any Accord or Dogel system.

The airfield was Blue Flight's initial target. The 13th's other two flights, and the 8th's air wing, had other tactical targets in and around the initial drop zone. The more enemy fighters Blue Flight could destroy on the ground, the fewer they would have to worry about in the air.

The Wasps were diving at 3.5 gees, their antigrav engines adding to rather than subtracting from Tamkailo's own gravity. The flight suits of the pilots had inflated to offset the effects of the gee-load, restricting movement. But the Wasp had been designed to need only slight movements by its pilot. A high gee dive, or climb, was unlikely to greatly inconvenience a pilot—as long as he kept his head. The planes *could* achieve greater acceleration than a human body could take.

"Start marking your targets," Zel said, flipping on his own TA systems.

They should have infantrymen guarding the airfield, Zel thought. Maybe other antiaircraft defenses. Infantrymen would have shoulder-operated missiles available. Those could be as deadly to a Wasp—or a shuttle—as a Boem's rockets. And there would likely be no warning of a TA system locking on first. Infantry rocket launchers depended on the eyesight of the man firing them for initial target acquisition. Then the rocket's television guidance system would take over, once it had been "shown" the target.

This should be the easiest run of the campaign, Zel reminded himself as his TA system locked on to its first two targets. The audible double click came just as the red lights on the head-up display went from blinking to solid. Later, there would never be this level of surprise. The enemy would know that the Accord was on the planet. They would be waiting.

He launched his first two rockets, and the TA system immediately locked on to two more Boems. Near the bottom of his dive, Zel could finally see men running around below, heading for their planes, or for cover. He launched the second pair of rockets and reversed the thrust on his antigrav drives, pulling up, the Wasp straining his ability to handle the gee-load.

"Start listening to your own warnings," he muttered through clenched teeth as he came close to graying out.

"Watch your damn controls."

He tilted the Wasp on its side and accelerated "up," parallel to the ground. Gerry Easton struggled to keep station on his wing. Blue Two had only launched one pair of missiles. He was still new to this business.

"You're doing fine, Gerry," Zel said over a private link. "Take a deep breath and let it out slowly."

There was a startled "Huh?" over the radio, and then the sounds of that deep breath. "What are you, psychic?" Easton asked after he had exhaled.

"I remember my own first time," Zel said. While he talked, he kept his eyes moving, watching his displays and what he could see on the ground. The routine was easy now, but the first time Zel had tried so hard to keep track of everything going on around him that there was no time to *do* anything.

On their first pass, Blue Flight had accounted for a dozen enemy fighters. It was a good tally, but Zel could see at least twice that number of undamaged fighters on the ground. And pilots had reached most of those.

Zel switched to the channel that linked him to his entire flight. "One more quick pass before they get those buzzards in the air," he said as he flipped his own Wasp around. "Then it's cat-and-mouse time."

Once a pilot got into his Boem, he would need only twenty seconds to strap in and another ten seconds to get his fighter in the air. They would bypass preflight checklists. It would be systems on and lift off, without waiting for the engines to warm up. In theory, computerized control systems should spot any problem in less than a second after the switches were thrown, far more rapidly than any human pilot could start to lift the plane off of the ground. The automatics would override the pilot, cutting power.

Zel saw no indication that any of these Boems were being switched back off. But then, he didn't have time to waste on fantasy. The Boems might still outnumber his Wasps three to one if this last ground attack didn't seriously cut into their numbers. Once the Boems were active, even before they got off of the ground, they were no longer

totally defenseless. Most of the Schlinal pilots immediately
activated electronic countermeasures.

The airfield was still a dangerous place for the Boems.
The incoming missiles were fired from too near to go wandering off into the sky because ECM measures confused
their targeting computers. All of the rockets hit something—planes, buildings, or the ground. Antigrav fighters
neither needed nor used a runway. The only level surface
they needed was enough for their landing skids to sit on,
and they had a lot of tolerance. Craters in the airfield
weren't even a nuisance. Nor were wrecked planes or other
debris.

"Here they come," Zel warned as he saw the first Boem
grow a shadow as it lifted off. That fighter spun on its
vertical axis, ready to directly challenge the invaders.

Zel was more than happy to take the challenge. He was
too close to risk a missile so he switched to his forward
cannons, a gatling gun arrangement of five 25-mm barrels,
each capable of spewing sixty hypersonic slugs per second,
fragmentation or—a new addition—armor-piercing rounds
for air-to-air combat. The older fragmentation projectiles
each separated into five heavy metal slivers in flight.
Though those rounds were murderous against ground
troops, they had proved less than lethal in a dogfight, and
combat in the air still did get very close sometimes. For
this flight, both the forward and rear cannons were loaded
with a 60–40 mix, AP to frag. The range was less than 120
meters when Zel hit the trigger. A four-second burst exploded the Boem. Shrapnel dinged off of Zel's Wasp as he
flew through the blast.

That was the last easy kill of the fight. The surviving
Boems were all in the air, their pilots ready to fight back.

Blue five was hit by two missiles. The rockets exploded
simultaneously, engulfing the Wasp in a dirty fireball. Remarkably, Verannen's escape pod shot clear of the mael-
strom. There was no response from Frank to Zel's call, but
the pod's parachute deployed and it settled toward the
ground, drifting clear of the air battle and the Schlinal airfield below it.

Zel reported the loss and the possibility that the pilot might have survived. If there was a chance, a rescue mission would be attempted as soon as there were Accord forces on the ground who could do the job.

The air fight went on.

It was not at all like a parachute jump. A chute provided both visible comfort and cause for concern. When you saw the sheet open above you, you knew that there was *something* up there slowing your descent, making it possible to drop several hundred meters and survive. But, in combat, it also provided an immense target for enemy gunners, an arrival announcement that could be seen for kilometers around.

Antigrav belts provided no additional target, but there was no sense of reassurance either. To the eye, you were simply falling, with nothing to prevent you from ending up crushed on the surface. The silence added to the eeriness. There was little sense of anything but the whisper of air. Despite the training, the assurances of experts, and practice jumps, Joe could not escape the sensation of falling out of control.

Joe looked around at the hundreds of men "falling" with him. The Corey belts had gyroscopic stabilizers, so the men were all falling feet first toward the ground. The formation wasn't nearly as precise as that of a drill team on the parade ground, but the men weren't nearly as scattered as they might have been. No one was plummeting out of control. That meant that there were no defective units—and that no one had panicked so much that they couldn't control their descent.

Left hand on belt controls. Right hand on weapon. A lanyard made certain that no one would lose his weapon on the jump. At worst, it might dangle a few centimeters out of reach.

The jump plan was, relatively, simple. The men of the 13th were to free-fall until they reached 150 meters, with their belts on the lowest setting, partially to keep the speed of descent from getting too high but mostly to keep heads up and feet down. A buzzer in the helmet warned the wearer when it was time to increase power to the antigrav units, one click at a time. Save most of the deceleration for the last three or four seconds of the drop. If you worked it properly, you would hit the ground with hardly any jolt at all, ready to move forward, or to drop to the ground for cover—unless you misjudged your descent badly enough to run the batteries dry before you reached the ground. That had been a significant danger with the Desperes belts. That was why they had never been used in large-scale operations. But the greater power of the batteries in the new Corey model was expected to—almost—totally eliminate that hazard.

Once on the ground, the infantry of the 13th was to secure a landing zone for their heavy equipment and for the other units, the ones who were riding all of the way in on shuttles.

Echo Company's section of the drop zone was in a rocky waste area five kilometers west of the edge of the Schlinal base designated Site Alpha in the attack plans, one hundred kilometers north of the southernmost tip of Tamkailo's southern continent, near the east coast.

Joe Baerclau searched the ground around the drop zone as carefully as he could during the descent, looking for enemy soldiers or emplacements. Anything he could spot from the air might save him, and his men, when they landed. Although there were no firm numbers on how many Schlinal troops were stationed on Tamkailo, the estimates had ranged from twenty-five thousand to four times that. Even in a best case scenario, the Accord was going to be outnumbered five to two. Joe had never accepted best case scenarios. Reality always seemed to favor the opposite.

The best he could say for the drop zone was that it looked too rough for enemy armor to operate in it. From above, it looked as if coarse stone had been laid in a bed of cement. Using the ranging sights in his visor, Joe estimated that the rocks ran from forty centimeters to two meters in diameter, mostly with half to two-thirds embedded below the surface. The rocks covered an area perhaps twenty kilometers in diameter.

In the last hundred meters, Joe started adjusting the angle of his drop to set down on a low, relatively flat, space he had spotted. The belt was not infinitely adjustable. The direction of thrust could only be altered by five degrees from vertical. For a second, Joe tried spreading his arms to present more surface to the light breeze, working to get more lateral distance than he could with the belt alone. Not enough work had been done with the belts for there to be any "official" doctrine on that.

It worked well enough that Joe almost overshot the target he had set for himself. For the last second, he pulled himself almost into a ball, drawing up his legs and holding his arms close to his body. He worked the thrust of his belt, feathering in to a perfectly gentle landing. Hitting the ground was softer than stepping from one stair down to the next.

Joe's perfect landing was spoiled when his feet slid out from under him and he fell—heavily—on his ass. The rocks were covered by a thin mossy growth that was more slippery than water-covered ice. The fall knocked the breath from Joe's lungs. He banged the back of his helmet on the rock. The padding in his helmet was enough to prevent injury, but there were still a few seconds of confusion, enough time for virtually all of the first drop team to hit the ground. Nearly everyone fell, some with more force than Joe had.

"Watch it," he said, belatedly. "This moss is murder."

Joe didn't try to get to his feet. Standing up was the wrong posture for an infantryman in most cases anyway. He slid a little more as he rolled over onto his stomach, all of the way to the bottom of the slight depression. This stuff is going to be a real pain, he thought. At least there was no incoming fire yet, no apparent reaction to the landing.

"Talk to me," Joe said over his link to his squad leaders. He tried crawling on all fours, looking to get to the top of the depression. It was slow going. It was almost impossible to get any traction on the moss.

"Who greased the ground?" Ezra Frain asked. "How

the hell we supposed to move on this?"

"Carefully," Joe replied. "You have any jump casualties?"

There was only a short pause before Ezra said, "Nothing that'll slow anybody down. We've all got bruises, though."

"I've got one man with a badly twisted ankle," Sergeant Low Gerrent of second squad reported. "Medic's patching him now."

"Third squad's okay," Sauv Degtree said.

"So's fourth," Frank Symes added. "Nothing serious, anyway."

"Pull the men in around me," Joe said. "Try to find an efficient way to move over this moss." Then he switched channels.

"Second platoon's mostly okay," he reported to the first sergeant.

"Mostly?" Izzy Walker asked.

"One twisted ankle, being attended to. Other than that, nothing but minor stuff from slipping on this carpet. Didn't anybody know about that?"

"Guess not," Walker said. "I'm hearing about it now, though, from all over."

"What next?" Joe asked.

"Just get your men together until we sort things out. Nobody's shooting at us yet. I'll be back to you in a couple of minutes."

Joe pulled out his belt knife then and started scraping at the moss. It was no more than a centimeter thick, with bare rock beneath it. Before First Sergeant Walker called back, Joe had cleared enough moss to get to the top of the depression so that he could look out toward the enemy buildings to the east. He didn't see any signs of Heggies coming out.

"Still following the plan," Walker said. "We're to move east and establish a perimeter, hold until the rest of the force lands. Take your platoon due east about a kilometer and take up positions. First platoon to your right, third to the left."

"Where are they bringing in the heavy stuff?" Joe asked.

"Farther west."

"I hope they've got something besides this moss to set down on."

Walker didn't bother to reply.

Joe relayed the orders to squad leaders and deployed the platoon. The footing remained treacherous. The slick moss seemed to cover every square centimeter of the rocks.

It'll make everyone keep their heads down anyway, Joe thought. The troopers scuttled along on hands and knees. Where there was any significant slope, they had to move on bellies, scraping away moss to get at the rock below in the worst places. It didn't take long for men to discover that the rock below the moss was extremely hot to the touch, almost scorching, even so soon after dawn. The moss itself did not feel particularly hot. Somehow, it absorbed sunlight and passed the heat on to the rock layer without holding much of it.

Joe stayed close to first squad, the squad he had led before he got the entire platoon. Even after more than a year as platoon sergeant, Joe still thought of first squad as "his." He knew the men in the other three squads better now, but that had not yet completely broken old habits. The men of first squad viewed it as a mixed blessing.

All eight infantry companies were on the ground now, spread over the western section of the rocky area and beyond. Shuttles were beginning to bring in the Havocs and support vans for the 13th's Wasps and Havocs. Other shuttles were bringing in the engineers and their equipment. The 8th SAT and one of the light infantry regiments were landing at separate locations to assist in taking Site Alpha.

Everybody rides but us, Joe thought.

The men of Echo Company had no chance to set up a defensive perimeter once they had covered the first kilometer of rock. New orders came through. They were to move another four kilometers east, closer to the enemy.

Crossing five kilometers of the slippery rocks was painfully slow. Long before Joe had covered the first kilometer, his knees were scraped raw beneath his battle fatigues. His elbows and hands were also cut and scraped.

Every muscle in his body ached. The forty kilos of gear he carried felt like a ton.

Echo was too far from the Schlinal depot to be in range of most small arms fire. Wire couldn't begin to reach. But there were clearly a few snipers with rifles that could strike at more than five kilometers.

"Keep down," Joe warned. "Those aren't mosquitoes whizzing around."

Second platoon suffered no casualties from the light sniper fire, but one man in third platoon was hit below his visor. The neck wound ripped the man's carotid artery. Before a medic could get to him, the man was dead.

After consulting with the first sergeant, Joe called a break for his men. Then he just flopped, cheek against the moss, while he dragged in several deep breaths.

Can't get enough air, he thought, uncertain whether the slight difference between Tamkailo's atmosphere and those he was familiar with could be that noticeable. *All in my head maybe,* he acknowledged.

After a moment, he rolled onto his side, almost on his back (his pack prevented him from getting fully supine). He lifted his helmet visor just long enough to wipe sweat from his face. The perspiration had been pouring into his eyes almost from the start of this crawl, stinging, burning.

Off in the distance, he could see aircraft fighting, more than a dozen planes. *I hope our guys keep 'em busy,* he thought. *We'd be easy pickings here.* The rocks might give decent cover against enemy rifle fire, but a strafing airplane would mow through them.

"Let's get moving again," he said over his link to the platoon's squad leaders. "We're too exposed here."

Zel sent three of his men to get fresh batteries and munitions as soon as he received word that their support vans were on the ground. He didn't want to take a chance that the entire flight would have to land at once. For ten or fifteen minutes, they would be shorthanded, but they would never have to concede the air to the enemy. The dogfight had been going on for twenty minutes—an eternity. Zel knew that Blue Flight had been lucky to have lost only one plane so far, though even one loss hurt. Finally, he had received a call from Frank Verannen. He was alive but had broken both legs. The bottom of the escape pod had been crushed by the explosion that destroyed his Wasp. Frank was still in the pod, on the ground, unable to move. At least no Heggies had come hunting for him yet.

In order to conserve ammunition, Zel had adopted a new tactic. He would approach a Boem as close as possible, then flip his Wasp end for end in order to use his rear-mounted cannons. Those were loaded strictly with armor-piercing rounds, meant solely for air-to-air use. They were intended as a deterrent, something to protect the previously vulnerable tail of the Wasp, but Zel's maneuver turned the cannons into an offensive weapon. The other pilots of Blue Flight quickly copied the tactic. The Hegemony's Boems had no rear guns.

Blue Flight was still outnumbered, more than ever once Zel sent planes in for servicing, but the Schlinal pilots never exploited their advantage. Most kept breaking away from the dogfight, apparently obeying orders to try to contest the infantry landings. Blue Flight didn't bother chasing them. There were other Wasp flights waiting, and after the first few minutes there would be mudders with shoulder-operated rockets waiting for Boems to appear. Not one of the Schlinal pilots managed to strike against the landings.

Twenty-seven minutes after launching his first pair of rockets, Zel scored his ninth kill of the battle with his last missile. With no more than ten seconds of 25mm ammunition left, he started looking for the three Wasps he had sent in for servicing. The rookies left with him had to be even closer to empty than he was. It took a pilot time—combat time—to learn how to stretch his ammunition. Zel finally used the radio, and heard that the three were on their way back, throttles to the stops.

Zel didn't wait. He ordered the flyers still with him to break contact and head in for servicing.

•   •   •

The 13th's four batteries of Havoc 205mm self-propelled artillery had as many new men as the air wing. Afghan Battery had lost five of its six guns in its last campaign, and the other three had all suffered at least 50 percent casualties. Afghan, Basset, Corgi, and Dingo: the dog names for the batteries were a play on words deriving from a line penned by William Shakespeare thousands of years before, "Cry havoc and let slip the dogs of war."

The crew of Basset two had remained the same for more than two years. They had had one Havoc destroyed under them without any of them suffering a serious injury. The commander was Gunnery Sergeant Eustace Ponks. The other three men—driver Simon Kilgore, gunner Karl Mennem, and loader Jimmy Ysinde—were all privates. They considered themselves to be the best gun crew in the 13th—and the 13th's artillery unit the best in the ADF. After all of the time they had worked together, their claim was not totally without merit.

Contrary to standing orders, they had landed on Tamkailo with their first round loaded, and Karl had the engines running before the shuttle pilot announced that they were on the ground and opened the cargo hatch.

Although the slick moss that covered the rocky area where most of the 13th's infantry had landed would not have bothered tracked artillery pieces and support vans, that area was too rough for other vehicles to operate. Landing just to the west, the artillery had more level ground. The nearer half of the Schlinal depot and camp was just within the range of the Havocs' guns, and there were avenues to the north and south that would permit them to get close enough to bring the entire enemy base under fire.

"Get us out and bear off to the left," Eustace ordered as soon as the cargo ramp was down. "Let's not waste any time."

Under the best of circumstances, a Havoc did not accelerate with any great dispatch, but Karl gave the twin engines as much throttle as the treads could handle. If the deck of the cargo shuttle suffered minor damage from the speed of the departing howitzer, it wouldn't be the first time.

"Basset two ready for action," Eustace reported to the battery commander as soon as he saw that Basset one was also out of its shuttle.

"Ponks, I've got a personal message for you from the colonel," Captain Ritchey said.

"Sir?" Ponks asked.

"He wants me to thank you and your crew for volunteering to stay behind if we come up short one shuttle because some careless crew damaged it on landing."

"I don't know what you're talking about, sir," Ponks managed. "We're strictly by the manual here."

Ritchey sighed over the radio. "I ought to at least make you take the round out of the can you stuck in there while we were still in the air."

"We would never violate SOP like *that,* sir," Ponks said, beginning to wonder if the Havocs had been modified to allow the battery commander to snoop.

"Never mind, Ponks." Ritchey paused for no more than two seconds before he said, "We're still following the original plan. We go north, then east. And we wait for all of the dogs to get out before we start firing. Unless we come under hostile fire first."

"Yes, sir." After closing his link to Ritchey, Ponks switched to the crew channel and whispered, "I think he's got us bugged."

"You're gonna have to quit calling the old man names, I guess," Simon said with a short laugh. "You'll never get that extra rocker for your stripes."

"Who wants another rocker?" Ponks said, as if he didn't. "The headaches ain't worth another twenty Corders a month."

CHAPTER 3

Rank offered no protection against the slippery moss of the drop zone. Like virtually every man who jumped with him, Colonel Van Stossen fell as soon as his feet touched the ground. Both feet went out from under him and he landed on his butt, hard. For more than a minute, he could do nothing but sit there, glassy-eyed, scarcely registering his surroundings.

"You all right, sir?" the sergeant who commanded the headquarters security detachment asked. Vince Cumminhow scrambled toward the colonel on all fours. He also had fallen, but had managed to break his fall. He had jammed his left thumb in the process, but that was too minor an injury to worry about.

Stossen nodded slowly. "I'm okay, Vin. Just had the air knocked out of me." He would never admit to the rather considerable ache in his seat or the headache that accompanied it. He blinked several times, trying to eliminate the sudden double vision. "What is this stuff?" He dragged his fingertips over the rust-colored growth.

"Some kind of moss, I think, sir," Cumminhow said. "A little slimy."

Stossen took time to look all of the way around a circle. His headquarters staff had, as always, landed in two separate groups several hundred meters apart, to make certain that no single enemy action or accident could completely cut off the 13th's leadership. Dezo Parks and the rest would join the colonel as quickly as they could now that everyone was on the ground.

"This stuff's going to play hell with the schedule," Stossen muttered as he tried to get to his feet. After several false starts, he gave up for the time being. "Let's see if that red stuff over there offers better footing." The colonel and his companions had landed—after jumping on belts—within fifty meters of the western border of the rocks.

"Has to be better than whatever *this* is," Cumminhow said.

Stossen gave no further thought to dignity. He scampered along on hands and knees just as the others were. He needed ten minutes to get clear of the moss. The hard red clay was hot, but at least it offered purchase for feet.

"Such an inviting-looking drop zone," Stossen muttered. He looked back over the extensive field of moss-covered rocks. "No wonder the Heggies didn't bother to defend it. They must know that no one can stand on that junk."

"I just wish *we* had known about it," Major Bal Kenneck, Stossen's intelligence officer, said as he walked up to the colonel.

"Couldn't tell without putting people down," Stossen said. He shook his head and turned to Kenneck. "You have anything for me yet?"

"Not much, sir. The only enemy activity has been pretty much limited to a few Boems. We're bringing in our heavy stuff already. But the Heggies are going to have plenty of time to get set to meet our mudders. Slow as that moss makes everything, it'll take a couple of hours to get our lines close enough to engage."

"You seen Teu since we landed?"

"Over there. He's coming," Kenneck said. Ingels and Dezo Parks were walking together.

"Get on to CIC and see what the reports are from the other landing zone. And find out where General Dacik is. Then we'll see just how far behind schedule we're going to be here."

Stossen shook his head and started walking to meet Ingels and Parks. His head still hurt, and there was a faint blurriness to his vision.

At first, the heat had been really intrusive only when the men scraped away the moss to get some purchase on the rock below. But as they moved west, crawling much of the time, toward the massive Schlinal depot, the heat grabbed at them, and it got more oppressive by the minute. There was only a very slight breeze, and that seemed to bring wave after wave of hotter air rather than any measure of relief. The more time the men spent flat on the ground, the hotter they got. One medic in Fox Company used a thermometer to determine that the ground temperature, just below the moss layer, was 39 degrees Celsius. *And this is as cool as it gets* was his thought. It was little more than an hour past dawn. The real heat of the day was still to come.

Echo Company was in the middle of a three-company skirmish line advancing toward the Schlinal base. Bravo Company was to their left, Fox to the right. Two of the 13th's sixty-man recon platoons were on the flanks, ready to move up to envelop the enemy positions when they got close enough. By the time the line moved to within two kilometers of the Heggies, the men could see artillery explosions hitting the Schlinal positions. Occasionally they could see Wasps attacking ground targets, or fighting Boems in the air.

At two kilometers, the men on the ground were still out of range of most ground fire. As they passed that distance, a few Schlinal automatic weapons, 12mm slug throwers, did open up on them.

"Get what cover you can," Joe Baerclau told his platoon. Switching to another channel, he said, "Sauv, can your people get a line on that center chopper?"

"Can't see the gun," Degtree replied, but I think we can give him some trouble. Hang on."

A few seconds later, one Vrerch missile was fired by a man in fourth squad. Almost as if that were the signal, Vrerchs were fired by another half dozen men in the three companies, homing in on the enemy machine gun positions.

All of the Schlinal guns seemed to stop firing before the first of the missiles exploded. A Vrerch could be seen in flight.

"Move on up," Joe ordered on his platoon channel. "Get a few more meters before they start shooting again." He scrambled forward, arms and legs sliding out from under him as he tried to get to the next low spot in the terrain. All three companies fought to make some more distance forward, to the next good cover—rock or depression.

Missiles exploded. Holes appeared in buildings. Stones tumbled. The 13th continued to advance—not rapidly, but steadily. Before the smoke of the Vrerch explosions settled, the Schlinal machine guns opened up again, more of them than before.

"They must be bringing new stuff to bear," Joe said, speaking on his link to Captain Hilo Keye, Echo Company commander.

"We're still too far out for them to do much damage," Keye replied. Even over the radio it was obvious that the captain was gasping. Hilo Keye was past the middle of his fifth decade. While that would be young for a civilian who was maintaining his age with medical nanobots, it was old for a soldier. Anti-aging technology was considered superfluous for a soldier, especially in wartime. Outside of the headquarters staff, Keye was the oldest man in the 13th. He had received his captaincy only after the Jordan campaign.

"We get a little closer, Yellow Flight is ready to make a few passes," Keye said after a considerable pause. He had switched channels so that he was speaking to all of the platoon leaders and platoon sergeants. "The more Heggies that get lined up nicely, the better hunting the flyguys will have."

"Rate we're going, it'll be dark before we close," Joe said. His transmitter was still on the private channel, so only Keye would hear him.

"Maybe it'll cool down by then. Look to your men, Joe." The captain's tone was soft enough that the words weren't quite a rebuke.

"Aye, sir. We're keeping our heads down." And roasting them in the process, he thought as he surveyed the platoon.

At a range of nearly two kilometers, even the Schlinal machine guns were making little impression on the 13th. There were a few minor wounds, more from flying chips of rock than from bullets. The rocky ground offered plenty of cover from enemy guns that were themselves at or near ground level. Bullets hit and ricocheted off.

The 13th mounted only sporadic return fire. The Heggies were too far away for Armanoc wire carbines to be of the slightest use, and even the heavier wire splat guns could do no damage at that distance. The only infantry weapons that could reach the enemy were Vrerchs and the Dupuy cough guns. Among the line companies, the RA sniper rifles were distributed two to a platoon. At that distance, the Dupuy riflemen rarely had clear targets. From time to time, the 13th used a few Vrerchs to help suppress enemy fire, but the company commanders became sparing of the rockets. If enemy aircraft managed to get past the Wasp screen, the Vrerchs would be essential to survival. They were the only ground-based weapon the Accord had that could be used successfully against enemy aircraft.

Fifteen hundred meters from the Schlinal lines, the three Accord companies stopped for a much needed rest. They had covered seven kilometers in the three hours since the landing—most of it on hands and knees.

Just a couple of minutes after the order to stop went out,

First Sergeant Iz Walker worked his way down the line to Joe's position.

"We've been on the ground three hours and we're already two hours behind schedule," Walker said.

"Not much we can do about it, is there?" Joe asked. Both men lifted their helmet visors so they could talk directly to each other without using their radios. It also gave them the illusion of having more air to breathe, and even the illusion was helpful.

"No, there isn't, and that's the hell of it," Walker said. "Captain just had a talk with the colonel. I gather that the colonel's been on to CIC and General Dacik about the mess. Nobody had any inkling about this moss. There's probably never been a single one of our people on this world before today."

"They didn't send in SI first?" Each of the SATs had a Special Intelligence detachment, and SI—a separate arm of the Accord Defense Force—had other assets that weren't assigned to specific units.

"I guess not. Not much place for even spooks to hide on these rocks. I suppose they thought that dropping SIs would give away more than it got."

Joe nodded. "Probably. But does anybody have a way for us to move on this moss without breaking bones and butts?"

"Maybe." Walker left it at just the one word for so long that Joe had to ask.

"What's that supposed to mean?"

"They're gonna load up a couple of Wasps with all needle rounds in their cannons. They'll make one, maybe two, passes from just in front of us in toward the Heggies. I guess they want to see if that'll open up a path."

"Crazy way to waste ammo," Joe said.

"Anything that gets us off of these rocks before high noon has my vote," Walker said. "Word is the air temp could climb to forty-two by then. These rocks are going to get hot enough to cause second degree burns by afternoon."

Hands, Joe thought. "Through battle fatigues?" he asked.

Walker shrugged. "It wouldn't surprise me."

"What happens when we get farther north?" The second phase of the battle plan called for the 13th and 8th to attack a second Schlinal base (called Site Bravo in the plan) that was a thousand kilometers closer to the tropics—at what was considered to be the very limit of human habitability on the planet. The base was located on the west coast of the southern continent, where prevailing breezes off of the ocean moderated the heat—a little. That operation had been scheduled to begin before midnight of the first day of the invasion. But with the delays already encountered, it looked very unlikely that the schedule could be kept.

"Let's get through this operation before we start worrying about the next," Walker said. "We'll be here another fifteen minutes, at least, before we start moving again. Now, I've got to check in with the rest of the platoons. Make sure your men are drinking plenty of water."

As if he hadn't thought of water himself, Joe took one of his canteens from his belt and took a long drink as the first sergeant crawled on toward the next platoon. Each man had jumped with two full insulated canteens, each holding a liter and a half. That wouldn't last long in the heat. And despite insulation, the water was already at body temperature.

Even with both air conditioners running full out, the temperature inside the turret of Basset two quickly climbed to 38 degrees and stayed there. Fans on high made the two compartments barely livable. All four men were sweating freely within minutes of firing their first round of the morning. But the cockpit of a Havoc was *always* hot, especially when the howitzer was being fired with any regularity. The gun's barrel was a radiator dispersing the heat generated by each shot throughout the interior of the gun carriage.

Jimmy Ysinde passed out after locking Two's fourteenth

round of the morning into the gun. Jimmy was the crewman who had the hardest job, physically. Although the loading system was virtually automatic, he had enough to do, nudging the proper round from its rack space onto the loader, to work up a sweat at any time. The system wasn't perfect. On average, he would have to manhandle about one round out of five into proper alignment.

Karl Mennem reached over the top of the howitzer's breech to splash water on Jimmy's face—and to check his neck for a pulse.

"Jimmy's way out of it," Karl reported. "He's breathing okay, but he's zonked."

"Do what you can for him," Eustace said. "Half the loaders have gone out already." And not a few of the other crewmen. Eustace had been monitoring the battery's command net.

All Havoc crewmen were crosstrained in first aid. Because they often operated away from any regular medics, that training could—almost routinely—mean the difference between life and death. But with one man out of action, the gun was also effectively out of action. A Havoc needed all four of its crewmen. Their stations were physically separated from one another. The only one who could be worked around was the gunner. The gun commander could work the howitzer from his location. But the commander had a lot of other responsibilities. His doing the work of two men slowed a Havoc's rate of fire considerably.

"Unless we can cool him down there's not much else I can do," Karl said. "He needs help or he's going to be in real bad shape."

"Take off his helmet and wet down his head and neck the best you can," Eustace said. Gun bunnies did have one advantage over their infantry cohorts. They could keep their water cool. Both of the crew compartments had small refrigerators. Cold water and the air-conditioned breeze would help them all, for a time.

"And salt," Simon Kilagore added. " 'Bout time we all took in a little salt."

After checking with Captain Ritchey, Eustace ordered

Basset two back, away from the line of guns that were still firing. With no counterbattery fire or aircraft attacks threatening them, the Havocs weren't doing nearly as much maneuvering as they would have in other circumstances.

"Best we can do is lay off on the shooting for a time," Ponks told his crewmates. "Give the air time to cool down a little in here. It's hot outside too, and no shade. If we can't cool Jimmy down in here, he's not going to get cool without evacuation."

Karl unstrapped his safety harness and squirmed around in the tight confines of the rear compartment to lean over the gun barrel. He was very careful not to touch the hot metal while he worked on Jimmy. Another five minutes passed before Jimmy opened his eyes and groaned.

"What happened?"

"Too much heat," Karl told him, splashing chilled water over Ysinde's head again. "Take it easy. We've pulled back."

"This world's gonna turn us all into mudders," Eustace grumbled in the front cockpit. "Another couple of hours, won't any of us be able to stay in here without being turned into road meat."

Al Bergon treated his first heat casualty of the day shortly after ten o'clock, barely four hours after the 13th landed. Mal Underwood, the new man, simply flopped forward on his face. Only the fact that he had his visor down kept him from breaking his nose in the process.

"Too much body fat in you," Al said when he finally brought Mal back to consciousness. "You'll do better when some of that's been baked out of you."

"I feel like hell," Mal said in a coarse whisper. "My stomach's playing up, and the world's still spinnin' around and around." His voice got a little dreamy. Al went back to work, recognizing the danger signal.

"We've got to do something for him, fast," he told Joe Baerclau over a private link. "We've got serious heatstroke here and I'm worried that he'll go into shock."

"You'll have to handle it for now," Joe told him. "We

can't get anything in to help for at least another hour. Any evac is going to have to be on foot, and you know how slow that's going to be with this moss.''

"I'll do what I can, but in another hour he may need a trauma tube to pull him back together. And how many more are going to drop in that time?"

"I'll check with the captain," Joe promised, and then he switched channels to do just that.

"The colonel said that he's working on it," Keye said. "I'll let you know as soon as I have word. In the meantime, watch for those Wasps. They're going to make their first ground-clearing runs any minute now.''

"Yes, sir.'' Joe looked skyward, but at least four times in the past hour he had been told that the runs were imminent, and they had yet to materialize. The planes had been diverted to meet more immediate needs each time.

Joe rolled half on his side so that he could look toward Al and his patient. Something dug painfully into Joe's side. He raised himself enough to move the obstruction and then started cursing, softly but with great intensity, under his breath. He called the captain again.

"Sir, I've got it. The belts.''

"What?'' Keye asked.

"We've been on the ground four hours now, an' then some. The antigrav belts should be recharged. We tie one healthy man with two casualties—hell, let them *fly* back to where they can get treatment. One man ought to be able to manage three sets of controls like that.''

Captain Keye hesitated for a moment, thinking through the idea, before he answered. "It should work,'' he admitted. "Somebody should have thought of that before we landed here. Hang tight. I'll have Izzy set it up. We've got to wait a couple of minutes, though. Here come those Wasps.''

At the moment, the Wasps were merely a distraction to Joe. He shouted the news over the radio to Al Bergon and the other squad medics. He scarcely noticed the lines of destruction that the Wasp cannons cut through the moss in front of the 13th's line. Fifteen hundred slivers of metal a second hit from each of three Wasps. Three clear avenues opened up through the moss, parallel lines leading directly toward the Heggie base.

Colonel Stossen heard the suggestion about using antigrav belts to move casualties from Dezo Parks, but the news did not really register. His headache had worsened and his vision remained blurred. Annoyingly, his left eye would tear up every few minutes, further limiting his vision. An analgesic soaker stuck to his neck had not significantly reduced the pain or helped his eyesight.

I need to check with a medic, Stossen had told himself at least a dozen times, but he had not done it. There were simply too many other things that seemed more urgent. The 13th was falling far behind schedule, not because of enemy resistance but merely because of the difficulty of the terrain. Now men were falling from heatstroke. He knew that more would fall victim in the next few hours, when the day reached its hottest.

"Get them back, and see if we have enough belts to . . ."

The colonel didn't realize that he had stopped speaking in the middle of a sentence. . . . *let the healthy men swap out and get back to their units* was how he meant to finish it. In his mind, he heard the completion. But the world simply seemed to fade out around him while he was talking. There was a sudden hollowness to his hearing, much as if he were holding a seashell to his ear. The sky and his surroundings seemed to take on a rosy tinge. For a moment, he even thought that he could hear waves crashing on a sandy beach, with a hint of some ethereal music in the background.

Dezo Parks saw his boss's eyes roll back, but he couldn't react quickly enough to catch the colonel before he fell forward and hit the ground hard face first. Van Stossen was unconscious before he fell.

CHAPTER
4

A field hospital had been set up at the far western end of the drop and landing zones, at the farthest point from the Schlinal base. An infantry company from the 97th LIR provided security. The surgeons and other medical personnel of the 13th and 8th SATs and the 97th had been busy for hours. In the early hours of the invasion, few casualties were inflicted by enemy action. More were from drop injuries or other accidents. But the overwhelming majority were heat exhaustion and heatstroke cases. Shock, dehydration, and—in some cases—delirium. The drop injuries had mostly been returned to duty before noon. Only a handful of men had hurt themselves badly enough that four hours of rest and soaker patches couldn't cure the problem.

Colonel Stossen was carried into the hospital tent just as the first of the men from the front line were being brought back on antigrav belts. Sergeant Vin Cumminhow brought the colonel in, helped by one of the privates in the headquarters security detachment.

"I think he hurt himself when we landed," Cumminhow told the medtech who was performing triage. "He fell. After that, he had a headache and complained that his vision was blurred. He didn't seem to feel too good all morning. Then, a few minutes ago, he just keeled over."

The medtech looked up from his examination just briefly. "Sounds like concussion, possibly even a skull fracture. He hit his head when he fell?"

"Naw, his feet went out from under him and he landed on his butt. The first time, at least."

The medtech shrugged and went back to his examination. "It could still be concussion. The second fall didn't help any." The colonel's helmet was off. The fall had snapped off the visor, which had been in the raised position. There were a number of cuts on the colonel's face. A nosebleed had already stopped, but it was obvious that the nose was broken.

"He'll be okay, won't he?" Cumminhow asked, his voice rising. Like most of the men in the 13th, the sergeant idolized his commander.

"Should be," the medtech said. "Now, get out of the way." He called for an orderly to help move the colonel.

Cumminhow stood where he was for a moment, watching. Then, with nothing better to do, he left. He reported to the executive officer by radio. When he left the hospital tent, he was shaking his head. He had never heard of anyone getting a concussion by falling on his butt.

"Nothing but farmers," Zel Paitcher complained as he led Blue Flight into another pass in front of the infantrymen. The initial passes had been so efficient at clearing avenues that headquarters had ordered several more runs, to clear a wider path. "Plowing the ground."

"Could be worse," Gerry Easton said. "We could be down there and somebody could be plowing us under."

"Only good thing about this is, the sooner the mudders get through, the sooner they'll be able to get to Frank." Verannen had quit answering calls. Zel didn't know if Frank was dead, unconscious, or simply had his radio out of commission. Blue Flight had already had another casualty. The Pitcher, Ewell Marmon, had gone down. Though no one had reached the wreckage yet, there was little chance that Marmon had survived. He had not managed to eject and the Wasp had gone in hard.

But, for the moment at least, there was no enemy air activity in the area. If the local Schlinal garrison had any Boems left in flying condition, they were on the ground, in bunkers.

Bravo, Echo, and Fox companies were on the move again, with the recon platoons out on their flanks, moving ahead to contact the units that were supposed to attack from the north and south. The Wasps had cleared five good paths through the slick moss. But as the infantrymen drew within a kilometer of the Heggie lines, they started taking more casualties from machine guns and sniper rifles. The bare rocks were too hot to keep crawling across, and it was dangerous to get up and run. Schlinal snipers were having a field day picking off men at leisure. They were too far away for the 13th's mudders to suppress fire with their own wire rifles, and the Accord snipers had more trouble finding targets than the Heggie snipers did.

Then the Wasps returned. This time they weren't opening paths. Each Wasp made its pass along the Schlinal perimeter, spraying cannon fire and laying an occasional rocket into a building that might harbor snipers.

The three-company skirmish line started moving forward again. Men scurried forward in a crouch, going down every few seconds. They stayed down only briefly, because lying on those rocks without the insulating layer of moss could be compared without much exaggeration to lying in a frying pan.

Schlinal machine guns homed in on the line of advancing Accord soldiers. The Wasps could not eliminate all of those weapons, and their range was enough to start causing casualties, even through net armor, at more than a kilometer. Unlike the Accord with its splat guns, the

Hegemony used slugs rather than wire in their heavy automatic weapons.

Ezra Frain dropped into the lowest depression within reach and rolled over onto his back so that his pack and canteens kept most of his body off of the scalding-hot rocks. Boots and helmet helped. The position was uncomfortable, but better than any of the alternatives he could think of.

Sweat rolling into his eyes had nearly blinded him, and the exertion of running had him gasping for air. Ezra needed a moment before he could even look around to see that his men were down and safe.

"Joe, there's got to be a better way," he said over his link to Baerclau. He was panting heavily, as if he had run several kilometers rather than only a few dozen meters since his last short "rest."

"You come up with it, you'll get a medal," Joe replied, equally out of breath. "Short of dropping gear to lighten the load, I can't think of anything, and you know we can't leave any gear behind."

"You thought of using the belts to get our casualties back to hospital," Ezra said.

"My idea for the year. Somebody else's turn now."

"If we could just use the AG belts to neutralize the weight of our gear, it'd help."

Joe hesitated for a second before he answered. The idea was tempting, but he quickly came up with a number of arguments against it. The one he mentioned was the gyro stabilizers. "Be hell trying to go flat in a hurry," he said. "Staying vertical in combat is a fast way to get dead."

The break was needed, desperately by many of the men. While most of them rested, keeping as much of their bodies off of the hot rocks as possible, those men with Vrerch rocket launchers or Dupuy RA rifles kept up the pressure on the Schlinal defenders in front of them. Those were still the only weapons the Accord infantry carried that could effectively reach the enemy. Their splat guns, heavy automatic wire throwers, had an effective range of no more than two hundred meters.

Joe switched to the channel that connected him with all of his squad leaders and assistants. "Get a good check on all of your men," he said. "Talk to everybody, make sure they're okay. I don't want anyone going woozy at a bad time."

The reports he got back were not heartening. While no one seemed to be in immediate trouble, everyone was feeling the effects of the heat and the "oppressive" nature of the air. Joe passed that on to the captain.

"Tell me something I don't know, Joe," Keye replied, sounding exhausted himself. "We just have to cope with it. Another five minutes and we make the big push. You might tell the men that it'll be a few degrees cooler in the shade of those warehouses up there. Maybe that'll help sustain them."

Joe glanced at the buildings. There were three visible from his position, and he knew from the briefings that there were a lot more—warehouses, barracks, a couple of small factories, hangars, and repair facilities—beyond the few he could see. And there were at least two regiments of Heggie infantry to guard them, men who had been on Tamkailo for weeks or months.

"I hope it gets easier once we get used to the heat," Joe said. "It ever rain here?"

"Who knows?"

Joe took a long drink of water. He had already emptied one canteen and started on the second. Then he checked his rifle: full power pack, full wire spool. The barrel was too hot to touch, even though he hadn't fired it since landing. Even the composite stock was getting uncomfortably hot to the touch.

He warned his squad leaders how much time they had left, then took another, shorter sip of water. The water no longer simply tasted warm; it was *hot*. "Hot enough for coffee," Joe mumbled as he screwed the lid back on. He considered dropping an instant coffee packet into the canteen. That might make the water more palatable. But then he shook his head. He could always put coffee into the water, but once it was in, he couldn't take it back out.

Joe looked up. What appeared to be two full flights of Wasps were approaching, ready to hit the Schlinal lines while the infantry advanced. Joe heard, but did not see, the Havocs as they opened up again. For the last hour or more, there had been very little action from the artillery. Now they were starting to hit the nearest line of buildings again.

Hit 'em good, Joe thought. *Make it easy for us.*

Time was running out. The five minutes were gone. First Sergeant Walker relayed the order for the attack.

Colonel Stossen was in a trauma tube suffering from concussion, dehydration, and fractures of the nose and skull—the latter injuries from his second fall. The medical nanobots did their work, replacing fluids, transferring heat, reducing swelling, and starting to knit the fractures. In the 13th's command post, Dezo Parks was in command.

"We'll move Alpha and Charley companies forward on belts," he told Teu Ingels. "Get them up to where the Wasps have cleared the way, then push forward so that they're just behind Bravo, Echo, and Fox. Put the other two recon units out on the flanks. Second, on the north, should be able to skirt the moss. First will have to use their belts to get as far as possible before they run dry. I want them in the gaps between us and the other regiments. Make sure that 3rd and 4th recon are getting where they're supposed to be. I want them on the east side of the base, ready to cause whatever confusion they can. Get them all moving now."

He waited while Ingels passed along those orders. "The 97th should be in position on the south now," Parks said then. "They'll attack when we do."

"They're in position. Bal just confirmed it," Ingels said. "And the 8th is almost ready on the north."

Dezo nodded. "Send George Company up as well, on their feet as long as possible. I want them close enough to bring them in wherever they might be needed. They might need their belts then." He shook his head. "And they thought those belts would only be good for landings." He was too drained by the heat to laugh.

• • •

The Wasps and Havocs did hold down the amount of Schlinal fire directed at the lead companies of the Accord attack, but no amount of fire could have stopped *all* of it for any length of time. The vast majority of Schlinal soldiers might be unwilling conscripts, but when faced with a combat situation, most did respond as their training had told them they should. Some individuals went beyond what even the most militant of their officers might demand. For the rest, officers and noncoms were there behind their men, demanding, threatening. Discipline in the Heggie armed forces was brutal, and quick. Every Schlinal soldier learned that lesson in the first days of boot camp. The lesson was always applied with a vivid thoroughness that insured that no one who witnessed punishment would ever forget the price of disobedience. Or failure. In combat, any infraction was liable to be met with instant execution. It was far safer for a Heggie soldier to take his chances with the enemy than to fail his superiors. That was as true for officers of every grade as it was for the rawest private.

As the men of the 13th moved nearer to the Schlinal lines, they thought less about the heat of air and rocks and more about cover and maneuver. Adrenaline dimmed the complaints of "heavy" air and burned hands and knees, even though some of the burns were severe. Company grade officers and noncoms cajoled and instructed, a constant presence in the earphones of all of their men. More importantly, they did their commanding from right in the advancing line, leading by example when necessary.

For one of the few times in his career, Joe Baerclau found himself wishing that he had one of the longer-range Dupuy sniper rifles, or that the Armanoc zippers hadn't been designed so thoroughly for up-close fighting— anything that would allow him to shoot back sooner without obviously wasting ammunition. It raised his hackles to be under fire and unable to return it. He could have fired his zipper, but that would have been a futile gesture, and much worse, it would have showed his men that he was not as cool and composed under fire as he tried to appear. That was perhaps all that kept him from emptying a spool or two of wire at several times its maximum effective range.

This advance was no mad charge. There was no running, not for more than two or three meters at a time. It would have been difficult in any case. Although the strafing that the Wasps had done had opened good paths, there were still slippery spots. Men needed to watch their footing. Even without the remaining bits of moss, the intense heat would have made running any distance impossible. Long before the 13th could have closed with the enemy, most of the men would have been incapacitated.

Up and down. Move forward a few meters and take cover to rest, sometimes for no more than ten seconds, just long enough to take in one deep, burning breath, and to lift a faceplate to wipe stinging sweat from bloodshot eyes and to try to get the slightest hint of an almost imaginary breeze.

"When we said we'd follow the colonel to Hell and back, I never thought he'd take us up on it," Mort Jaiffer complained during one of the longer breaks. Echo had closed to within three hundred meters of the nearest enemy positions.

I know what you mean, Joe Baerclau thought, but what he said was "Save your air. We get up this next time, it's going to start getting even hotter."

"I'd feel a lot better if we had the tropical forest to go with this tropical heat," Mort said. "A little shade would be welcome, and trees would give us better cover."

This time Joe didn't say anything, didn't bother to voice his thought: *This isn't the tropics; it's damn near polar.* He didn't have to voice the thought. It occurred to Mort as well. Mort was too educated to miss something that obvious. He had also paid attention to the prejump briefings.

What happens when we do *go closer to the tropics?* Mort asked himself. *If it's this miserable here . . .*

He wiped sweat from his face and lowered his visor. He had taken a drink before talking. He was thirsty again, or still, but decided not to use any more water at the moment.

He had little enough left, and there was no telling how long it would be before there might be a chance to refill canteens. Being left without water for any significant time would be suicide in this heat. Literally. He shifted his position just enough to let him look over the crest of the rock he was behind. He tried to remember just what path he had chosen for himself before going down this time. He didn't want to have to think about where he was stepping when they started out again. He would be looking farther ahead then, mostly at the enemy lines.

At least we don't have to worry about mines or booby traps, he thought. The moss was surety for that, along with the strafing runs that the 13th's Wasps had done. If there had been any explosives planted, the cannon fragments would have detonated them. As long as they stayed on the stretches of rock that had been cleared of moss, they would be fine—that would keep them clear of the slick growth without worrying about explosives.

We just have to worry about cover, and not hitting a patch of that moss and breaking our butts.

"Check your weapons," Joe said over the platoon channel. "Wire and juice."

Mort automatically complied, even though he was absolutely certain that his Armanoc was ready to go. He had already looked several times. That too was automatic. Mort spoke to Wiz Mackey, the only man left in his fire team since Mal Underwood had been evacuated. Wiz confirmed that he had a full spool of wire and one hundred percent showing for his rifle's power pack. Then Mort switched channels to report to the squad leader.

"Wiz and I are set, Ez," he said.

"Take it easy then," Ezra Frain replied. "I just got the word. We're going to have another ten or fifteen minutes here. We're waiting for the other units to get in position before the attack. We're all going in at once. When we start this time, we keep going until we get there." *Or until we can't go any farther* was the unspoken qualifier.

• • •

Blue eight, Will Tarkel's fighter, lost power without warning as Blue Flight was heading east for another strike against the Schlinal defensive positions. Both antigrav drives quit at once. There was no time to attempt diagnostics, scarcely time for one try at restarting the engines. The Wasp had the glide characteristics of a six-ton rock without power. There was no possibility of landing one safely without the drives. Will managed to eject behind the 13th's line. His fighter's momentum carried it almost to the first warehouse in its path. It crashed about twenty meters short.

A squad from Echo's 4th platoon picked up Will Tarkel within two minutes after the escape pod landed.

Zel Paitcher watched the pod float down, in constant contact with Will until he was certain that Will was safe and unhurt. Then he turned his attention back to the Heggies. The fight for Tamkailo was barely six hours old, and he had already lost three-eighths of his flight.

Ezra Frain was barely twenty-one years old. At that, he missed being the youngest sergeant in the 13th SAT by nearly a full year. He had been in the military since his eighteenth birthday, first in his homeworld defense force, on Highland, and then in the 13th. He had been Joe Baerclau's assistant squad leader, then moved up a slot when Joe took over the platoon. Ezra did not feel twenty-one. Combat and responsibility had made him feel ancient. Every step he took toward the Schlinal defenders at Site Alpha added a year to the way he felt.

"Keep marking possible cover," he warned his men. "Know where you're going to dive before you have to." Advancing across open ground, even when it was as uneven as this rocky stretch, made him feel particularly vulnerable. It seemed to be something out of military ancient history, a style of combat that had been impractical—and excessively bloody—hundreds of years before men first left Earth to settle other worlds. The fact that standard-issue weapons were not intended for this sort of combat made the feeling of exposure even worse. Ezra no longer thought about the heat that made each breath difficult and uncomfortable, or about the sun-heated rocks that had burned his hands, arms, and legs. Those pains had faded long before, even though his hands were blistered. The enemy was only 150 meters away now.

Wire could be a hazard on unprotected areas of the body at this distance. Ezra crouched a little lower and kept moving forward. Olly Wytten and Pit Tymphe flanked their squad leader, Olly to the left, Pit to the right. The men were spaced no more than four meters apart. The entire line was like that, but that line did remain fairly straight, as near as the terrain permitted.

Olly advanced in his usual intense manner. Anything he did, he gave it his all. Of the replacements who had come to first squad since its first time in combat, Olly was the best. He had all of the tools and knew how, and when, to use them. Pit had to hold himself back. He was well below average in size, almost as short and thin as Joe Baerclau. He tried harder, as if he constantly felt the need to prove himself. Recklessness was never far from the surface for Pit Tymphe. But this was his second campaign. He was getting better.

Al Bergon was to Pit's right. In the SATs, a medic was just a rifleman with additional duties. In combat, being a medic took precedence when there were casualties to treat. At other times, the medic was expected to pull his weight as a combatant. Al kept his place between the two fire teams of first squad. None of ''his'' men had been hit. So far, the only casualty of the day had been Mal. The last time Al had checked, Underwood was recovering from his heatstroke, but was not ready yet to rejoin his comrades.

Wiz Mackey was to Al's right. Wiz had once been a hothead like Pit, but combat and the loss of his best friend had tempered his recklessness. In close combat, he was still the most ferocious man in the squad, but he no longer took unnecessary chances. His anger had tempered him, made him coldly methodical, even in fury.

Mort anchored the squad on the right. He was his usual steady, reliable self. He had always approached his work methodically, as if being a combat infantryman was no more exceptional than being an associate professor teaching introductory courses in history and political science. He had been good at that. He was better at this.

Joe Baerclau was no more than two steps behind the line now, sometimes closer, between first and fourth squads.

Heggie wire started ricocheting off of the rocks around the men of first squad with some regularity. They were still somewhat more than a hundred meters away from the Schlinal rifles, so the wire no longer carried enough momentum to penetrate net armor, and the ricochets would do no more than scratch exposed skin. A direct hit on unprotected skin would be different though.

"Cover!" Joe shouted over his platoon channel, repeating a command that had come over the company channel from Captain Keye.

On the noncoms' net, Keye had additional instructions. "When we start up again, it'll be fire and maneuver, by squads. Keep the jumps short."

Joe gave his orders quickly. The squads would move odd and even. "Start using wire when we go," he added. "Even if we're not close enough for it to do much damage, it'll give them something to think about."

This was no long rest break. Joe had scarcely finished his instructions before the order came to start moving again. He got off a three-second burst of wire as he got back to his feet. His wire had a lot of company. In both directions.

The fight was finally going to be joined at close quarters.

CHAPTER
5

All of the buildings in the Schlinal compound had been constructed of native rock quarried near the base. For the most part, it appeared that the builders had used very large square-cut blocks. Even in the buildings that appeared to be barracks, windows were few and small. The only breaks in the walls of the warehouses and other buildings appeared to be doors.

The rusty color of the stone testified to its high iron content. That there were other metals and minerals present was of little interest to anyone on either side at the moment. A foundry and mill had been built on the site. Steel girders and trusses had been fashioned to frame the stone buildings. Stone cut into sheets as much as fifty centimeters thick had been used for roofing. The Accord intelligence estimate was simple: "Left to themselves, those buildings might last as long as the Egyptian pyramids back on Earth. The slightly lower oxygen content of the atmosphere (and low average humidity) suggests that even the interior steel framing might last almost indefinitely.'' Schlinal construction was not routinely designed to be that permanent. But the use of prison labor and the lack of more ephemeral building materials on Tamkailo had made these exceptions possible, almost mandatory.

It certainly made for unusually solid construction. Those buildings could stand up to a lot of abuse, even the abuse of rocket warheads and artillery shells. Missiles exploded and punched holes, scattering stony shrapnel (more outside than in), but it would take a great many such hits to inflict serious structural damage.

The Schlinal designers of the compound had given little thought to providing a solid defensive perimeter around the base. The installation had originally been built as merely a depot on an otherwise uninviting world, not a base for an occupying force. The mesh fencing had been intended to contain garrison and prisoners, not to keep out an enemy or to provide more secure firing posts. There *were* automatic weapons positions at the corners, and spaced at wide intervals in between. And small pavilions had been spaced inside the fence to give sentries a place to get out of the heat of Tamkailo's sun. On this world, the pavilions were no luxury, but necessity. But those defensive measures were pro forma, to give soldiers something to do. The Schlinal overlords had no real concern about escaping prisoners. The only escape from penal servitude on Tamkailo was death.

Long before the leading units of the 13th got close to the base perimeter, there were extensive gaps in the fence. Most of the pavilions had been destroyed, as well as those machine gun positions on the three sides of the base that the Accord was attacking.

One unavoidable result of the air attacks was that there were plenty of shallow craters to give cover to the Schlinal defenders, and they were quick to take advantage of them. More were sheltered within and between the nearest rank of buildings. Again, shell damage had provided a few gun ports, holes in the sides of buildings. Other troops were on the roofs now, behind low parapets, many of them armed with rocket launchers to take their toll on any aircraft that returned.

The 13th's Red Flight lost two Wasps within seconds of each other, leaving the flight with only five planes. Yellow Flight lost its third plane of the day. At the moment, Blue Flight was away from the action, heading back to land and replenish munitions and get fresh batteries. The air wing of the 8th SAT and two squadrons of the 17th Independent Air Wing were coming in as well now, attacking the northern and southern sections of the perimeter and striking at targets in the middle of the base. The 97th LIR was attacking on the ground from the south. The 8th SAT was moving against the north side of the base.

On all three sides where they were attacking on the ground, the Accord infantry had closed to within one hundred meters of the Schlinal defenses. It was seven minutes past local noon. The first Accord soldiers had landed five hours and fifty-three minutes earlier. The invasion was already more than four hours behind schedule.

Up and forward, down and shoot. Concentrate. Wire rifles show no muzzle flashes to guide return fire. Spot likely shooting positions. Concentrate fire on holes in the walls and at the lips of craters on the ground. If you see movement of any kind, shoot. Anything in front of you is hostile. Maybe you won't hit anything vulnerable. Maybe you will. In either case, you'll give the enemy something to think about. You'll reduce the amount of enemy fire coming at you, and you'll make the fire that does come less accurate. The better you do your job, the harder it'll be for the enemy to do his. You know the statistics: hundreds of meters of wire expended for every casualty inflicted. Do your share. And then some.

None of the 13th's troopers really had to think about those things. They were the basics of combat training, instilled through hard repetition and swift discipline throughout the weeks of boot camp, reinforced constantly on training maneuvers in every unit—and brought home by deadly example in actual combat. Recruits were taught to go into training exercises with the battle cry "Kill, kill, kill!" Lectures told them about the evils of the Schlinal system and the dangers to any world that fell to them. *The enemy is evil. We are the force of Good in the galaxy.* Men being put through long hours of very intensive physical training were especially receptive to such psychological preparation, on deep subconscious levels. Under stress, the mind held to those precepts.

Joe Baerclau felt oddly peaceful. His earlier jitters had disappeared as soon as he was close enough to return fire with some hope of scoring telling hits on the enemy. His concentration was total, balancing the needs of his own fire and movement with the continuing need to keep an eye on what his men were doing. There was no useless radio chatter now. He gave terse instructions, and received them. He took reports and gave them. Each man in the 2nd platoon of Echo Company knew his job. And did it.

Joe moved his aim from target to target, limiting himself to short bursts of wire. He left fire suppression to others, preferring to conserve as much ammunition as possible for times of greater need. Across a 40-degree zone in front of him, he shot at anything that looked as if it might be an enemy soldier. The 13th's forward movement was slow now. A single squad would scuttle forward two or three meters, from cover to cover, while the rest of the platoon provided covering fire. The rest of the companies in the skirmish line were moving in the same methodical fashion.

But the cover of the rock field ended sixty meters from the Schlinal perimeter. Beyond that point, the ground had been leveled prior to the construction of the base. The ground beyond the mossy rocks was a combination of clay and stone, and there was no vegetation of any sort. There was, in particular, none of the moss that had proved so treacherous. But there would be no cover at all for the 13th once they got clear of the rocks.

Ezra Frain marked one Schlinal helmet in a shallow crater. Very little of the helmet showed behind the soldier's wire rifle. When Ezra first spotted it, there was only a thin sliver of the helmet showing, perhaps two centimeters high in the center. And no rifle. Ezra waited. The Schlinal soldier came up just far enough to squeeze off a short burst and then ducked again. The pattern repeated. The man moved a little to one side or the other before he came up each time.

"I'll get you yet," Ezra said after shooting at the vanishing helmet for the third time. He slipped a fresh spool of wire into his Armanoc, saving the old spool. There were still a few meters of wire on it, too much to waste.

Ezra held his breath, silently counting off the seconds since the helmet had disappeared. Fourth squad moved forward and took new positions. "Let's go," Ezra told his squad.

He started forward without looking to make sure that his five remaining men were moving with him. He knew that they would be, no matter how frightened they might be. While he crawled to the next slight cover, Ezra kept his eyes on the crater ahead. That helmet had stayed down longer than usual this time. Any second now . . .

When the helmet popped up the next time, Ezra raised himself to his knees and held down the trigger on his zipper, ready to pour an entire spool of wire into the helmet and the lip of ground in front of it if he had to. More of the helmet appeared, pushed back and up as wire sprayed off of it. Wire might not damage a helmet, but the impact would be felt by the man wearing it. Ezra extended himself, getting one foot out in front of him, lifting a little more, trying for a slightly better angle of fire.

Wire from at least two Heggie rifles found Ezra as the man in the crater came up and went down. Ezra didn't see the Heggie fall, dead. More than fifty snips of wire had cut into Ezra at the same time. Some had found the gaps in his net armor. The rest had penetrated it.

Al Bergon saw Ezra go down and stopped firing immediately. He crawled sideways to the squad leader. Before Al got to him though, Ezra Frain was too far gone for help. His eyes were open, expressionless, as Al slid him back to better cover.

Then the eyes closed and Ezra was dead.

Joe Baerclau swallowed hard when he heard the news from Al Bergon. After acknowledging the medic's report, Joe switched channels to talk to Mort Jaiffer.

"You've got first squad now, Professor. Ezra's dead. We'll run first squad as a single fire team for now, reorganize when we get a chance."

On the other end of that call, Mort squeezed his eyes shut, hard, for just a second. "I hear you." Mort glanced toward where Ezra had fallen. Al had already moved back into his place in the line.

"Be careful, Prof," Joe said.

"Yeah." Then Mort switched to the squad frequency. "Let's spread out to cover the gap," he said after confirming that they had lost Ezra. "And keep your heads down." There was always continuity. The gaps in the table of organization always slid to the bottom of the unit. Whenever an officer or noncom went down, there was always someone to replace him.

In the TO at least.

Major General Kleffer Dacik and his headquarters staff had landed twenty minutes after the first assault waves. The general had established his command post west of the landing zones for the attack on Site Alpha. With two concurrent operations going on, Dacik had plenty to keep him occupied. During the first hours, he left operational control of the attack on Site Alpha to Colonel Stossen, the senior regimental commander, and then—after Stossen became a casualty—to Colonel Napier Foss, commander of the 8th SAT. Foss had only recently been promoted to full colonel, and he was new in command of the 8th, but he was the next senior man. On the other continent, Colonel Jesiah Kane of the 5th SAT was in local operational control.

"I hope Stossen's not out of commission long," Dacik

told Colonel Ruman, his operations officer, after learning that Stossen had been taken to the hospital. "Foss may be good, but he doesn't have Van's experience."

"I've already sent a man over to check with the doctor," Ruman said. "Should be hearing from him soon."

"Van's going to miss this first fight in any case, and that's bad enough." Dacik looked down at the large mapboard laid out on the ground between them. "This whole operation depended on timing, and that damned moss screwed it from the first pair of boots that touched down. There's no way we can make up five hours."

"We knew we'd have to improvise, General," Ruman said. "You emphasized that hard enough. Besides, the 8th and 13th are used to improvisation."

"But it's that much longer that the 5th and 34th are going to have to hold on without reinforcements on the northern continent," Dacik said. "As far under strength as they are, it's going to be dicey as hell."

Colonel Ruman didn't say anything. This entire operation had been dicey from its inception.

An hour past noon, the Accord had moved its lines within sixty and seventy meters of the Schlinal defensive lines on three sides. Recon platoons from both the 8th and 13th were operating on the fourth, the east, side, to keep the Schlinal garrison from getting out where they could maneuver and endanger the entire Accord line. Sergeant Dem Nimz had the 13th's 3rd recon platoon. SAT recon platoons were twice the size of line platoons, sixty men— at least in theory. None were at full strength for the landing on Tamkailo. Of the four in the 13th, only the 1st recon platoon had a lieutenant, a platoon leader. The rest were commanded by sergeants. Junior lieutenants were in short supply throughout the spaceborne assault teams, and reccer lieutenants had to be a cut above their peers in the line companies. Just as enlisted reccers were an elite within the elite SATs.

Third platoon's four squads were operating independently, not a rare circumstance. Dem stayed with first squad. Sergeant Fredo Gariston was the nominal squad leader. The two men had worked together closely during the 13th's previous campaigns. Each knew how the other thought, what he was likely to do in almost any situation. It made them extremely effective together.

"Best thing we can do is find a way to get in the middle," Dem whispered to Fredo. Both men had their visors up and their radio transmitters switched off. The squad was concealed in a shallow ravine eighty meters from the southeastern corner of the Schlinal base. "Create as much confusion as we can."

"And hope our own people don't clobber us?" Fredo replied. "That place is a free fire zone, if you recall."

"We're not going to be that big a target," Dem said. His grin was tight. "We get in a bind, we can always get our guys to lay off."

"Don't forget, we're not supposed to give the Heggies a chance to capture that new rifle." Fredo pointed at the weapon Dem was carrying. A new rifle: Dem was one of a dozen men giving the weapon its first combat test. It too was a product of the research that the Corey team had done in their hidden laboratory on Jordan. The rifle didn't even have an official name yet. For the moment, it was simply the XAG-1.

"I know," Dem said. "Long as we've got three seconds, we can turn it into something nobody could analyze. In the meantime, it might give us the edge we need."

"We're gonna have to liberate a few Heggie explosives if we're gonna do much damage," Fredo said. "What we've got with us won't do a hell of a lot to those stone buildings."

"So we'll help ourselves. This place is supposed to be loaded with munitions. Maybe we can put one or two of their warehouses in orbit."

Fredo just shrugged. He had seen the pyramids on Earth. His father had been a trade representative, stationed on "the Mother World" for five years while Fredo was growing up. To Fredo's thinking, it would be as easy to put the Great Pyramid of Giza in orbit as one of these buildings.

Dem called the rest of the squad in close and started giving instructions. He used hand signs more than words. Reccers worked in silence whenever they could. It made them less . . . conspicuous.

Blue Flight strafed the Heggie line on the west side of the base from south to north. With Accord soldiers now less than seventy meters from the enemy, the flyers had to be particularly careful. They attacked in a vertical echelon this time, with each Wasp behind and below the fighter in front of him. All six fired in unison, their cannons raking along a hundred meters of the enemy line at a time. There was no escape for the men in their path; no chance for them to turn and fire missiles at the planes.

"Empty your guns," Zel instructed. "We'll turn around and give them rockets on the next pass. Give the mudders a chance to close."

Ten seconds for each pass. As Blue Flight turned west, several rockets came up after them, aimed more from the roofs of the buildings than from the Heggies on the ground. The men on the roofs had been out of the line of fire.

The five Wasp pilots pushed their throttles all of the way forward, shooting straight up, as they keyed in their full repertory of electronic countermeasures. At the moment, their most effective defense was to push for altitude as rapidly as they could stand. If they could get above ten thousand meters, they would almost certainly be able to elude the enemy missiles.

Zel kept his eyes on the head-up display. That showed each of his Wasps and the oncoming rockets, blue for Wasps, red for missiles. The last plane in the flight was no more than fifty meters in front of the closest rocket, but Blue seven wasn't losing any ground. And, after ten seconds, he actually started to widen the gap.

"Watch your gees, Kwill," Zel warned. "You black out and you'll get that bastard up your tail anyway."

"I'm . . . o . . . kay," Kwillen said, so slowly that Zel knew that Ilsen was pushing himself too close to the limit.

"Flip left, then dive and flip left again," Zel ordered.

Kwillen obeyed without comment and the rocket went past him.

"Now do a one-eighty and head west just above ground level," Zel said. "We'll pick you up in about ninety seconds."

Zel was beginning to feel the pull of gravity himself. He checked his display again before he eased off, ever so slightly, on both throttles. "Odd left and even right," he ordered, and the remaining Wasps of Blue Flight split apart, feathering away from one another as if on display at an air show. All were still climbing, but the sudden blossoming of flight paths helped to confuse the Schlinal missiles. One quickly started to wobble, showing that it had lost its target lock. The rest fell farther behind.

"Ease off and maneuver independently," Zel said next. He tilted his Wasp to the left so that he could spot Kwillen's Blue seven as it streaked west, a black shadow racing over orange rocks behind the Accord lines.

"They must have tanks here somewhere," Dezo Parks said. He had moved the 13th's command post east, closer to the fighting. Not a single Nova tank had been spotted by the spyeye satellites, by the Wasps, or by anyone on the ground. And there had been no incoming cannon fire anywhere around the base. "It just doesn't figure. Those tanks *have* to be here."

"Not battle ready?" Bal Kenneck suggested. "This is a depot, a staging area. It is possible that they haven't got them fueled up or stocked with ammunition. The crews might not even be on planet."

"That's too much to hope for," Teu Ingels said. "They had Boems on alert status. There must be at least *some* tanks ready to roll. The Heggie commanders here can't be *that* incompetent."

"No rows of tanks drawn up in a parking area," Kenneck said. "If they've got the armor we think they should have for this force, it can't all be indoors. You don't do that with battle tanks."

"At least we don't do it with our Havocs," Hank

Norwich said. Though he was commander of the 13th's artillery, he no longer rode a Havoc himself. He only regretted that part of the time. His deputy commander rode Afghan one now. "This is our first time on a Schlinal world like Tamkailo. We simply don't know what the Heggies might do here."

"But after six hours on the ground . . ." Dezo shook his head. "By now, they could have a dozen battalions fueled and armed, out raising hell. If there are tanks, and there have to be, they've had plenty of time to put in an appearance."

"Again," Bal said, "maybe the crews aren't on planet. They couldn't just stick infantrymen in the cockpits and tell them to learn as they go. Right, Hank?"

Norwich nodded. Then he cleared his throat noisily and the others all looked at him.

"There is another possibility," he said. "Just occurred to me. Even with air conditioning, our men have been having trouble in this heat. Maybe the Heggies have learned that they simply can't use their Novas here. At least not during the day. Do they have air conditioning in the Novas?" He looked to Bal Kenneck.

"I don't know," the intelligence officer admitted. "I'll check with CIC, see if anyone does."

Even at extremely close range, the Accord battle helmet was secure protection against wire. The helmet itself, and the faceplate, would stand up even to heavy bursts of wire from as close as ten meters. At that range, though, the head inside a helmet could get battered severely, with enough force to cause concussion. At ranges above fifty meters, a helmet might even deflect a heavier slug, such as those fired by Schlinal sniper rifles, or by the Accord's Dupuy RA rifle. The helmet was the most reliable piece of an Accord soldier's protection. Net armor was considerably less secure. In theory, the Accord standard operating procedure was to replace battle fatigues after seven days of exposure, more often under particularly trying conditions. In practice, that wasn't always possible—and in extreme conditions, seven days could be six days too long. Accord battle planners took some satisfaction in the fact that Schlinal practice provided replacement battle fatigues no more frequently than every fourteen days.

Although helmets were sufficient against most of the munitions that an enemy might aim at them, a helmet *was* a target, and a rocket-propelled grenade exploding within ten meters of an exposed helmet was almost certain to make a casualty of the man under the helmet.

When the Accord advance stopped on the west side of the Schlinal base, the leading companies of the 13th were little more than sixty meters from the enemy. The firefight was fierce. Men in static lines took what opportunities they could to fire at the enemy. Sixty meters was close enough for hand grenades to become part of the action. Smoke, white phosphorus, and fragmentation grenades exploded on both sides. Only the volume of rifle fire kept the grenades from being thrown with any special accuracy.

There were casualties on both sides, extremely heavy for some units. The Accord was stopped cold. They couldn't advance another centimeter without taking prohibitively high casualties.

This stalemate had been going on for nearly two hours, well past midday, when a fragmentation grenade landed twenty-five meters from Joe Baerclau, nearly wiping out his platoon's third squad, leaving only Sauv Degtree and one private alive and unwounded.

CHAPTER
6

"Tell the flyguys that we're going up on the roofs, Major," Dem Nimz told Teu Ingels. The 13th's 3rd recon platoon had finally made it to the edge of the Schlinal base. The men had pushed themselves to the limit to get through the gap between the 13th and the 97th. They had—somehow—managed to penetrate the Heggie line without being observed during a Wasp attack. Despite the rigorous training that reccers went through and their oft-repeated claim to be able to move within ten meters of an ememy in daylight without being seen, even Dem was more than a little surprised at his platoon's complete success. They hadn't drawn a single shot from the enemy.

First squad had taken a long rest once it could, inside one of the warehouses just behind the Heggie perimeter—four buildings west of the spot where they had infiltrated the Heggie lines. Dem and his men had simply crawled into the most confined spaces they could find, and collapsed.

Twenty minutes passed before Dem made his radio call to report what they had done.

"You're *inside* the base?" Major Ingels asked.

"Yes, sir," Dem confirmed. "Inside a warehouse and unobserved. I figure the safest way for us to head is up. With all of the Wasps hitting this place, my bet is that most of the Heggies, if not all, have gone lower."

"I hope you're right. Give me two minutes to clear this with the air people, then go ahead."

"Two minutes," Dem repeated, then he switched to the squad's channel. This was one of the rare instances when he figured that the radio would be safer.

"We go back outside and use our belts," he told the others. There was an interior stairway visible along one wall of the warehouse, open. But there were Heggies in the warehouse with the reccers. The reccers would be visible far too long if they climbed stairs. Besides, going up on the outside would give them a chance to surprise any Heggies who might still be on the roof. Despite his conviction that the roofs would be unoccupied by now, Dem liked to hedge his bets. Then he told the others squads what they were going to do and cleared them to take whatever action seemed appropriate where they were.

"Anybody on the roof, just blast away," Dem said when he returned to first squad's channel. "Don't give 'em time to let the rest know they've got company. All the racket outside, nobody's going to notice our gunfire."

There were no questions. Dem waited another minute before he gave the order to move. He liked to think that he was the fittest man in the ADF, but six hours on Tamkailo had him wondering about his conditioning. He felt as if he had already run a marathon in full kit.

"Fredo, get back to that door and make sure the coast is clear." Dem waited until Gariston was up and halfway to the door before he gestured for the rest of the men to come out from their cover and move in that direction. The team was used to working together. Men watched on every side, alert against the possibility of accidental discovery by their unwitting hosts. The men divided the work naturally, a glance or a hand signal enough to make certain that there was no confusion within the squad.

Fredo opened the door just a few centimeters, slowly, looking out through the widening crack to scout as much of the terrain as he could. To check the other way, he looked through the crack along the hinge side of the door rather than stick his head out in the open. The door was set midway in the meter-thick stone wall, which restricted his field of view considerably. Fredo watched for nearly a minute before he used a hand signal to let the others know that the way was clear.

"Right against the wall and straight up," Dem said as the squad moved. He detailed two men to face outward, covering them from that side. The rest would be facing the building, ready to take on anyone they found on the roof.

The antigrav belts were as silent as Wasps. The squad paced themselves by Dem's rate of climb—one hand on belt controls, the other holding a weapon at the ready. They needed only two seconds to reach the level of the warehouse roof.

It was empty . . . except for the bodies of four Heggie soldiers, and a trail that showed where the 25mm cannon fire of a Wasp had swept across the roof.

There was a low parapet around the edge of the roof, no more than fifty centimeters high. In several places that parapet had been shattered by cannon fire or rockets. There was also a hole, not quite a meter in diameter, where the wall and roof met, on the west side of the building, near its northern corner. Near the northern wall, there was also a small kiosk where the stairway came out.

Dem used hand signals to position his men—one to watch the door leading to the stairwell, two to cover the north, south, and east sides of the building from the corners. Dem and the other seven men went to the west wall.

Cautiously, Dem raised his head to look at the ground below. There were hundreds of Heggies, perhaps a thousand or more, in the line west of the buildings. But they were all facing west or south, away from the roof where the reccers were, concerned only with the Accord attack coming in from those two sides.

Now what? Dem asked himself. He had not bothered to make detailed plans before. *Go up on the roof and see what havoc we can create* had been the extent of his planning. To this point, he had been concerned only with getting into position.' After that, improvisation. He glanced at the rifle in his hands. And smiled. *At least we'll see what you can do,* he thought.

"We'll work off to the left first, the men in front of that next building," Dem told the others. "If they do start looking, I want them to look in the wrong place first. Soon as Heggies start to show an interest in the roofs, we hightail it across and jump to the next roof east. On belts," he added after a slight hesitation. That next roof was twenty-five meters from this one.

"You sure we're gonna have enough juice to make it?" Fredo asked.

"There and back again," Dem replied.

He gestured for the men to take their positions and promptly put them out of his immediate thoughts. They all knew what had to be done. Dem moved up to the position he had staked out for himself behind the parapet. Before he could do anything more, though, there was a call for him.

"Nimz."

"Yeah."

"Ingels. You in place?"

"Yes, sir," Dem said. "Just about ready to make things interesting."

"Hold off a bit if you can. Anyone likely to spot you?"

That almost demanded a sarcastic reply. Anyone likely to spot a *reccer*? Especially after they had successfully sneaked into the center of a Heggie base? But Dem suppressed the urge. "No, sir. We appear to be all alone up here."

"Let's coordinate things then," Ingels said. "We're going to hit those Heggies with everything we've got, all at once—air, artillery, and infantry. We've got to get the men off of these rocks and tie off Site Alpha as quickly as pos-

sible. Wait for the air and artillery, unless you come under
fire first. When the big guns start, you go to work from
behind. There'll be so much hell breaking they shouldn't
even have time to look for you.''

''How long?'' Dem asked.

''Not more than five minutes,'' Ingels said, mentally
crossing his fingers. ''Air and artillery, then you. After
thirty seconds, we push the infantry forward, all three regiments.''

''We'll be ready. I just hope the flyguys and dogs don't
knock this building out from under us.''

''Turn your locators on so they know where you're at.''

Dem hesitated before he said, ''Yes, sir.'' As usual, the
reccers had all turned off the beacons that identified them
to the mapping system run out of CIC. Without those locators on, they could only be picked up when one of them
transmitted. Dem switched his on, then switched channels
just long enough to tell the rest of the platoon to do the
same. Then he was back to Major Ingels.

''We're set, sir.''

''Good. The Wasps are rendezvousing now. Less than
five minutes. Out.''

Joe Baerclau felt a tightening in his throat when Captain
Key relayed *the Word* to the platoon leaders and sergeants.
It was going to come down to a mad charge after all, across
sixty meters of open ground, directly at an enemy that
outnumbered them. That was a nightmare to any soldier.
There would be little margin for error, all around. The
Wasps and Havocs were going to concentrate their fire right
on the Heggie perimeter. While they were active, the
mudders would have to get up and run right into that
mess—and hope that nobody's aim was off, and that the
heavy stuff was halted before the mudders ran into a rain
of ''friendly'' shrapnel.

''Fire suppression,'' Joe whispered, belatedly checking
to make sure that his transmitter was off. ''With a
vengeance.''

But then the transmitter had to go back on. He hit the

platoon channel and told everyone at the same time. "Wait for the order," he cautioned. "Soon as the bombardment starts zapping them, we go, full out."

Joe looked back toward the west, wondering where the Wasps would come from. After a couple of seconds, he gritted his teeth. *Not from that way*, he thought. *From north or south, so they can rake the enemy line.*

He closed his eyes, but scarcely longer than a slow blink. *Rake 'em good*, he thought—almost a prayer. He opened his eyes and checked the load on his Armanoc. Then he felt for the knife on his belt.

"We're going all the way in, whatever it takes. That was what the captain had told him. There would be no stopping short of the enemy, not as long as a single man was able to move. "We've got to overwhelm them in a hurry, before they have a chance to regroup," Keye had said. He hadn't needed to add, *It's our only hope.*

Joe looked along the line, a quick glance in either direction. *My men*, he thought. And then the Wasps were on their way in, from the south, totally silent until their guns started to fire and the first rockets were launched.

Dem had laid three magazines for his rifle at his side, where he could reach them in a hurry without looking. The test rifle did not shoot wire or rocket-assisted slugs. It shot 20-gram 7.75mm fléchette bullets, rounds with tiny razor-sharp vanes that popped out in flight. The propulsive charge was an antigrav drive, the same sort as was used in the new Corey belts. The thrust was funneled into the rear of the rifle's chamber, with enough power to give the bullet a muzzle velocity of nearly three hundred meters per second. Dem also had a neat little stack of five hand grenades within easy reach. No matter what happened, he would find time to use those five grenades. Even if the squad had to abandon the rooftop in a hurry, he would find the few seconds it would take to throw those grenades.

A deep breath. Burning air. Dem had an instant to wonder whether there was more to the atmosphere than heat, too much carbon dioxide, and too little oxygen—

whether there also might be toxic trace elements, enough
to add a little chemical burn to the heat.

Too bad we don't have planet-cookers, he thought. *They
just want all of the Heggie assets here destroyed. If we
coulda done it from space, without landing* . . . But that was
an idle wish from pulp adventure videos, and then the
Wasps arrived, and there was no more time for fantasy.

Rockets and cannons. The Wasps raked the perimeter of
the Schlinal base. The first artillery rounds exploded at
almost the same instant as the first rockets, an unusually
precise coordination of assets. Flames and shrapnel,
followed by showers of debris, hurtled into the air to fall
back to the ground. Some of the detritus was human flesh.

Dem started firing instantly, raking one section of Heggie
soldiers, giving them an entire thirty-two-round magazine.
His test rifle's cyclic rate wasn't as great as some other
automatic weapons he had used, but it was faster than
squeezing off individual shots the way a cough gun
required. Before he reloaded, he tossed two of his ready
grenades, one as far to the left as he could, the other equally
far to the right. Then he ejected the rifle's empty magazine,
stuck a fresh one in, and jacked a shell into the chamber.

The range wasn't extreme, wouldn't have been even for
a zipper, but the results were still impressive. The vanes of
the fléchette rounds went through net armor as if it were
thin cotton, spinning, chopping everything in their path. A
concentration of bullets seemed virtually to puree flesh.
Dem picked one man at random and put the entire second
magazine into his back, stitching a line from side to side
that cut the man completely in half. Dem's only interest
was clinical. It was his job to test the rifle thoroughly.

Two more grenades went out before Dem loaded his
third magazine.

The scene below was bloody chaos. The Heggies hadn't
had time to think about men behind them on the roofs of
buildings that they thought sheltered them. But the Heggies
did not simply die. They fought back, as well as they could,
against the infantry charging toward them and against the
aircraft. Dozens of surface-to-air missiles were launched at

the Wasps. Although Dem wasn't paying attention to that phase of the fight, he did note three Wasps hit by those shoulder-fired rockets.

While Dem switched to the last of the magazines that he had laid out, he looked farther off for the first time, to the line of men advancing toward the Heggie positions from the west.

"Watch where you're shooting," he told his men, an unnecessary bit of advice, perhaps, but one he could not restrain. "We've got friends moving in."

The pace of the advance was slower than Joe Baerclau had anticipated. At least, it felt slower with adrenaline pumping and the inevitable edge of fear behind it. It seemed that drill-field marching would have been faster. But the amount of enemy fire had fallen off to almost nothing as soon as the Wasps and Havocs opened up. The Heggie soldiers were far more concerned with staying alive. Secondarily, they tried to bring down the aircraft that were decimating their ranks. The line of advancing Freebie infantry was, for the moment at least, an exceedingly minor concern for most of the Heggies.

Joe kept both hands on his rifle to keep his shooting as accurate as possible. There *were* targets out there: a few Heggies who were shooting at the Accord infantry, and others who just exposed themselves to ground fire in their attempts to escape the air attack or to fight back against the Wasps. Twice, Joe warned his men to be careful of their fire, to pick targets while they had that luxury.

"Keep your heads. Make your wire count," he urged.

Sixty meters. The line of chain-link and razor-wire fencing had been shredded by the earlier air and artillery attacks. It would not pose much of an obstacle in most spots, though—perversely enough—there *were* a few sections still standing undamaged.

One man in second squad went down. Within forty meters of the enemy line, Joe could spare no more than the briefest sidelong glance. A call on the radio told him that it was second squad's medic who had been hit. Al Bergon hurried over to help. He only needed a second to check the man and report that he was dead.

Two men in fourth squad went down next, including Frank Symes, the squad leader. Fourth squad's medic reported that both men were alive, not too badly hurt, and dragged them back to some slight cover.

Twenty meters. There was no more artillery fire coming in. The kill radius of a Havoc shell was twenty meters. The Wasps were pulling away from their last strafing run. For just an instant, there was relative quiet all along the perimeter.

Captain Keye shouted, "Charge!" over the company channel, a command that might not have been heard in combat for a thousand years. Not a man in Echo Company was confused by it, though. They knew what was needed. They were on their own now, and it wouldn't take the Heggies long to turn their attention back to them now that the Wasps were gone.

They ran, straining lungs and muscles to the breaking point.

In first squad, Wiz Mackey went down to his knees. He dropped forward to support himself on all fours, and to present less of a target. "I'm okay," he said on the squad channel. "Just . . . a . . . minute."

Joe went down to one knee himself, fairly close to Wiz, providing covering fire. When he spared himself an instant for a glance, he could see that Wiz was gasping heavily, panting, out of air. Joe was gasping himself. Then Wiz took in one deep breath.

"I'm okay now," he said, and his voice didn't sound nearly as winded as it had before.

"Okay, let's go," Joe said. Talking hurt, interfered with breathing. Wiz and Joe were eight meters behind the rest of the line when they got up and started forward again. Bravo, Echo, and Fox companies were crossing the Schlinal perimeter, moving right into the first line of Heggies.

Armanoc carbines were not equipped with bayonets. Even after several years of warfare, Accord military thinking had not recognized that hand-to-hand combat might yet be something to provide for. *Use wire as a bayonet blade,* the SOP and training manuals urged. *A quick burst of wire will cut better than any knife ever forged.* Joe had used that line in training, but he had always had his doubts. Fifteen or twenty centimeters of cold steel on the front end of a rifle struck him as an exceptionally good idea.

From their positions just behind the line, Joe and Wiz—and perhaps twenty other men along the front—were able to continue providing covering fire for the men who were more closely engaged with the enemy. Many of the officers, and more than a few platoon sergeants, held back, on orders, until Alpha and Charley companies moved up into position and joined the closer battle.

Joe slipped a fresh spool of wire into his zipper. Whenever he saw a clear target—most no more than two or three meters away now—he let off a short burst, just enough to drop a man. Joe was down on one knee again, presenting as little target area to the enemy as possible.

More Heggies came toward the fight, pouring out from between the buildings and coming out of doors. Now that the air and artillery attack had ended, the Heggie infantry was returning to the fray quickly. The Accord's advantage faded.

Joe was changing spools again when a Heggie trooper got clear of the mess in front and leapt at Joe, his rifle held out in front of him in both hands. Joe got his own rifle up to counter the attack, but the force of the Heggie's leap knocked Joe over backward. Both men went to the ground. A knee in the stomach forced the air from Joe's lungs. For an instant, he was unable to do anything. He did manage to keep his grip on his rifle, kept that weapon between him and his assailant. The Heggie was equally reluctant to let go of his wire rifle. But neither man was able to bring a muzzle around to face his foe. Without wire in the chamber, it would have done Joe no good in any case.

As soon as he was able, Joe tried to roll the Heggie off of him, pushing upward with his right arm and drawing his left arm back, just a little. At the same time, he brought his right knee up. He didn't connect with the Heggie's groin, his target, but the shift of weight was enough to roll the two men to the side, though not enough to free Joe of his attacker.

The Heggie pushed back, trying to regain his position on top. The two men's helmets butted together. Joe could make out the face of his opponent through the tinted visor of his helmet. Heggie infantry helmets were not routinely equipped with faceplates or the sophisticated electronic displays that Accord helmets had.

Again, Joe pushed, trying to roll his foe over. This time he moved toward the right. When the Heggie countered, Joe let go of his rifle's pistol grip with his right hand and grabbed for his knife. Before the Heggie could adjust to the change in tactics, Joe had the blade in the man's side.

The Heggie stiffened, then went limp, collapsing on top of Joe.

His weight seemed intense. Joe made one attempt to push the body off of him, but the effort was too much. He couldn't force in enough air. The light disappeared and Joe lost all awareness.

CHAPTER
7

Dem Nimz moved all of his men to the north wall. Fredo took half of the squad, and they jumped to the next roof on antigrav belts. The two halves of the squad combined their fire then, concentrating on the avenue between the two buildings. They managed to contribute to the fight without having a single round returned for another minute or more. It was apparent that no one on the ground had any idea where the fire was coming from.

Eventually, though, someone looked up. A shouted warning on the ground led to a sudden flurry of gunfire directed at first the one roof and then at both. Heggies moved for cover, to the east end of the buildings and into doorways. The reccers pulled back from the parapets for a moment.

"We move?" Fredo asked Dem.

"No," Dem replied. "Spread out along the walls. On my count, everybody drop a grenade over the edge. Give them something to think about."

One, two, three. The grenades went out. By another

count of three, they exploded, twelve blasts that sounded as one. The reccers moved back to the edges of their roofs and looked down. Just below them, there were no Heggies left on their feet. Forty or fifty bodies, few of them whole, were clustered together. Most of the Heggies had been moving toward the ends of the buildings. The pattern of bodies was almost an image of an hourglass.

The reccers brought their rifles up again, finding targets farther off, left and right. They had only another twenty seconds of clear shooting before more of the enemy took them under fire. A rocket-propelled grenade arched up toward the roof where Dem and his half of the squad were. It went high and hit fifteen meters behind the reccers, rolling farther away before it exploded. All of the reccers had time to drop to their stomachs before the explosion. The shrapnel arched over them.

"*Now* it's time to move," Dem said as he got back up to his knees. "Fredo, cross to the far side of your roof. See what's there. The rest of us will go east, then north. On belts."

Lateral movement was tricky with the belts. The only effective way that the reccers had found was to jump at an angle, switching the belts on as they jumped. The gyro stabilizers needed a second to force a man upright. Further manipulation of the drive units themselves took care of the rest.

No one spotted Dem and his companions as they made their first leap.

"Hold on. Let's give those mudders our greeting card," Dem said after they landed. There were clusters of Heggies in the lane they had just leapt over, clustered at the ends of the building the reccers had just left. A couple of the Heggies were firing down the lane toward the 13th. More were watching the roofs where the shooting had been coming from. The rest were waiting their turn—or waiting for an order to advance down the avenue where so many of their comrades had been killed.

Dem and his men started with a volley of grenades. Before those exploded, the six reccers all opened up with their rifles—one Dupuy cough gun, four Armanoc zippers, and Dem's XAG-1 rifle.

"I think this thing is penetrating three layers of net armor," Dem said. He had his link to Fredo open, but he was speaking more to himself. "Through both sides of one man and into the next." Of course, that was at a range of no more than thirty or thirty-five meters. "We get everyone equipped with these and nobody'll stand up to us."

"One battle at a time," Fredo said. "There's a lot of work left here."

The reccers had only a few seconds of grace before they were spotted this time, especially Dem's group. Farther back from the front, the Heggies they attacked looked up more readily.

"Time to jump again," Dem told the five men with him. There had still been no casualties in the squad.

" 'Bout one more jump is all we have on these batteries," one of the others said. "Let's make it to someplace besides a roof."

Dem hadn't yet considered abandoning his rooftop strategy, but he hesitated long enough to think about the suggestion. "You're right, it is time for us to get back to ground level," he conceded. "But we'll jump to that next roof east, then go down the stairs. It's about time we made some big noises. Find something very explosive to touch off." Then he switched channels again, to let Fredo know what they were going to do.

"You're going to be on your own for a bit," Dem said. "Work east and north. We'll rendezvous as soon as we can."

"Just let us know when you're going to put a building into orbit," Fredo said. "I don't want to be on the roof when you do."

"I've got your blips on my visor," Dem said. Then he notified the other squads in his platoon, and the other recon platoon sergeants. All of them had also infiltrated the Heggie base by this time.

Several grenades tossed over the side of the building marked the farewell for Dem and his companions. While the explosives were going off in the lanes on the north and west side of the building, they ran across the roof and launched themselves toward the next building east. It was quite clear that this would be their last belt jump for at least four hours. Half of the team heard the low-power warning on their belts sound before they landed.

The door leading from the roof into this building was locked. Dem stuck a small chunk of plastic explosive over the lock and blew it. Inside, they found an open stairway leading down along the side wall. This warehouse seemed to be void of Heggies. At least, no one was visible from the stairs, and no one shot at the reccers. The building consisted of one large open space, fifteen meters by thirty and ten meters high. The lanes between stacks of supplies were two meters wide, enough to allow forklifts to maneuver. Two of those were parked at the end of adjacent aisles.

Halfway down the stairway, Dem paused to survey the interior. The other five men took up defensive positions, their weapons spread to cover the most likely avenues for Schlinal workers or soldiers.

The contents of several stacks were obvious: missiles for Boems and shells for Novas. The rest of the stacks consisted of crates, and there was no way for Dem to tell from a distance what was in them. The only legends on the crates were numbers.

"They *do* have tanks somewhere," Dem whispered. "Where there's shells, there's guns."

"How much of this stuff you figure we can cook off?" Coy Mueller asked.

"Let's see what's in the crates first," Dem said. He started down the stairs again, moving quickly. At the bottom, Dem used hand signals to indicate where he wanted each of his men. "Pry open a few crates. Those numbers on the first line look to be part numbers. Identical crates, identical numbers—should have identical contents."

The six men fanned out quickly. Dem used his belt knife to pry open the nearest crate. It contained rocket-propelled grenades. He helped himself to a half dozen. Dropping his visor for a minute, he said, "Somebody find launchers for these grenades. We can use them later.''

There were several crates of launchers in the next stack. Each of the reccers took one launcher and as many of the RPGs as he could carry.

Five minutes of searching gave the team a good idea of what the warehouse contained. Five minutes of more delicate work let them arm a dozen of the Boem missiles and aim them at other stacks, mostly at the tank shells. Strategically placed shaped charges would, if everything worked properly, ignite the rockets. The men pulled safety pins from the heads of as many missiles and shells as they could, arming the explosives.

''Give us enough time to get the hell away from here,'' Coy said when Dem started sorting through his selection of fuses.

''Remember, we're going to be on foot,'' Abe Junger added. ''No rocket man stuff.''

''The only caps we've got enough of are five-minute,'' Dem said. ''That's going to have to be time enough. Coy, you check that door on the east. Make sure we're going to be able to get out of here before we clip these caps.'' He didn't want to get caught in a firefight at the door of the warehouse once the timers were activated. ''Abe, you check the door on the north, just in case we need a different way out.'' Those were the only two exits that Dem had spotted.

Dem and two of the remaining men put the timed caps in place on the charges, but they waited for reports from the doors. Both were clear—clear enough for reccers.

''Abe, move around to the east door,'' Dem said. ''We'll take that.'' He watched until Abe was as close to the other exit as Dem was. Then he nodded at the men with him. Very quickly, they clipped the fuses to arm the charges they had placed.

No one needed an order to run for the door.

Mort Jaiffer pulled the dead Heggie off of Joe Baerclau. At first, Mort thought that the Bear was also dead. He knelt next to the platoon sergeant and felt his neck for a pulse. The relief Mort felt when his fingers detected a steady beat made him light-headed for a moment.

"Al, get over here!" he shouted into his radio. "The Bear needs help."

For the moment, most of Echo Company was out of the fighting. The heaviest action had moved into the avenues between the warehouses and other buildings and, in some cases, inside the buildings. It was a brutal kind of combat, but only so many men at a time would fit in the lanes between the buildings. Mostly, the 13th—and the units coming in from the north and south—were waiting for the Wasps to return and clear out the areas between the buildings. They were fighting a containing action, content to hold their own and keep the enemy from escaping or regrouping.

Al Bergon ran past a pile of Heggie bodies to Joe Baerclau. Mort had the sergeant's visor up and had already poured water over the Bear's face.

"I think the heat got him," Mort said. "I don't think the blood is his. At least I can't find any trace of a wound."

"He skewered the Heggie right enough," Al said, giving the dead man only a glance. Mort retrieved Joe's knife, which was still sticking in the man.

"You're right," Al said after he had checked Baerclau's vital signs. "Just the heat. Heat and exertion. He's starting to come around now."

Joe's eyes opened, but they were not focusing. They seemed to track separately at first, only slowly coming to some sort of accommodation with each other. Joe blinked once, then again.

"Sarge?" Al spoke loudly, even though his mouth was only a few centimeters from Baerclau's face. "You hear me?"

Joe blinked twice more, slowly. His head moved a little to one side, then back. He blinked again, trying to force his mind back to alertness.

"Sarge?" Louder.

"No need to shout," Joe said, his voice cracking. "I hear you."

"You took a nap," Al told him. That seemed to go right

past the sergeant. "Heat exhaustion and then some. You're dehydrated." *Like the rest of us,* he thought. He gave Baerclau a drink of water, then swabbed down his face with an alcohol-soaked patch. "Best I can do for now. I'm all out of IV bags. Doc Eddles is on his way up with what he needs to take care of all of the heat casualties."

Joe took in a long breath that was almost yawn. "How long was I out?"

"Don't know," Al said. "Mort found you under the Heggie you knifed. Just lie still," he added when Joe tried to sit up. "Don't complicate this."

"What's going on?" Joe asked as he went limp again. Obeying was much simpler than insisting on having his way.

Mort gave him the news, as briefly as he could. "Sergeant Degtree's taking care of the platoon for now," he added. "He's the only one left from his squad."

"What about the others?" Once more, Joe started to try to sit up, forgetting that he had just decided to obey Al and stay down. Al just put his hands on Baerclau's shoulders and held him down until Joe quit trying.

"I don't know. We lost men." Mort hesitated. "Pit's dead. Wiz is down, wounded. He's gonna need a few hours in a tube, I guess."

"Definitely," Al said, finishing his work on Baerclau. "But he'll be okay. And so will you, as long as you just lie there until Doc Eddles gets up here. We'll try to rig you a little shade."

Joe closed his eyes. There didn't seem to be much else he could do.

Dem and his men ran across one avenue and into the next building. He was certain that at least a few Heggies outside saw them, but the reccers weren't in the open long enough to draw fire. It didn't matter whether or not there were any Heggies inside the building that they ducked into. Even if there was an entire battalion of Heggies waiting, running into them was preferable to remaining too close to the building that had been rigged with explosives. That blast *might* not amount to much—but then again, it might be monstrous. A lot depended on luck, how many secondary explosions their preparations started. Dem didn't want to take chances.

There were only a handful of men in the building that the reccers ran into, and they appeared to be civilians. At any rate, they weren't in uniform and they weren't armed. As soon as they saw the reccers, the five men quickly raised their hands as high as they could. Dem used his rifle to motion them out into the open, away from any cover.

"Any more in here?" he demanded.

The response was almost unintelligible, but clearly a negative. Dem didn't recognize the dialect, but it was far from any of the language variants common in the Accord.

"Down." Dem gestured with his rifle to make sure that the men got his meaning. They went down rapidly, spreading arms and legs. All of them kept their eyes on their captors.

"Abe, you keep them covered while the rest of us move across to the far side. Don't get too far behind us. We've only got about ninety seconds left before. . . . " He didn't finish that, in case the prisoners might understand him better than he understood them.

"We gonna leave these jokers here?" Coy asked. "Colonel might appreciate some prisoners."

"Can't take the chance," Dem said. "Let's go. Abe, give us twenty seconds, then follow as fast as you can. We'll cover you."

Twenty seconds and then another twenty seconds to cross to the far side of the warehouse. Near the far wall there was a line of tanker trailers, all labeled as water. Dem eyed the nearest trailer for a moment. The temptation was too much.

"This ought to be safe enough," he said. "We're close to the door. Hunker down under whatever cover you can find. We'll try to take time to fill our canteens before we leave, if this place doesn't go up with the other building." *And if these cans are really full of water,* he thought.

He glanced at the time line on his visor display. Less

then ten seconds left. He got down in a hurry. So did the others, Abe skidding under one of the water tanks. As far as Dem could tell, none of the Heggie civilians had moved. He could see two of them, still spread-eagled on the floor.

The first sound that the reccers heard was a dull thump, an explosion baffled and damped by thick stone walls. Then the secondary blasts started. It was quite like an artillery barrage heard at a distance—for perhaps twenty seconds. One *crump-thump* followed another, the intervals decreasing.

Then there was one major blast. The warehouse in which the reccers were hiding shook violently. Two water trailers started to roll. Neither got far. Each bumped into a neighbor and stopped. Dust fell from the ceiling and from the girders that held it up. Somehow, clear against the immensity of the explosion, there were sharp, lighter sounds of glass breaking and small objects falling. The audible assault seemed to encompass the entire sound spectrum, from tones so low that they were felt rather than heard, to squeals that went right up to—and past—the upper limit of human hearing. The level crescendoed until some of the reccers clapped hands over the sides of their helmets, as close to their ears as they could get.

Fredo Gariston and the other half of the recon squad had one—questionable—advantage over the reccers who were hiding in the warehouse. They could see some of what happened. Two roofs to the north and one to the east of the explosions, they were much closer than they wanted to be.

Almost concurrent with the first sounds of the blast, the air itself seemed to compress around them. Dust rose from several rooftops. The stone roof over the explosion visibly bowed up, but before anyone could remark on that, the blast tore through the roof, scattering heavy chunks of stone and metal. With that barrier gone, the sound level doubled, trebled. Flame and debris shot skyward, seeking release through the line of least resistance. More of the roof gave way, collapsing. The secondary explosions continued for more than five minutes. Balls of flame jumped out of the breached roof, as if a succession of tiny new suns were being born.

The rooftop reccers lost interest in the show very quickly as debris started to rain down all around them: stone and metal—and more that couldn't readily be identified.

"Let's get out of here!" Fredo shouted at his companions. They were on the northeast corner of their roof, but debris was still falling around them—and far beyond.

"No juice for our jump belts," one of the others shouted back.

"We'll go down on ropes," Fredo said. Each reccer carried a twenty-five-meter rope. Half of them had grappling hooks. There were Heggies on the ground, hundreds of them in sight, but they had suddenly become the lesser evil. And the Heggies were equally intent on escaping the volcanic aftermath of the explosions.

As Fredo went over the side of the building, a last glance toward the warehouse that was exploding showed two walls collapsing, one inward, the other outward. He didn't wait to see if the rest of the building would fall as well.

Another shock wave shook the building that concealed Dem and his companions. A stack of crates near the west side of the building tipped over, starting a chain reaction that stopped only after three other stacks had fallen. Chunks of stone fell from the ceiling. One, perhaps several, of the civilians screamed in pain. Two got up and started running. They went right past Dem and his men without seeing them. The reccers moved farther under their cover.

Then the interior of the warehouse rang as if it were a gong. Dem looked up and saw the western wall sag inward. A long, vertical crack appeared and widened.

"Let's get out of here!" he shouted. He turned around on his belly and scrambled out from under the water trailer, heading for the nearest door. His companions were less than a second behind him.

Abe was the last man out, just before the building's west wall collapsed.

CHAPTER
8

The Schlinal prisoners were assembled into work gangs after the garrison surrendered. More than eleven hundred men had surrendered, about 20 percent of them civilians—prisoners or the descendants of prisoners. Even the female ten percent of the population were either prisoners or the descendants of men and women who had been sentenced to penal exile. Only in the rarest of circumstances did anyone descended from a penal exile make it off of a prison world. In the Hegemony, it was a crime to be born of criminals. And the sentence was life.

A half dozen of the highest ranking Schlinal officers, including the commandant of the penal colony and the commanding general of the army that had been staging on Tamkailo, were found together, their hands bound behind them, their throats slit. The commandant had been disemboweled and sexually maimed as well. More than thirty other officers and noncoms, mostly of the colony garrison, were also found dead in suspicious circumstances.

Not many Heggie officers of any rank survived. Two Accord Special Intelligence teams questioned those few officers, and a sampling of the enlisted men and civilians, through the remainder of the afternoon. Few of the prisoners were willing to say much, but the SI men learned enough—often by piecing together hints dropped by several different individuals—to know that in the last minutes of fighting there had been a mutiny coupled with a rebellion by the penal exiles. "Life's impossible here anyway," one private said sullenly. "We thought the whole place was going to blow up."

All of the munitions that remained in the depot were carried out into the open. The engineers burned what could be destroyed that way. Charges that had to be detonated were handled in small batches. Repeated explosions eventually gave the engineers a shallow pit to help contain later detonations. It was slow work. The depot had held tens of thousands of tons of tank shells, Boem and surface-to-air missiles, grenades, other explosives, and ammunition for rifles and machine guns, as well as thousands of those weapons.

Captain Hilo Keye limped into the field hospital that had been moved into one of the first buildings that had been emptied of its stores. Nearly three hundred Accord soldiers, and half that number of Heggies, were being treated. The warehouse did offer one very important advantage over the tents that had been used before. In addition to the insulation provided by its thick stone walls and ceiling, the warehouse had been air conditioned to help protect the munitions that had been stored in it, a luxury the Schlinal barracks did not enjoy. And the power supply had not been destroyed in the fighting.

For a couple of minutes, Keye stood just inside the door, off to the side, taking deep breaths of the interior air, luxuriating in the coolness of the interior. He leaned back against the wall to take his weight off of an aching left foot and ankle. Objectively, the temperature inside the building was still about 30 degrees Celsius, but the late afternoon temperature outside was closer to 40, without any shade except that available on the east and south sides of the buildings.

Echo Company, or as much of it as survived and wasn't in the hospital, was camped on the east side of one of those buildings. More than four hundred thousand liters of water had been liberated from the Heggies, and engineers were already making repairs to the water supply system. That had been seriously damaged in the battle. Accord troops were making liberal use of that water, not merely drinking it but standing under makeshift showers, just to cool off—a little. Sunset was still three hours away, and the air temperature had shown no indication of beginning to drop.

"Something I can do for you, Captain?"

Keye opened his eyes. He hadn't really been aware that he had shut them. He stared at the medic, a man he didn't recognize even though he had the 13th's patch on his collar. Keye blinked several times and dragged in one more deep breath before he spoke.

"Jammed foot, sprained ankle. Left foot."

The medic glanced down—the top of the boot was loose and a medical soaker had been wrapped around the ankle—then brought his gaze back up to the captain's eyes. "You can walk, sir?"

"I made it this far. If you'll give me a little help, I think I can make it the rest of the way. Doc Eddles busy?"

"Over in this corner, I think." The medic pointed, then pulled the captain's left arm around his neck and took a fair share of the weight "We've gotten pretty well organized."

It seemed to Keye that the journey from door to corner took forever, but—logically—he knew that it could hardly have been more than two minutes, even shuffling along and detouring around stretchers, trauma tubes, and working medtechs and surgeons. Long before he injured his foot and ankle—that had been done after the fighting had ended, in a stupid accident (at least Keye considered it stupid)—his mind had been wandering. Although he had paced himself as best he could, the heat had started to get to him. If the fighting had continued for even fifteen minutes longer than it had, Keye thought that he would have been down, out of action, just from the heat. *I'm too old for this crap* was little comfort. Somewhere along the way between his men and the hospital, he had already decided that he really was too old to continue in a field unit. It was a job for younger men. *If I can't transfer to some sort of staff position, I'll have to get out.* It was a painful realization, more painful than his ankle. And he was certain that he would not change his mind later, when the ankle—and the heat of Tamkailo—were no more than bad memories.

Doc Eddles, Echo's medtech, saw the captain being helped toward him and broke away from what he was doing to go to the medic's aid.

"Captain?" Eddles said.

"Ankle and foot," Keye replied. "And the heat. I was starting to lose it"—he had to drag in a long breath before he could complete the sentence—"before I hurt myself."

The two men laid the captain on a stretcher. As soon as he was down, Hilo closed his eyes and again let out his breath. Being flat on his back came as a distinct relief. He could feel tension draining away. He heard Eddles thank the medic and then sensed that the medtech had knelt at his side. A medtech was more than a medic but less than a surgeon. Eighteen months of specialized training equipped him to perform anything less than major invasive surgery, but medical nanobots and trauma tubes meant that major invasive surgery was seldom necessary. And the military training would qualify Eddles for a civilian medtech's license when his contractual tour of duty was over.

"I'm going to set up a drip before I work on your ankle, Captain," Eddles said, his voice soft enough that it seemed to Keye to be almost part of a dream. "Got to get you rehydrated."

Keye didn't bother to answer. He felt as if he could slide into sleep, or something even deeper, but he felt no concern. Whatever happened . . .

•   •   •

Joe Baerclau felt sixty kilos lighter as he picked his way through the confusion in the hospital, heading back to his platoon. Since all of his combat gear had been taken off of him before he was carried to the hospital, he *was* significantly lighter. Rifle and gear added up to thirty kilograms, even allowing for the wire and grenades he had expended and two empty canteens. Dehydration would have accounted for perhaps another couple of kilos. Joe felt as if he were about to float off of the ground.

Other than feeling as if he were in low gravity, Joe felt exceptionally well. At the moment, he didn't even feel particularly hot. Fluids had been pumped back into his body. Even now, medical nanobots were coursing through his system, neutralizing toxins and completing their repair work. But the heat was just beyond the next door.

Although Joe didn't know it, the stretcher that he had vacated had been occupied less than three minutes later by Captain Keye, before Joe got across the room. Joe was eager to get back to his men, to show them that he was still in one piece and ready for duty, but he did hesitate before opening the door that would take him out of the hospital. The memory of the heat was almost as oppressive as the real thing. It wasn't until the door opened and two men carried in a stretcher with yet another heat casualty on it that Joe took one last breath of the air-conditioned air and went outside.

He had been given precise directions on where to find his men, and he had also been assured that the entire compound had been secured, that there were no more Heggies armed and on the loose. He wouldn't have let words alone reassure him, but the obvious presence of Accord soldiers along the side of the building did. If there *were* still Heggies around, there were more than enough friendlies to take care of them.

Looking along the avenue, Joe saw what remained of the warehouse that had been blown up from inside. Not much, that is. The buildings on the two nearer sides were both seriously damaged as well. Joe looked for a moment, then turned and walked the other way, north. He went to the corner, then crossed the open space to reach the shady southern side of the next building. Echo was supposed to be on the east side of that building.

Mort Jaiffer was the first man in Joe's platoon to spot him. Mort was the only man in the platoon on his feet, leaning against the building while everyone else was sitting, or lying, in the growing patch of afternoon shade.

"We expected you a half hour ago, Sarge," Mort said. His voice was flat, without the usual bantering tone.

"Couldn't tear myself away from the good life," Joe replied. "You got my gear stashed somewhere?"

"Better than new." Mort pointed to a rather disorganized-looking pile. "Right with mine. Even loaded your canteens for you."

Joe nodded. By that time Sauv Degtree had gotten to his feet and moved to meet Baerclau.

"The platoon's yours again, Joe," Sauv said softly. "And welcome to it." None of the men had their visors down. This was as close to "off duty" as they were likely to get on an enemy-held world.

"Give me the report," Joe said. He looked around for a place where the two of them might speak privately, but the shady zone along the side of the building was crammed from one end to the other, and Joe didn't relish moving out into the sunshine any sooner than he absolutely had to.

"Twenty effectives now that you're back," Sauv said, lowering his voice. "Two men in hospital."

Joe couldn't help the narrowing of his eyes. Twenty plus two: that meant that the platoon had lost seven men killed.

Sauv waited until he saw Joe's eyes start to relax. "Captain's in the hospital. Twisted his ankle. Underwood's back for duty. You know that I'm the only one left from third squad," he said.

Joe nodded again. "We'll have to reorganize. You'll take over first squad, at least until we get off this cinder. I don't have any idea what'll happen then. Mort will be happy to go back to being assistant squad leader. Hang on." He gestured for Mort to come over and told him what he was doing.

Mort's nod was almost gleeful. "You can give somebody my corporal's stripes too. Let me go back to being just a plain mudder."

"It doesn't work that way," Joe said. That was a continuation of a discussion that had been going on between the two men for more than a year.

"Jaiffer, I'm going to need your help getting to know what the others in the squad can do," Degtree said. "*You* I know about."

Mort almost blushed. "My reputation precedes me." He had been feeling as low as he ever got. The talk was starting to revive him.

"It does," Degtree agreed. He turned back toward Baerclau. "You need me for anything else right now?"

Joe shook his head.

"Come on, Professor. Let's go talk to the men," Degtree said. He let Mort lead him over to first squad.

Joe trailed along. He strapped on his web belt, put the Corey belt over it, then picked up his rifle and other gear. He slung the rifle over his shoulder but just carried the backpack and the items that normally hung from it. He pulled down his visor long enough to make a quick call to the first sergeant.

"Where are you?" Joe asked.

"North end of the wall, just before the shade runs out," Walker said. "How you feeling?"

"Good as new. I'll be there in a couple of minutes."

Joe walked slowly. Even in the shade, it was oppressively hot, and there seemed to be no particular hurry. It was obvious that no one in the company had any news of impending action. *I guess nothing is going to happen before the captain gets back,* Joe thought.

"Take a load off," Izzy Walker said when Joe got to him. The first sergeant indicated a patch of ground next to him, against the side of the building. His visor was up and his helmet tilted back at an angle. "This wall is almost cool," he added. There was a space of almost three meters to the next man along the wall, the largest opening along the entire length of the building.

Joe sat before he spoke. "I've got seven dead and two in the hospital."

Walker sighed. "I know. Degtree gave me the platoon report thirty minutes ago. The rest of the company's been hit just as bad. Almost thirty percent killed or too badly hurt to get back to duty in the next twenty-four hours."

Any injury that required more than four hours in a trauma tube was rare, and *serious*. Those were life-threatening injuries, the type that were usually saved only because of very prompt treatment.

"Why couldn't we just sit back and let the flyguys and gun bunnies do the work? Hell, we coulda stayed on the ships until they leveled this place, just come in to clean up," Joe said, his voice somewhat plaintive. "That frontal attack . . . ." He shook his head. "That was just plain suicide."

"Time, Joe," Izzy said. "These stone buildings, it would have taken days for the Havocs and Wasps to bring them down. The reccers cooked off a whole warehouse full of explosives, and hell, that didn't do much damage to anything else but two buildings just on either side." He paused before he added, "We've got a schedule here, and we're far enough behind it now."

"Farther north," Joe whispered.

"Hopefully, that'll still be a night action," Izzy said. "There's another reason why we had to get Site Alpha taken before dark. *Somewhere* around here, there's got to be a whole fleet of Nova tanks."

"I heard that SI's interrogating prisoners. They find out where those tanks are, or why they haven't been used?"

Izzy shrugged. "Not as I've heard. The reccers are out looking for them. And every eye in the sky. One thing for certain, they're not in this compound."

"Where the hell is there to hide tanks on this rock pile?"

"Man who comes up with the answer to that, before the tanks come out and hit us, is likely to get a promotion on the spot, and enough medals to build a Havoc. Only thing anybody can figure out is that they must be underground—somewhere."

"Scuttlebutt was that they can't operate Novas in this heat, 'cept maybe at night," Joe said after the two men had been silent for a minute or more.

"You noticed the Havocs weren't spittin' very fast," Izzy said.

"I thought it was just me."

"Even with cold air pumping at full speed it got so hot inside them buckets that they had to back off. Had a lot of heat casualties. I've talked to men who've looked over the insides of Novas. No air conditioning."

"So, as soon as it gets dark, we're apt to have trouble?" Joe asked.

"Wouldn't surprise me."

"We staying here tonight?"

It was time for another shrug. Izzy stretched this one out. "According to the plan, we're supposed to be back on the shuttles before sunset today, moving to attack that next Heggie place on the west coast, north of here, northwest. Site Bravo." He glanced at the sky, then out at the length of the shadow stretching away from the building. "Nobody's saying anything about moving now, though. I checked with the CSM." The command sergeant major was Friz Duke, the ranking enlisted man in the 13th SAT. "Everything's on hold."

"For how long?"

"Until somebody says different. I just don't know. I hope they're not gonna try a dawn landing at the other spot. We try to work during the day at Site Bravo, it'll be a hundred times worse than today."

"And if we wait for tomorrow night, they'll have that much more time to get ready for us."

"That's about the size of it," Walker agreed.

Joe got to his feet slowly. "I'd better get back to my men." He was shaking his head as he walked away.

CHAPTER
9

Although oceans had ceased to be commercially important for human settlements thousands of years before, men still sought locations near them, on almost every world that was settled. Oceans were a constant: if a world was suitable for humans, between 50 and 80 percent of its surface would be covered by water. No matter the vagaries of weather, and the often serious threat of tropical storms, men sought the sea. The first settlements on any newly settled world were almost always near the mouths of major rivers as well. There were always excuses for both choices, some of them valid. Oceans tended to moderate climate. Rivers provided abundant sources of fresh water and made the natural growth of crops possible. In addition, if the local waters did not contain edible fish and other seafood, terrestrial varieties could be introduced and established. Although food replicators could provide virtually any crop, or meat, that humans had ever cultivated or craved—as well as novel varieties that had never existed in nature—few social groups cared to subsist totally on the provender of nano-factories, preferring to keep at least a portion of their diet "natural."

Even on Tamkailo, a world where no human food crops could grow, where no terran animals could graze, the Schlinal settlers had chosen sites near the sea. All three Heggie bases were within a few kilometers of ocean, situated on or near major rivers. The rationale, in addition to natural tendency, was clear on Tamkailo. All three settlements had started out as penal colonies. Oceans provided a clear limit to the directions an escapee might take. To a lesser extent, so did major rivers.

It had scarcely occurred—or mattered—to the planners of these penal colonies that there was no place for an escapee to run to on Tamkailo. Leaving the isolated settlements was certain suicide. *Absolutely* certain. If the heat didn't kill the escapee, he would die of hunger. Nothing grew on the world that would sustain human life. But proper reverence had to be paid to the traditional Schlinal methods of operation.

Only four Wasps were in the air. The 8th SAT was currently providing that air cap. The rest of the planes were on the ground undergoing routine maintenance. Their pilots did what they could to remain cool. They had eaten. Most tried to sleep while they could, but the heat made that difficult. Still west of the captured Schlinal base, the pilots and their support crews did not have cavernous stone buildings to shelter in. They had to make do with tents and open pavilions for cover from the late afternoon sun. Mechanics had jury-rigged a few large fans, but those provided only minimal relief.

The Havocs of the two SATs were also idle, parked around the Schlinal base. The artillery crews were inside buildings, or on the shaded sides of those buildings. Nearly a third of the men from the gun crews were in the hospital being treated for heat exhaustion or worse. The Havocs had suffered no losses from enemy fire during this attack—they had never been close enough to enemy infantry to worry about shoulder-launched missiles, and the Wasps had kept all of the enemy Boems well away—but one loader in the 8th had died from the heat before his crewmates could get help for him.

Jimmy Ysinde was back with the rest of Basset two after spending two hours in the hospital. He still looked pale and felt weak, but the medtech had cleared him for duty.

"I was off in some neverland," Jimmy said as he sat in the corner of a building that contained a dozen industrial food replicators, stacks of raw materials for them, and finished meal packs. The others stared at Jimmy. For a moment, he stared at the floor between his feet. When he did look up again, he said, "It was hell coming back." The strained look on his face was more than just a reminder of his physical suffering.

"But you are back," Karl Mennem said, worried at the way Jimmy sounded—almost as if he regretted the return trip.

"Yeah. But what about next time?"

"Hey, they know how vulnerable we are now," Eustace Ponks said. "Some of the crew chiefs are working on a way to make things easier for us. Rosey said there ought to be a way to rig a third air cooler in each of the guns." Rosey Bianco headed the maintenance crew that serviced Basset one and Basset two.

"There enough spares for that?" Simon Kilgore asked.

"Rosey says yes," Eustace said. "Maybe even a fourth in some of them, but I think the chiefs want to keep a few handy for replacements."

"That might help here," Jimmy said, "but we're going closer to the equator for the next operation. Will it be enough?"

No one could answer that.

The chief regimental surgeon kept Colonel Stossen in the hospital for nearly six hours. The only way he could do that was to keep Stossen unconscious until right near the end. No sooner was Stossen awake than he wanted his helmet so he could get back in touch with what was happening. He still had a minor headache. Still, or again. Stossen was aware of it as soon as the nanobots scrubbed the last of the sleep patch's medication from his system and he woke up.

"Just take it easy for a few minutes, Colonel," the surgeon said. "You came close to not waking up at all."

"But I *am* awake," Stossen said. "And I've got a command to see to."

"Soon enough. Look, this battle is over. You're inside what used to be the Heggie base. We're secure. The exec knows what shape you're in. He'll be here to pick you up in a few minutes. Until then, you just lie there and let the knitting finish. I should have kept you out and in the trauma tube for another hour. In any case, I'm not releasing you for duty until Parks gets here."

Stossen took a deep breath. The surgeon did have that authority, even over him. "So I'll stay," he said. "At least let me communicate."

"Not a chance, Colonel. A radio puts you back on duty." He looked around, as if he hoped to spot Lieutenant Colonel Parks coming into the hospital. Actually, he hoped that the executive officer would stall as long as possible.

"Just a link to General Dacik then."

"Colonel, you've had a rough time. You spend much more time trying to wheedle me out of doing my duty and you're not going to be fit to do yours. Is that clear, sir?" The surgeon stared at the colonel without blinking until Stossen nodded.

"I get the message." Stossen closed his eyes and took a deep breath. *Maybe it's just as well,* he thought. *We're in the Heggie compound. Things must be going okay here, or the doc wouldn't keep me down so long. Maybe.*

As he relaxed, the ache in his forehead started to ease. Faster than he would have thought possible, Stossen started to drift back toward sleep. He didn't even try to fight it. Then, just as he was ready to cross the divide, he felt as if he were suddenly falling, and that snapped his eyes open.

Dezo Parks was standing over him.

"Doc tells me you haven't been very cooperative," Parks said.

"That's his business. Mine's running the 13th," Stossen growled. "You here to spring me?"

Parks nodded. "We've got a briefing to attend in about twelve minutes."

"Dacik?" Stossen asked as he sat up—slowly, cautiously.

Parks nodded again. "HQ's in the next building north of here."

"Any idea what we're going to hear?" Stossen was relieved that he didn't feel dizzy or light-headed, and the pain didn't return. Standing was the next procedure to attempt, but he did plan on taking his time about it. Despite what he had told the chief regimental surgeon, he did know that he was still shaky. The medical nanobots of a trauma tube might repair damage in a hurry, but there was always a little left to get through afterward.

"Other than that we're more than ten hours behind schedule, no," Parks said. "I imagine we'll get a new schedule, maybe find out what's happening with the 5th and 34th on the other continent."

"Give me a hand, Dezo. I don't want to fall on my ass again."

He really didn't need much help. He used Parks more for balance than real support, and he let go as soon as he was on his feet and confident that he could stay there.

"How badly were we hurt?" Stossen asked as he experimented with easy movements. He had to look fit moving, at least until he was away from the hospital and the watchful eyes of the surgeon.

"Pretty bad," Parks admitted. As they walked across the warehouse to the door, he told him just how badly.

It was an unusually large meeting for a combat zone, even if there seemed to be little immediate prospect of continued fighting. It would have been much more normal for only the most essential of people to gather in one place for the conference. The rest would participate by radio, with linked mapboards. But Major General Kleffer Dacik preferred to be able to have eye contact. He and his staff were all present for this meeting, along with the commanders, and the executive and operations officers for the 8th and 13th SATs, the 97th LIR, and the 17th Independent Air Wing. The subsidiary air and artillery commanders for the two SATs were also in attendance. Van Stossen and Dezo Parks were the last to arrive.

"Good to see you back on your feet, Van," Dacik said as he gestured the two men to seats. The seats were packing crates. The conference table was a collection of crates that had been covered with a tarp.

"I feel kind of foolish about it all, General," Stossen replied. "Hell of a way to get injured."

"There aren't any good ways," Dacik said. "I assume your exec's brought you up to date on the basics?"

"Yes, sir, as much as there was time for on the walk over from the hospital."

Dacik leaned back and let his gaze drift around at the faces that had gathered for this briefing. All were career military men, but until the start of the war with the Schlinal Hegemony, none of them had had actual combat experience. There were privates who had seen as much or more battle than these men. But they were the best that the Accord had, and the past few years had made them all experts. The hard way.

"I've been on the line with CIC for the better part of a half hour, running our options through the computers," Dacik said when he had finished his visual survey. "There's no mistaking the fact that our timetable for Tamkailo has been shot full of holes." He shrugged. "We more or less knew that it would be DOA, one way or another. The 13th's problems on those rocks . . . well, that's something we couldn't possibly have planned for. SI has been collecting samples. A shuttle's already taken those up to the flagship. There's a chance the lab people might make something useful of it."

"I'd settle for a way to counter it," Stossen said. The laughs that came from the men around the "table" told him that everyone knew exactly how he had suffered his injury.

"I'd rather have a way to deal with the heat," Napier Foss, the commander of the 8th SAT, said. "We know about the moss now. Some of us better than others." He didn't bother to wait for the laughs. "We can avoid the moss or run Wasps across again if we come up against it. What we can't avoid is the heat if we're going to operate on a world like this."

Colonel Luro Bones, C.O. of the 97th, snorted. "Unless someone's got air-conditioned skivvies, we're out of luck on that."

"As a matter of fact, sir," Captain Lorenz, Dacik's aide, said, "that *has* been tried. Not here, and not skivvies, but air-conditioned battle fatigues. The idea was discarded as totally impractical, something we weren't likely enough to need to spend the necessary money."

"Skimping on Corders. That figures," Bones said. He snorted again. It was a trait he was rather noted for, especially among his own officers. Some claimed that they could distinguish among at least a dozen different snorts that the colonel used regularly. And decipher them.

"We're not here to discuss the failings of the Quartermaster Corps," Dacik said pointedly. "We make do with what we have, as always."

There were no apologies. That would have upset Dacik even more than the digression, and everyone at the conference knew that.

"The immediate problem remaining at Site Alpha is that we still have two regiments of Heggies unaccounted for."

"Two?" Stossen asked.

"One regiment of armor, Nova tanks, and one regiment of armored infantry and their APCs."

"Hasn't Intelligence managed to find out where they are from the prisoners?" Bones asked.

"Only in the most general fashion," Major Jorgen Olsen, Dacik's Intelligence chief, said. "Within twenty-five kilometers of here, in some sort of underground complex drilled out of the bedrock. There was no sign of that sort of thing on any of our surveys from space, and we haven't been able to pick up anything even now that we're looking for it. We hope to avoid active seismic mapping. We'd have to bring gear down from the fleet for that, and it would mean more delay. There are no piles of debris or anything else to give us a clue. Apparently, the rock quarried in the construction of the underground complex was used in building this base. It's been here since the beginning, according to our sources at least.''

''And we didn't have a glimmer as to its existence until we started looking for the missing Schlinal armor,'' Dacik interjected. When Olsen looked at the general, Dacik made an impatient gesture for him to resume.

''Our guesses this morning that the Heggies had realized that they couldn't use their armor during the day appear to be accurate. But that's still conjectural. On all three bases, the Heggies have apparently done most work at night, leaving the daylight hours for sleep. More to the point,'' he said, with a quick glance at Dacik's impatient look, ''the soldiers who manned *this* base had virtually no contact with the armor and mounted infantry regiments in this underground base we're looking for. All they could say for certain was that they had never seen Novas during the day, except when they were brought off of the shuttles. The chain of command connected only at the very top on Tamkailo, and the separation was enforced with the usual Heggie rigor.''

''An elite corps?'' Foss asked.

''We're not sure,'' Olsen said. ''It might be nothing more than the usual Schlinal paranoia of keeping absolute separation between units so that they can't conspire to overthrow their leaders.

''We've had Wasps looking, and the reccers are out as well. We will find the entrances to this underground complex, possibly any second now. It is a matter of some importance that we find the armor before dark, and sunset is now''—he looked at his watch—''two hours and thirteen minutes away.''

''Listening gear?'' Stossen suggested. ''They start an

engine, we ought to be able to hear it, even if they've got thirty meters of solid rock on top of them.''

"We've got gear on the ground and the most sensitive laser mapping eyes in orbit scanning the area around here," Dacik confirmed. "Just nothing sophisticated enough to do anything more active. Either the Heggies are too deep for either sort of equipment to detect them or they're being cagey as hell. We assume the latter. The second we locate entrances, we'll move our forces to cover them, artillery standing off, infantry in close, Wasps staging overhead. Everything we've got at Site Alpha. There's no way that those Heggie troops and vehicles can break out and do serious damage if we keep our eyes and ears open. At most, they'll have two or three exits. Even if each one can handle three vehicles abreast and they come out racing at full speed, we should be able to stop them almost instantly, block the entrances with their own wreckage. It wouldn't matter if they outnumbered us a hundred to one as long as they've got tight bottlenecks to come through to get at us.''

"Wouldn't it be, ah, safer to simply plug the entrances as soon as they're found?" Bones asked. "We've got engineers and a lot of explosives around, don't we?''

"We won't know if that's even feasible until the engineers get a chance to look at the entrances," Olsen said. "The type of rock around here, we simply might not have the capacity to plug all of the exits thoroughly enough to solve the . . . problem.''

"And we have to account for all of those Heggies, one way or another?" Van Stossen made it a question only for form's sake.

"Affirmative," Dacik said. "Destroy or disable. We can't leave those two regiments, men or equipment, behind after we leave in any condition where they might be used by the enemy.''

"What does it do to the timetable?" Stossen asked. "I know we're already behind schedule. And how are the 5th and 34th managing?''

"The 5th and 34th are doing their job, holding," Dacik said. "The Heggie defense at Site Charley is active and unified.'' It sounded like a press release, saying very little, and the general's tones made certain that there were no follow-up questions on the subject. When he wanted them to know more, he would tell them.

''We were supposed to be embarking for our second landing this evening, by now or before,'' Bones pointed out. ''Have you decided what we're going to do about that part of our mission, sir?''

''It has to wait until we finish up this operation,'' Dacik said. ''Since we don't dare try to operate at Site Bravo during daylight hours, it looks as if we'll have to move that forward until tomorrow night.'' He paused before he added, ''And hope that we can get the job done in one night, before daybreak.'' It was more than just the impossibility of operating during the day there. A one-day delay in the operation was bad enough. He didn't want to contemplate losing a second day. The 5th and 34th might not be able to hold on that long.

''We are getting more intelligence on Site Bravo,'' Major Olsen said. ''More passes with the spyeyes. That's the one advantage to the delay. We'll have a better idea what we're getting into there than we did here.'' Olsen glanced at the general, then started to say something else, but he stopped before the first word was entirely out.

''The enemy tanks,'' he said after a moment, holding up a hand to stop any questions while he listened to more of the report over his helmet radio. ''The 13th's reccers and SI have found two entrances and think they know where there's a third.'' Another silence. ''The two places they've seen are nearly three kilometers apart, and more than twenty klicks from here, northeast, closer to the shore.''

Dacik stood while Bones said, ''Three klicks? That's one hell of a big hole in the ground.''

''Gentlemen, we have work to do,'' the general said. ''Get back to your units as fast as you can. By the time you've got your people assembled, we should have your orders ready. Jorgen, get enough shuttles down here right now to move everyone into position.''

''Shuttles, for twenty kilometers?'' Olsen asked.

Imp -2

SD 1-1

Ben

Mini -2

2　　➲　[Grant
1 800 - 896 - 1669　[Det
[

<u>A 211 => 206</u>

		⊗ Dallas 10-4
Buffalo	9-5	Phil 9-5
Indi	8-6	Arizona 4-10
[miami	7-6	Ny G 5-9
NE	6-8	Wash 4-10
Ny Jet	3-11	

		*GB 9-5
⊗ Pitt	10-4	Det 8-6
· Cinn	6-8	Minn 8-6
Hou	5-9	· Chi 7-7
Cleve	4-10	*TB 7-7
Jacksonville	3-11	

		SF 10-4
[KC	11-2	Atl 8-6
Oakland	8-6	St. Lou 7-7
- Denver	7-7	Carolina 6-8
SD	7-7	NO 6-8
+ Seattle	7-7	

"I want everyone in position around that complex before dark," Dacik said. "There's not enough time for us to walk that far. Let's get this business finished as quickly as we can."

Dem Nimz and his recon platoon had been joined by the Special Intelligence team headed by Sergeant Gene Abru for this hunt. Nimz and Abru didn't waste time congratulating each other when they spotted the first of the entrances to the underground facility. They confirmed their discovery less than thirty seconds before one of the other search teams found a second opening. The ramp leading out was sculpted so carefully that a Wasp flying an overhead search pattern at only a hundred meters had missed it completely. The line of the ramp leading down to the entrance pointed almost directly at the late afternoon sun, which meant that there was only the narrowest strip of shadow along one side of the ramp. The walls were angled and smooth.

"A savvy piece of work," Abru commented, studying it through binoculars at a distance of no more than fifty meters from the upper end of the ramp.

"Better than I would have expected from Heggies," Dem said.

Gene nodded. "A hell of a lot of thought and work went into that. They didn't build this in a day, or in a year—if it's all one piece from here to the other exit."

"Makes you wonder, don't it?"

"I'd sure like to sneak a look inside," Gene said. "This has got to be more than just a parking garage, that's for certain. There *must* be more to it than that."

"Want to try to get in for a look-see?" Nimz suggested. "Your guys and a couple of us?"

Abru wanted nothing more. If his mouth hadn't been so dry from operating out in the heat all day, he would have salivated at the prospect. But after a moment, he took the binoculars away from his eyes and shook his head. This was no time for heat dreams.

"Even *I* don't think that's possible, and that's saying

something," he said, turning to look at Nimz. "They've got to have those entrances covered with enough firepower to wipe out a battalion, and probably electronic alarms as well. A mosquito couldn't get in unobserved."

"Just a thought," Dem said. "There probably won't be much left afterwards, if we stick around long enough to look then."

We will, Abru thought. *No way we can go home without finding out what the Heggies have been up to down there.* With or without General Dacik's approval, Special Intelligence was going to have a look around.

"We will have to get a little closer, in any case," he said. "Try to see what kind of fortifications they've got at the bottom of that ramp. The more we can learn now, the easier a time the rest of the force will have."

"You're the boss here," Dem said easily. Theoretically, he and Abru were the same rank, both platoon sergeants. But rank meant something entirely different in SI. Even Colonel Stossen treated SI sergeants as equals.

Abru made his dispositions quickly. The SI team and one squad of reccers would go forward for the look. The rest of the recon platoon would spread out to provide cover for them, just in case they stirred up something.

"Keep a sharp eye for mines and bugs," Abru warned everyone before they started out. "Not just to keep ourselves together. The general's sending out a welcome party for these gophers."

The reccers and SI men were all experts at this sort of drill, detecting even the slightest hint of a mine or booby trap. But all of the expertise in the galaxy wasn't enough this time. The lead team had gone no closer than thirty meters from the side of the ramp's end when a perfectly camouflaged mine popped up a meter off of the ground and exploded in front of half of the reccer squad.

CHAPTER 10

Simon Kilgore maneuvered Basset two into position. It was still extremely hot inside the turret. He couldn't touch the ceiling without burning his fingertips. He had found that out by accident. Sunset was a few minutes away. There had been some very minor easing in the outside temperature, but the Havoc's air conditioning had not yet caught up with the demand. Three air conditioners now. The extra had been installed in the rear compartment, but close to the one open connection between the back and the front, near the barrel of the howitzer. Jimmy and Karl, the two men in back, said that they could feel the difference that the third unit made.

"I've got a nasty itch about this," Simon said on the crew's radio channel. "Lining us up like ducks in a shooting arcade."

"You and me both," Eustace agreed, the statement almost a growl. "But unless the Heggies have armor stashed somewhere besides the holes the reccers found, we should be okay. Even if they come popping out of those holes, we're outside the range of a Nova right now." Not by much. The Nova's smaller main gun had an effective range of about ten kilometers, half that of a Havoc, and Basset Battery was positioned eleven kilometers from the nearest of the exits from the underground complex.

The 13th's Afghan Battery was slightly closer, and directly in line with one of the ramps. All but one gun of Afghan Battery had been destroyed in the 13th's last campaign, so the colonel had given them the "honor" of having the most direct shot at any Heggie vehicles that came out of that exit. If the Heggies didn't try to come out, Afghan was positioned so that its guns could zero in on the doors at the bottom end of the ramp.

Eustace was more than willing to concede that honor to Afghan, or to anyone other than his Fat Turtle—the name painted on the side of Basset two's turret. Eustace was much happier being a little to the side. A Nova would have to traverse fifty meters of the ramp from the underground door to get high enough to rotate its turret to get a shot at the Fat Turtle. Long before that could happen, Basset two could have a shell on its way—and be moving fast, in any direction.

Captain Ritchie, Basset Battery's commander, doubted that any Nova could get far enough up the ramp to be any threat at all. "There's mudders out there too, with Vrerchs. We might not even get a chance to fire a shot."

Eustace hadn't argued the point, but he didn't accept the captain's optimism either. *We don't ever get off that easy,* he had thought.

Ponks used a periscope to check the infantry's movement. Shuttles had moved them in to within five kilometers of the entrances. They were moving closer on foot, slowly, as if they expected the enemy to pop right out of the rocks in front of them. *Or mines,* Eustace conceded mentally. He had heard scuttlebutt about a reccer patrol caught by a bouncer. News like that always traveled fast.

"Jimmy, you be sure to yell if the pace starts to get to you once the shooting starts," Eustace said on a private channel. "Don't be foolish. We don't want you dropping again."

"I'll be okay, Gunny," Ysinde replied. "They fixed me up good as new this afternoon, and the extra cooler does make a difference back here."

"Guys have cooked in these cans even on worlds that weren't as bitchin' hot as this one. Just be careful."

"Yeah, yeah. How long we gonna have to wait here? The boredom's gonna get me long before the heat does."

"Once it gets full dark, I don't think the colonel will wait long, or the general," Eustace said. *I sure as hell wouldn't,* he thought. If worse came to worst, the Havocs might sit in front of the ramps and pour rounds in through the doorways until there was no chance of anyone inside surviving. The batteries could take turns, spelling each other so that no one would get *too* hot. It wouldn't be possible for all of the Havocs to get in line with the doors at once.

Dem Nimz had been talking to himself a lot. He wanted to be back out where the action was going to be, not sitting in a field hospital with a trauma tube locked around his left arm. Fredo had nearly had to coldcock him to get him to a medic in the first place. With his left arm hanging useless and bleeding from a dozen shrapnel wounds, Dem had still tried to help men who were hurt worse that he was. Five of his men had been killed by the mine, and two of the SI men as well. Nearly everyone else in both groups had been wounded. Dem wasn't certain, but he thought that Gene Abru might have been the only man not killed or wounded by the explosion.

Man's got more luck than anyone I ever saw, Dem thought. Abru's battle fatigues hadn't even been touched. *I got his load as well as mine, I guess,* Dem decided. If he had been standing just a few centimeters to one side or the other, Abru would have been hit as well.

Dem tried to look around, but with the trauma tube anchored next to him and his arm held tightly by the device—all of the way to the shoulder—his mobility was limited. Fredo had been with him a few minutes before, but now he had gone off to talk to the other injured members of the squad. Two men, according to Fredo, had already been treated and sent back to the platoon. Fredo had scarcely been scratched himself. He had been at the far end of the line when the mine went off. Both of his hands had been cut up, a little, but no shrapnel had been imbedded in the cuts. Small soakers had killed the pain and would heal the cuts soon enough.

Dem's helmet was sitting on the floor next to him, out of reach, so he couldn't even use the radio or see what the time was—how much longer he had to spend in the tube. Two hours, the surgeon had said, minimum. If the nanobots hadn't transported all of the bits of shrapnel to the surface by then, it might be twice as long.

"Fredo, you'd better take good care of my new rifle," Dem muttered. The experimental weapons couldn't be left lying around, even in a hospital. Dem couldn't protect it while he was being treated, so Fredo had it.

Dem's mind drifted back to the instant just before the explosion. He had been watching the ground closely. It was all bare rock. How had the Heggies managed to conceal a mine on that? He would have sworn that he could not have missed so much as a grain of sand on that surface. But he could see the mine pop up to waist level in his memory. There had been no warning at all, not a glimmer.

"We're not the only ones coming up with new gimmicks," he muttered. Then his system gave in to the medication being released in his bloodstream. He slid into an empty sleep.

Kleffer Dacik had dragged his staff to the roof nearest the enemy's underground complex.

"We should have gone in with the troops," he mumbled. The entrances weren't even visible from this distance. He couldn't even see the troops who were closest to the nearest ramp, at about twenty kilometers. Only Dacik's aide was close enough to hear.

"We'll have video from the Wasps once they get into it,

sir, and more from the line companies,'' Hof Lorenz said. ''Down there on the ground, we wouldn't have a much better view of the whole operation than we will from here.'' *Unless we got right down with the front-line mudders, we wouldn't see anything,* he thought. That wasn't something he was apt to say to the general. Dacik was much too likely to decide that he wanted to be that close. Lorenz had spent virtually his entire military career in staff positions. Every superior he had ever worked for had agreed that he had a particular knack for staff work. He worked hard to maintain that evaluation. Staff work brought him as much danger as he might ever desire. On Jordan, it had very nearly killed him.

Dacik pulled his visor down to take advantage of the night-vision systems built into it. The sun had finally set. Evening dusk was rapidly turning to full darkness. Already there was a vivid star field visible overhead, though neither of Tamkailo's two moons was out at the moment. One would rise in a half hour, the other not until nearly two hours later. The two moons combined did not have the surface area of Earth's one moon, and their albedo was slightly lower, but when they were combined with the thick star field around Tamkailo, the night could actually be slightly brighter than a clear full-moon night on Earth.

''Olsen, there any word yet on movement down any of those ramps?'' Dacik asked.

''Not a glimmer, sir,'' Olsen replied. ''We've got bugs in close enough to hear the slightest sound. No matter how silent those doors are, we'd hear residual sounds from inside. A big cave complex like that, the echoes of even a boot scraping on rock would carry if one of those doors opened.''

''It'll still be a few minutes before the last of the dusk line fades from the west, sir,'' Lorenz said. ''They'll probably want every bit of darkness they can get. I guess that means before the moons rise.'' *Poor bastards,* he thought. The Heggies waiting underground had to know that they had virtually no chance once they came out, and no better chance staying where they were—unless their comrades at one of the other sites on Tamkailo managed to stage a large rescue effort. That was, at best, highly improbable. "Maybe the conscripts will mutiny again."

Dacik glanced at his side. *They might,* he thought. Then he blinked several times, rapidly. Two regiments of prisoners? They'd be more trouble than they were worth. The prisoners they already had were a major inconvenience. Transporting them off planet would strain the fleet's resources. But they couldn't be left behind. Trained soldiers were a valuable military asset. This entire campaign was designed to deny the Schlinal warlords military assets. All of them on Tamkailo. The general recognized that the notion was primitive, almost inhuman, but it would be far more . . . expedient to finish this off militarily.

"We'll wait another thirty minutes," he said. "If they haven't surrendered or made their move by then, we'll do what we have to do." None of the men around him made any comment. And no one suggested that they try to establish radio contact with the Schlinal commander to demand a surrender.

"Thirty minutes," Dacik repeated.

The infantry established their perimeter two hundred meters from the nearest end of the ramps, and left wide avenues in front of those exits. There was little cover available, and the rock and hard clay of the terrain made it impossible to dig foxholes with hand tools.

Echo Company was in a second line, fifty meters behind the first. It was not necessary for the Accord to draw a complete perimeter around the enemy complex. By this time it was certain that there were only three exits. Men were arrayed in arcs facing those, with only occasional listening posts scattered around the rest of the area. Besides, this show would belong to the big guns and the flyers. Unless something truly unforeseen happened, the infantry would have nothing to do until the fight was completely over.

"Spectators," Mort Jaiffer said. He was on a private link to the Bear. "You know what kind of hell this is going to be for the men down in that hole, don't you?''

"I know," Baerclau replied. His throat was tight. For all of the years he had spent fighting the Heggies, he could find no joy in the prospect. Three, maybe four, thousand men had to be down there, and unless they showed a white flag very soon, they were going to be subjected to the most intense bombardment anyone had experienced in the war. Even if most of them were deep enough that they would be safe from the rockets and shells, they would suffer. *Shell shock.* It had never been anything more than two words to Joe. Now he was beginning to imagine what it might really be like.

The evening remained silent, right up to the expiration of General Dacik's deadline. Ten minutes before the half hour was up, word went out to all units, advising them when the action was to begin. West of the captured aboveground base, the Wasps of the 5th and 8th SATs, and the 17th IAW, began taking off and assembling into their individual flights. Each flight leader had his objectives and had decided how he wanted his men to proceed. The rockets that Wasps carried had one large advantage over artillery shells: they could be guided by the pilot right up until the instant of impact, by video. Once the massive gates sheltering the entrances to the underground complex were breached, missiles could be directed inside—just as far as they had a relatively straight path to follow.

From his rooftop vantage point, Dacik continued to stare into the growing darkness. He kept the visor of his battle helmet down now. The time line kept him apprised of how close his deadline was. At need, he could flash overlays on the visor that showed where each of the units getting ready for the coming battle were. He had reports from the air and artillery commanders. Their units were all ready for his signal. The infantry was in place, for whatever residual role they might have when this action was begun. Or ended.

Come on, start something! Dacik urged silently. But there was no response from the Heggies.

Ninety seconds before the expiration of the thirty minutes

he had stipulated, Dacik asked, "Anything from the listening posts?"

"Not a hint, General," Major Olsen replied. "I don't think they intend to come out."

"Ru, give the air and artillery people the sixty-second alert," Dacik said. Colonel Ruman had been waiting for that. He already had the regimental, air, and artillery commanders on link.

After that, there was silence again on the rooftop. Dacik watched the seconds tick off on his helmet time line. Around him, the members of his staff were all doing the same, lost in whatever personal thoughts they might have. Only Ruman watched the general more than his own visor display.

Exactly as the last second passed, Dacik said, "Go," softly and Colonel Ruman repeated it on his link to the commanders.

The gates leading into the underground Schlinal base each consisted of two large doors, four meters wide and five high. Constructed of the best steel and resin composites known, the doors were seventy-five centimeters thick, reinforced on the inside by six girders. The doors and their frames were as secure as any bank vault's door.

Each gate was hit by six 205mm armor-piercing rounds. The Accord targeting systems were accurate enough at eleven kilometers that each round hit within fifty centimeters of its target point. Two doors to a gateway: each door was hit high, middle, and low, slightly closer to the center than the hinge sides. In no case was the elapsing time between first and sixth round hitting a gate greater than nine one-hundredths of a second.

The Accord gunners did not wait to see how their first rounds had scored. Before the first volleys hit, the guns had all been reloaded, with high explosive rounds this time. The targeting points were the same. With the doors gone—and no one in any of the Havocs had any doubt that the doors would be gone—these rounds would travel inside the underground complex to explode there, spreading shrapnel—and death—to any Heggies within reach.

As soon as the second artillery volley had been fired, there was a flight of Wasps making a run toward each of those gates, low, no more than fifty meters above the ground. Each aircraft launched four rockets, the most that a pilot could track and guide effectively. At the entrance on the southeast side of the complex, a missile collided with an artillery shell along the ramp, twenty meters short of the now open doors, but other than that, every missile and shell exploded inside the entrance to the underground complex. Most of the missiles reached in a hundred meters or more before they were allowed to impact.

Balls of flame erupted from each gate, rolling up the ramps and climbing into the sky. Sheets of fire brightened the night, but only for a moment.

"A lot depends on the way that place was constructed," Olsen said, an offhand comment. He had been thinking of the kind of engineering that would have been needed for such an extensive underground facility. The blasts were on the horizon, visible a noticeable instant before the sound arrived. "Unless it's all just one open chamber, we might pound away all night without completely disabling the units down there."

Dacik turned and stared at his intelligence chief for a moment without saying anything. Then he turned back to watch the distant battle. He let the bombardment continue for another hour before he finally called a halt to it.

Dacik turned to his staff, lifted the visor on his helmet, and said, "Let's see what we've got in there. Probe all three entrances."

CHAPTER
11

There would be more surprises from mines popping off of the ground to explode in the faces of the infantry that moved in to investigate the underground complex. Engineers had come up and cleared lanes to the sides of each ramp, using fifty-meter lengths of explosive cable. Small mortars fired the end of the rope. Once it was stretched out on the ground, the cable was detonated with enough force to clear a path several meters wide. Even if the mines couldn't be detected with the naked eye, they responded to explosive persuasion. At least twenty were detonated.

Delta and Echo companies of the 13th were given the task of probing the western entrance to the underground complex. They were accompanied by 3rd recon and a platoon of engineers. Gene Abru and two of his SI men went along. He only had the two left fit for duty. Another was still in the field hospital. The rest had been killed in the earlier mine blast.

The patrols moved toward either side of the ramp, Delta

on the left, Echo on the right, each with half of the reccers. The engineers came up behind. Their job wouldn't begin until the line platoons had secured working areas for them.

If there was any work left for the engineers to do.

Echo's second platoon eventually found itself over the far end of the ramp, thirty meters above the pavement. Joe Baerclau slid forward on his stomach to look over into the trench. Gene Abru and Dem Nimz—Dem just out of the hospital in time to join this patrol—flanked him.

There was no mistaking the stench rising from the entrance. Burnt flesh.

"Literal Hell," Joe whispered. He was on a channel that linked him with the two men who flanked him and also with Captain Keye.

"You hear any sounds of life?" Keye asked. He was along the side of the trench, some thirty meters from the gutted doorway. Men lined both sides of the ramp up above.

"All I hear is fire sounds," Joe replied, "and not much of that. If there's anybody left alive in there, they must be a long way from this gate."

"We're going to have to go in," Keye said after a pause. "You men up above the gate, drop down on your belts. You get in place, the rest of us will come down the ramp. Any firing, get out the same way, full blast. Soon as you're out of the line of fire, we'll open up."

"Lot of good that'll do us," Dem muttered after raising his visor to avoid broadcasting the complaint.

"Don't worry about it," Gene said. "Baerclau was right. Anybody left alive in there, they sure as hell aren't going to be sitting near the gate waiting for us. Any trouble will come farther in."

It took a couple of minutes to get everyone ready. The first and second platoons of Echo, plus the reccers and SI men with them, would go over the side together.

"Jump off backwards," Abru advised. "That way you'll be facing into the cave as you go down." Abru was an old hand with antigrav belts. SI had used the previous model extensively in the war. They had also done most of the early testing of the new Corey belt.

"Have your weapons ready," Joe added. "We don't expect any trouble at the door, but no chances. You even *imagine* you hear or see anything, shoot it fast."

When his feet hit the surface of the stone ramp, Joe cut the power to his belt drives and went flat on his face, rifle out in front of him. There was still no indication of enemy activity inside. The only evidence that there were—or had been—people inside continued to be the stink of burned meat. That was even stronger at the bottom of the ramp.

"Move on in, Joe," Captain Keye said. "The rest of us will be coming in behind you. Keep this channel open and tell me what you're seeing."

"By squads," Joe told his platoon. He moved in first, with first squad. Abru stayed at his side. They stopped in the doorway and let the first squad of Nimz's recon platoon move past them. For the time being, the reccers were under Joe's command.

There was a confused pile of twisted wreckage in and just beyond the gateway, the remnants of the doors and, possibly, whatever had been nearest to them. The floor, walls, and ceiling had all been pitted by the bombardment. Some of the craters were more than a meter deep and two or three in diameter. The metal of the smashed doors was hot enough to burn skin. Heat signatures inside nearly overloaded the infrared sensors in Joe's visor night-vision system. Contrast was terrible. If it hadn't been for the second system, which worked by concentrating available light, the visors would have been useless.

"About what you'd expect from a confined space where so many explosives went off," Joe told the captain. "It's a miracle the ceiling didn't fall in, more than it did, but I don't see any structural damage from here, nothing obvious other than the smashed doors. We're looking down what appears to be a tunnel, just a little wider and higher than the doorway. I can see what appear to be gaps on either side, other tunnels, I suppose, or doors leading into chambers. There is no, repeat no, sign of anyone moving in there."

Keye told Joe to wait. When he returned to the channel, he said, "We go on in, as far as necessary. The general wants to know what is, or was, in there. Map it out. The whole works."

"That means us," Dem said. Some of the reccer helmets had one additional system that the standard infantry issue didn't: tiny video cameras that could link directly to CIC's computers. The SI men were similarly equipped. In the line companies, only officers' helmets had the extra system.

"Divide your men among second platoon's squads, Nimz," Keye said. "We want a good look at everything. Any heavy work comes up, let my people handle it."

In most circumstances, Dem would have argued those orders, but there didn't seem to be enough chance of meeting opposition to make the argument worthwhile.

"Yes, sir," he said, more meekly than anyone who knew him would have suspected possible.

Joe got to his feet and motioned his men forward. First squad hugged the left side of the tunnel, second squad the right, taking full advantage of the cover available. Fourth squad came up behind, half on either side. Not even the inclusion of the reccers made up for the missing third squad and the other casualties that the platoon had already suffered on Tamkailo.

The entrance tunnel, which went on straight for more than three hundred meters before splitting into two tunnels, which branched off to northeast and southeast, was littered with debris. Parts of the doors had been blown more than a hundred meters down the corridor. Joe wasn't certain where all of the metal and other debris had come from. Bits of stone had been blasted from roof, walls, and floor, but that hardly seemed to account for all of it that littered the corridor. The men had to go around and, in many cases over, obstructions. It wasn't until Joe reached the first of the openings along the sides of the main passage that he saw any sign of the men or equipment that had been in the complex. Looking to the right, there was a five-meter-long side tunnel that opened up into a large chamber. Another ramp led down to the floor of this chamber—a room that was easily eighty meters square and ten high.

"How the hell did *that* happen?" Joe asked, turning to look at Dem Nimz. "None of our shells or missiles could have made a ninety-degree turn to get down there."

Dem shrugged. He was too busy scanning the garage area—obviously what the large chamber was—to get a complete video record of it.

On the other side of the entrance, Abru spoke. "They must have had flammables stored up here, munitions or fuel. Probably hydrogen tanks. Flash fire. Secondary explosions. Something down there caught and caused the rest of the damage."

Dem moved away from the wall and stepped out into the middle of the ramp leading down into the parking area. There seemed to be no danger in that move. There was no sign of anyone alive in the chamber below. Dem held his rifle loosely at his side, pointed more at the ground than into the garage. Dem had seen a lot in his life, and not just as a soldier. There was no precedent for this. After a couple of minutes, he started walking slowly down the ramp.

Gene and Joe followed. Behind them, their men tagged along. Engineers came in and set up two small but powerful searchlights at the entrance and got them playing back and forth across the scene below.

As if seeing it through night-vision gear wasn't bad enough.

Joe did try to estimate the number of vehicles in the room, part of his running commentary to Captain Keye. Forty-eight Nova tanks, a half dozen armored personnel carriers, and four other vehicles, crowded together, with little room between vehicles in each row, and less room between the rows. It would have taken considerable time—and no small amount of skill on the part of the drivers—to get those vehicles out of the garage and up the ramp. All of the vehicles were scorched. At least a dozen of the tanks had had their turrets blown off. Ammunition and fuel in the tanks had apparently gone up as a result of the flash fires caused by the assault above. The walls and ceiling of the chamber were also scorched black.

The three sergeants were nearly to the bottom of the ramp before they saw any human bodies, though: two figures crouched next to the treads of one of the tanks—figures that had been incinerated in that position, unable even to fall flat in death. They remained like charcoal sculptures, perhaps fused to the metal of the tank by the flames.

More bodies were discovered. Some groups, it was impossible to tell exactly how many bodies there were. Men next to their tanks, men in their tanks, or in their APCs.

"Not enough of them here," Gene Abru said after the Accord group had worked its way from one end of the garage to the other. "They weren't mounted up ready to roll."

"There must be barracks rooms somewhere else down here," Dem said. There were a half dozen doorways leading out of the garage on its level.

"We're going to have to break up to explore all of these exits," Joe said, not just to his companions, but also to Captain Keye, who was still up in the main tunnel. Other platoons were exploring the other side passages off of that. Two more large parking areas had already been discovered. Both showed the same sort of damage that Joe and his companions had seen.

"There's still a chance we'll find live Heggies down here . . . somewhere," Dem said. "Even if they didn't have fireproof doors between here and the living areas."

Joe listened to Captain Keye for a moment, then reported to the others. "The orders are nothing smaller than a squad. Any hint of opposition, withdraw and wait for orders." He hesitated, then added, "That comes straight from General Dacik."

For a second, Joe thought that Gene Abru was still going to argue the order. It was clear that the SI team leader had his own ideas about exploring the installation. But Abru closed his mouth again and said nothing.

Echo didn't find any surviving Schlinal soldiers, but one of the platoons from Delta, exploring off of one of the other garages, did. And so did some of the men exploring off of the other two entrances to the complex. Altogether, almost four hundred men had survived the explosions and fires. The rest, more than three thousand, had died. Not all had burned. Many had died from smoke inhalation. Others had merely suffocated when all of the oxygen was sucked out of chambers where they were hiding.

The night was more than half gone when everyone but the engineers and SI men made their way back out of the underground complex. The engineers were there to finish the work of destroying the physical complex, planting massive charges at strategic locations, to be detonated after everyone was out. The SI men were there to discover whatever they could of what the Heggies might have been up to under so much rock.

Echo Company waited outside the western entrance to the complex.

"We wait for the SI men and the engineers, then we get back on the shuttles," Joe told his men.

"How long, any idea?" Sauv Degtree asked.

"Not more than a half hour," Joe replied.

A little apart from the rest of the platoon, Mort Jaiffer stood, looking back down the ramp. He just stared, without a conscious thought in his head. Eventually, he lifted his visor. Both of Tamkailo's moons were up now. He could see well enough, better than he really wanted to, without his night-vision systems.

Eventually, Mort became aware that tears were running down his cheeks. He had a notion to wipe them away, in case anyone might notice, but the effort needed was just more than he could muster. One hand came up, just a little, then fell back to his side. His stomach was knotted up, a tight pain that intruded more and more on his awareness.

After a time he could not measure, one conscious thought finally forced itself on his attention: *What the hell are we doing here?*

He sat down and continued to stare down the ramp. The tears continued to fall.

CHAPTER
12

General Dacik ordered nearly all of the troops that had taken part in the southern landing on Tamkailo back to the transports rather than keep them on the ground through another full day or move them directly to the Heggie base that the attack plan designated as Site Bravo. Nine hours aboard ship might not be much of a reward, but it was appreciated. Simply being moved off of the sweltering planet was important. The men would remain aboard ship until it was near sunset on the west coast of the southern continent. The only exception was the 17th IAW. Their Wasps boosted back to the fleet in orbit, and then, immediately after receiving fresh batteries, they were dropped to go to the support of the 5th SAT and the 34th LIR at Site Charley on the other continent. Their support group was loaded aboard shuttles and transported directly to the other action from Site Alpha. The 5th and 34th needed help. The 5th's air wing had already lost half of its Wasps.

"Thirty minutes until chow call," Joe Baerclau told his

platoon as they filed into their compartment aboard ship. "Get yourselves cleaned up. We get back from chow, I want weapons cleaned, gear cleaned and checked. Squad leaders, inspect your men. Find out what's missing, what's damaged. We'll get everything repaired or replaced before we drop again. I want everybody ready to go before I hear the first snore. And while we're up here, I want everyone to do a *lot* of drinking—water, juices, coffee." There was no alcohol aboard ship, except for medical stores. "We're all short on body fluids. Get them replaced before we jump again."

Joe moved through the troop bay to the corner that was reserved for the platoon's sergeants. A head-high partition walled off that section. Joe's bunk was the lower in the far corner. As ranking noncom, he had had the first choice. By the time he got to his bunk, he had already stripped off his combat gear and was half out of his fatigues. The fatigues would go into a recycler. Even though the net armor in the battle clothes hadn't come near its full week of service, no one would go back into combat in the same kit.

Ezra Frain had slept in the bunk above Joe. Stripped to bare skin, Joe stood next to the bunks and looked at the one that would have no one in it going home. There would be a lot of empty bunks, but for the moment, this was the only one that seemed to matter. Joe and Ezra had been close friends. While Joe was first squad's leader, Ezra had been his assistant. When Joe became platoon sergeant, Ezra got his third stripe and became squad leader. They had worked together, played together, laughed together.

"Home," Joe whispered. Home was Bancroft, but Joe hadn't been there in four years—with no prospect that he might get back anytime in the foreseeable future. Bancroft was an abstraction, a place of vague memories. His family still lived there, but even they seemed part more of a dream than of any reality. If Joe did have a place called home now, it was more the 13th Spaceborne Assault Team, or Albion, the world that the 13th called home.

"You just gonna stand there buck naked all day?" Frank Symes, fourth squad leader, asked.

Joe blinked and turned. Symes, Gerrent, and Degtree were all looking at him.

"You just been standing there for five minutes," Degtree said. The squad leaders had all dropped their gear and started to strip for the trip to the showers. Joe hadn't even heard them file in behind him. They had seen to their squads first.

"Just thinking," Joe said softly.

No one asked what he had been thinking about.

Out in the main section of the troop bay, there were a lot of men thinking. The Accord Defense Force had no place for mindless automatons. No one had been on the ground long enough to settle into the battle numbness that might have muted intelligence—and imagination. It might have been better if they had. The mind's ability to suppress long, harsh conditions might have made it easier to deal with the denouement of the battle. But most of the men did not let dark thoughts distract them from the prospect of getting clean, and then getting fed. Routine maintenance. Keep as clean as possible. Eat, give your body fuel for the next time. Those were drilled into recruits as forcefully as any other lessons.

Mort Jaiffer just sat on his bunk, though. He had dropped his pack and web belt, tossed his rifle to the mattress, and then plopped down next to it. He didn't ever bother to start undressing. As a corporal, he had rated a lower bunk. Back—ages ago, it seemed—he had stated loudly and often that the guarantee of a lower berth on the transports was the only thing of real value in his promotion from private to corporal.

Mostly, what Mort felt now was an exhaustion so complete that he couldn't even wonder at it, a depletion more of mind and soul than body. It was, perhaps, the same sort of numbness he had felt on other, longer campaigns after many days of fighting and walking, of danger and boredom, of too little sleep. But, if he had had the energy to think about it, he would have been the first to doubt that explanation.

Mort sat with his eyes open, staring straight ahead without blinking. What he *saw* was a play in his mind, a memory, perhaps constructed in the moment rather than real. He was back in the university, teaching the second semester of his freshman course in political science. Words and phrases tripped over each other but scarcely made an impression. *Realpolitik.* *"The continuation of diplomacy by other means."* Back then, in that other life, those words had come trippingly off his tongue, part of the currency of his profession, concepts studied with intellectual rigor, as sterile as words in a dictionary.

The faces in Mort's memory were anonymous. Perhaps he was recalling actual students. More likely, his mind was projecting stereotypes, amalgams drawn from imperfect memory. There were probably no more than a half dozen of the students he had taught in his years at the university who might stand out enough in his memory to be present as themselves. The students had come to him eager for learning, trusting what he said, young men and women— scarcely more than boys and girls—seventeen or eighteen years old for the most part. But every semester there would be one, or a few, who were older. Some had even come back to the university after a term in the defense forces, back in the days before open warfare between Accord and Hegemony had meant that few enlistees were getting out when their term of service expired. Mort had stood in front of them and lectured. Three-dimensional video cameras had captured every word and nuance, every gesture and facial expression, to be transmitted to satellite classrooms in other towns, and to private homes. At the beginning of each lecture session, Mort had always set aside ten minutes for questions, particularly for the students viewing him by remote.

Hesitant questions, self-assured answers.

Mort had taught political science in the morning, history in the afternoon. There was always some overlap in the student body between courses, even though Mort wasn't the only professor teaching either course. Aspiring young politicians, academics, and lawyers took the courses. A few came simply to satisfy their own interests. Others took the classes to fulfill humanities requirements while they pursued technical degrees.

Some students left to go into the Accord Defense Force. It had been clear that war with the Schlinal Hegemony, perhaps also with the Dogel Worlds, was coming. More than once, Mort had had a student drop out to join the military. Toward the end, he had even found it possible to predict when such defections were likely, simply from watching the morning news. By that time, it was no longer an intellectual game, even for him.

Mort had waited until the end of the spring term at the completion of his third year on faculty before he told the department chairman that he was taking an extended sabbatical for government service. A new law guaranteed the jobs of people who left other occupations for government, especially military, service. The Accord and its member worlds were gearing up.

For this?

A hard, stinging slap on his shoulder brought Mort out of his trance. He blinked rapidly, several times. Joe Baerclau was standing in front of him, a wet towel wrapped around his middle.

"You'd better hurry and get cleaned up, Professor," Joe said, speaking softly. "Chow in fifteen minutes."

Mort looked around, then sucked in a deep breath. "I guess I'm just about zonked," he said, unwilling to share what he had been thinking.

"Shower, eat, then sleep," Joe said, squinting at Mort. "Save the thinking for the ride home to Albion." The look he saw in the Professor's face wasn't sleepiness, but something more troublesome.

Roo Vernon was not yet comfortable being an officer. If pressed, he would state flatly that he didn't like it much at all, that he would be much happier going back to the ranks. He had been supremely satisfied as a Wasp crew chief, a technical sergeant with the reputation of being the best mechanic in the 13th. But a good idea, and hard and heroic work at a difficult point in the 13th's campaign on Jordan, had brought him to the notice of Colonel Stossen and, through the colonel, General Dacik. After his battlefield improvisation turned the tide of battle, Roo could not escape his reward, the Accord's two highest medals (one for his idea, the other for managing to put it into successful operation under severe battlefield conditions) and a field commission. Stossen and Dacik had not been content to make Vernon a mere lieutenant. His commission was as a captain, arbitrarily placed two-thirds of the way up the list for promotion to major. Roo did find himself occupying a major's slot in the table of organization, senior maintenance officer for the 13th—not just over the Wasp wing, but over all of the vehicles in the regiment. The major who had occupied that slot previously had been transferred to the 7th SAT. What Major General Dacik had not told Colonel Stossen or the new Captain Vernon was that when Roo did make major, the general intended to move him to his own headquarters staff as senior aircraft maintenance officer.

Captain Roo Vernon found management frustrating. He liked working with his hands, and he claimed—with more than a little justification—that he knew the workings of the Wasp better than the people who had designed and built it. After returning to the fleet from the first phase of the campaign to neutralize Tamkailo, Roo wanted very much to get inside one of "his" Wasps, to see what the extreme temperature conditions had done to the birds. Only thirteen of the wing's twenty-four Wasps had survived the day's fighting. Thirteen planes, sixteen pilots. That was a better ratio than usual, but it didn't ease Roo's concerns.

"How can we make the Wasps safer for the lads?" he asked his mechanics as they prepared to do quick maintenance inspections back aboard ship. "Any time a pilot dies because we haven't done everything possible to protect him, it's as bad as if we shot the lad ourselves."

It was not the most tactful thing to say to the crew chiefs and mechanics, even if most of them had known Roo for ages. Most "ground" crews developed close relationships with their pilots. Those who had lost pilots—in the last twenty-four hours or in earlier campaigns—felt bad enough about their losses without having Roo harp on it.

"We've never run our birds in a place like Tamkailo," Roo said. He pronounced the world's name Tam-ky-lo rather than the proper Tam-kay-lo. "We don't know what that kind of heat can do to a Wasp, despite what the computers say. The programmers who wrote that program never experienced a world like this either. Don't just *look* at parts when you do your inspection, touch 'em, *smell* 'em. That'll give you a better idea than looking or even electronic scanning, I'm thinking. You know what the cables and connections are supposed to feel like. Anything feels not one hundred percent, or you get any kind of burnt smell, pull the part and replace it. Myself, I'm going to be working with two crews to completely disassemble Yellow Three. It's not going back into action. It received too much battle damage."

There were a half dozen spare Wasps aboard the fleet carrier, and enough repair parts to—conceivably—build another six fighters. Although the technical manuals made a point of saying that a maintenance crew could not, repeat *not*, build a functional fighter from repair parts without the specialized construction facilities of a factory, Roo knew better. He had already done it once, in a maintenance hangar on Albion—mostly out of boredom.

"Let's get to work," Roo said, softening his voice. "If we can get the birds ready to fly again in six hours, that'll give us another three hours to catch some sleep before we go dirtside again." Obviously, the planes had to come first.

Zel Paitcher's Blue Flight had been cut in half by the day's fighting. Two of his pilots were dead. Ewell Marmon had gone early. Ewell's wingman, Tod Corbel, had gone in the final assault on the main base. Frank Verannen and Will Tarkel had both had their Wasps shot out from under them. Verannen had been trapped in his escape pod for hours before he had been rescued and taken to the field hospital. It was uncertain whether or not he would be ready to fly again when Blue Flight returned to the surface. There were new planes ready for both Frank and Will. Besides the direct battle casualties, Ilsen Kwillen had nearly put himself out of action by pushing his Wasp at too high a gee-load. He had needed two hours in a trauma tube to repair internal injuries and might not be certified for duty in time for the second phase of the campaign.

Zel might have consoled himself by thinking that of the three pilots in the 13th who had survived the destruction of their Wasps, two had come from his flight. But he didn't. It wouldn't have helped.

"Decimated means you've lost ten percent," he muttered to himself as he walked back to his quarters from the mess hall. "*I* lost fifty percent. In one day." Marmon and Corbel had worked well together. "Almost like Reston and Paitcher," Zel whispered. He had flown as wingman to Slee Reston for more than a year before Slee was killed on Jordan.

It still hurt to think about Slee.

Kleffer Dacik refused to let himself think about the men he had lost taking Site Alpha on Tamkailo, or the men still being lost at Site Charley half a world away. He knew the numbers. But he would not let himself dwell on them, not now. If he did . . .

"The first operation was a fiasco, gentlemen," Dacik said, addressing his staff and subordinate commanders from the three ground units that had taken part. "It started with low comedy and ended with too much tragedy." He shrugged. "A lot of it we couldn't help. Some we should have."

He did not waste much time rehashing the mistakes of the first day. Brief mention of a couple of the worst preventable errors sufficed.

"We can't afford any screw-ups at Site Bravo," he said after he had finished his recapitulation. "There is absolutely no allowance for error. We'll have only the one night to complete that operation. In just after local sunset, we absolutely *must* be off the ground by dawn tomorrow morning. We can't protect our men against the daytime heat at Site Bravo. Jorgen, you have the latest intelligence update?''

This conference was taking place in the Combat Intelligence Center on *Capricorn,* the flagship. All of the commanders were physically present—to the annoyance of those quartered on other ships in the fleet. The transit time came out of what little time they would have had for sleep.

"It looks better than it did twenty-four hours ago," Olsen started. "Sure, the Heggies have had extra time to prepare for us, but that preparation does not seem to have been designed to strengthen the defenses at Site Bravo. Quite the opposite. Our estimate is that nearly half of the forces that were there have been transferred to Site Charley on the northern continent. Site Bravo was always the smallest of the three Schlinal facilities on Tamkailo. Conditions there are . . . simply impossible for large numbers of men. Our current estimate is that there might be seven hundred civilians there—prisoners, penal exiles, and their descendants, individuals of no military value to the Hegemony—and quite possibly a security threat to them. As far as *military* assets, no more than one very short regiment, light infantry, perhaps fewer than one thousand men. Those soldiers are, moreover—as far as we can deduce—strictly garrison troops, not part of the force that the Hegemony was marshaling on Tamkailo for its next offensive against the Accord. Garrison troops who were, according to every intelligence estimate I've seen, chosen for this duty either as a result of, or in lieu of, disciplinary action. But they *are* acclimated to local conditions, insofar as that is possible." Jorgen looked up from his monitor and glanced around at the others. All of them were watching him.

"We're not absolutely certain why the Heggies even bother with such an impossible location. They've made what accommodation they can with the climate. What work has to be done is done at night, local routine completely switched about, but even so . . . '' He shook his head. "There is evidence of mining. Since there is also mining done around the other two sites, we have to assume that

Site Bravo offers some metal or mineral that isn't available at the other places. What that, or those, might be, we can't say. The suggestion is that the Heggies might be mining radioactive elements at Site Bravo.''

"Is there a storage depot, like at Alpha?" Colonel Foss asked.

"A much smaller facility than either Alpha or Charley," Olsen said. "*Much* smaller. We feel that ninety percent of the storage is for the use of the garrison and inmates— civilian residents." "Inmates" was as good a word as any for the civilian population of Tamkailo. "There seems to be one building that is particularly well isolated and circled with its own defensive measures. Whatever is in that building must be the key to the operation."

"Okay, Jorgen, that'll do for now," Dacik said. "You can key the rest of it for them." Olsen nodded and Dacik turned his attention to the others.

"We're going to deviate significantly from the earlier plan for Site Bravo," the general said. He looked at each of the commanders in turn, ending up with Van Stossen. He stared without blinking at the commander of the 13th.

"I'm going to lay primary responsibility for Site Bravo on you, Van."

Stossen barely had time to think, *It doesn't surprise me. The 13th always draws the short straw,* before Dacik continued.

"We're going to try to take Site Bravo with just the 13th. Your lads have the new Corey belts. They'll land right on top of the enemy. The infantry, at least. The Wasps will go in to provide cover. Use half of your recon platoons to establish an LZ for the Havocs and the support crews for air and artillery, within gun range for the howitzers. With a little bit of luck, though, you won't even have to use the artillery.

"The 8th and 97th will stand by up here," Dacik continued. "If you get into a bind, I'll send them in as reinforcements, or as a rescue party. But if the 13th can handle Site Bravo alone, the 8th and 97th will be diverted straight to Site Charley. Things are getting a little too sticky there. The 5th and 34th are in trouble.''

"We'll do what we can, sir," Stossen said.

Dacik nodded. ''The belts are our edge, Van. Make it count. You get done at Bravo, the 13th will be lifted directly to Site Charley. The Wasps will boost back up here and get dropped again right away. We need everything we can get for Site Charley.''

And hope that it's enough, Dacik thought.

CHAPTER
13

After two full meals and, for those who could manage it, as much as six hours of sleep, the troops aboard the fleet transports prepared for another combat landing. While the men of the 13th knew that they were destined for Site Bravo, the men of the 8th and 97th could not be sure where they would be landing. Shuttles were ready for the reserve units. The men were dressed and ready to go, though still in their barracks bays aboard ship. They would move to the hangars and landers once the 13th was away.

Thirty minutes before their scheduled departure, the men of the 13th filed through the ship toward the shuttle hangars. For the most part, the men were silent, almost sullen. It wasn't simply the prospect of more combat that affected them. It was more the knowledge that they were jumping back into the most oppressive climate that any of them had ever experienced. They had been warned that Site Bravo would be even worse than Site Alpha, that they absolutely had to be finished before sunrise brought impossible temperatures.

There was not a man in the 13th who had not successfully faced the usual fears of combat before, if only during the one day that they had already spent on Tamkailo. Human enemies could be fought, and beat. The heat of the tropics of this world could not be fought effectively, could not be beat—except by retreat, by going underground or into well-insulated buildings during the hours when the sun was above the horizon. Long before midday, the heat at Site Bravo would be literally enough to fry a brain, to kill.

This time, none of the troop shuttles were crowded. Normally, going into a campaign, a single SAT line company filled two shuttles, with the men crammed against one another, side by side with scarcely room to fall over. Two of the 13th's companies had lost so many men in the conquest of Site Alpha that each fit into a single shuttle. Other companies managed to squeeze two companies into three shuttles. Only three of the eight line companies still came anywhere near to filling two shuttles with their men.

"Squad leaders, one more check of your men," Joe Baerclau ordered as Echo Company waited to board its shuttles. Echo still needed two, but it would not crowd either one.

The platoon's three squad leaders moved among their men, looking at power settings on antigrav belts and Armanoc carbines, testing helmet circuits, talking to their men. When that was done, the squad leaders checked one another, and Sauv Degtree checked the platoon sergeant. The routine was more to occupy minds than because of any real need. Keep everyone busy, thinking about immediate—and manageable—tasks. Don't give them idle time to worry about things beyond their control. Keep them thinking as *soldiers*.

First squad, second squad, fourth squad. As Joe received the expected positive reports, he had to think again about the third squad, wiped out except for its sergeant, who now had first squad. A fourth of the platoon gone right there, in addition to its other losses.

Joe checked his own gear again, for at least the tenth time. Then he looked toward the door at the head of the passageway. It was time for Echo to be moving into the hangar to board their shuttles. While he stared, the door opened and a naval rating gestured the soldiers through. Four platoons into the shuttle on the left, four into the shuttle on the right. Once the two lines started moving, it didn't take long for the company to board the shuttles, for the men to strap themselves in place along the bench seats in the troop bay.

Then it was time to wait again, but not for long.

The hatches were sealed. Many of the men felt a momentary pressure on their ears as the shuttle was put through its own checks. Two minutes later, the green lights over each hatch were replaced by red lights. That meant that the hangar was being depressurized. The air was being pumped out of the hangar so that the huge outer doors could be opened safely. When the interior air pressure was down to less than a tenth of "normal," the doors would be opened and the two shuttles ejected with the rest of the air and by small catapults. The shuttles had to be clear of the hangars before they could turn on their own antigrav drives.

"Prepare for separation," the shuttle pilot warned, giving his passengers the customary thirty seconds' notice.

Joe took a deep breath and held it for a count of ten. He could not have recalled what had started the ritual, or when it had begun. Somehow, it had become part of his personal routine. Another deep breath was held to a count of five. He looked around at the men of his platoon. The faces were hidden behind visors now, the tinted surface a mask for the expression beneath.

"Five seconds," the pilot warned.

Joe blinked a couple of times, then looked up at the bulkhead across from him. There were monitors spaced around the troop bay. At the moment, the cameras feeding those monitors were divided between a view of the exterior door and the opposite side of the hangar.

The outer door opened. It always seemed to "pop" open to Joe, who had never been able to suppress his amazement that anything so large could be moved so quickly. Or so silently. He knew that sound could not travel through a vacuum, but the outer doors were connected to the hull of the ship, and when the doors opened, the shuttle was sitting on the hangar deck. There *was* a solid connection. But there was no sound, no physical rumble or vibration.

There were several minutes of weightlessness once the shuttle was clear of the ship, while the fleet of shuttles formed up for the assault. Although the shuttles were powered by antigravity drives, no specific provision had been made for providing artificial gravity for the people inside. But all of the troops were strapped in, and they knew how to deal with zero gravity. It took some of the pressure off where straps and gear confined the men. And added different, lesser pressures where their harnesses held them in place.

Once the shuttle was under acceleration, they would know the feeling of weight again.

Joe closed his eyes. He had actually come to enjoy the sensation of losing track of up and down—as long as it didn't last for long. The shuttle pilot was short on commentary. Some pilots kept up a running account of what they were doing in these early moments. Not this one. After announcing separation, the pilot didn't speak again until it was time to warn the troops that the power descent was about to begin.

An attack descent was like nothing any civilian passenger was ever likely to experience. Civilian shuttles providing service between passenger liners or spaceport satellites and the ground would merely use enough power to set them in a fuel-efficient glide, using engines minimally to adjust course and cushion the landing. Troop shuttles carrying men into a combat landing, or a drop, were more profligate with fuel. Instead of trusting to a planet's gravity to bring them down, pilots accelerated toward the surface. The surfaces of military lander were designed to take the extreme heat that was generated pushing down through the atmosphere, and the entire structure was able to withstand far more stress during braking maneuvers than any of the humans who rode it were.

The weight of acceleration moved above two gees for most of the ride in and topped out over three. The men in the troop bay could judge their approach as easily by which way seemed to be "down" as by watching the monitors on the bulkheads. Some stared at the screens. Others kept their eyes shut throughout the descent.

On most previous descents, Mort had been one of the watchers, keeping up a running commentary—on almost anything but the coming fight. This time, he remained silent. He glanced at the monitors only rarely. He spent much more time staring at the piece of deck immediately in front of his feet. He stared and concentrated on that small area of metal, using it as a focus to try to keep his mind blank. He did not want to think, not about the coming fight or the fight of the day before, not about anything. The only time he snapped out of his near trance was when Sauv Degtree or Joe Baerclau spoke to him, for the necessary squad checks. He was still the leader of a fire team. He had duties.

"Take care on landing," Joe warned the platoon. "We're going to be aiming for rooftops. Watch the edges. Give yourself as much leeway as possible, away from the sides. You get too far over to maneuver safely to the roof, go for the ground and jump up, if you've got the juice in your batteries. If not, attach yourself to whatever platoon you're near until we can get you back." On the buildings and in between them. The 13th hoped to have so many men in the middle of the base that the Heggies would be unable even to begin any significant defense. They hoped that there would be no real battle at all at Site Bravo.

"Unstrap!" the jumpmaster said over a radio channel that reached everyone in the troop bay. Men hit the releases on their safety harnesses. Down was below their feet now. The gee-level was high, but declining.

"Stand in the doors!" was the next command. Every man knew which of the four exits he was to head toward.

"Thirty seconds!" This jumpmaster shouted everything, although that was totally unnecessary. For all practical purposes, he was speaking directly into the ears of every man aboard.

Second platoon would jump through the left rear hatch in two columns. First and second squads would go out together, left and right. Fourth squad filled out both lines behind them.

When the hatch opened, Joe Baerclau and Sergeant Low Gerrent, second squad's leader, would be the first men out. At the right front exit, Captain Keye and First Sergeant Walker would be first out.

"Opening up!" the jumpmaster announced, and as soon as the hatches were up, he shouted, "Go!" even louder than his earlier commands.

Joe Baerclau took a deep breath and jumped out into the slipstream.

"This is going to be tricky," Zel Paitcher whispered to himself. He had said that to the squadron commander during the preflight briefing, had repeated it to his men as they moved to their hangar and their Wasps. It was something they had never practiced, even in simulators—taking close ground support to what Zel hoped would not prove to be its reduction to absurdity.

"We need to get our licks in against the Heggies at Site Bravo, but we don't want to give them a second more of warning that we're coming than we absolutely have to," Major Tarkel had told the 13th's pilots. "And since the mudders are going to be jumping in on belts, right on top of the enemy, we're going to have to get under them and make one quick pass just seconds before they ground. Between the jumpers and the rooftops."

"And let them fry in the explosions of our missiles?" one of the pilots from Yellow Flight asked.

"That's where timing comes in," the Goose said. "Missiles first, then cannon. Judging from our efforts at Site Alpha, you're unlikely to start any secondary explosions. The construction at Site Bravo is just as solid, thick stone and concrete. Just get in and out, crack open doors, break windows, give the mudders entry points and confuse the hell out of the Heggies.''

That was the point where Zel had cleared his throat and said, ''This is going to be tricky,'' for the first time.

The more he thought about it, the trickier it looked. The only bright spot was that there was no evidence that the Heggies had any fighter planes stationed to protect Site Bravo.

The 13th's Wasps followed the troop shuttles down, staying close enough so they would be able to dive past and make their runs ahead of the jumpers. The landers carrying the artillery and all of the support equipment—as well as regimental headquarters—veered away from the rest early on, aiming for a landing zone some dozen kilometers from the Schlinal base. Two Wasps from Yellow Flight went along to provide air cover for them. It would take a little time for the Havocs to get out and ready to lend their long-range support to the mudders, though. By that time, the Wasps would be looking for a chance to land and replace batteries and munitions. The descent from orbit took a lot of power, even this descent with the pilots holding back, staying with the shuttles instead of accelerating past them.

As shuttles approached their drop altitude, three hundred meters, they shifted formation. That was the signal that Zel and the other Wasp flight leaders had been waiting for.

''Time to get into position,'' Zel told Blue Flight. ''Follow me in.''

He took a slow, looping curve to the left, losing two hundred meters of altitude in the process as he lined up to make an east-to-west run across the base. The other five planes of his flight (spares had been brought out for the two pilots who had lost their planes at Site Alpha) spread out to either side of their leader. Blue, Yellow, and Red: the three flights would crisscross one another's path over the enemy base, hitting it from three directions. That would leave only one side of each building free from attack. Major Tarkel had ruled out splitting the three flights four ways. ''This is complicated enough as it is,'' he had said. ''Three sides will have to do.''

At least the Schlinal base was laid out on a perfectly rectangular grid. There were nine primary buildings, three by three, with four smaller buildings in a separate row along the western side. The avenues between buildings were a uniform fifteen meters wide. At this site, the Heggies had even foregone the customary fences. It was too obvious, even to them, that there was no escape for anyone confined to the location. The spyeyes had only pinpointed ten guard posts: bunkers at the corners of the rectangle, two additional bunkers along either of the long sides, and one in the center of each of the short sides. Bunkers: low, stone structures that seemed to be contained more underground than above. They also appeared to be connected by tunnels to the buildings. The Wasps planned to ignore those bunkers. With the mudders landing inside the perimeter, they would be tactically irrelevant.

"Remember, if those bunkers *are* connected underground, it's likely that all of the buildings are connected the same way." The pilots had been told that during the briefing. It seemed to be a logical conclusion, even though there had been nothing of the kind at Site Alpha. "The Heggies know they can't venture outside during the daylight hours."

Neither can we, Zel thought as he waited for word to come from the shuttles that the mudders were about to jump. *We've got no more than nine hours to wrap up this operation to give us time to get off before sunrise.*

Zel was listening to the jumpmaster in the lead shuttle, the man who would set the timing for the entire flotilla of landers. Thirty seconds. Ten.

"Here we go," Zel warned his flight while he mentally counted off those last ten seconds. "Into position."

With their antigrav drives, the Wasps could hover in place, waiting for just the right instant, then loose their missiles from that position or accelerate into the attack. With no enemy aircraft, and no sign of ground fire, they did just that. In the dark, it was virtually certain that they wouldn't be sighted before they switched on their target acquisition systems, if then. If they were spotted, it would take the Heggie forces time to get that word to men with surface-to-air missiles. The Wasps represented the pinnacle of more than three millennia of technology designed to make aircraft as nearly invisible to enemies as possible.

Infantrymen started jumping out of their shuttles. In the first second or two, the men were blown by the landers' slipstreams. As they fell clear of those, the antigrav belts took hold. Some men swayed like pendulums until their stabilizers locked them in proper attitude.

Blue Flight moved under then, across the Heggie base, firing rockets and cannon, trying to open ways into each building—as many ways as possible. There was absolutely no return fire. Like a practice run on the range back home, Zel thought, delighted at the lack of enemy fire—but worried just the same. It wasn't like the Schlinal military to take without giving back full measure.

"Okay, now we go cover the LZ," Zel told his men after they, and the other two flights, had completed their one run across the target area. "Make sure we've got someplace safe to land."

Joe Baerclau felt an instant of panic after jumping out of the shuttle, worse than he had experienced since the first time he had done a practice jump with an antigrav belt. In that moment, he managed to bite through his lower lip and draw blood. He seemed to swing back and forth for an impossibly long time, enough to start him worrying that the gyro stabilizers on his belt had failed. Only slowly did the pendulum motion dampen and stop. Joe worked at his belt controls, slowing his descent to fifteen meters per second. Jump altitude had been three hundred meters. He had fallen fifty meters before he got his drives adjusted. He had a couple of seconds before he would have to slow his descent again.

The Bear swallowed hard and looked around for his men. They were where they belonged, most a little higher than he was. No one was falling out of control. Once assured of that, Joe looked down. He didn't see the Wasps streak by beneath him, except as shadows that eclipsed the ground and the buildings, but he did see rockets explode, the flashes coming back out of door and window openings along the sides of buildings.

Joe slowed his descent again. Two more seconds passed as he made certain that he and his men were over the building they were supposed to hit.

"I don't see any sign of Heggies on the roof," he said over the platoon channel. "No ground fire coming up at us."

After that he had to devote nearly all of his attention to manipulating his belt controls. He was rather too near the western side of the roof. He reached down and twisted the thruster on the left side of his belt to move him a meter or so farther in, then slowed his descent to come in for a smooth landing.

Baerclau was the first man on that roof. The rest of his platoon was no more than two seconds behind him, though, landing with rifles at the ready.

"First squad to the door," he ordered. As on the buildings at Site Alpha, there was a small kiosk with a door leading to interior stairs. "Second squad behind them. Fourth, spread out around the perimeter until we go in." The men were already moving when he gave the orders. The prejump briefing had covered this much of the operation. After that, it would be a little more ad lib. *Get inside. Get down the stairs. Deal with whatever you come across. Link up with the units covering the outside.*

Even though it was two hours past sunset and there was a breeze off of the ocean, the air on the rooftop was stiflingly hot. The stone-and-concrete roof radiated heat. After one deep breath, Joe started to breathe more shallowly, as if that might minimize the discomfort. *Got to be close to 40 degrees even now,* he thought. That gave new urgency to the order that they had to finish their work before first light.

Joe went over to first squad. Sauv Degtree had already tried the door. "It's not locked," he reported.

Joe looked around. All of the rifles of first and second squad were pointed at the door. The men were down on one knee or flat on their stomachs in an arc facing the door.

"Yank it," Joe said, getting down himself.

Sauv pulled the door open and moved to the side, out of the way. There was no one on the landing inside. No gunfire came out. Joe waved second squad through, onto the stairway. One fire team stayed on the landing at the top. The other went down far enough to see into the interior of the building.

It was empty.

"All the way to the bottom," Joe ordered. "Second squad, then first. Cover the exits. Look for anything leading underground especially."

Second squad moved down the steel metal stairs as quickly as they could. First squad was no more than ten steps behind. Before Joe followed first squad in, he called fourth squad over to follow them. There was no need to leave men to guard the roof behind them.

Primed for a fight, Joe worried at the lack of any opposition at all. The muscles in his forearms were knotted tight. He had to consciously hold himself back on the stairs. He kept trying to speed up. The press of men in front of him made that impossible. But the greatest danger at the moment seemed to be of falling.

There were two doorways leading outside at ground level. One had been blown in by a rocket. The other hadn't been touched. At first, Joe had trouble spotting the door leading to the suspected underground tunnel system. It was in a corner of the building, a doorway next to a pair of doors leading to rest rooms in a small cubical protrusion.

The door leading underground was markedly different from the doors leading outside. It was solid metal, set in a frame that looked as if the door had been designed to resist being forced—a smaller version of the vaultlike doors that had led to the underground complex near Site Alpha.

"Check those crates. See what's in them," Joe ordered fourth squad. "Look for anything we can use." Then he switched channels to talk to Captain Keye. "We've secured this building and located the door leading below, sir."

"Hold tight for a few minutes, Joe," Keye replied. "I

haven't heard from everybody yet.''

"Any resistance at all, sir?''

"George Company's had a little shooting. That's all I've heard of. Now let me deal with the other platoons. I'll get back to you.''

"First squad, I want every eye on that door leading down. Second, you watch the ground-level doors.'' Joe looked around to make sure that he wasn't missing anything obvious. The warehouse was nearly empty. None of the stacks of crates were more than head-high, and there was a lot of empty room between them.

Joe moved to one of the stacks. One crate had been dragged off and the lid pried open. A coil of fence wire. He moved to the next stack. Bedding.

"Anybody find any munitions?'' he asked on fourth squad's channel. He received a chorus of negatives. "Keep looking. Weapons, ammunition, medical supplies, anything like that.''

Within five minutes, he knew that there were none of any of those items in this particular building. There wasn't even any food.

Joe went over to the door that had been blasted open by the Wasps. There seemed to be no activity anywhere near it. After listening for a moment and hearing nothing but a few distant zipper sounds, Joe moved into the doorway. The wall looked to be nearly a meter-and-a-half thick. The passage was two meters wide, wide enough for a work vehicle to get in and out.

Careful to expose as little of himself as possible, Joe looked each way. There were Accord troops at either end of the warehouse, covering the intersections. Neither group had encountered any Heggies, civilian or military. Neither had come under fire.

"They must all be underground,'' Joe said over his noncoms' circuit when he moved back inside.

"Oh, no,'' Mort whispered. He sounded as if he were in pain. "Not again.''

I know what you mean, Joe thought, but he couldn't say that. "I don't think it'll be the same'' was what he did say, on a private link to Jaiffer. "This time, we'll have to go down and get them." That might be a bloody mess, but it would be easier to take than the other—what had happened at the end of the operation at Site Alpha. Joe didn't have time to get any further in his musing. Captain Keye was back on the line.

"We're going to try to break into the tunnel system at two points. Alpha and Fox companies have the honors. The rest of us are just to keep the other exits guarded, stop any Heggies who try to break from them."

"Stop them in the doorway or let them come out and surrender?" Joe asked.

"If they want to surrender, let them."

Glad to hear that, Joe thought. "Yes, sir," he said.

Joe passed the news to his platoon and arranged everyone so that they were all watching the door leading below ground.

"They come out shooting, I want a half dozen grenades and a kilometer of wire in the doorway in the first second," Joe instructed. "If they don't shoot, we don't. That's straight from the captain. We're just supposed to contain them. Somebody else got the short end of the stick this time."

After that, it was simply a matter of waiting. Very rarely, Captain Keye or First Sergeant Walker would provide a few words about the progress of the fight. Two entrances to the tunnel system were blown open. The 13th fought its way underground. The Heggies fought back.

For a time.

Then, for no discernible reason, they couldn't surrender fast enough. The rest of the exits were opened and Heggies came out, hands raised. There were far fewer of them than CIC and intelligence had suspected, no more than six hundred altogether, and two-thirds of them were civilians.

"Get rid of their helmets," Joe instructed his platoon. Forty Heggie soldiers had come out of the door 2nd platoon was watching. "Frisk 'em to make sure nobody's carrying any weapons or spare communication gear. We've got to march them to the LZ, ship 'em up the fleet. The rest of this is up to SI and the reccers."

CHAPTER
14

The Schlinal base designated Site Charley by the Accord was located on the northernmost point of land on Tamkailo. It was situated near the far end of an eighteen-kilometer-long peninsula that was ten kilometers wide at the base, tapering to four kilometers at its northern end. Over their decades of occupation, the Heggies had blasted a canal through the rock, turning the peninsula into an island. The channel was twenty meters wide, with sides from six to nearly fifteen meters above water level, and steep. The cut was deep enough to put more than five meters of water through. The canal was crossed in two places by truss bridges constructed of steel and composite beams and paved with concrete and stone slabs. The northern ends of each bridge were fortified with gates and guard posts. The gun emplacements were aimed north, though. Their purpose was to keep people in, not to keep invaders out. The southernmost kilometer of each side of the peninsula was also equipped with barriers and guard posts. Site Charley was still, at heart, a prison, like the other two bases on the world. Lengths of razor wire and other obstacles lined both sides of the canal, though that was hardly necessary. A man in the water could scarcely hope to climb the steep southern wall of the canal, even if there were anyplace to run to, anyplace where survival was even remotely possible.

The terrain around Site Charley, and on south of the peninsula, was considerably different from that around the other two Heggies bases on the planet. Site Bravo had appeared to be devoid of any macroscopic native life forms. In the short time the 13th had been there, no one had seen any sort of plant life, and not even a single insect. Site Alpha had displayed a number of varieties of ground-hugging moss and a considerable selection of tiny insects. The biggest animals seen around Site Charley were also insects, but some of the species were rather larger—comparable to a common housefly in size if not in appearance. But the real difference was in plant life. Besides mosses, there were several distinctive types of fungus, including at least three species of giant mushrooms or toadstools. The largest grew to be as much as three meters high and spread canopies up to four meters in diameter. There was even, in a few places, ground cover that looked—at a distance—like grass but which was actually another sort of ''hairy'' moss with blades up to ten centimeters high.

The peninsula was rocky and uneven, offering considerable cover for infantry and vehicles. There were rocky ridges and stretches that looked as if a mountain had been broken up and its pieces strewn around at random, boulders from a meter in diameter to chunks that were larger than an artillery shuttle. There were several roads leading from one end of the peninsula to the other—not paved roads, but lanes that had been cleared of smaller obstacles, with detours around the larger ones.

South of the peninsula, which was primarily rock, there were considerable areas of soil, mostly clay. The terrain was gently rolling, with long valleys running northwest to southeast. Some of those valleys showed evidence that—occasionally at least—they held running water. Gradually, the land became higher to the south, reaching eventually to mountains that peaked at slightly more than two thousand meters.

Coming in by shuttle, the 5th SAT and the 34th LIR had been forced to land south of the canal. The Schlinal garrison, and the troops that had been gathered for the next offensive, were prepared, waiting for the Freebies to show. The Heggies had fiercely defended the line of the canal. The Schlinal warlord responsible for all of the troops that had been gathered on Tamkailo had his headquarters at Site Charley, and when the orbiting satellites were knocked out simultaneously, he had immediately ordered his troops on alert. Men and tanks were being rushed south from the northern end of the peninsula within minutes. Boem fighters were in the air even faster. At Site Charley the aircraft were not caught on the ground.

When General Dacik and his staff finally landed behind the Accord positions south of Site Charley, the 5th and 34th still had not managed to cross the canal in force. Two patrols by recon platoons and SI teams had been forced to retreat with heavy casualties, recrossing the canal by rope, under fire. Three attempts to cross the bridges had been repulsed, with casualties heavy on both sides. The duels in the air and between armor and artillery on the ground had been battles of attrition. The 5th's Havocs had been forced to withdraw beyond the range of Nova main guns—and that put the main Schlinal base at the north end of the peninsula far out of range for them.

"They're just sitting there, and there hasn't been a thing we could do about it," Colonel Jesiah Kane, commander of the 5th, reported when he met the general's shuttle. Kane had been in tactical command of the forces at Site Charley. "Before 17th Air got here, we couldn't even contain their Boems. *With* the 17th, we managed to keep at least parity in the air, but we still haven't been able to use our Wasps to significant advantage. Those stone buildings will take anything we can throw at them from the air. It's like trying to knock down the pyramids back on Earth." Kane, alone of the senior officers under Dacik's command, was from

Earth. Less than one percent of the Accord military came from the mother world.

"I know," Dacik said. He looked at the situation as shown on Kane's mapboard. "The 8th and 97th will be moving into position with the next few minutes, and the 13th will be here in six or seven hours—with a little luck." At that point, Site Bravo had not yet been secured. Dacik had headed north immediately after the 13th's shuttles had dropped toward Site Bravo. By the time his shuttle landed, he knew that the 13th was not running into significant opposition and had cleared the 8th and 97th for the final operation.

"I don't know yet how much armor the Heggies have here, but it must be at least two full regiments, perhaps a lot more," Kane said. "We've destroyed at least forty Novas, but they keep bringing more into play."

"They never used their tanks at Site Alpha," Dacik said, a bit absently. He was listening to an intelligence report over his helmet radio at the same time.

Around the two commanders, Dacik's headquarters staff was setting up shop. For the moment, Dacik planned to operate out of his shuttle, but duplicate operations were set up outside it, and two hundred meters away. A shuttle on the ground would be too inviting a target if any enemy aircraft got through the Wasp shield. If and when he moved away from the landing zone, General Dacik had an armored personnel carrier to serve as a mobile command post.

Kane started to say something, but Dacik held up a hand to stop him. He wanted to hear the end of the report he was getting over the radio. When it was finished, he let out a long breath and looked at Kane.

"The 13th is closing things up at Site Bravo. No opposition at all, to speak of. It appears that the Heggies moved most of what they had out of there before we got to them. Here?"

Kane nodded. "There was considerable activity the first night, shuttles landing right out toward the end of the peninsula, out of reach of our Havocs." He shrugged. "The Wasps didn't have any luck getting to them either. That was before the 17th arrived. Since then, they haven't been able to get any shuttles into the air.'' His laugh was sour. ''Maybe I should say that they haven't been able to *keep* them in the air.''

''We'll try the same thing with the 13th that we did at Site Bravo,'' Dacik said. ''Drop them right on top of the enemy. We'll stage the rest of our forces here. No matter what the cost, we're going to have to force a crossing over the canal to get up the peninsula in a hurry once the 13th lands. They won't be able to hold out forever up there, especially since we'll have to bring their Havocs and support elements out here.''

''General, the Heggies have at least six thousand men on that peninsula. That's SI's estimate. My own guess is that the number might be twice that, mostly military. This is the easiest climate on the world. It's where they staged the bulk of the invasion force they were gathering. The 13th, even if they were at full strength . . . '' Kane stopped and shook his head. ''They won't be able to hold out very long at all.''

''Then it's up to us to make sure that they don't have to. We'll start our push an hour before sunset, hit the Schlinal defensive line with everything we've got, and keep at it. The 13th will drop on the Heggie base ninety minutes after sunset. By that time, I hope that the Heggies will have moved the overwhelming bulk of their forces south to face us. I'll have the 13th's Wasps come in from the north as well, just ahead of the infantry. Hit 'em from behind. Work to get as much confusion going as possible.''

''And hope we confuse them more than we do ourselves?'' Kane asked.

The 13th stayed on the ground at Site Bravo until very nearly dawn. The artillery and the support units were lifted first. The Wasps were fitted with the auxiliary modules that would give them enough power to boost to orbit and rendezvous with their carrier. There they would be given fresh batteries and have their munitions topped off for another descent, this one at Site Charley. The pilots would have a few spare minutes aboard ship, while it moved into position for their third attack descent of the campaign.

By the time the 13th's infantry boarded the shuttles at Site Bravo, half a world away from their next destination, there was a faint line of light on the eastern horizon, the first hint of a new day. They had already taken time for a meal and a couple of hours of rest. Not many men had actually managed to get any sleep.

"We're not going back to the ship this time, are we?" Wiz Mackey asked as he filed past Joe Baerclau, boarding the shuttle.

"No, we're going straight to Site Charley," Joe replied. His visor was up, but he spoke loudly enough that most of the platoon heard him. "We're going to hit them there the same way we did here." Captain Keye had relayed that news just minutes before.

"I just hope it turns out as simple," Mort said, giving Wiz a nudge. Mackey had stopped in the doorway.

"Don't count on it, Professor," Joe said. "From what I hear, the Heggies have been putting up a real fight up north. That's why they need us to finish 'em off."

"Yeah, any manure detail comes along, send for the 13th," Jaiffer said as he followed Wiz into the shuttle.

So far, there had been time for only the most preliminary of briefings. Colonel Stossen had given the company commanders the first instructions he had received from General Dacik. More detailed plans had to wait until they were formulated. That was what Colonel Stossen and his staff were trying to do at the moment. The conference was being held in the open, between two shuttles, with the entire command staff physically present. They would split up between the two landers, as usual, for the ride north and the coming combat jump. Colonel Ruman, Dacik's operations officer, was on link, trying to follow what was being said.

"It won't be as simple as it was here," Stossen admitted. "Too many buildings, for one thing, and too spread out." His mapboard was open and on the ground in the middle of the group. The view was a three-dimensional representation of the northern base. ''And the Heggies have shown every intention of fully defending Site Charley. There's been no sign of mutiny or revolt, no indication that surrender is a realistic expectation.''

''We can't count on the same level of surprise either,'' Bal Kenneck warned. ''We've jumped twice here. The folks at this location might well have had time to radio news to Site Charley of how we hit them. If it had been me, that's the first thing I would have done.''

Stossen nodded. ''We'll put the recon platoons on these roofs here, at the northern edge of the complex. The rest of us will land on the ground, half here''—he adjusted the mapboard to show a two-dimensional view from overhead and pointed—''on this open ground right at the end of the peninsula, on the north side of the complex. The rest will land over here, on the east, at the airfield, as close to these hangars as they can get. Those will be the first objective for that section. Tie off any ground support for the Heggies' Boems.''

''Which companies where?'' Teu Ingels asked.

''Cut 'em straight down the middle,'' Stossen replied. ''Alpha through Delta at the tip of the peninsula, Echo through Howard at the airfield.'' Under most circumstances, Stossen would have been horrified at the thought of dividing his command so cavalierly, but he was too spent to be able to think straight enough to look for the minute differences between one group of soldiers and another that might make a particular company better suited for one objective or the other. ''Senior company commander in each group to take immediate tactical control.''

''That's Captain Cavite from Charley and Captain Digby from Fox,'' Dezo Parks said, supplying the names instantly.

Stossen nodded. Once he heard the names, he knew that Parks was right. Recalling them first had been simply too much for his tired mind. ''Tell them,'' he said.

In addition to being the two senior company commanders in the 13th, Ives Cavite and Jak Digby had been close personal friends since their days together in the military academy on Bancroft. Cavite's nickname at the academy had been "the Cavity," an obvious mispronunciation of his name, while Digby had inevitably been called Digger. Once out of the academy and serving together, those nicknames had soon metamorphosed into Hole and Mole—though rarely to their faces.

"One thing," Bal said. "It looks as if we can count on slightly more moderate weather at Site Charley. For what it's worth, it's winter in the northern hemisphere. That gives us a couple of degrees. The prevailing wind is from the northwest, polar, as well." Tamkailo's axial tilt was only six degrees, and there was very little eccentricity to its orbit, so the differences between summer and winter were minimal. "The Heggies *have* been using their armor at Charley, day and night."

"Small blessings," Parks mumbled.

"Maybe not so small," Stossen said. "I'll take a little less heat in exchange for enemy tanks any day here. We outrange the Novas with our Havocs. There's damn little we can do about the heat."

"This might be the last place we have that advantage," Bal said. "The latest rumble I've heard is that the Heggies have finally come up with self-propelled artillery that's in about the same class as our Havoc. They haven't used them against the Accord yet, but there are indications that they're testing them against the Dogel Worlds. One report suggests that these new Heggie SPs might even have a couple of klicks in range over the Havoc."

Stossen forced out a sigh. "As long as they don't have those guns on Tamkailo—that's all we can worry about now."

"And if we finish the job we started out to do here, we may never have to face them—if the general was right about crippling Schlinal offensive capability," Parks said.

"Don't hold your breath," Stossen suggested.

Hilo Keye spent most of the shuttle flight in a conference with regimental headquarters and the other company commanders. The plan of operations was drawn up en route. As soon as something almost solid was agreed to, Keye relayed it to his platoon leaders and platoon sergeants. Twice there were significant alterations that required new briefings.

"I wish they'd make up their minds," Frank Symes grumbled after Joe Baerclau passed along the latest changes. The shuttles were close to their objective. This journey had been much slower than most assault runs. There would be no screaming descent from orbit. Most of the way, the landers had flown less than two hundred meters above the ocean, as they followed a great circle route over Tamkailo's north polar region.

"Time is making up their minds now," Mort said. "Unless they put us in a holding pattern, we're within fifteen minutes of our jump now."

The reflex was automatic. Each of the sergeants and corporals on the link checked the time line on his visor.

"Do an inspection of the belts," Joe instructed. "Make sure you see one hundred percent power on every indicator." There were a few spares aboard the shuttle.

While he waited for reports on the inspection, Joe stared at the mapboard on his lap again. The captain had indexed the views available for the assault area, the base, the airfield, and the terrain in between. CIC had had plenty of time to get all of the information on the Schlinal installation and known forces into the mapboard network. Details of the battle plan were being added even as Joe studied his board. Light yellow ellipses indicated the drop zones for each of the platoons. Bright blue lines showed the anticipated lines of advance, the buildings—primarily hangars for Echo Company—that were to be the initial objectives of the company.

Dropping in the middle of an airstrip bothered Joe. There would be absolutely no cover for his men. If the Heggies were waiting for them . . .

Eustace's smile showed gritted teeth. The 13th's artillery had come by a slightly different route from the one taken by the infantry, moving more rapidly. The Havocs had been put right into the battle as soon as they came out of their shuttles south of the canal. The long-range duel had been going on for forty-five minutes now. Out on the peninsula, the Heggie tankers were showing more spunk than they usually did. With only half the range on their guns, they had to expose themselves to Havoc fire for at least eight minutes before they could get close enough to return it. But they were doing it. Despite heavy losses, they kept coming south along the peninsula, forcing the Havocs to stand back, out of range of the Schlinal base on the northern end of the peninsula.

The Novas did their best to follow erratic courses on their way south, using fire and maneuver as best they could. By the time a Havoc shell got to where they had been, they were somewhere else. Boems were occupying Wasps in the air. That part of the battle was as much a standoff as this one, but with the aircraft on both sides suffering heavier losses.

"Not a very efficient way to run a battle," Karl Mennem said after the Fat Turtle "spoke" again. CIC was plotting position and course on a single Nova, or a company of them, at one time. Then as many as two full batteries of Havocs would saturate the area where CIC expected the tank or tanks to be by the time the artillery shells reached the end of their ballistic paths.

Sometimes it worked. More often it didn't.

"We do what we can," Eustace replied. "Jimmy, how you doin'?"

"Just fine," Ysinde replied. "This is almost like a winter exercise on Albion." There was a short pause before he added, "Compared to Site Alpha." It would be a long time before he would be able to forget the heat.

"Yeah, well keep an eye on the thermometer, and if you start feeling the least bit woozy, let me know."

"Right, Gunny," Ysinde said. "Just find us something to hit."

"Fair trade," Eustace said. "Maybe we can't box them in, but they can't do any better against us."

"We might do better just picking a spot and firing at random," Karl suggested. "Don't even look for the Novas first."

" 'I shot an arrow into the air,' " Simon quoted as he moved the Fat Turtle toward its next firing point. With the Novas moving south, the Havocs had to fire and move after each shot to keep the Heggies from zeroing in on them. "Like a cat that knows exactly how far the dog's leash will let it go," Eustace had said earlier.

It was time for another salvo. Fourteen howitzers fired almost at once—the "almost" because they were co-ordinating for "time on target," looking for all fourteen rounds to hit simultaneously.

This time, the dogs found something to bite. "Two Novas hit!" Eustace shouted, relaying a report from a Wasp. The pilot didn't have time for more. There were two Boems chasing him, and his own wingman had been shot down not more than thirty seconds before.

Approaching the northern end of the peninsula from three different directions, the shuttles carrying the 13th's infantry companies and recon platoons came in low, skimming the negligible waves for the last fifty kilometers. The landers were not quite as "invisible" to enemy detection devices as Wasps. The bulky shapes necessitated by their purpose limited their stealth. Flying at wave-top levels helped.

The armada of shuttles had separated to approach the three jump zones. The plan called for the shuttles to boost to drop altitude only in the last few seconds, almost as they reached the shoreline.

Dem Nimz sat next to one of the shuttle doors. For the last fifteen minutes, he had kept his eyes closed. His head was back against the bulkhead. As far as anyone around him could tell, he might have been asleep. He wasn't. The tableau was only partially a pose designed to make everyone think that he was as cool and collected as possible. Dem *was* cool and collected. It had been a long time since he had felt any real jitters before action, and he couldn't even remember anything that might reasonably be called fear.

He went back over the plan of attack in his mind. His memory was excellent. He no longer needed to look at mapboard views of the base to see it clearly. He knew where his men were supposed to drop, where the other recon platoons would be, and where the line infantry would be hitting.

Dem waited for the sudden increase in apparent weight that would come when the shuttle pilot accelerated to climb to drop altitude. When it came, he opened his eyes, sat up straight, and looked around—as casually as he could manage. Just a few steps away, the jumpmaster was already on his feet. The jumpmaster's orders came quickly. The reccers unfastened their safety harnesses, stood, and moved to the doorways. The reccers had plenty of room for this ride. One platoon to a shuttle. That left a lot of empty space.

The hatches opened. The jumpmaster gestured to Dem and shouted, "Go!" Dem dove forward, propelling himself away from the lander. His right arm cradled his experimental AG rifle. His left hand was on his belt controls. He counted to three before he turned the antigrav belt on. Dem wasn't in the least worried about jumping out of a shuttle. Counting training, he had made well over a hundred jumps, first with parachute and the older antigrav belts, now with the new Corey belt. There was always something of a thrill to the start of a jump.

Down. Dem looked to the building below. As usual, the shuttle pilots had dropped them perfectly. Dem marked the roof that his platoon was to occupy. Straight below. There seemed to be a bit of a breeze from the northwest, but it was blowing him more toward the center of the roof than toward an edge.

He was within fifty meters of the rooftop when he spotted movement there, and heard the first sounds of enemy wire coming up toward the jumpers.

The Heggies were waiting for them.

CHAPTER
15

Echo Company landed too far away from the reccers to hear the initial rifle fire directed at the men jumping for the roofs, but within seconds an all-hands alert had been broadcast. Joe had already been scanning the ground around the drop zone, paying more attention to the hangars than to the open space immediately below him and leading over to the ocean. There had been no hint of enemy movement around the airfield. No lights showed from the hangars.

As he dropped below eighty meters, Joe aimed his carbine toward the nearest building, holding the zipper one-handed so he could work his belt controls with the other hand. Joe's right index finger rested lightly over the trigger guard of the Armanoc. If he had to fire on the drop, he knew that he was unlikely to actually hit what he aimed at, but he might keep the target from hitting him.

"I want skirmish lines as soon as we touch down," Joe said. "First and second squad watching the hangars. Fourth, cover the rest of the circle." Two ahead, one behind.

Echo Company was on the left flank of this assault, closest to the buildings of the main base. Echo, Delta, Fox, and George—south to north. It would be up to George Company to take the north end of the line of hangars and secure that flank. Echo would have to set up posts to cover the gap between the other end of the line and the rest of the installation. The southernmost hangar was over two kilometers from the nearest corner of the grid of buildings at the main base.

Joe was no more than twenty-five meters off of the ground when the first enemy fire came close. The sound of wire zipping by was unmistakable, but Joe couldn't see where it was coming from. Wire rifles showed no muzzle blast.

"Where's it coming from?" he demanded over the platoon channel as he got ready to land.

"Looks like the end of the last hangar," Mort said. "I thought I saw something moving there."

The platoon was hitting the ground by that time. Everyone went straight down into prone firing positions even though the hangars were too far away for wire coming from them to be a serious danger.

"Move it!" Captain Keye ordered over the company net. "Up and at 'em."

"By squads!" Joe ordered, switching to his platoon channel. "I want the cough guns zeroed in on the end of the last hangar and the gap between that building and the next to the right. Vrerchs and RPGs as well. Keep their heads down if you can't blow 'em off."

Fire and maneuver. One squad advanced a few meters, then went prone while the rest of the platoon gave them covering fire. Then another squad moved. The men with sniper rifles, Vrerchs, or grenade launchers used them from resting positions, then moved when it was their turn. The rest of the platoon sprayed wire, even though they were more than a hundred meters from the nearest possible enemy positions.

Before Joe had run a total of twenty meters, he was soaked in sweat. But that did cool him off. There was enough of a breeze coming toward Echo Company to make the temperature bearable. For a time.

The platoon's first casualty was Frank Symes, fourth squad leader. A heavy burst of wire caught him in the chest and throat just as he was getting up to lead his squad forward again, about eighty meters from the nearest point of the hangar that the platoon was moving toward. Just a few extra meters might have made the difference for Frank. The squad's medic was with him in seconds, but there was nothing he could do for his sergeant.

"Can't be more than fifty Heggies shooting, all along the strip," First Sergeant Walker said over a channel that connected him to all of his platoon sergeants. "Mechanics and guards is my guess." Soldiers who might be less than fully proficient at basic combat skills. "Let's blow 'em over in a hurry, before they get reinforcements."

That would make the odds four short companies of SAT troops against a handful of Heggies, hardly a fair fight— not that anyone would insist on a fair fight. A few seconds later, Walker was on the radio again.

"First and second platoons, take the end of the line. Looks like maybe a half dozen Heggies there. Secure that corner."

Joe spent ten seconds on the line with first platoon's sergeant, then switched channels to talk to his own men. "On my signal. Up and all the way." Ten seconds later, he gave the signal. He was already getting to his feet as he gave it.

First and second platoons were no more than sixty meters from the near corner of the hangar. The thirty-seven men left in the two platoons sprinted that distance, spraying wire at any spot that looked as if it might conceivably hold an enemy. Along the line, the rest of Echo and the other three companies with it were doing the same thing.

There simply were not enough Heggies to defend the hangars, though they did manage to cause several dozen Accord casualties before they broke and ran toward the buildings of the main base.

● ● ●

Dem Nimz's test rifle proved to be ill-suited for use during a jump. He gave it a good test, returning the Heggie fire. But the gun's mechanism could not completely damp its recoil. That set him swaying like a pendulum and made accurate fire impossible. Dupuy cough guns—two men in each reccer squad were equipped with the rocket-assisted rifles—were similarly "flawed," but the Dupuy was only semiautomatic, and its muzzle velocity was much lower than the new weapon's.

The rest of the reccers were still armed with Armanocs, though, and the recoil of the zippers was negligible. The reccers gave a good account of themselves, even in the air.

Dem hit the roof off balance and fell backward as he cut power to his belt. Under the circumstances, falling flat was the safest possible move.

Four reccers were either dead or unconscious when they hit the roof. They provided a macabre spectacle. The gyro stabilizers on their belts kept their torsos upright, but their legs were splayed out and their heads sagged forward or back, lolling around in response to movement. The thrusters of the belts scooted their bodies around, hands dragging, almost at random until they ran out of power or until someone managed to hit the shut-off switch.

It was several minutes before any of the reccers on the roof with Dem had any opportunity to worry about their fallen comrades. They had dropped into the middle of a Schlinal infantry platoon. A lot of the reccers were wounded, but still conscious, able to defend themselves to some degree.

Once the reccers were on the roof, knives became as important as rifles, often more so. Although Armanocs weren't equipped to take bayonets, Dem's test weapon was. So was the standard-issue Heggie rifle. Unlike this rooftop's defenders, though, Dem had taken time to get his bayonet in place. Few of the Heggies seemed to think about using bayonets, except as hand knives.

Roughly equal numbers of Heggies and Freebies fought for control of the roof. The free-for-all was a series of independent duels, with the balance turning only slowly from the Heggies to the reccers.

Dem pulled his bayonet out of one Heggie's gut, twisting the blade to increase the size of the wound. He spun left, seeing someone come at him from the side, rifle at high port, ready to swing the rifle butt toward his head. Dem didn't have time to get his own rifle aimed at the Heggie, to end the duel with a quick shot. All he could do was bring his rifle up to meet the other weapon. As the rifle stocks collided, Dem brought his knee up toward the Heggie's groin. The man twisted to the side, so all Dem hit was his hip, and the Heggie was able to press forward while Dem was off balance.

Dem let himself fall, bringing his rifle around as he did. As the bayonet came into line between the two men, the Heggie couldn't jump on top of Dem. The split second that the Heggie hesitated was fatal. Dem pulled the trigger and blew a hole high in the Heggie's chest.

Nimz was slow getting back to his feet. The fall had taken the air from him. But the fight was almost over. More reccers had been killed. Dem's sixty-man platoon had dwindled to the size of a line company platoon. He only had twenty-nine men left, and more than half of them had at least minor injuries.

Frank Symes was the only man killed in Joe's platoon during the assault on the hangars. There were several minor injuries in the platoon, but nothing that a medic couldn't handle. None of the wounded were hurt too seriously to continue.

"Joe, get your men on the roof. Set up your platoon's splat gun at the back corner, covering the approach from the main base," Izzy Walker said. "First platoon will be on the ground in front of you."

"Right," Joe replied. "Unless you want us to go inside and up by the stairs, we'll have to go up on ropes. Nobody's got enough juice on their belts to do it the easy way."

"Hang on a second," Walker said. It was closer to two minutes than one second before the first sergeant came back on the link. "Bring your men on in. We've got the inside secured. The stairs are along the wall on the south end of the building."

Echo's 1st platoon was already establishing its defensive line west of the hangar. With ground too hard to allow much excavation, the line was spread out to take best advantage of the irregular terrain.

Joe gathered his men, and they started back around the end of the hangar to one of the doors. There were lights on inside now. Someone had flipped the switches; the Heggies hadn't cut power to the building. The inside of the hangar seemed vast—eighty meters long, forty wide, and fifteen high, plenty of room for thirty Boems or more. There were only four fighters in the hangar, but they were all armed and loaded with fresh batteries. Obviously, the 13th's landing had caught those few Boems between missions.

"That's four buzzards that won't be giving our guys any more grief," Wiz Mackey commented. He raised his visor to spit in the general direction of the nearest Boem. None of the other men from first squad bothered to reply.

"Every building has stairs to the roof," Mort mentioned on the noncoms' circuit. "But we haven't seen any evidence that they really *used* the roofs for anything. No regular defensive emplacements, nothing. Too damn hot to start with. Why'd they bother?"

"Just be glad they did," Sergeant Degtree said. "Maybe they went up at night for a breeze."

As first squad neared the door leading out onto the roof, Joe whistled shrilly on the squad's channel, a signal that caused the men to freeze in their tracks.

"Hold up! This is no damn lark," Joe barked. "Who told you that the roof's secure? Figure there might be a platoon of Heggies out there with their guns trained on that door until you know better."

Sauv Degtree muttered under his breath. Nobody noticed, but there was embarrassment as well as guilt in his *I should have known better.*

"By the book," he told his squad. "My fault," he told Joe, switching channels just long enough for the confession.

Only Mort glanced his way, just briefly. "Check your weapons for full load and power." He looked at his own. The charge was nearly full. He had better than half a spool of wire left in the rifle as well.

"Mackey, you yank the door and drop. I want everybody else aiming through the opening. Any hint of opposition, shoot first and we'll forget about the questions."

Second and fourth squads were lower on the stairway, guns also trained on the door. Baerclau was between first and second squads. He checked his rifle as well. He really did not expect Heggies to be waiting on the roof, but he had experienced a sudden sinking feeling in his stomach when he saw "his" squad racing for the door as if there weren't the slightest chance of opposition.

Degtree looked around at his men. He took a deep breath. Wiz was watching him. Sauv nodded, and brought his rifle up at the same time. Wiz hauled the door open and dropped to the landing in front of it, bringing his rifle to bear as he fell.

The lights inside the hangar made it impossible to see anything out in the darkness on the roof, but no fire came in through the doorway.

Joe counted silently to five, then said, "Go," on first squad's channel.

One fire team at a time, the squad went through, followed almost immediately by second squad. Joe moved to the side of the door and waited until both first and second squads were in position outside.

"It's clear," Sauv reported.

Joe moved outside the door and stood next to the kiosk while he directed the rest of the platoon out and got everyone in position, two squads on the side facing the main Schlinal base and the other squad spread out facing the landing strip.

"We're in position, Captain," Joe reported. "No opposition up here."

"Don't get too comfortable, Joe," Keye replied. "As soon as we've got the airfield secured and the Heggies' ammo and the planes we caught on the ground blown up or booby-trapped, we're going to be moving again.''

"Yes, sir. As long as nobody blows this roof out from under us.''

"If we blow it, I'll give you time to get clear,'' Keye said dryly.

"The Novas are withdrawing, pulling back up the peninsula,'' Eustace Ponks told his crew, relaying news he had just received. "Let's get moving, Simon. We follow them north until we're just three klicks behind our lines.'' Three kilometers: that would keep them out of the range of shoulder-launched rockets coming across the canal and allow their main gun to reach very nearly to the Schlinal base at the northern end of the peninsula.

"On the way,'' Kilgore replied, pushing the throttles forward.

"We'll keep our interval with the Novas on the way,'' Eustace said. "Just out of their range. Karl, Jimmy, fire mission coming in now. We're gonna hurry those Novas along.''

General Dacik watched the withdrawal of the Schlinal armor on his large mapboard. The blips might be several minutes out of date by the time they moved, but it did give him some idea what was going on.

"They've heard about our landings at the far end of the peninsula,'' Jorgen Olsen guessed. "They're pulling the Novas back to dislodge the 13th.''

"I want every effort made to be sure that they pull back all of the armor,'' Dacik said. "Get Wasps in as close as possible to hurry them along. We'll give them a few more minutes, then hit both bridges with everything we've got. We've got to force our crossing quickly now, get north before the Heggies have time to neutralize Stossen's command.'' *Neutralize:* that was the polite staff word for "destroy.''

"We've got all of our ground assets poised,'' Colonel Ruman said quickly. "Just waiting for the word to go.''

With the Heggie armor pulling north in a hurry, the

bridge crossings might be a little less costly than they would have been otherwise, but if the Heggie infantry continued to defend the bridges with as much determination as they had so far, it would still be a bloody engagement.

"As soon as the tanks are twelve klicks north of the canal, and Jorgen can tell me that they've *all* gone north," Dacik said. "That's when we go."

Olsen was already busy on his radio links to CIC and to the Wasp flight leaders. He broke away from a radio conversation long enough to say, "It should be about nine minutes until all of the tanks we know about are past that twelve-klick line. So far, it looks as if they're all going north. Still checking." It would be impossible to know for certain, but nothing in combat is ever certain.

Dacik pulled his visor down just long enough to glance at the time line on the display. Nine minutes.

"Ru, get on link and notify Kane, Foss, Bones, and LaRieu that we jump in ten minutes." Lieutenant Colonel Saf LaRieu had assumed command of the 34th LIR the first day of the attack against Site Charley, when the regiment's previous commander was killed.

Dacik's plan for the breakthrough, such as it was, had been finalized only forty-five minutes earlier. The regimental commanders all knew what was expected of them. The 5th and 8th SATs would spearhead the attempts to cross the two bridges. The 34th LIR would continue to support the 5th SAT. The 97th would back up the 8th. The two light infantry regiments were to maintain pressure along the canal first to prevent the Heggies from moving all of their assets to the bridges. Once the SATs established a bridgehead on the peninsula, the light infantry would cross behind them and move to the flanks, to clear Heggie opposition along the canal.

The 5th and 8th would drive north as fast as the opposition permitted. After covering the breakthrough from almost point-blank range, the Havocs of all three SATs would cross the canal as soon as the Heggies were far enough from the bridges to be out of rocket range of the artillery.

•   •   •

The 13th's 3rd recon platoon was pinned down on its rooftop. After disposing of the Heggies who had been there when they arrived, the reccers were taken under fire by more Heggie infantry—men on the ground and on roofs that hadn't been directly assaulted by air.

"Good thing we jumped with our locators on this time," Fredo Gariston told Dem. "We can tell who's who." Fredo was flat on his back, his left arm and hand bloody. Dem was wrapping medicated soakers over a dozen wire cuts.

"Try making a fist," Dem said after he had the last patch secured.

Both men stared at Fredo's left hand. The fingers twitched, but did not close. Dem shook his head.

"I was afraid of that. Doesn't feel like any broken bones, but you've got serious muscle damage in that arm, maybe even nerves cut."

"I don't suppose you've got a trauma tube in your back pocket," Fredo said. He was able to joke. The med patches had numbed the pain almost instantly. He didn't feel a thing in his left arm now.

"No, and I don't know how long it's gonna be before we can get you to one."

"No problem. I can fire a zipper one-handed. And reload it too. Just don't expect speed records."

"Never mind that. You just keep your ass, and your head, down," Dem ordered. " 'Less the Heggies get right on this roof with us again, you're out of it."

"They were waiting for us," Fredo said, his voice starting to go dreamy. It had taken three soakers to cover all of the wounds on his arm. The heavy dose of analgesics was starting to make him drowsy. It wouldn't be enough to put him out, but it did take his mind several steps away from full alertness.

"They were waiting for us," Dem agreed, pondering whether or not to hit his friend with a sleep patch as well. Fredo's left arm was in very bad shape. The wire had torn away a lot of meat, and Fredo had lost considerable blood before Dem got to him. Dem decided against the sleeper.

Between loss of blood and the soakers, Fredo would almost certainly lose consciousness on his own soon enough.

"How many?" Fredo asked, fighting a losing battle to stay awake.

"Couple hundred on the roofs," Dem said, speaking slowly, softly, watching Fredo's eyes now. They were barely open. "More on the ground."

"Watch . . . the . . . door," Fredo said. The last word was almost unintelligible as he finally went into limbo.

Watch what? Dem thought before that last word penetrated. *Door.* He turned to look at the door leading in from the roof. It was shut. Two reccers were kneeling beside the kiosk, using it for additional shelter, but they weren't watching the door.

"Good thinking, Fredo," Dem whispered, knowing that Fredo could no longer hear him. "They could blast us good there." Quickly, he put two men to watch the door. "Keep your zippers right on it. It opens, don't wait to see who's there. Start shooting, then toss grenades in."

The rooftop fight was a cat-and-mouse game that showed no promise of ending quickly. Pick your moment. Get up just high enough to aim a rifle at the next roof. Spray a few meters of wire and duck before an enemy popped up to spray you. It worked the same for Heggie and Freebie. The most either side could hope to do was to keep the enemies' heads down.

Men guessed wrong, on both sides. They raised up to spray and got sprayed. If they were lucky, all they had exposed was a helmeted head. Accord helmets and faceplates would stop wire even at short range. Schlinal helmets did not have visors. That made them more vulnerable.

Twenty minutes after hitting the roof, Dem's platoon was down to nineteen effectives. There were three men hurt too badly to continue fighting. The rest were dead.

Dem looked up at the sky. *I hope the line companies get to us in a hurry,* he thought. Then he got on the radio and started asking about timetables. "We can't hold out long," he told Major Parks.

CHAPTER
16

Near both bridges, Wasp maintenance teams had used aircraft ordnance to create ground weapons, the innovation that had gained a commission for Roo Vernon. Everyone had heard about his novel use for aircraft cannons and rockets. Now he had explained to his counterparts in the other two SATs on Tamkailo what his men had done on Jordan. All that General Dacik was interested in was the cannon mounts. The 25mm five-barreled cannons were set on tripods made from repair parts that the Wasp ground crews could assemble. Loaded with fragmenting anti-personnel rounds, a single gun's five barrels could spray fifteen hundred metal needles per second.

Four guns had been assembled and hauled into place near each of the bridges. One minute before the two SATs were to begin their assault, the makeshift guns opened up, playing back and forth along the Heggie lines near the north ends of the bridges. Those cannons, added to the rest of the weaponry that four regiments could bring to bear, suppressed most of the Heggie fire. The 10mm-long metal shards that the 25mm round separated into could cut through any body armor.

The 5th and 8th ran for the bridges, massed charges. They had narrow approach lanes. The bridge deck itself was not being fired on by the Accord. Fire zones on either side left a triangle that was safe from friendly fire. On the Heggie side of the canal only men with RPGs were getting in much work. Grenades could be launched from behind cover, sent out in arcs across the canal—or onto bridges. By the time the first Accord troops reached the bridges, something new was added. Tank rounds started exploding. At least a few Novas had not gone north with the rest, or they had turned around and come back within range of the canal.

Then the Heggies turned loose their remaining Boems for one last attack.

Zel Paitcher had been unable to get rid of a hollow feeling in his gut. It wasn't hunger. It wasn't even fear . . . exactly. "Just a nasty little itch," he had whispered to Gerry Easton the last time they had been on the ground for new batteries and ammunition. *A nasty little itch that tells me this is my last campaign* was the full thought, but he hadn't shared the rest of it with his wingman.

The 13th's Blue Flight was down to four planes now. Four planes and four pilots. Zel and Gerry. Ilsen Kwillen and Will Tarkel. The rest of the 13th's flights were in similar condition. The 8th and 17th had been hurt, but not quite as badly. The 5th's air wing had been chopped to pieces in the early fighting, when they were the only Wasps at Site Charley. Only five of its twenty-four Wasps had still been intact when the 17th IAW arrived. And two of those five had been shot down since.

Like the rest of the Accord forces south of the canal, the Wasps had a part to play in the general's desperate assault against the bridges. The Wasps were primarily assigned ground support missions, flying along the Heggie lines north of the canal, trying to put as many of them out of action as possible. Part of the 17th was higher, its mission to keep Schlinal Boems away.

They weren't entirely successful.

The 13th's ten remaining Wasps were concentrated on the Heggie positions guarding the western bridge. They came in from farther west. Prior to the attack they had rendezvoused over the ocean, twenty kilometers away, and only twenty meters above the water.

"We'll stay down as long as we can," Zel told his men while they waited for the signal to start their attack. "Low and fast. Until we get close to the bridge, stick with cannon. We'll use both rockets and cannon approaching and leaving the area of the bridge. We run dry, we turn straight south and beat it, just high enough off of the ground to stay out of the way of artillery shells."

Zel led his flight in, climbing as they reached the shoreline, maintaining their relative altitude as the ground rose. The targeting diagram on Zel's head-up display had been keyed to show the line of Heggie defenses in green. Zel cut back on his forward speed. When the ground-speed indicator dipped to 500 kph, he locked it in.

And gave the first touch to his trigger. Three hundred meters ahead, the metal slivers fired from five barrels converged on an area no more than two meters wide. The long diameter of the elliptical pattern was right along the main Heggie trench. No body armor could stand up to the hypersonic assault of that much sharp metal.

Zel kept his bursts short until the bridge came into easy range of his missiles. He emptied his racks quickly, aiming not at the bridge itself but at the defenses at its northern end, across the roadway and to either side. Then he switched back to cannons and kept his finger on the trigger as he flew over rocket explosions and past the bridge. When his forward cannons fell silent—out of ammunition—he accelerated sideways and up. The antigrav drive meant that there was no need to *turn* the Wasp in order to change direction, and Zel didn't waste the time to turn until he was far enough out of range of a ground-launched missile to afford it.

Only three planes from Blue Flight made it away from the canal. Ilsen Kwillen's Wasp was hit by a rocket while it was north of the canal. It broke into three main pieces. The escape module did separate, but the parachute failed to deploy.

Kwillen's escape pod slammed into the rock wall of the canal's south bank at more than four hundred kilometers per hour.

There were two roads leading from the hangars and landing strip to the main Heggie base at the north end of the peninsula. Although they had not been paved, the routes did show that tracked vehicles had moved along them. In a couple of places, irregularities in the ground had been leveled out.

Echo Company was given the road at the south end of the hangars. Howard Company had the other road. Fox and George were in the middle, spread out in a loose skirmish line to make certain that no Heggies were missed, left to take them from behind. On the north, Howard could keep a watch on its flank all of the way to the water. Echo could not be nearly as certain of *its* exposed flank. The rough terrain ran all the way south to the canal. Entire battalions of Heggies might be hidden there.

"Nothing we can do about it," Izzy Walker told Joe Baerclau. "Keep an eye on what you can see. We've got to get to the base as quickly as we can. We *know* there are Heggies there, and our reccers need help fast."

One Boem had tried to land at the airfield before the 13th left the hangars. It had been hit by three Vrerchs when it was no more than twenty meters off of the ground. There had been no need to look for the pilot.

Joe's platoon was moving forward in a column on the left side of the road. First platoon was forty meters ahead of them. Fourth platoon was level with second, on the other side of the road. Third platoon was in front of them. The rest of the company, fifth and sixth platoons, came farther back.

Echo was under half strength now. Joe had already

reorganized again: two squads instead of four, or the three that the platoon had been functioning with since the end of the first battle on Tamkailo. Sauv Degtree still had first squad. Low Gerrent had second, the squad he had led for more than a year. The survivors of fourth squad had been divided up between them.

"Let the guys up ahead worry about what's in front of us," Joe told his men. "I'm more worried about our left flank. The rest of our people are nearly twenty kilometers away." Then he switched channels to speak privately with Mort, who had the point for the platoon, as usual. "*You* worry about what's in front of you, Professor. Don't take it for granted that first platoon will spot any mines or booby traps. You heard about those bouncers that the reccers couldn't spot in daylight on bare rock."

"I heard. I'm watching," Mort replied.

Despite his own advice, Joe couldn't completely ignore what was in front of Echo—far in front. The signs of fighting at the main Heggie base were all too evident. Wire at a distance produced a sound almost like that of a mosquito whizzing close by. But there were the explosions of grenades to punctuate that, easily audible over the couple of kilometers of open ground that separated Echo from the fighting. And the buildings of the main base were on higher ground.

Despite the need for haste, the pace of the 13th's advance was relatively slow. The companies on the roads might easily have moved faster, but they held back even with the companies moving cross-country in the center. And, occasionally, the line encountered a pocket of Heggie riflemen.

Although the temperature was still above 34 degrees Celsius, it felt . . . almost cool. Every now and then Joe lifted his visor for a moment to get a touch of the breeze coming from the northwest. That dried sweat quickly. The slow pace of the advance helped as well. Carrying full combat kit was hard work regardless of the temperature.

The four companies had only covered two-thirds of a kilometer before they ran into more determined opposition.

There was a flurry of gunfire from wire rifles and slug-throwing machine guns, and the blasts of several grenades.

"Hit the dirt!" Joe shouted over his platoon channel—a needless order since most of the men had already dropped.

"Roadblock," Captain Keye announced over the noncoms' channel. Then he switched channels. "Joe, take your platoon around to the left. The Heggies are two hundred meters in front of you—two machine guns, maybe a dozen zippers. Fourth platoon will be moving up on the right so be careful where your people are shooting."

"On the way," Joe replied. He used his platoon channel to pass along the orders. "Sauv, Low, we'll do an el. Take a forty-five-degree heading from the road. We'll go out a hundred and twenty meters, then make the right angle. Column on the first leg. Skirmish line when we make the turn."

Second platoon started forward, running low, the men crouched over to minimize their exposure. They might be too far from the enemy for wire to do much damage, but the bullets fired by Schlinal crew-served automatic weapons could take a man out at a lot more than two hundred meters.

Joe maintained his position between the squads. Mort was still on point. Sauv Degtree had needed no lessons on the Professor's value at the front. Once away from the road, the platoon was able to take some advantage of terrain. For most of the first leg of their flanking maneuver, they were able to keep a low ridge between them and the enemy roadblock.

There was no thought of heat or cooling breeze now. Joe's mind was entirely on the problem of getting around into position on the enemy's flank, and keeping his men as safe as possible in the process.

"Don't assume that the one batch is all of the Heggies waiting," he reminded Mort on a private link. "They have to know that we'll try to flank them."

"You think you can handle this better than I can, you're welcome to it," Mort replied—an uncharacteristically testy response.

Mort took five minutes to cover the first leg, moving enough beyond the 120-meter mark to center 2nd platoon on that distance. Joe took a second to confirm the bearing on the enemy guns before he signaled for the platoon to start heading directly for it. Then he called 4th's platoon sergeant.

"We gonna hit 'em together?" Joe asked.

"Sounds good to me," Dieter Franzo replied. Franzo had been a squad leader when the 13th first dropped on Tamkailo, and not even the senior squad leader in his platoon. He had become 4th platoon's third platoon sergeant in three days. "Just say when. We're about one hundred twenty meters out from them now, and maybe fifty meters north of the road."

"We're a little closer to them and farther from the road," Joe said. "They haven't spotted us. At least, they haven't started shooting at us. Hang on a second." He changed channels long enough to get his men down. Just over a hundred meters from the enemy, they were close enough to be vulnerable even to wire if the enemy spotted them.

"Let me know when you get within a hundred meters," Joe said when he returned to the link with Dieter. "We'll go in together then. I'll let the captain know what we're up to."

"I heard it, Joe," Captain Keye said, demonstrating that he had been monitoring the channel. "As soon as you two start firing, we'll move forward on the road as well, hit them with everything we've got."

"Everything" included three Vrerchs targeted against the two Schlinal machine guns as well as a dozen RPGs, and rifle fire from the half of Echo Company that could bring their weapons to bear.

The firefight ended quickly. Echo started moving forward again.

"Joe, you stay out there on the flank," Captain Keye said. But he had to bring 4th platoon back to the road. They were in front of the rest of the skirmish line.

• • •

The 5th and 8th SATs moved across the bridges. Despite all of the supporting fire on the ground and in the air, the toll was still expensive. The Heggies defending the canal line fought as if they were long-term professionals rather than conscripts. The Accord's dead were left where they fell on the bridges. Bodies could be recovered later, when—if—it was safe. Medics worked on the wounded. Other men worked to carry those wounded back to the south side of the canal, to the relative safety of the fixed positions there.

But the two SATs did make it to the north end of the bridges. Hundreds of men rushed into the narrow bridgeheads and fought to expand them. The Schlinal force continued to resist. More Novas came close enough to bring their main guns to bear on the bridgeheads. From the south, Havocs continued to duel with the Schlinal armor.

Both bridges took hits from the Novas, but the bridges had been built too well to collapse without massive damage. Holes were blown in the decks. Sections of the low ramparts along the sides were knocked into the canal. Truss sections were bent and warped. More men were killed making the crossing.

"Start moving the 34th and 97th across," Dacik ordered as soon as all of the SAT infantry companies had made it to the north side. "We've got to free up the SATs to move north. Start moving the Havocs into position in case we need to move them across the canal." Theoretically, the Havocs could cover the entire peninsula from positions near the south bank of the canal, but in combat, their accuracy did increase as ranges decreased.

The recon platoons on the rooftops noticed when the enemy fire directed their way fell off to almost nothing. Those few reccers who were left alive on the roofs. After more than thirty minutes of heavy fire the enemy had, apparently, decided to abandon them, at least for the moment.

"I think they're moving away," Nimz reported.

"They've just left enough marksmen to keep us pinned down."

Dezo Parks took the report. "Probably moving to intercept the line companies," he told Dem. "We've got men advancing from both directions. The companies coming from the airfield should be within about five hundred meters of your position by now. If you get a chance, give them a hand, but don't take extreme chances. We'll get to you soon enough."

"We're in pretty good shape for now," Dem replied. "As long as the heat stays off. But if the Heggies want us bad enough, they could take us in two minutes. I don't have many men left here, and the other platoons are at least as bad off as we are."

Parks started to say something else, but a quick gesture from Bal Kenneck stopped him. "Hold on a second," Parks told Nimz. Then he lifted his visor.

"I just had a call from Olsen," Kenneck said. "CIC has detected a new fleet coming in-system full blast. *They're not ours.*"

CHAPTER
17

The physics of interstellar travel are complex. A full development of the Loughlin-Runninghorse equations—the theoretical breakthrough that had made possible both antigravity (or projected artificial gravity fields) and hyperspace drives—can take days to run even on a network of the fastest molecular supercomputers in the galaxy. As Einstein developed upon Newton, with relativity becoming important only under extreme conditions, the Loughlin-Runninghorse expansion becomes necessary only where the equations of relativity and quantum mechanics start yielding infinities. The earlier systems remain valid, of course, within their proper domains.

It is not, however, essential to understand the mathematics of hyperspace to notice some of its practical results. Of military importance is the fact that a ship, or a fleet of ships, entering or exiting hyperspace, must do so at a certain minimal speed and at a certain minimum distance from any large concentration of matter . . . such as a star or a planet. Below the minimum speed (which also depends on the mass of the ship), there is simply no transition from space to hyperspace. The distortions inflicted by extraneous collections of matter can lead to more chaotic results—in both the scientific and mundane meanings of the phrase. The precise safety margin remains uncertain. In the course of the Accord-Schlinal War, that margin had been shrunk, in practice. Where once a ship would not have dared emerge from hyperspace within less than eight hours' normal space travel time from a planetary mass, four hours was now considered standard.

A daring skipper might shrink that to three-and-a-half hours.

Admiral Benjamin H. Kitchener had been sleeping when the Schlinal fleet emerged from hyperspace. "Suddenly emerged" would have been a melodramatic redundancy. The transition between normal space and hyperspace was always abrupt, in either direction. An object was either in normal space or it was in hyperspace. There was no gradual appearance as it moved from one to the other, no "ghostly" transformation. To the limits of measurability, the transition was instantaneous as the drives realigned from one medium to the other.

The admiral had been sleeping after more than sixty hours of being awake with no more than a handful of ten-minute naps. If the campaign had gone according to schedule, the troops would already have been back aboard the ships of the fleet and the fleet would have been on its way out of the system already. If.

A call from the bridge woke Kitchener. He had, at least, been sleeping in his clothes. He had done no more than peel off his shoes before collapsing across his bunk, only forty-five minutes earlier. His feet had been aching from all of the standing he had been doing. He didn't bother to put his shoes back on before hurrying to the bridge.

"Talk to me," Kitchener commanded as he entered the bridge.

Capricorn's captain, Marley Quince, pointed at the largest monitor in the chamber. "Twelve vessels, all large,'' he said. ''Coming on fast. They'll reach us in three hours and forty-one minutes and be in position to launch shuttles within minutes after that.''

''*If* they're carrying troops,'' Kitchener said. ''They might just be transport for the troops already there, ready to take them on for whatever the Heggies staged them here for.''

''No, sir,'' Quince said. ''Neither empty troop ships nor commercial freighters would have come out of hyperspace that close, that fast.''

The admiral nodded his agreement. ''Well, in any case, they couldn't have received word of our attack until they came out. That means they've had no more than a couple of minutes to start making their plans.'' He moved to a compsole and started keying in demands for data. ''A scheduled arrival,'' he added.

''They'll still have their complement of space fighters and heavy weapons,'' Quince pointed out. ''They're a threat to us.''

Kitchener called CIC. ''Give me a plot to intercept the incoming vessels as far out as possible. The object is to slow down any reinforcement for the Schlinal forces on planet without taking unnecessary chances with our ships.''

He turned to face Quince again. ''Has Dacik been notified?''

''I called him immediately after I paged you, Admiral, but I didn't have many details for him.''

Kitchener studied the screen of data on the monitor in front of him. ''All capital ships. We could be talking about four regiments.''

Quince whistled softly. He had been following the news from the surface closely enough to know what that would do to the Accord's land forces.

''I think I'd better talk to Dacik myself,'' Kitchener said. ''I'll do it from my cabin.'' He glanced down at his feet. ''I seem to find myself out of uniform.''

Kleffer Dacik turned away from his staff and walked a dozen paces. The general had felt blood draining from his face at the first sentence out of Captain Quince's mouth.

Kitchener's confirmation and the extra details didn't make Dacik feel any better. He listened without comment to the admiral's recital. It didn't take long. Afterward, Dacik remained silent for nearly thirty seconds before he responded.

"I hope you can handle the majority of them before they get to us, Ben. Three or four regiments hit the ground, we're in big trouble. I mean *big*!" *That,* he thought, *is understatement, not hyperbole.*

"We'll do what we can, Kleff, but you know what it's like," Kitchener said. "We're unlikely to do major damage to the enemy fleet. They're unlikely to do major damage to us." The thorn and the rose. Battle in space was difficult and, at least in Accord experience, rarely decisive.

Kitchener paused for so long that Dacik felt compelled to stick an "I know" into the silence.

"There is one option I think you should consider, Kleff," the admiral said then. "We've got three-and-a-half hours before the Schlinal fleet reaches us. Three-and-a-half *safe* hours. Can you evacuate before then?"

Dacik closed his eyes, squeezed them shut. Evacuate. Withdraw. Retreat. He took a deep breath and let it out. He *could* make a case for it. They had already destroyed considerable enemy war matériel, inflicted thousands of casualties, taken nearly two thousand prisoners. They had already done enough damage to cripple whatever plans the Schlinal warlords might have had for the people and supplies they had been caching on Tamkailo.

"We'd have to get the last of our people off of the ground in, what, two-and-a-half hours?" he asked.

"About that," Kitchener said. "Takes about fifty minutes to get a shuttle up and docked, especially with traffic. If the last of your people are off the ground in two-and-a-half hours, that will give us perhaps twenty minutes to start boosting out to a jump point before the Heggie fleet can get to us. With that kind of a lead, we'll be home free."

Tempting. Dacik thought. But ... "I don't think it's possible. Two hours ago, yes; maybe even ninety minutes ago. But I've got men inside the Heggie base, trapped. And the rest of the 13th is right around the base at the north end of this peninsula, too close to the enemy to get shuttles in and out safely, and there's not much chance of either ending opposition on the ground or withdrawing in two-and-a-half hours. Especially the reccers pinned down inside the enemy base.''

''I still think you should consider evacuating what you can, Kleff,'' Kitchener said. ''You have to balance the loss of a few men against the possible loss of your entire command. And my fleet.''

Behind Dacik, the members of his staff stood and stared. They couldn't hear either side of the conversation. From its length, though, they could easily deduce that it wasn't good news. The general had mentioned the enemy fleet as soon as Captain Quince passed along the first report.

''No,'' Dacik said after more than a minute. ''We don't withdraw.''

''Kleff—'' Kitchener started, but Dacik cut him off.

''It's not just that I don't want to abandon men to the Heggies, though that *is* part of it. The Heggies don't take prisoners. They kill anyone they capture, as far as we've ever seen. No POWs have ever come home in this war. But, still, that's only part of my reasoning.'' This time, he paused only very briefly. The admiral waited him out.

''You remember the briefings before we started out on this campaign,'' Dacik said. ''A chance to stop a major Schlinal invasion . . . somewhere, maybe a chance to bring the war to an end. If we withdraw, the war goes on for certain. We've done a lot of damage, but there are still two or three regiments of Heggies on the ground, plus however many are coming in, and at the stores in Site Charley. If we stay, even if we end up getting wiped out, there's a good chance that we'll do enough damage to the Heggies that they won't be able to mount another offensive against the Accord anytime soon. It might end the war. *That* is what I've got to put into the balance, Ben. That's our mission here.''

''Okay, Kleff.'' The resignation was obvious in Kitchener's voice. ''We'll make our stand here, win or lose. I'll do what I can to cut down on the odds for you. And

I'll get a message drone on its way out before the Heggie fleet reaches us. Things go really bad up here, you might have to wait a couple of months for a ride home.'' Radio messages were limited to the speed of light in normal space. For more urgent communications over interstellar distances, small unmanned rockets equipped with hyperspace drives could be launched with documents or recordings. It would take weeks for the message to get through, but not the years that radio would have taken.

''I'll make sure my exec has transmitted the latest additions to our battle log to CIC,'' Dacik said. ''Send that along with your message, Ben.''

''Right. Good luck, Kleff.''

''The same to you. I'll buy you a drink when we get back to Albion.'' He almost said *if*.

The nearest building of the Heggie base was only 250 meters from Echo Company. But there was a line of Heggie defenders between them, on higher ground than Echo. A series of machine gun emplacements with overlapping fields of fire was the clincher. The advance by the four companies of the 13th that had landed at the airfield had come to a complete halt.

''We're going inside,'' Dem Nimz told what was left of his platoon—sixteen men, not including himself. Barely more than a fourth of the number he had started with. ''We'll set four small charges on the door, blow it off, then take on whatever we find on the other side. We're sure not doing anything out here but dying.'' He had already heard about the incoming fleet but did not share that news with his men. It was not, Lieutenant Colonel Parks had informed him, for general dissemination yet.

Dem detailed his men, watched as the explosives were placed over the hinges and latch on the door—enough to blow it completely across the kiosk. If there were any Heggies behind that door, they wouldn't be there for long. The problem would come from enemy soldiers farther down, on the stairs, or on the floor of the building.

Dem slipped a fresh magazine into his rifle. Despite all

of the use he had given the weapon, he still had a couple of hundred rounds left. He had carried all of the ammunition he could. Around him, the others checked their weapons—zippers and cough guns.

"We've been here long enough to get about a half charge on our belts," Dem said. "We get on the stairs, we're going all of the way down. We hit much Heggie wire, jump. Get to the floor as quickly as you can without breaking bones."

The men all looked at the power indicators for their belts. A half charge did not mean that they would get exactly half the time or distance that they could get from a full charge. In practice, it was less, perhaps no more than a third of what a full charge would permit.

"Clip the fuses," Dem said. He took a quick but deep breath and forced it out. Ten-second fuses. The shaped charges would direct virtually all of the explosive force inward, but when the door went, there might still be debris blasted back. The reccers got as far back as they could, prone on the roof. Half had the sides of the kiosk to shelter them. That was built of stone. There was little chance of *it* going in the blast.

The four charges went off together. The metal door crumpled and blew inward. There was little smoke, more dust. A sharp report. The sound of the door crashing against the inside wall and the top of the metal stairway was lost in the ringing of ears from the initial blast.

"Go!" Dem screamed, even though his visor was down and he was shouting into his microphone. He pushed himself to his feet and into a sprint, as if he had fifty meters to cover instead of just five.

He was the first man through the doorway. He dove forward, sliding through hot debris, and came to a stop with a rifle aimed down the stairs. There were several Heggies visible at the bottom of the stairway. They were simply staring upward, not yet recovered from the surprise of the explosion. Three of those men fell to Dem's rifle before the last two men in the group dove for cover. By that time, three more reccers were at the top of the stairs spraying wire. Those last two Heggies went down hard.

Dem jumped to his feet and started down the stairs, scanning as much of the warehouse's interior as he could, shooting at any hint of movement, even when it was only his imagination. This warehouse appeared to be nearly full of supplies. That meant that there were a lot of sections of the floor, aisles between the stacks, where Heggies might be hiding, invisible to anyone on the stairs.

One of the men behind Dem tripped and sprawled forward. The man thought fast, though. Before he could start to tumble into the men on the stairs below him, he got a hand to his belt and switched it on. The gyro stabilizers righted him as he hooked the pipe that served as a railing at the side of the stairs and swung himself sideways over the bannister, then started a rapid descent to the floor of the warehouse. Farther up on the stairs, three other reccers jumped on their belts, spraying wire as they dropped.

Dem stayed on the stairs. There was very little wire coming toward the reccers. Apparently, there were only two Heggies still shooting. Dem got one of them. The other ducked around a stack of crates and ran. Before Dem reached the bottom of the stairs, he heard a door slam. He went to cover behind the nearest stack of crates, on the floor, his rifle out, covering two aisles while he waited for the rest of his men to get down the stairs and into position.

That was easier than I expected, Dem thought, but he wouldn't say it. There was still enough superstition in the man that he would not "jinx" the team by voicing such optimism.

"Let's give this place a quick scan," Dem said as soon as his team was in place. "See what's here. Make sure there are no more Heggies waiting to surprise us."

They spread out along the wall where the stairway was, then worked their way across to the other side, two or three men to an aisle. They paused at each intersection to make certain that there were no enemy soldiers on the cross aisles, then went on through the next section. Since they never came under fire, the operation only took a couple of minutes.

"Lot of munitions here," Fredo observed after they had finished and set men to watch the two exterior doors and an inner door that they suspected led to another underground tunnel complex. Dem had kept Fredo close to him. Gariston was still woozy from the medpatches, unable to do much with one useless arm, but he insisted on taking part. "We gonna blow it the way we did at the first place?"

"We might have trouble getting out of the way this time," Dem said. "Let's rig it, in case we get a chance." *Or in case we get to the point where getting out doesn't matter,* he thought.

Basset three exploded before it got off its first round on the new fire mission. It had been hit right under the front lip of its turret. Gun and turret had flipped off, backward. There was no need to wonder about the fate of the crew. They didn't have a chance.

"Those Novas are too damn close," Simon Kilgore said as he brought Basset two to a stop so that Karl could fire. At close to maximum range, Eustace didn't want to fire on the move. There were friendlies too close to the target coordinates, on two sides.

"They're Dingo's responsibility for now," Eustace said after the round was out and Simon had the Fat Turtle moving again. "Let's make sure we get *our* job done."

The howitzer moved left seventy-five meters, then pulled back fifty. Long before Simon brought the Havoc to a halt again, the next round was in the chamber and the targeting computer needed only the last few decimal points to correct its aim. That round went out and the Fat Turtle started to move again. This time, the jaunt would be a little longer, to a place no closer than two hundred meters from any of its previous firing positions. A *good* Havoc driver really didn't need the help of his navigating computer to keep away from previous firing positions, but most used it at least as a backup.

Basset two got off two more rounds before they were switched to a new target—and allowed to move farther back from the canal.

• • •

Echo Company had moved two hundred meters south in its attempt to outflank the Heggies defending the roads leading from the airfield to their main base, but there were still Heggies in front of them.

"Get your heads down," Joe warned his platoon. "Artillery fire coming in."

At first, the Havocs concentrated on the sections of the Heggie defenses that blocked the two roads, and the area between those roads. Then the line of incoming shells marched farther south. The explosions were placed about twenty meters apart. Havoc targeting systems were *good*. Since the kill radius of a Havoc HE round was more than twenty meters, that left a fifty percent overlap.

"Up and at 'em!" Captain Keye ordered as soon as the artillery blasts moved farther south. Echo got to its feet and moved forward, shooting on the run.

They covered more than half of the distance before a few of the Heggies recovered from the barrage and started shooting again. The Schlinal fire was light and uncoordinated now, though. Echo kept moving. Keye did not waste time explaining why. He knew about the incoming Schlinal fleet but had not shared that knowledge with anyone in the company but his executive officer and the first sergeant.

There was a low rampart of rocks and clay, only a meter high, in front of the Heggie defenders. Numerous gaps had been blown in that by the artillery barrage. The few Heggies who remained on the line were quickly overwhelmed by Echo and, farther along the line, by the other three companies coming in from the airfield.

"Back behind the wall," Keye ordered as soon as enemy resistance at the line ended. "We've got to wait for the others to get in position."

Most of the men were already moving behind the slight cover offered by the remains of the Heggie rampart when they came under fire again, this time from right at the edge of the nearest row of buildings inside the enemy base. From the start, this fire was heavier than what Echo had experienced from the outer line, but it still was not coordinated. A flurry of gunfire would come from one section of the Heggie defenses, aimed in the general direction of Echo, but—as often as not—too high or too low.

"Looks as if they're not certain where we are," Joe whispered to Mort. They were next to each other, speaking with visors up. Behind one of the surviving sections of the outer rampart, they were sheltered from direct fire.

"Maybe they're not," Mort said. "Those night-vision goggles they use—just infrared, right?"

Joe nodded.

"Temperature must still be within a couple of degrees of body temp," Mort said, "at least of what would be apparent through our clothes and gear. Heggies probably aren't seeing too clearly. Broad, fuzzy patches. All they'd have to go on is movement, at least until the moons come out."

Joe looked at the sky. "Any idea when that'll be?"

Mort had none.

Before the two could speculate any further, Joe had a call from Izzy Walker. All of the platoon sergeants were on the link.

"Sit on this for now," Walker started. "Until the captain or I say different. This info is just for you." That was enough to assure the attention of all of the platoon sergeants. Walker told them about the new Schlinal fleet coming toward Tamkailo. "If our ships can't stop 'em, these new Heggies'll be in orbit in less than three hours. They could be down on top of us forty-five minutes later. Before that happens, the general wants us inside this base and the Heggies there out of action."

"What about the rest of the army coming up from the south?" Joe asked. "They gonna get here in time?"

"I don't have any idea," Izzy admitted. "We're gonna have to play this as if they won't."

CHAPTER
18

Not even General Dacik had any idea whether or not his units would be able to link up before the new Schlinal forces arrived. The 5th and 8th SATs had established costly bridgeheads north of the canal. Both had managed to expand their perimeters enough to allow some units of the two light infantry regiments to cross. They had taken heavy casualties—and inflicted even heavier casualties on the Schlinal forces trying to hold them back.

But then the advance ground to a halt.

"I don't understand it," Colonel Ruman said. "We've always been able to crack a Heggie line when we put enough pressure on them."

"These Heggies have obviously been told that reinforcements are on the way," Major Olsen said. " 'Hold on, help is coming.' " He paused, then added, " 'If you don't hold on, you'd better be dead, because there'll be a reckoning afterward.' That's how it would go in their army."

Dacik nodded. "If what we know about the Heggies is

accurate. The people who might give us a different story don't usually end up as prisoners.''

"Still, if we don't break this line pretty soon, we might as well forget it and start worrying about defensive positions to meet the reinforcements,'' Ruman said. "If we don't do something, we'll be up the creek. We sure as hell don't want Heggies on both sides of us.''

Dacik stared at his mapboard while he thought. The map gave him no clues. Finally, he took a deep breath and looked up.

"You're right,'' he said. "We've got to do something in a hurry—concentrate on breaking through at one point instead of trying to force both bridgeheads. Bull through no matter what it costs. We'll leave the 5th to defend the eastern bridgehead and put both LIRs behind the 8th. Well, not quite everything. Leave one battalion of the 34th on the north side of the canal with the 5th. The rest to spread out to cover the rest of the south side of the canal. Use all of our Havocs and Wasps to blast a hole through the Heggies and cover our flanks until the 8th really gets moving.''

"The air is ours now, General,'' Olsen said. "At least until the Heggies manage to bring in new fighters. If this fleet is carrying any. The last of the Boems that were here are down. The ones we didn't shoot down had to land because of dry batteries, and there are no fresh batteries at the airfield for them. The 13th blew the chargers and drained or destroyed the batteries that were waiting. They've been destroying the fighters that came in as well.''

Dacik nodded slowly. "We'll use the 13th's Wasps to hunt tanks. The rest to cover the breakthrough and provide whatever support we can spare for the 5th. How long will it take to get the 97th in position to cross over behind the 8th?''

"Their first battalion is already across,'' Ruman said. "Part of the second, as well. The rest of second is spread out along the south bank, from the bridge west to the sea. Third is about half-and-half. Part is marshaled behind the bridge ready to cross. The rest is along the south bank east of the bridge, over to where they meet the 34th.''

"How long?" Dacik repeated.

"Could take thirty minutes to get all of second battalion in place to cross the canal. Thirty minutes for third."

"Get them moving now. And I want them *all* ready to cross in fifteen minutes," Dacik said.

Colonel Ruman got busy on the radio.

In the last hour, Dem Nimz had talked with the ranking reccer in each of the 13th's other recon platoons. First and second recon were now led by men who had been squad leaders three days earlier. Fourth recon was being led by a corporal who had only been an assistant squad leader at the start of the Tamkailo campaign. Four recon platoons: their normal complement was 240 officers and men, 60 to a platoon. The total manpower left was 68, scarcely more than a single platoon. And they were scattered.

They had, at least, all managed to get off of the exposed rooftops. They were inside warehouses and not currently under fire. The Heggies were making no attempt to rout them from their temporary havens. But there was no way for the reccers to escape from the middle of the Heggie base.

"The first thing we have to do now is get together," Dem had told the men leading the other platoons. He ordered the corporal commanding 4th recon to stay put and wait for the rest of them. He told 1st and 2nd to prepare to blow up what they could in the buildings where they were, as 3rd had already done. Blast or burn: the building the 1st platoon was in contained no munitions; the building 2nd was in had some munitions but more of the space was taken up by clothing and other spare gear.

"I've asked the colonel to set up a diversion for us," Dem said the second time he talked to the noncoms leading the other platoons. He *had* spoken directly with the colonel, after pleading with Dezo Parks for the help for five minutes first. "The Havocs will drop a short barrage around us, right in the center of the base. At the same time, our line companies will pick up their fire and make another attempt to get in. While all that's going on, we'll set off our three

buildings and make for 4th platoon's hideout.'' After that
. . . Dem hadn't done much thinking past that. Even trying
to get the remnants of the platoons together was likely to
be an expensive maneuver. There was a real chance that
the Heggies might finish off the 13th's recon detachment
completely. Dem hoped that they would be able to link up
with the line companies soon, if any of the reccers managed
to survive this. For one of the few times in his military
career, Dem Nimz wanted as many men around as possible.
Men who wore the same uniform he did.

The artillery would be the key. When it started hitting,
the reccers would clip their fuses or start their fires and
make for the exits closest to the building where 4th platoon
was waiting. And hope that the Heggies weren't also
waiting for them.

The wait not only seemed long, it *was* long. Dem didn't
know how much trouble the colonel had had persuading
General Dacik to release the 13th's Havocs for even the
few minutes they would be needed for the diversion. More
than once, Dem started to call the colonel again. Each time,
he held back. Stossen had not given him a specific time,
just that it would be as soon as possible. *Wait!* Dem told
himself. *You're safe for now.*

Men were posted to clip the fuses. The rest were gathered
near the exit they would use, spread around just enough to
cover the building's other doors. They would wait to spring
the door and go out until there were only ten seconds left
before the detonations inside the building.

It wouldn't matter if there was an entire battalion of
Heggies just the other side of the door. The reccers would
go out and to either side, leaving the door open. Even if
there were significant numbers of Heggies waiting, a
massive explosion channeled through that doorway ought
to give them pause.

If it didn't, 3rd recon—and perhaps 1st and 2nd as
well—would simply cease to exist.

The artillery rounds started falling. Inside the building,

the fuses were clipped. Dem watched the seconds tick away on his visor. Then . . . "Go!"

Fredo yanked the door open with his one good hand. Dem was the first man through it. He stepped to the right. There were perhaps a dozen Heggies in his immediate field of view. He sprayed a burst from his rifle across the group. Two of his men got out and added their wire to the assault. All of the Heggies went down.

But there were more of them, off to either side. Fortunately for the reccers, those Heggies seemed to be more concerned with the artillery rounds that were exploding, moving toward them from either end of the street. Third recon sprinted to the right of the door they had come out of. Each man was counting down the seconds, and before he reached ten, he went down, just in case the explosion inside the building proved to be more violent than they expected.

The sound of the explosion—explosions—was more muted than Dem had anticipated, but flame and debris shot out through the open doorway. Behind that first eruption, there were sounds of more explosions inside, and a continuing roll of smoke and flame coming through the doorway.

Dem didn't wait for more. He whistled over his platoon frequency, then shouted, "Let's go!" as he got to his feet and started running again. The building where 4th platoon was hiding was across the next intersection and on the far side of the lane. Dem didn't time himself, but he thought that he might have set a record for the hundred-meter dash, even loaded down with more than thirty kilograms of gear. Even Fredo, injured and still groggy, kept up with the group.

The Schlinal army had another low rampart just outside the nearest line of buildings. Rocks and soil cleared away when the construction sites were leveled had merely been shoved out of the way, heaped up along a line. Like the other line, this one had resulted mostly from construction workers moving material simply the regulation number of meters away from their work site and leaving it, rather than from any conscious design for defense. Time and weather had done most of the "work" of improving that original "construction."

The rampart did provide cover against rifle fire. The ground sloped downward, gently, from the base toward the airfield and the sea in front of the rampart. That gave the Heggies the high ground as well. They had another line of defense on the rooftops, all of the roofs that had not been cleared by the reccers.

Echo through Howard companies of the 13th had reached the first line less than a minute after the artillery barrage lifted. Their advance had stalled again there as the Heggies behind the second line and on the roofs kept up heavy fire.

"We need the artillery again," Teu Ingels told Colonel Stossen. "It's the only way we're going to get in there." Stossen and his staff had moved around from the north side of the base to the east just a few minutes before. They were almost directly off of the northeast corner now, slightly more around to the east. The two halves of the 13th had finally met.

"I don't think we're going to get our Havocs, at least for a bit," Stossen replied. "The general's using all of the artillery to force a breakthrough at the canal. That's why I had so much trouble getting them for even a few minutes before. Right now, I guess the other is more important. It's the only hope for the rest of our people to make it out here before the new fleet gets in."

"We've got to do *something*," Dezo Parks said. "We have to take this base before that new fleet arrives. Destroy the stockpiles the Heggies have here, or take them for our own use. Especially if the 8th and 5th don't make it out to us."

"We're outnumbered already," Stossen reminded him. "Maybe two to one or worse, with just the Heggies inside the base trying to keep us out. They have the defensive positions. Without artillery or air, we don't have any leverage at all. The general has preempted all of the Wasps as well."

"At least the Heggies don't have any air left either," Bal Kenneck noted. "And they've been using their tanks strictly against the units at the canal."

"What about the reccers?" Ingels asked. "Enough of them left to help us open a way into the base?"

"I'm waiting to hear from them now," Parks said. "They were going to try to consolidate during the barrage. Altogether, they only equal one recon platoon now. Maybe less. If there are enough of them left to matter . . . " Parks just shook his head.

"Colonel, I think we should consider just sitting tight until the 8th gets here," Bal suggested. "Get the reccers out if possible, so they're not in the way. Let the general use all of the air and artillery to clear the streets in there once the breakthrough is established south of here. Do what we can to establish a perimeter of our own in case they don't get to us in time."

"The new fleet could be overhead by then, more Heggies on their way down," Ingels pointed out. "If we get stuck between them . . . "

"The general wants to avoid that as well," Stossen said. "Who's commanding the reccers now?"

"Nimz," Parks said, "3rd recon's platoon sergeant."

Stossen nodded, remembering Nimz's hoarse pleas for artillery support. "Good man. He calls again, I'll talk to him myself, Dezo. In the meantime, let's do what damage we can. Vrerchs and RPGs. Splat guns to clear the lanes between those buildings. Tell the platoons to get their snipers busy as well, to clear away as many of the Heggies on the near roofs as they can."

A frontal attack into prepared enemy positions is the deadliest form of assault infantry can make, something that most commanders have avoided whenever possible for thousands of years. The 8th SAT moved north along the road leading from the western bridge. The first minutes of the attack were especially brutal. The first company to storm the Heggie line was completely wiped out, every man either killed or wounded too severely to continue. The second company thrown against the defenses was very nearly destroyed as well.

But the rest of the 8th continued to move forward, two companies—what was left of them—at the point of a wedge, pushing against the Heggie defenders in front of them. The rest of the 8th moved forward on the flanks, widening the assault. Behind them, the 97th LIR moved forward as well.

At first, the Heggie line held solid. That line was crowded, men "stacked" three deep. Noncoms and officers were close with their disciplinary squads to make sure that no one retreated. Then the line bent from the continued pressure. Men moved north, but not far. The Heggies formed a new line across the gap not more than a hundred meters behind the first. To either side of the road, the rest of the Heggie line adjusted itself. The line did thin out somewhat. A lot of bodies were left behind.

The 8th and 97th pressed the attack. Just in front of them, the Wasps of the 5th and 8th SAT, and the 17th IAW made repeated runs back and forth. From farther back, the Havocs of all three SATs made their contribution.

Wasps fell from the sky on every pass. Nova tanks returned artillery fire. The tanks were close enough to take out some of the Havocs, though they lost as many tanks in return.

In the middle, infantrymen fought and died.

And died.

General Dacik had moved his command post closer to the western bridge. As soon as possible, he wanted to move across the canal—but not just yet. He watched the fighting through binoculars, lying flat just behind the last ridge south of the canal.

Along the rest of the front, fighting was light. Dacik had moved as much of his army as he could to put it across the one bridge. The enemy had moved forces to counter that. At the other bridge, to the east, the 5th and the 1st battalion of the 34th did what they could to tie down Heggies. If the Schlinal warlords moved too many of the men guarding that bridgehead, the 5th would be able to break through.

Can we do it in time? Dacik asked himself. He could see the carnage on the north side of the canal. Even without the reports he was getting from the 8th and 97th, he could tell how badly his units were being hurt.

Can we do it at all? Even that wasn't certain. He closed his eyes, just for a second. Even if they did manage the breakthrough in time and got to the base at the far end of the peninsula, would it do any good?

Will we have anyone left to face this new army when it lands?

"We're through!" Colonel Foss's voice shouted in Dacik's ear. Over the radio. "We've got our hole through their line."

Dacik felt his heart thumping loudly. "Go for it, Nape," Dacik said. "Get north as fast as you can. Take the 97th with you. Don't worry about anything else. Just get up there and link up with the 13th."

CHAPTER
19

The primary reason why so few battles are fought in space is a matter of physics. Changing direction is not merely a matter of spinning a steering wheel or control yoke and immediately speeding off on a new heading. There are direct analogies between space navy and the older sea navies—wind and sail. It takes time and energy to change the course of a ship in space. That is true for a ship in orbit with a speed of less than 30,000 kilometers per hour. It is much more evident when the ship is braking after emerging from hyperspace at more than 120,000 kilometers per hour. The geometry of plotting an intercept course in real time is beyond the capabilities of the unaided human mind. Powerful computers working in parallel are used to plot the course and the engine requirements for achieving the interception. The capabilities of ship thrusters, measured against momentum and local gravity—as well as the speed and course (subject to change) of the vessel to be intercepted—restrict what *can* be done, and how quickly.

Ships in space must be *close* in order to do battle at all. Despite millennia of weapons development, none of the available weapons are of any particular value against enemy ships at any real distance. Energy and particle beams, even though they operate at or near the speed of light, will do little damage to a capital ship. Hulls designed to protect travelers against the dangers of cosmic radiation need little additional hardening to protect against energy weapons, and that technology is older than interstellar travel itself. Ship-to-ship missiles travel more slowly. They can almost always be intercepted before they can travel much more than half of the distance to their target. Two capital ships rarely get close enough for missiles from one to reach the other before interception.

That fact had led to the design and deployment of fleets of small fighter spacecraft, vehicles given over to payload and propellant. With less mass and higher accelerations, a flight of fighters could hope to get close enough to launch more missiles than the enemy's defenses could handle—*if* the attack fighters could get past the enemy's defensive fighter screen.

Improvements were slow in coming, and incremental. Better offensive weapons were met by improved defenses. In the few years of fighting between the Accord and the Hegemony, neither side had yet managed to tip the balance. The usual result of battle was the destruction of flocks of fighters, with crippling damage to the capital ships of either side rare.

Over Tamkailo, all that the Accord really wanted was a chance to destroy significant numbers of Schlinal shuttles before they could land reinforcements on the world below.

Intersection was still more than an hour away.

General Dacik released the 13th's Havocs to support the 13th again—for five minutes. Major Norwich acted as spotter. He was with Colonel Stossen at the north end of the peninsula. Norwich directed the fire against the outer rampart and against the walls of the outer buildings. High-explosive and armor-piercing—the latter against the buildings.

Ten seconds before the expiration of the ten minutes that the general had allowed, Colonel Stossen ordered his infantry forward.

Blue Flight accelerated toward the Schlinal base. Zel and his remaining Wasps had been hunting Novas along the peninsula. Major Tarkel had called to ask if they were close enough to make a single pass—without getting approval for the mission from General Dacik. Zel had agreed instantly. Goose Tarkel didn't even mention it to Colonel Stossen until the Wasps were ready to start their strafing run. He saw no need to tell the general at all.

Three Wasps came in from the east, each following a lane between buildings. They used their cannons, sweeping from one side of the Schlinal base to the other. It could only be once through. Then the Wasps turned south again, heading back to their tank hunting.

Nimz waited until he heard Wasp cannon fire move past the building. It was a distinct sound—a metallic rain—plain even through the building's thick stone walls. Dem had his men posted and ready. He had done a little quick reorganizing. The reccers would operate as a single platoon now. The four squads did not, quite, correspond to the original four platoons.

"Let's go," he said softly, as soon as the metal rain passed the door. He had been warned of the Wasp pass only some ten seconds before it started.

The 13th's reccers moved through the one doorway, rapidly, into the land that had just been cleared of Heggies. Dem led his men east at a run, to the next intersection. With half of his men on either side of the east-west lane, they started shooting at the Heggies to the north and south in the cross street. They had ten seconds of pure target practice, shooting at men who weren't expecting an enemy on the ground behind them, ten seconds to do as much damage as they could before they came under fire again.

Dem and his men were reccers. They made the most of their opportunity.

Echo Company was up and moving west behind the artillery barrage and the Wasp runs that coincided with the end of the barrage. The two rough ramparts were 120 meters apart. Echo came under only light and sporadic fire as they raced across those 120 meters.

When they reached the inner rampart, Echo paused for only an instant. Commanders checked to make certain that the units on their flanks had also reached the rampart. Then Colonel Stossen gave them another "Go" and the 13th started moving forward again, into the Heggie base.

Echo was at the extreme left of the 13th's attack. They climbed over the rampart and scores of bodies, then turned left, firing into the area between the rampart and the wall of the nearest building. They moved south, aiming for the next east-west lane through the base.

Joe Baerclau got his platoon over to the right, along the building's wall. That kept them out of the line of fire of the Heggies on the roofs. They couldn't lean over and shoot directly down without exposing themselves to Accord riflemen farther out. When the platoon reached the southern end of the building, the men had to wait at the corner. One fire team started shooting around the corner, as far as they could without exposing themselves. Farther out, the company's 1st and 3rd platoons went back across the inner rampart to move farther south. First came back over once they were covered by the next building. Third stayed in the gap to shoot straight down the lane.

"Hey, cut that out!" a voice said over the company noncoms' channel. "This is Nimz, 3rd recon. We're up this street."

All three platoons stopping shooting down the lane. Dem Nimz and two other men came running down the lane. Captain Keye and First Sergeant Walker moved along the east wall of the building past Joe's platoon.

"I've got about fifty men left," Nimz said. "We're covering the next intersection, Captain. I'd suggest securing these two buildings. I think a lot of the Heggies have gone inside.''

Captain Keye took a moment to relay the news that Echo had contacted the reccers and to explain the situation to Colonel Stossen.

"Okay, Nimz,'' Keye said then. "For the time being, consider yourselves part of Echo.'' That had come from the colonel. Keye turned and gestured to Joe. "Baerclau, you take your platoon into this building. Secure the interior and the roof. I'll send 1st platoon to take the next building over. Nimz, you stay with Joe until we can get you back to your platoon. You've been inside here. These men with you will go over with 1st platoon for now.''

Nimz just nodded. Baerclau was already talking to his squad leaders.

"What can we expect inside?'' Joe asked Dem as he started moving 2nd platoon down the east-west lane toward the nearest door leading into the building.

"I think the buildings on this side of the base are all warehouses, the first two or three lines anyway,'' Nimz said. "Our guess is that any factories are in the middle and that the smaller buildings over on the west side are barracks and mess halls and other support services. You get inside any of the warehouses at the first site?'' When Joe nodded, Dem said, "These are about the same. Big interior space. Stairs to the roof along one wall. Stuff stacked neatly. I think we've got a tunnel complex underneath, like at Site Bravo. No idea how extensive *that* is.''

"We'll worry about that when someone tells us to,'' Joe said. He took a deep breath and glanced at the recessed doorway. The door was closed. He positioned first squad on the east side, second on the west.

"Any suggestions?'' he asked Dem.

"Explosives,'' Nimz said without hesitation. "Blow the door in and run in behind it, shooting all the way. They might be waiting for a break-in, but the blast should give us a couple of seconds to cut down the odds. I've got a couple of charges left.''

Dem didn't wait for Joe's nod. He pulled the charges

from his pockets and moved into the recess on hands and knees. There was no window in the door, but he wasn't taking any unnecessary chances. He only needed ten seconds to affix the two explosives and clip the fuses. He scooted back out of the recess and dove to the side.

The others didn't need any orders. Everyone pulled back from the opening and got as close to the wall as they could.

The fuses had only a ten-second delay. When the charges blew, Dem allowed no more than two seconds before he started into the doorway. Not all of the debris had settled yet. Joe Baerclau and Wiz Mackey were in just behind him, with the rest of the platoon moving in as rapidly as they could.

The first men in started shooting before they knew whether or not they had any living targets. Dem stopped where the wall of the doorway gave him a little protection and fired out into the interior of the warehouse. Joe and Wiz went past him, diving off to the side, careful to get under Nimz's gun level.

There *were* Heggies in this warehouse, at least a platoon of them. That was Joe's initial assessment as he dove to the floor and rolled to cover next to a stack of crates. But for as much of the interior as he could see, there might have been three or four times that number.

The explosion that had blown the door into the warehouse hadn't hit anyone, but it had given Joe's platoon the couple of seconds Dem had promised. Then the Heggies started shooting. Some obviously pulled their triggers from reflex, before they had the weapons pointed toward the doorway. There was little accurate fire on either side during the initial seconds of the firefight.

Joe pulled the pin from a grenade and lobbed it. From the corner of his eye, he noted two other grenades going away from the doorway. He scrambled forward on his stomach, heading for the next stack of crates. When the grenades started to explode, he stopped, pulled his arms and legs in as close to his body as he could get them, and hunched his shoulders up, covering the vulnerable junction between helmet and fatigue shirt.

Once the grenades had blown, Joe got to his hands and knees and scuttled across the aisle. That drew fire. He felt a burning sensation in his right hip and knew that he had been hit. At the ranges available inside the warehouse, he had no doubt that his net armor had been pierced. With wire, he expected that there would be several wounds.

The pain took a moment to reach his awareness. Joe had little time to fret over it, though. Al Bergon was already at his side, examining, then slapping a medpatch over the wounds. The analgesic in the patch worked quickly. The blood clotters worked even faster, stopping the bleeding.

"Doesn't look too bad, Sarge," Al said while he worked. "All in the meat. Shouldn't even slow you down for more than a few minutes."

Joe blinked a couple of times. "You mean I've got a fat ass."

"You said it, I didn't," Al said. He slapped Joe on the shoulder and started looking for his next patient.

Joe sat up, too quickly, when he realized that the shooting inside the warehouse had stopped. Sauv and Low had their squads moving across the building, toward the northwest corner.

"What's going on?" Joe asked over his link to the squad leaders.

Sauv answered. "The Heggies worked their way out of here in a hurry, Joe. Looks like they've gone underground."

"Make sure, both of you, then set guards over all of the doors. Where's Nimz?"

"West wall, near the door." It was Dem's voice on the radio. "My guys are in the next lane so this side should be secure."

"Get some backup before you open the door, just in case," Joe said.

"I know what to do," Dem said, keeping his voice neutral at the cost of some effort.

"Mort, take your fire team over to support our reccer," Joe said after switching channels. "His guys should be on the other side of that door, but don't take chances."

"On the way," Mort said.

Joe stayed down for a moment longer, thinking, trying to make certain that he hadn't forgotten anything that might be critically important. His wounds no longer hurt. A medpatch didn't take long to neutralize local pain, even worse pain than he had felt from the wound in his hip—his butt, rather. Once he was as certain as he could be that nothing essential had been omitted, it was time to find out whether or not his wounds were going to slow him down.

He got up to his knees cautiously, then straightened up, sitting on his haunches. There was stiffness but no pain, more a tightness that might have stretched the new scabs over his wounds. Using his rifle as a support, he got to his feet. He felt no dizziness, no discomfort. The slight limp when he tried walking was more psychological than physical. It faded away after just a few steps.

Then he called Captain Keye. "We've got the interior of this building secure. The Heggies who were in here have apparently turned mole, gone through an interior doorway we think leads to a tunnel system. Nimz is getting ready to contact his men on the far side of the building. As soon as we finish checking what we've got, we'll go for the roof."

"Give the roof to the reccers, Baerclau," Keye said.

"Yes, sir."

"Joe," the captain said after a slight hesitation.

"Yes, sir?"

"We don't have much time left to get the job done here."

"This is the last base, isn't it?" Joe asked.

Keye let out a long breath. "Yes, but we've got complications." Hilo didn't like keeping information from his people. At least his platoon sergeants and platoon leaders had to know.

"More Heggies?" Joe asked.

"A new fleet coming in," Keye admitted. "For the time being, this news doesn't go any further. You understand me, Joe?"

"Perfectly, sir. How much time do we have?"

"Can't be certain. From the briefing I had, certainly no

more than an hour before the new fleet is in position to start launching shuttles. And fighters. Maybe less than an hour now. I'm not sure. You can figure out the rest.''

''Any idea how many of them?''

''Just guesses with nothing to base them on. Anywhere between two and four regiments is possible from the number of ships reported. Until we know better, we have to assume the worst.''

The worst? Joe thought. *We couldn't even handle the best end of that estimate.* ''I hope our navy lads take care of a good share of them, sir'' was what he said.

''So do I. Remember, Joe. This goes no further, not even to squad leaders. I really didn't have clearance to tell you, but I want my platoon sergeants to know what's coming.''

''I appreciate it, sir. What about Nimz? He's the reccer platoon sergeant.''

Keye hesitated before he answered. ''You tell him, Joe. Face-to-face, not over the radio. Make sure he knows not to tell anyone else without orders. Far as that goes, he may already have the word.''

''One hour. Sixty minutes,'' General Dacik said. ''I want every man and every piece of equipment north of the canal by then.'' He had his entire staff and all of the senior unit commanders except Colonel Stossen on the link for this session. ''And then I want both bridges blown.''

''We might have trouble getting across that quickly,'' Saf LaRieu said. ''The 5th has widened their bridgehead a little, but not enough.''

''Then bring the rest of your people across to the other bridge and turn east once you get over the canal. We've got to break this end of the peninsula loose,'' Dacik said. ''Whatever it takes.''

''Yes, sir,'' LaRieu replied.

''If we can clean out Heggie resistance on the peninsula, we're got a chance to hold on for quite a time,'' Dacik said. ''These new Heggies will have to come to us. And without bridges to cross the canal . . .'' He let that hang for a moment. ''I'm sure that this fleet wasn't coming in expecting that they would have to fight for Tamkailo. That's our only advantage. No doubt they know what's waiting for them now. That people here were probably in contact with them within minutes after the fleet emerged from hyperspace. And even if they weren't, the new fleet would have spotted our ships soon enough. But a few hours to plan an operation with whatever troops they happen to have on those ships isn't the best way to work. If we're particularly lucky, they won't even have any great stock of ammunition. With all the stores we've found here, the newcomers might have no more than standard issue.''

This time Dacik paused long enough to give the others time to throw cold water on his hopes, but no one spoke. ''We need to have the Havocs and all of the support vans for the artillery and air far enough north that they'll be out of range of any Novas that the newcomers might have with them. The howitzers close enough to support any action along the canal.''

''What if they drop out on the peninsula?'' Luro Bones asked. ''They know what the situation is. That's probably their best bet.''

''We'll blow as many of their shuttles out of the air as we can,'' Dacik replied quickly. ''Try to deal with the troops from any that get through as expeditiously as possible. If we can break the 5th free in time, we'll use it as a quick reaction force. And use all of our Wasps to back them up.''

''We're going to have our butts stickin' up in the air here, General,'' Colonel Ruman said. ''There still might be three or four thousand Heggies on the loose on the peninsula. No way in Hell we can neutralize all of them before the new fleet unloads.''

''We'll concentrate on the ones between us and the Heggie base,'' Dacik said. ''Stossen reports that the Heggies there are withdrawing underground again, fighting all of the way. The 13th can sit on those Heggies. If they're down in tunnels, they're irrelevant.''

''Unless they've got bolt holes prepared,'' Major Olsen said. ''If they've got exits out somewhere that the 13th hasn't found, they could raise real Hell.''

CHAPTER
20

In space the dance continued.

Within fifteen minutes of emerging from hyperspace, the Schlinal fleet had stopped braking for a routine orbit around Tamkailo. A few minutes later, the incoming ships accelerated, increasing speed and changing course. The individual ships also moved a little closer to one another, maneuvering slowly into battle formation. Ships did not make hyperspace jumps too near one another. Even the mass of a ship complicated that process.

Closer in, the Accord fleet accelerated out of its parking orbit, away from Tamkailo.

Both fleets wasted copious amounts of energy, opting for maximum movement rather than fuel-efficient trajectories. At the moment, propulsive energy was the least of the concerns of either commander. There would be no shortage of antimatter for their engines and weapons systems. In CICs in each fleet, the other's course was plotted. During the early stages, the time required for light to travel from one fleet to the other was greater than the amount of time that the CIC computers needed to correct and project the enemy's course, and to evaluate possible changes in course and time of interception.

The opposing commanders made their own adjustments to those of the enemy, which were met with further refinements. And so forth. Plans for the engagement were made, refined, and changed again: a simplified version of chess with fewer pieces and movement possibilities.

Nearly two hours before the fleets could come close enough to begin the actual fight, it was clear that the battle would take place between forty and fifty thousand kilometers above the northern hemisphere of Tamkailo, above and east of that world's northern continent. The fireworks, if there were any, would be visible from the peninsula that held the Schlinal base designated Site Charley by the Accord. It would still be night on the ground when the battle in space started.

The 13th's Havocs followed those of the 8th across the western bridge. The few Havocs remaining to the 5th would be the last to cross the canal, and they would cross the eastern bridge to support their infantry and the parts of the 34th LIR that had crossed there.

It would have taken an observer several minutes to be certain that the Havocs were indeed all aiming for a bridge crossing. As usual, the gun crews worked hard to avoid showing a pattern to their movements, and there was certainly nothing recognizable as a formation. The howitzers continued to fire and maneuver on the way, only gradually moving into a wedge-shaped area leading up to the bridges.

Primarily, the targets that the 13th's Havocs were aiming for were enemy Novas. There were still at least two dozen of those roaming the peninsula, firing at the Havocs and at the Accord infantry. The 8th's artillery divided its attention between enemy tanks and the infantry that the 8th was attempting to push through as it headed for the Schlinal base at the far end of the peninsula.

"Where the hell is everyone?" Simon Kilgore demanded as he steered the Fat Turtle toward the bridge.

"Your guess is as good as mine," Eustace replied, one of the few times that he might be willing to concede that anything anyone else could do might equal his own abilities. "North of this ditch, that's for sure. And our guys are at the far end of the peninsula. They need help."

"We can help them from down here and be safe at the same time," Simon said.

"Not for long," Eustace replied. "Captain Ritchey says we got more Heggies coming in. The general wants us where we can hold 'em off." Eustace was far from crazy about the idea that the battery commander had outlined, but Eustace tried not to worry about anything larger than the crew of his own gun. That was more than enough trouble for any noncom.

"Why not just get out while the gettin's good?" Simon asked.

Eustace didn't have an answer for that. Getting out seemed to be the smartest move to him as well.

Kleffer Dacik wasn't certain that his answer for that question was the right one. At one time or another in the couple of hours since they had learned of the approaching Schlinal fleet, nearly everyone on his staff had made the suggestion at least once. Their arguments were valid. They had already inflicted major damage to the Schlinal depots on Tamkailo, totally disrupting any plans the Schlinal warlords might have had for using the stores of matériel and the thousands of troops that had been collected on Tamkailo for their next invasion. The Accord had killed or captured at least five thousand Heggies, perhaps as many as six or seven thousand. They had destroyed or captured thousands of tonnes of munitions and other supplies. And destroyed about three regiments of Nova tanks.

"We've already scored a major victory here, General," the argument went. "Why jeopardize what we've done already? Why risk losing the rest of five front-line regiments and an air wing for what little more we might accomplish?''

"We haven't finished the job," Dacik replied, with a bulldog persistence that belied his own doubts. "There might be another three thousand Heggies on the peninsula, plus most of the supplies in Site Charley. And whatever that fleet is carrying. I want it all, or as much of it as we can get. We have a chance to end the Schlinal threat against the Accord, if not permanently, at least for a good long time."

It was a desperate gamble, and no one was more aware of that than Kleffer Dacik. He watched the time line on his visor display. He listened to frequent updates on the progress of the two fleets from CIC. It came as something of a relief when one important deadline passed, when there was no longer time to get friendly shuttles down and all of the men back up to the transports before the enemy fleet arrived within striking distance.

As another military commander had written thousands of years before, on taking an equally desperate gamble, the die was cast. Withdrawal was no longer an option.

Site Charley was silent. Echo's second platoon was in another warehouse, doing little but standing around. Or sitting. A few of the men were eating. The platoon's wounded had all been treated. There had been no deaths in second platoon in the fight for the main base. A team of engineers was welding the door leading from the warehouse into the underground complex to its frame. There were thirty-seven buildings in the main base, thirty-seven metal doors that did not open onto the outside. One team had gone back to the airfield to see if there were openings to the tunnel system there. If so, those would be sealed as well.

"Burying them alive," Mort commented. His visor was up about halfway. Even though he was a dozen meters from the welding, he didn't want to look toward the welder's arc without eye protection. The faceplate of a battle helmet would not be sufficient for that up close, but at a distance, it would do. "There could be a regiment or more of them down there."

"I doubt that it's that final, Professor," Joe said. "Even if they don't have exits that we haven't found, they've almost certainly got gear down there with them that will let them break out. Sooner or later. If nothing else, they'll have explosives. We're just doing what we can to make sure they don't get out too soon. If they escape once we've left this cinder, that's fine with me."

Mort shook his head, unconvinced. "We came here to kill Heggies, and we're certainly doing that. Wholesale. Regular combat is one thing, but this is going to be like the underground garage at Site Alpha—simple slaughter."

"Them or us," Wiz Mackey said. "An' I'd rather it be them any day, and twice on Sunday."

"This Sunday?" Mal Underwood asked.

"Beats the hell out of me," Wiz said. "I'm not even sure what month this is."

"By our time, I think it's Wednesday," Olly Wytten said. "Or it's Wednesday back on Albion."

"Totally irrelevant here," Mort said. "In any case, the Hegemony uses a different calendar than we do."

"Enough," Joe said in a tired voice. "Before anybody gets too carried away, let's appropriate a few of the goodies." That got everyone's attention. "Hand grenades," Joe said, raising his left hand shoulder high and extending the index finger. "Stuff 'em anywhere you can. One man in each fire team grab an RPG launcher and grenades for it." He raised a second finger. "One man in each fire team take a bundle of these Heggie rockets and a launcher." A third finger. "They may not be as good as our Vrerchs, but they'll do in a pinch. Everybody else, grab either RPGs or rockets to help supply the men with the launchers. Load yourselves down with everything you can carry and still function. We've got a shuttle coming up from south of the canal to bring in more wire for our zippers, so we can forget about Heggie rifles this time."

Very softly, Mort asked, "You trying to tell us something, Sarge?"

Joe hesitated before he answered. "I'm trying to tell you that you're still soldiers in a combat zone and that there are still plenty of Heggies around. We may have corralled some of them here, but there's mudders and armor coming at us from the south, maybe a couple of regiments. The 8th and the 5th are driving the rest of them our way. Reason enough?"

"That'll do until something better comes along," Sauv Degtree said before Mort could speak. Jaiffer looked from one sergeant to the other, then shrugged.

"Reason enough," he said.

By that time the welders had finished sealing the door to the tunnels. They had their gear collected, and the corporal in charge of the group came over toward Baerclau.

"We're ready for the next one, Sarge," the corporal said.

Joe nodded, then lowered his visor. "Grab that stuff and lets go," he said over the platoon channel. "We've still got three more doors to plug." There were only five welding rigs available. Joe's platoon was shepherding one of the welding teams.

The confusion on the peninsula escalated, on both sides. The 8th pushed north as quickly as its infantrymen could walk or, in some cases, run. The 97th LIR came behind them, spread out to try to drive any remaining Heggies north ahead of them. To the east, the 5th had finally broken through the Heggie line that had been containing them and they were moving north also, several kilometers behind the 8th. The 34th was trying to regroup on the move, trying to get its battalions back together and complete the line across the peninsula. At the same time, the Heggie units that were retreating continued to fight, and they were obviously trying to regroup on the move as well.

General Dacik met his self-imposed deadline for getting his command across the canal. His headquarters wasn't the last unit to cross, but it came very near the end. Once he got to the north side of the water, he waited while engineers planted explosive charges on both bridges and blew them—decks, trusses, and piers. Only after the dust had settled and he could see for himself that both bridges had been destroyed completely did he get back in his APC and head north, in a hurry now to catch up to the bulk of his army.

"We've got less than an hour before the fight starts up there," Dacik told his aide, Hof Lorenz. "Maybe less than another hour before we've got more Heggies down here with us." He shook his head. "Not much time to secure this peninsula, is it?"

Captain Lorenz knew better than to attempt any answer to that.

For a moment, Zel wondered if Blue Flight was even going to have a place to land. All of the 13th's support vans were on the move, north of the canal . . . *some*where. And Blue Flight needed to land within the next few minutes. The three remaining Wasps were low on munitions and—more critically—low on juice in their batteries. If the squadron's ground support didn't find a place very soon, the Wasps would just have to land wherever they could and wait for their vans to find them— not the most ideal of alternatives.

Zel had lost track of how many hours he had been in the air, how many kills he had scored—Boems and Novas— and how many thousands of rounds he had used strafing infantry. Since coming north to Site Charley, the 13th's Wasps had been in the air almost continuously, landing only to take on recharged batteries and fresh loads of rockets and 25mm ammunition.

It was Roo Vernon who came on the radio to tell Zel where to set his flight down, even though Roo was no longer Zel's crew chief.

"You keeping busy, Roo?" Zel asked, after passing the landing information on to Gerry Easton and Will Tarkel.

"Busy and then some," Roo said, still new enough as an officer that he had to bite off the automatic "sir" at the end. Technically, he now outranked Zel, since his commission as Captain predated Zel's promotion to that rank.

"Your guns still working on the ground?" Zel asked. He

was homing in on the vans. In another forty-five seconds he would be on the ground.

"Fair enough," Roo said with justifiable pride. "We've used 'em tonight. Next step's to figure a way to mount 'em on APCs. Maybe on Havocs too, give the big guns something to defend themselves with."

"You keep doin' all this fancy thinking, you'll get yourself a cushy job back in some R and D thinktank," Zel said. He hardly heard Roo's horrified disclaimer. It was time to set Blue One on the ground.

Ground crews ran to service the three Wasps. Zel didn't bother to get out, or even to open the canopy on his fighter. It was too much trouble. As soon as new batteries were installed and the rocket racks and cannon magazines refilled, Blue Flight would be back in the air. The pilots all knew what was coming—the new Schlinal fleet and, perhaps, more Boems. The Heggies on the ground had to be taken care of first, as far as possible. Sleep? Zel yawned. Just thinking the word made him sleepy. He blinked several times, then lifted his visor to rub his eyes. They had started to water. Again.

Blue Flight had been on the ground for less than ninety seconds—the gun magazines were open, the battery hatches as well, and the old batteries were being lifted down out of the sockets, the new ones at hand, ready to snap in—when the first incoming shells exploded. During the first ten or fifteen seconds of the barrage, Zel was hardly aware of what was happening. The noise and the flashes startled him so badly that his sleep-starved brain needed time to catch up. Not that there was anything he could have done, without fresh batteries in place and the hatches sealed over them, he couldn't even take off.

Smoke and flame and noise. The ground shook. Blue one was rocked violently, almost tipped on its nose . . . by a near miss. The Wasp was not hit directly. Still, Zel's head was snapped forward and to the side. His helmet whacked against the side of the cockpit. He blinked again, several times. The light of the blast had hurt his eyes. The crack on the head put "stars" in front of them. Zel shook his head to clear his vision. Roo Vernon had been walking toward Zel's Wasp just before the barrage hit. When the shells stopped coming in, there were still several fires burning—two of the maintenance vans were ablaze. Zel didn't see anyone standing, anywhere around him.

He popped the canopy open and slapped the emergency release to free the straps of his safety harness. If nothing else, he needed to get away from the plane before the next round of shells came in. The Heggies obviously had them perfectly targeted.

Zel pulled himself up out of the cockpit. He permitted himself only a second to look around before he jumped to the ground and ran—staggered—around his Wasp toward where he had seen Roo just a moment before. The sounds of the shells exploding were still ringing in his ears, but there seemed to be nothing new coming in.

Roo Vernon was unconscious, sprawled out at least ten meters from where he had been standing. He had so many shrapnel wounds that Zel didn't even try to count them. He screamed into his helmet radio for medics, not knowing if there were any around. He didn't hear any response.

He looked up, then around. His Wasp appeared to be the only one that hadn't been directly hit. Though neither of the others had burned, there was major damage to both. There was no movement in the cockpits of either.

Zel was unable to get the canopy open on Blue two. Gerry Easton was slumped inside, showing no signs of life. After more than a minute of futile effort, Zel got down from that Wasp and went to the other. By the time he popped the canopy on Blue eight and cranked it open manually, Will Tarkel was starting to move—a little. His head fell from one side to the other. He groaned.

"Hang on, Will. I'll have you out in a second," Zel promised.

It took thirty seconds for Zel to get Will's safety harness unfastened. Then he lifted the wounded pilot—who outweighed him by fifteen kilograms—out of the cockpit and carried him out on the "wing." He laid Will down, jumped to the ground, then picked Tarkel up again and carried him over to where Roo was lying. Once more, Zel screamed for a medic over his radio. There was still no response.

Zel switched to the channel that connected him with Goose Tarkel, Will's uncle. "Major, we got hit hard after we landed. I've got badly wounded men here, including Will. We need medical help and we need it right now."

"A van from Yellow Flight is already on the way, Paitcher. Two minutes or less. Do what you can until they arrive."

Zel went back to the two wounded men he knew about. Will needed a tourniquet on his arm to stop the bleeding. Zel used his belt to take care of that. Roo seemed to have a profusion of small cuts. All were seeping badly, but there seemed to be no way to stop them other than with medpatches.

Medpatches. Zel looked at the three vans that had come to service the planes. There would be—or would have been—first aid kits in each of them. All of the trucks had been hit. Two had caught fire. One was still burning. Zel wasn't particularly optimistic, but he went looking.

He couldn't get into the one van that was still burning, but the first aid kits in the other two trucks had both survived—though the case of one was smoking when Zel got to it. He carried both cases over to where the wounded men were lying and started cutting away uniforms and slapping medpatches over the worst concentrations of cuts. When he had done what he could for Roo and Will, he got up and started looking around to see if there was anyone else left alive.

He found one mechanic who had been blown more than twenty meters from where he had been standing before the attack. The man was unconscious but wasn't bleeding. His heartbeat was weak and thready. Zel didn't try to move him, suspecting broken bones—perhaps even the spine.

After finding no one else from the ground crews alive, Zel went back to the Wasp he had been unable to get into. Gerry Easton still hadn't moved, but Zel couldn't tell if the man was dead or alive unless he could get to him. Once more he tried to pop the canopy manually. Without success. He was still trying when the new van arrived.

"Somebody give me a hand here!" Zel shouted. The crew chief and one of his men went to work on the wounded men after Zel pointed out all three of them. The other mechanic brought a tool over to Blue two.

"He alive in there?" the mechanic asked as he poked the business end of the meter-long tool in a notch at the rear left of the canopy.

"Can't tell," Zel said.

"I'll have it in a second, sir." The mechanic leaned on the tool, a pry bar with a specialized attachment intended for just this operation. There was a loud popping noise and the canopy came up out of its lock. Together, the two men got it all of the way off. Then Zel reached in to put fingers against the side of Easton's neck, feeling for a pulse.

There was none. Gerry Easton was dead.

CHAPTER
21

There were only minor differences between the Wasp airplane and the Accord's Bat spaceplane, and for the most part, those differences were stylistic rather than functional. The primary exception was in weapons systems. The Bat was never equipped with the 25mm cannons that were a staple of Wasp armament. Partly in place of that, the Bat was normally furnished with a rack of small antimissile missiles, a more important defensive weapon in space.

The power plant of the two fighters was identical, two battery-powered antigravity drives. The cockpit/escape module was also identical. But the designers of the Bat took extensive liberties with the exterior design of the fighter. Since neither the Wasp nor the Bat depended on aeronautical efficiency to fly, that was a "minor stylistic" difference. The Bat did not even have the appearance of a wing. The cockpit sat atop and between two rounded rectangular solids—rather like something baked in a loaf pan—that housed the drives, batteries, and controls. The space below the cockpit, between the two sections of fuselage, was equipped with the necessary fittings and control linkages for the variety of weapons that the Bat used.

While the Wasp could operate in space as easily as the Bat, the Bat was never deployed less than 180 kilometers above a human-habitable world, high enough to ''fall'' around that world if it should happen to lose power. Suddenly deprived of its engines, the Bat's glide characteristics—in an atmosphere, that is—would be even more rocklike than the Wasp's. The Bat also, according to the most sophisticated simulations, would have a tendency to tumble in an atmosphere without working power plants.

Although the Bat's batteries provided it with no more than the approximately ninety minutes of power that the Wasp's batteries provided, without the drag of atmosphere and the greater gravity close to the surface of a world, that ninety minutes of power could—under the proper circumstances—allow the Bat to operate for as much as twelve hours—and conceivably much longer—before it had to return to its carrier for fresh batteries. The Bat carried enough air to see a pilot through eighteen hours.

In outward appearance, the Schlinal spaceplane was identical to its airplane. Provision for more air and different armaments were the only real differences between the two versions of the fighter. And, of course, the model designation number. The *air*plane was the Boem A3. The *space*plane was the Boem S3. In practice, the two were interchangeable.

As the two fleets drew nearer to each other, the relative angle between their vectors was 27 degrees. There were no precise ''rendezvous'' coordinates at the apex. They would never actually pass through the same point in space. At their nearest approach, providing both fleets remained on their same courses, they would be eighty-seven kilometers apart. The battle would be carried to the enemy by the fighters each fleet carried.

Aboard the Accord's ships, the fighter pilots had been sent to their Bats as soon as the van of the Heggie fleet came within three hundred kilometers, still ''above'' the

Accord fleet and moving at a slightly greater speed on their almost converging course. Flight control computers tracked a variety of potential enemy sorties, travel time, trajectory, and how soon the Bats would have to be launched to meet each possible scenario. Each TIC (threat intercept computer) could handle all of the variables connected with more than a thousand targets simultaneously. With the Bat pilots already in their fighters and the hangars already partially depressurized, the Bats could be launched within thirty seconds of the order, giving them plenty of time to accelerate away from the fleet on a course to intercept Boem S3s as far off as possible.

On the Accord flagship, the Constellation class *Capricorn,* Admiral Kitchener had already moved to CIC, which served as his flag bridge. A dozen officers and ratings manned the intelligence-gathering equipment and compsoles. Kitchener was in constant communication with the skippers of each of his ships and with their launch control officers. He also kept a link open to General Dacik on the ground. Unless the Schlinal fleet acted first, Kitchener had decided that he would launch the first defensive element of his fighters when the two fleets approached to within 200 kilometers of each other. He would wait until the fleets were no more than 150 kilometers apart before he sent out his attackers—unless the Heggies struck first.

"We'll hold back one-third of our Bats to strike against Schlinal shuttles and their escorts in any case," Kitchener informed the captains and launch officers. "No matter what happens to us, we have to do what we can to cut down on the number of Heggies who reach the ground intact."

He looked at a bank of monitors that relayed the view of the enemy fleet from each of his ships. In his more wistful moments—safe in a friendly port with a few drinks under his belt—Kitchener sometimes regretted the impersonal silence and distance of war in space. A student of military and naval history, he wished at times that he had been alive back on Earth sometime in the last century of men-of-war powered by sails, by the movements of air. It

was a wish he had never shared with anyone, in or out of
service, not even his wife.

Kitchener smiled at a chance memory. He was almost
certain that his wife at least suspected. Both of his sons had
been given toy sailing ships and models, at the earliest possible ages, and introduced to computer games set in that
milieu. They became interested because their father had
made certain that they had every opportunity to become
interested. Both of those sons were now in the space navy,
though neither had ever served under their father's command.

Kitchener hid his impatience well. That was more than
simply the habit of command. After more than forty years
of service, he knew firsthand the inexorable nature of space.
There was nothing to do but wait. Either speeding up or
slowing down could only delay the eventual confrontation.
Changing course would have the same effect now. It would
take the expenditure of prodigious amounts of energy to
hurry the battle by even seconds—to little effect. There
could be no tactical surprise.

But the battle *would* begin soon. Kitchener glanced at a
clock, then at a readout of distances. The gap between the
fleets had almost narrowed to two hundred kilometers. The
Schlinal fleet had not launched any fighters yet, neither an
attack formation nor a defensive screen.

"Ready the shield patrols," he said, the order going over
the radio to the necessary commanders. "Commence
launch . . . now!"

Then, for just an instant, he allowed himself to relax.
The next move would belong to his opposite number, two
hundred kilometers away.

"Baerclau!"

"Yes, Captain?" Joe replied.

"The fleet battle is about to begin, sometime in the next
fifteen minutes or so, according to Major Ingels."

"I tell the men now, sir?"

"Go ahead. Our fleet is larger. The numbers are about
three to two in our favor."

"Glad to hear that," Joe said. "Maybe our ships'll save us the bother of facing any of those Heggies down here."

"Don't count on it."

"Just hoping out loud, sir."

"We've still got plenty of work to do. We're going to spread a line all the way across the peninsula, just south of this base. George and Howard will mount patrols behind us, north of the line, to make certain that none of the Heggies sneak out behind us. The rest of us will take the best defensive line we can find and hold it until the rest of the army gets to us."

"We're the anvil?" Joe asked. Hammer and anvil: it was an age-old tactic. Keep part of your people stationary, waiting. Use the rest of your army to drive the enemy against your prepared positions. Put the enemy in a cross fire and keep up the pressure until they surrender—or cease to exist.

"We're the anvil," Keye agreed. "I hope you had your people stock up on some of these Heggie munitions."

"All we could carry, sir. I thought it wise to, under the circumstances."

"Very wise, Joe. Colonel's given orders for everybody to stock up on rockets and grenades. Heggies bump into us, they might still have a few Novas in working condition." The Heggies would still outnumber the 13th, possibly by more than two to one. The 13th would need whatever edge it could find to keep from being overrun.

"If they know they've got reinforcements on the way in, they won't surrender," Joe said after a short pause. "They'll be more afraid of their own warlords than they are of us."

"That's the way I read it too, Joe," Keye said. "They're going to be in a panic, and fighting might seem less dangerous than surrendering. Panicky men are capable of just about anything."

"Yes, sir."

Keye gave Joe specific orders for 2nd platoon. Joe passed those orders on, giving his men the rest of the bad news as well.

"We're up shit creek," Wiz Mackey said, disgust in his voice.

"All we've got to do right now is take care of the Heggies coming north toward us," Joe said. "That might not be as hard as the big shots think."

"What do you mean?" Mort Jaiffer asked.

"They've been fighting for quite a while out there already," Joe said. "Facing four regiments. And *we* are sitting between them and their supplies. The only ammunition they're going to have left is what they haven't used yet, what they've got with them."

"You think they're going to run dry," Mort said. "Like we did on Porter."

"It's possible," Joe said. "Depends on how much they were carrying, when the last time was that they got supplies before we jumped in, and how much shooting they've been doing. And they've been doing a lot of shooting, according to the captain. It took our guys a long time to break across the canal and start the Heggies running our way. Heggies aren't superhuman. They can't carry much more than we do. It had to run out sooner or later, and it might already be later."

"Sounds like you're trying for a slot in Intelligence," Mort said. "I just hope you're right."

"Me too," Baerclau admitted. "But if we can take care of the Heggies on the ground before the reinforcements start trying to land, we might still come out of this okay." Joe felt a little disgusted with himself, acting like a cheerleader when he wasn't certain that he believed a word he was saying.

Major General Kleffer Dacik had too much sense of dignity ever to admit to feeling anything so plebeian as "the thrill of the chase," but he did feel it as his command APC raced north along the peninsula. Only a handful of armored personnel carriers had been landed on Tamkailo, all for use as command posts or medical treatment facilities. Most of the APCs that had been carried to Tamkailo remained about the ships, and the fleet had not carried the usual complement of the vehicles. That would have required another three or four ships, and there had never been any expectation that the vehicles would be required for this campaign. With the planned in-and-out nature of the mission, APCs had seemed mostly irrelevant.

The 8th and 5th were now moving north almost as quickly as if they had simply been on a training hike back on the worlds where their home bases were. The 97th and 34th were spread out behind them, also moving forward as quickly as the terrain—rather than the enemy—permitted. On the rare occasions when a Schlinal unit tried to stand and fight, they were hit with massed fire from the Havocs and Wasps.

For a time Dacik had kept his command post behind the skirmish line that was intended to clear the peninsula thoroughly. But he could restrain himself for only so long before ordering his driver to hurry north, to get as close as possible to the 8th's spearhead.

"We've still got to pull rabbits out of a couple of hats," he confided to his aide. "Clear the peninsula, then get men posted to be able to respond in case the Heggie reinforcements try to land on this side of the canal."

"And we won't know where they're going to land until they're more than halfway down, right, General?" Lorenz asked.

Dacik shrugged. "They'll be a lot lower than that before we can we certain where they plan to ground, but we'll be able to start narrowing it down earlier."

"You don't suppose they'd go for one of the other sites, do you, sir?" Hof asked. "Figure on regrouping on the ground before they take us on?"

Dacik hesitated before he said, "If they land at one of the other sites, it could only mean that there are more of them coming that we don't know about yet. Ships that haven't come in-system yet. If this fleet is all that's coming—I mean in the next few days—then they have to engage us immediately. Anything else would help us and hurt them, and any Schlinal warlord who's managed to get high enough to command that many men is going to know that as certainly as I do.''

''If they *do* land at one of the other sites, what do we do?''

Once more Dacik hesitated before he answered. ''If they land at either of the other sites, we finish the job here on the peninsula and get the hell off Tamkailo as fast as we can.'' There *were* limits.

Van Stossen wasn't interested in races. He was looking for a good stretch of ground to defend, a line running all of the way across the peninsula. He didn't care if that ground was a hundred meters south of the Schlinal base or two kilometers—except that he hoped it would be closer rather than farther off, to give his men a chance to dig in and set up crew-served weapons before the mass of Heggies hit the line, and before the peninsula grew too wide for what was left of the 13th to adequately man that line.

Spread across the peninsula, the 13th's line was already too thin by half. Each company had to cover 800 meters at the southern edge of the buildings, and the farther south they went, the longer the line would get. Stossen had scarcely needed to tell his staff, ''We'll stop at the first suitable place.''

That proved to be only 250 meters south of the last walls of the Schlinal base. The line was not quite straight east-west across the peninsula. The lay of the land demanded a slight angle, northwest to southeast. A low ridge ran most of the way across. There was sandy beach along the eastern shore, large rocks at the western end. There were several gaps in the ridge, and in other places it dwindled away to less than a meter in height, but it was good enough. Stossen decided that they were unlikely to find anything more suitable.

''This is it,'' Joe Baerclau told his platoon as soon as he got the word. ''Dig in the best you can.'' Along the stretch of ridge that Echo Company was given, there was solid rock below no more than ten centimeters of clay that was almost as hard as the rock it covered. ''You'll probably have to look for rocks to pile up in front of you," he added. "Do what you can in a hurry."

Second platoon broke down into two squads, four fire teams, now. Joe put each fire team by itself, with ten meters separating them. No one would be able to sneak through a gap that size, not even in the dark, and the fire lanes would overlap. But if the enemy came on in sizeable numbers, with determination, they would be able to break through without difficulty. There was no help for that.

Joe situated himself with first squad, on the end nearest second. He worked as hard as any of his men at preparing the best defensive position he could in a hurry, knowing that the Heggies might be on them almost any minute. He wasn't nearly finished when Al Bergon came over to him.

"How's your hip feel, Sarge?"

Joe stopped working for a moment and blinked. "Forgot all about it. Didn't have time to think about it."

Al smiled. "I guess that means you're doing okay. When this is over, we'll take a look and make sure there aren't any bits of wire left in there that'll have to be cut out." If the medical nanobots in the medpatches had done their work fully, any wire would have been transported up to just below the surface, encased in pimples that could be "popped" to get the metal out.

"Yeah, sure," Joe said absently. He wasn't ready to start thinking past what he was doing. His wounded posterior wasn't hurting. That was all he could worry about.

"You got your position ready?" Joe asked the medic.

"As ready as I can get it." Al shrugged. Medics had very low life expectancies in combat. Al had lasted longer than most. "We have any action, I probably won't get to spend much time in it anyway." He turned and walked away then, without waiting to see if Joe had a reply.

"Sauv? Low?" Joe said, switching to his link to the squad leaders. "Do a quick check on your men. It sounds as if the fighting is getting close. We're likely to have Heggies in our laps in a few minutes."

The sounds of fighting had been there, in the distance, for some time, a constant background noise that was beginning to get noticeably louder—which meant closer. There might be a few Heggies on their own first— "stragglers" wouldn't be the right word; these would be men who were running faster than their comrades, away from the fight they had been in—but the bulk of the Heggie forces might not be far behind.

Joe moved up on top of the ridge—it was a meter-and-a-half high where he was—and stood there looking first one way and then the other along the line. The ground sloped away a little in front of the ridge, not much, but even a little might help.

Not a bad place to make a stand, Joe thought, transiently amazed that his platoon had actually pulled such a lucky placement. The Heggies'll have to do the hard work to get to us.

He looked south, scanning slowly from side to side, a little farther out on each pass. There were tanks out there yet, and who knew how many Heggie mudders—perhaps a couple of thousand of them.

A 205mm artillery shell burst no more than two kilometers south of the ridge. Joe happened to be looking almost directly at the place where it exploded. In the brief glare of the blast, he saw the outline of a Nova tank silhouetted against the light, moving north, toward the ridge.

"Here they come!" Joe shouted on his platoon channel. He jumped back down behind the ridge.

CHAPTER
22

Faro Malmeed used the time of waiting for meditation. That discipline from his childhood had always stood him in good stead in the military. The admiral had ordered all Bat pilots into their fighters, to wait . . . for whatever. Faro did not know about the squadrons on the others ship, but the Bat pilots of the Constellation class *Orion* had done nothing but sit in their planes for nearly two hours now. *Orion* was the lead ship in the fleet, even in front of *Capricorn*. The Constellations—there were twelve of them in this fleet—were the largest ships in the Accord inventory. Nothing, civilian or military, was larger. That applied not only to the Accord and its member worlds but also to the Schlinal Hegemony and the Dogel Worlds, although the Doges had a ship that was very near the same size. That was—or had been before the tensions between Doges and Hegemons erupted into open war—strictly a civilian freighter.

"Hurry up and wait," Faro mumbled, remembering to

make certain that his transmitter was off. Then he switched it on. "Commander, how long are we going to sit here?" he asked.

Lieutenant Commander Osa Ximba, commander of *Orion*'s Indigo Flight, was just as bored by the wait as his pilots were, but he didn't have any *good* answers, so he gave the standard *military* answer. "We sit here until they tell us to do something else. Then we'll do the something else."

"But what's going on out there? Have you heard anything at all?" The questions had finally imposed themselves on Faro's meditation a few minutes before, distracting him too much to continue.

"It's about to start out there," Ximba said. "That's all I know."

It wasn't much consolation to Faro. His brother Vign, a Bat pilot aboard the *Cetus,* might be out there somewhere.

Three seconds of boost after the Bats of *Cetus*'s Purple Flight were ejected from their hangar was all that was required. After that, they had nothing to do but coast into position. Vign Malmeed, Purple six, had been a Bat pilot for more than two years, but he had yet to come under enemy fire—or get off a shot at any Schlinal vessel, of any size.

This was the first time he had even *seen* a Schlinal fleet.

The dozen Heggie ships had spread out into battle formation. From end to end, the formation covered more than forty kilometers: three columns of ships in what was called—with less than perfect accuracy—a battle cylinder formation. The nearest vessel was more than 140 kilometers away from *Cetus*'s Purple Flight.

At that distance Vign could not truly *see* the Boem S3 spaceplanes in the defensive screen around the capital ships. Like the Bat and the Wasp, the Boem did not reflect light. The blips that his targeting system showed him were built up from information cross-linked from nearly every ship in the Accord fleet—movement and computed vectors derived as much from the way that the shadows of Boems occulted sections of the ships they were defending, as from more direct observation.

"They're coming out to meet us," Purple one said. There was certainly no surprise in his voice. The Heggies were expected to intercept them as far out from their ships as possible. The was the purpose of a defensive cap. "Arm all weapons systems."

Vign did not expect to have a shot at any of the Schlinal capital ships. If Purple Flight got through, it would mean that the Heggie defensive screen had broken down completely. The job of this flight, and a half dozen others, was to draw the Schlinal defenders out, engage them, destroy as many as possible, to allow other flights a better chance to get through to the big ships.

Battle in space is not only silent, it is much less exciting visually than many people anticipate. Partly for the same reason. Sound needs a medium, such as air, to carry it. Fires need oxygen—air—to support combustion. Some types of explosives are built with their own oxygen supply. Others depend on rupturing hulls to feed on the oxygen in the atmosphere maintained on the ship . . . or plane. The fiery trails of rockets are supplied by oxygen carried by the rocket as part of its propellant. That can be the most visual aspect of a duel in space.

The other reason why space battles are so . . . dull is that they always appear to occur in slow motion. The actual speeds of the ships and planes might be great, but the distances are also great.

"Time to check their reaction time," Purple one said. "Thirty degrees left, thirty degrees up, full thrust."

There *was* a slight physical rumble within the Bats as their antigrav drives cranked up to maximum. Vign enjoyed the extra sensation of weight pressing him back into his seat. He ran a complete check of his weapons and navigation systems. The computer diagnostics took only a couple of seconds. Then he watched the display on one of his monitors as the Heggies reacted to Purple Flight's acceleration. The Boems changed attitude and went under thrust again.

Both sides were ready for a fight.

Zel Paitcher was surprised to wake up in the back of a support van, pressed up against the side of the narrow aisle that gave access to bins of tools and parts. There was someone else lying in that aisle with him.

I guess I passed out, Zel thought. His mind seemed unusually clear. It wasn't like waking up from sleep. He felt perfectly alert. But there was a gap in his memory: *I wasn't here before; I wasn't injured . . . was I?*

When he tried to think back, his memories were a patchwork of sights and impressions, slow to appear, and they did not seem to connect into a meaningful whole. Shells exploded around the Wasps. Men were running. Roo Vernon was waving, smiling. Lights. Sound. Somehow, all of the bits of the picture started spinning, scene by scene, and all of it together. Zel thought he was going to fall, but then realized that he was already flat on the floor of a van and there was nowhere for him to fall *to.*

"What happened to me?" He heard the words, so he assumed that he had spoken them out loud. Just to make sure, he repeated the sentence.

"Concussion, sir—I think," an unfamiliar voice said. "That's what the medic said on the radio. You was helping us take care of the others, then you just sorta keeled over. You feeling okay now, sir?"

Zel lifted a hand to his head and touched it experimentally several times. "I don't feel any pain," he said after a moment. "My mind seems to be working, after a fashion."

"We'll have you and the others to a medtech in just a couple of minutes, sir, soon as we find where they are. Things are pretty confused. Last I heard, the Heggies had stopped retreating."

"What happened?" General Dacik asked on a link that included the commanders of the four regiments moving north along the peninsula, as well as his own staff.

"It's like we hit a brick wall with a rubber band, General," Colonel Foss of the 8th said. "They had prepared fallback positions ten klicks north of the canal—mines, trenches, gun emplacements. I think the line was already manned as well, at least with a skeleton force. Their troops hit that line, and we had organized fire coming at us much too soon for anything else."

"When did they have time for that?" Dacik demanded, turning to look at his Intelligence officer.

Olsen shook his head, then shrugged his shoulders. "We never saw any of it, sir."

"Our experience was exactly the same on the east side," the 5th's commander, Colonel Kane, added as soon as the others left him an opening. "Prepared positions. Troops waiting for us. It's going to take time to break through this new line, time we don't have."

"What about the 13th?" Foss asked. "Can Stossen move south to nip the Heggies from behind?"

"You men put out reccers to see if this line extends all of the way across the peninsula?" Dacik asked.

Foss and Kane said, "Yes, sir," in unison.

Dacik continued to stare at Major Olsen, who was standing right next to him, about four hundred meters south of the line where the Heggies had stopped to fight. "What's the gap between our line and the 13th, Jorgen?"

Olsen looked down at his mapboard, used a cursor to draw the line, than hit a key along the side of the screen to get the distance. "Just short of seven kilometers, General. The 13th reports enemy activity close to them as well, tanks moving in, presumably infantry as well."

"Nape, Jesiah, we've already targeted the Havocs against the enemy line, and I'm working to bring the Wasps back in." He *had* been saving the Wasps to meet the new Heggies who could be arriving in little more than an hour, but this had to come first. "The 13th has its own problems. I'll talk to Van and see what he can do, but we're going to have to break this line the way we broke the line at the canal. Head-on, straight up. We can't give the Heggies seven kilometers of this peninsula to let them land their reinforcements. Remember, we've cut the bridges behind us.''

Neither of the SAT commanders replied immediately. It was Foss who finally broke the silence. ''Frankly, General, I'm not at all certain that we *can* break through this time, not and have anyone left to meet the newcomers when they get here. I'm down to less than forty percent effectives as of fifteen minutes ago, and Jesiah's been hurt even worse. We might not have the strength to break through this line in less than an hour. Or in a week.''

''Find weak points and punch through,'' Dacik said. ''We don't have any choice. We've got to move, and we've got to move fast.''

There was another pause before the commanders conceded their assents.

Overhead, more or less, the Boem S3s of the Schlinal defensive screen had to kill speed to intercept *Cetus*'s Purple Flight, to keep the Bats from sliding behind them and getting a straight shot at two of their capital ships. Purple Flight went to full thrust again as it closed to within missile range of the Boems.

''I want two missiles targeted against each of them,'' Purple one said. ''We'll boost straight through the flight. By the time they get turned around—any that our missiles leave—we should have the distance and speed to outrun anything they shoot after us.''

It was the rockets that the Heggies would shoot off while the two groups were racing toward each other that Purple Flight had to worry about. Those would cover the gap in a hurry.

Vign got his targets lined up and waited for the command. First pass: the entire flight would fire its missiles at once. In theory, at least, that would overload the Boems' ECM and missile-intercept capabilities and make it much more difficult for the Heggies to evade destruction.

Both sides fired at once. There was scarcely time for the pilots of either flight to switch their weapons selectors over to the smaller, high-speed, anti-missile missiles that were their only active defense. Tiny electronic decoys were jettisoned almost as quickly to try to deflect targeting systems.

There were a total of twenty-seven unspectacular explosions. Twelve of those resulted from missiles hitting missiles and scattering debris. Nine were exploding Boems. The rest were Bats.

Vign Malmeed did not see them. He had less than a second to realize that Purple six was going to be part of the show.

"Nimz, I've got to send you and your men out again," Colonel Stossen said. "The rest of the army's got themselves stuck, seven klicks south of us. The Heggies had prepared positions."

"I was beginning to suspect something like that, Colonel," Dem said. "We'da had more Heggies hitting us than the few who did get this far otherwise. What do you want us to do?"

"Get down behind the Heggie line and make them think you're the whole regiment. Raise a little Hell. Distract them enough to let the 8th and 5th punch through."

"Yes, sir."

"And, Nimz . . . we don't have much time. We could be seeing shuttles and fighters from this new fleet in less than an hour. We need to secure the peninsula first, or at least get our whole force linked up. If you've got enough juice built up on your belts, use them to get south fast."

"We'll do what we can, sir," Nimz promised.

No more than three minutes later, the fifty-four men remaining from the 13th's four recon platoons slipped over the ridge, breaking into two groups and moving apart. Behind them, the line companies on either side adjusted their positions to cover the gap. The reccers moved in two groups, Dem leading one, Fredo the other. Fredo's left arm was in a sling. A medic had treated his wounds, but he needed time in a trauma tube to complete the repairs. But he would not stay behind.

At first the reccers crawled, doing everything they could to avoid showing a silhouette. Schlinal night-vision gear was inferior to the double system that the Accord used, but it was not totally useless. Slow movements, low to the ground, were the best way to trick the Schlinal gear. Having ground that was almost body temperature helped confuse infrared night-vision systems. The contrast was too low.

Once away from the 13th's line, the reccers made their way to the lowest area of ground around before getting to their feet and hurrying south, jogging. It was too soon yet to switch over to antigrav belts. They were too close to the line. Dem wanted to get at least a kilometer south first. That would, he hoped, put them behind any Schlinal mudders posted to watch the 13th.

The reccers saw several Heggie patrols and observations posts. But reccers were trained in movement that won't be seen. The Heggies weren't. In one case, Dem and his men passed within twenty-five meters of a squad of Heggies without being seen or heard. A couple of minutes later, they walked past a Nova, not more than six meters from the tank. There was no sign that either of the Nova's crewmen spotted them, even though the Nova carried better night-vision gear than Schlinal infantrymen wore.

Dem waited until his men were a hundred meters south of the tank before he decided that it was time to hurry along. "Don't get carried away just 'cause we're on belts," he cautioned. "Stay low. I'd rather hear toes scraping the rocks than see heads sticking way up in the sky. We fly south until the first belts start showing a low power warning, then we all land and go on from there."

With luck, he thought, they might cover half of the remaining distance to the new Schlinal line before low-power lights started to come on. If they got within four kilometers, they could cover the rest of the distance on the ground in little more than a half hour, if they pushed themselves. And reccers knew how to push themselves.

That still wouldn't leave much time. By then there could be Heggie shuttles and new Boems on their way down from the Schlinal fleet.

"Push it," Dem said as he switched on his own belt.

Manipulating a Corey antigravity belt for horizontal travel required the use of both hands and considerable coordination. The gyro stabilizers fought it all of the way. They were only designed to permit a 5-degree deviation from vertical. The men had to hold the drive units and twist them so that they thought "up" was at an angle in front of them, and then manipulate the power settings almost constantly to keep from rising too high above the ground. A third hand would have made the operation considerably easier. There was certainly no way to keep a weapon at the ready during the process. Rifles were slung, with the slings clipped to one of the straps on each man's pack harness so that it wouldn't be lost in transit. Remarkably, Fredo Gariston, with only one usable hand, still managed to keep his place with the patrol. Even Dem Nimz had trouble believing that.

Dem had been sweating before—it seemed to him that he had been sweating continuously since landing on Tamkailo, hundreds of liters of the stuff—but there was a new outpouring now as he worried at his controls. Right now, Dem and his reccers needed luck more than anything else. If their course chanced to take them right over a concentration of Heggies, they would have little opportunity to defend themselves. Before they could land and get their weapons into play, they might lose half of their already seriously depleted force.

The need constantly to adjust speed and angle took deep concentration. It kept the reccers from building up any great speed. It also seriously compromised the distance they would be able to travel before running out of power for the miniature AG drives. Before his men had traveled a single kilometer on belts, Dem was worrying that he had seriously overestimated how far they might get before batteries started to get dangerously low.

At least they wouldn't be high enough for a fall to do much damage. "Push till we start running dry," Dem told his men. That might give them an extra hundred meters over stopping when the first low-power indicator came on.

Dem kept glancing at his power gauge, glaring at it as if he thought he could make it hold power a little longer by force of will. Whenever his feet brushed a slightly higher piece of ground, he would push off of it or take a couple of running steps. Although Dem didn't waste time thinking about it, he would have assumed that most of his men would likewise be doing everything they could think of to extend the distance they could travel on the belts, even for a few extra meters. It took a certain kind of soldier to volunteer for recon duty, and reccer training took care of the rest.

When one of the reccers announced that his low-power indicator had come on, Dem figured that they had already moved to within three-and-a-half kilometers of the main enemy line—closer than he had hoped. "Give a shout when you run dry," he told the man. "We're doin' good. Let's do better. I figure this is our last time on belts here." One way or another.

Still, there wasn't much time left in the air for the reccers. Within twenty seconds, every low-power indicator was on, and ten seconds after that, belts started running dry.

"Ground and form up," Dem ordered. He glanced at the time line on his visor. It would be four hours before the belts would have a full charge again, if they did need them again. Four hours. *We should live so long,* Dem thought.

Although the two groups of reccers were spread out over rather large areas after their "flight" south, it took no more than a minute for them to form up again. Once the groups started to coalesce, the men communicated with hand signs, the way reccers preferred. Having split the team in half before, Dem and Fredo now split each of those groups in half. Finally, Dem got on the radio just long enough to give rather broad instructions. Reccers didn't need a detailed blueprint. Even if a man got separated from the rest of his team, he would continue to fight on alone until he could get back to the others—or until he could no longer fight or move.

"We get as close as possible and raise as much hell as

possible," Dem said. "Remember, our guys are on the other side of the Heggies, so don't get *too* rambunctious with the RPGs and rockets. They make their breakthrough, we'll tag along with them, back to the rest of the 13th."

The patrols moved forward, and farther apart from one another. The sounds of battle were clearly audible now. The reccers were less than three kilometers from the front line.

Dem moved his patrol more to the west. The farther apart his reccers were, the more confusion they ought to be able to sow among the enemy once they made their presence known. The Heggies wouldn't be certain just how many Freebies had come up behind them—and they would have to worry that the entire 13th had moved south. That was exactly what Colonel Stossen wanted them to think.

We'll sure find out what these guys are made of, Dem thought with a grim smile. He was walking point on his patrol. That was no place for a squad leader, let alone the 13th's ranking reccer, but it was where Dem wanted to be. He trusted his own senses and talents more than he trusted anyone else's, especially at a time like this.

The patrol had gone just over a kilometer on foot when Dem spotted a Heggie machine gun emplacement. The gun did not start firing, which meant—almost certainly—that the reccers hadn't been spotted.

"Down!" he whispered over the channel his patrol was on. He waved up the two men nearest to him and showed them the enemy position. He pulled out a grenade and indicated that the other two should do the same.

"Together," he whispered when all three of them were up on their knees in position to hurl the grenades. The others aped his movements exactly, pulling the pins from their grenades, then throwing them and dropping forward onto the ground. The Heggie post was less than forty meters away. Shrapnel could reach that far and do damage.

The grenades exploded together. "At 'em," Dem said over his patrol's channel. The reccers got to their feet, rifles blasting before they could know whether or not any of the Heggies had survived the grenades.

Two men were still moving, wounded but alive, in the

trench that had held the machine gun. One of the reccers ended the movement with a very short burst of wire.

Dem looked around quickly, wondering how close together the Heggie positions were on this side of the line. There was no fire coming in at them. After a moment, he climbed out of the trench on the south side.

"Let's go," he said. He hadn't given a second thought to the way that the Heggie wounded had been killed. After all, the Heggies never took prisoners. And the reccers were in no position to take prisoners now, especially not wounded ones.

Ten minutes later the reccers could see the main Heggie line, six hundred meters in front of them. Dem took a moment to confer with the leaders of the other three patrols.

"We'll all hit them at the same time," he said. "Let's try to cut the distance at least in half. Give 'em a volley of rockets then and move forward until we're close enough for RPGs and the sniper rifles." His own test rifle would score effectively from three hundred meters. The Dupuy cough guns could reach a lot farther. "Another quick burst from there and then we'll try to get close enough for zippers."

If necessary. Dem hoped that before they could get that far the 5th and 8th would be on the move again, coming through—over—the Heggie line. That way a few of the reccers might actually survive the night.

CHAPTER
23

Orion had finally launched its Bats. The hangars were spaced around the hull at 120-degree intervals. Indigo Flight emerged from the ''bottom'' of *Orion,* facing Tamkailo. It wasn't until the Indigo Bats were clear of their own ship that they could see the Schlinal ships—now almost as close as they were likely to get to the Accord fleet, little more than ninety kilometers away. Two of the Schlinal ships had clearly fallen out of formation. One was broken in half, an extremely rare degree of damage. The other did not show any obvious major wounds, but it was obviously out of action.

Faro Malmeed did not concern himself with the possible fate of the—perhaps—fifteen hundred or two thousand Heggies who might have been on those ships. Even on the vessel that had broken in half there might still be considerable numbers of survivors in gastight compartments that had not been compromised. And if there weren't . . . Faro still wouldn't worry about them, even though he had not heard yet that his brother had been killed in action. The

Heggies were, after all, the Enemy.

"We're going buggy hunting," Osa Ximba told his flight. "And any fighters they send along to protect them. Landers are our first priority."

In Indigo three, Faro nodded. It made obvious sense to go after the largest number of *them,* the enemy, that you could.

"They haven't launched yet," Osa continued, "but they're going to have to start within the next few minutes if they're going for a landing anywhere near Site Charley." If they were going for a direct landing anyway, without letting the shuttles ride through a complete orbit on the way down, and *that* was unlikely. It would leave the shuttles vulnerable for far too long.

Ximba gave his pilots their vector and acceleration orders. The initial speed and course were neutral, allowing a variety of responses, depending on what the Heggies did in the next few minutes. Minimal power usage. If the Bats had to go low in pursuit of the shuttles, they would need every bit of juice they could save in order to boost back to a rendezvous orbit for *Orion* . . . or one of the other ships in the fleet.

Faro looked around his Bat. There were no nearby threats, nothing on his head-up display or monitors. His look outside was only partly to confirm that there were no Heggies or incoming rockets anywhere in his vicinity. The Bat's "eyes" were far more reliable than his own. Bats were flown on instrument, almost never by anything so primitive as a pilot looking out and making judgments based on what he saw. Mostly, he was just trying to see what kind of damage had been done so far in the battle. He had noticed the two Heggie ships that were out of action. As his Bat moved farther away from *Orion,* he could see some of the other ships in the Accord fleet.

The Accord ships were in three columns with the center column, the one that *Orion* led, sticking out in front of the other two. The three columns were "stacked" above Tamkailo, each farther out than the one "below" it. The two fleets were close enough now that the angle between their courses was finally apparent to the naked eye.

At first, Faro could see only the nearest few Accord ships. Those were between him and the rear ends of the columns. Indigo had been out for nearly five minutes before he could finally see the last ships in the two outer columns. One of those, the ship at the tail of the "highest" column, seemed to be dropping behind, falling out of station. The fleet, even that last ship, was still accelerating, but the one ship was not, apparently, accelerating as rapidly as the rest.

"Shuttle launches from nine ships," Ximba announced. Faro checked his navigating monitor. The Heggie fleet was shown on that. The two crippled ships had not launched any shuttles. The third ship that was not spitting out landers was the second one from the front of the formation. The shuttles came out, spent no more than two minutes moving into their own formations, and then started away from the ships, heading for the ground. They were running "hot," accelerating toward Tamkailo—a standard assault descent.

It only took another five seconds before the computers gave Indigo Flight their intercept instructions. Around them, the rest of *Orion*'s Bats, and the Bats from *Capricorn*, swiveled onto their intercept course and pushed throttles forward, boosting toward an empty point in space—a point that the Schlinal shuttles should reach a fraction of a second ahead of the Bats.

Both groups would need approximately twelve minutes to reach that point. For at least half of that time, the Bat pilots would have virtually nothing to do. They wouldn't be able to strike at the Heggies, and there were no Heggies in position where they would be able to strike at the Bats.

There were a lot of other blips around both fleets: the cordons of fighters on attack and defense, electronic decoys, and mines that could be controlled remotely and detonated if an enemy vessel came close enough for the blast to do damage. But Indigo Flight could ignore all of those other fighters with impunity unless they showed significant changes in course and speed. It was only the Boems accompanying the shuttles that might be a major threat to Indigo.

"Any word on escort for those shuttles yet?" Faro asked.

"Just that there are at least some Boems with them," Osa replied. "CIC hasn't got them all sorted out yet. There are at least sixty-eight small blips out there. Figure that at least half of them are fighters, maybe two-thirds."

Just before *Orion*'s Bats reached the halfway point on their intercept course, Faro happened to look back toward the Accord fleet and see another group of Bats heading off on what appeared to be an intercept course. He mentioned that to Ximba.

"Affirmative," Osa replied. "We hit 'em first. Anything left, that lot can worry about them. About three minutes after we make our pass."

Faro Malmeed was not normally given to levity, particularly on duty, but he could not help himself this time. "Are we *supposed* to leave a few for them?" he asked.

"The one thing I *don't* need just now is someone trying on a new pair of shoes," Ximba said on a private link to Malmeed. "You get my meaning?"

"Aye, sir," Faro replied, quickly. "It just slipped out."

"I want my pilots loose, but not so loose that they start losing parts," Ximba continued. To him, death was nothing to joke about, not even enemy deaths.

Forty-five seconds later, the Bats made a very minor correction to their heading.

This fight would not be the confused melee that atmospheric air battles still could be. The planes and shuttles had too much speed behind them for the acrobatic maneuvers of a dogfight. The Bats would have once through the formation of shuttles and Boems. As soon as they were beyond their Schlinal targets, the Bats would flip end for end—only a change in attitude, not in course—to get more time to launch missiles. They would, however, increase their speed as rapidly as they could, to carry them out of range of any Boems that survived their attack.

Indigo Flight started getting target locks for its missiles a full minute before they were near enough to launch and give the missiles good odds of getting through without being intercepted or decoyed away from their targets. Each pilot armed six rockets for the first strike. On the far side, they would try to get six more off. That would leave each Bat with four strike missiles to use for defense—as a backup to the smaller, faster antimissile missiles they also carried—or for targets of opportunity, in the unlikely event that any of those might arise.

"Just like a drill," Osa Ximba told his men as they approached the release point. "Just like a drill." He kept his voice soft, easy, giving every appearance of being totally relaxed with his job.

"Steady . . . *now!*"

Indigo's missiles raced forward just a second ahead of the missiles launched from the other Bat flights accompanying them. Their velocity relative to the Bats was deceptive. The missiles were not starting out from zero—or from only a few hundred kilometers per hour as they would have been if they had been launched by Wasps deep in a planet's gravity well and atmosphere. Rather they added their acceleration to the velocity carried by the Bats, more than 20,000 kph. Even without warheads, those missiles would be able to penetrate the hulls of a landing shuttle on both sides. Opening a shuttle to vacuum would be as fatal to the people inside as a thermonuclear device—had such things remained in use.

Explosives merely insured that the hulks would not be salvageable afterward.

The Boem S3s with the shuttles also launched missiles, theirs aimed at the Bats or at the missiles that the Bats had fired. Most of the shuttles activated their electronic countermeasures. At the distances and speeds involved, those would likely be of little use, but pilots took every measure they could.

Missiles hit and exploded. Brief flares of light presaged the spewing of debris. That debris could, and in some cases did, hit other shuttles or fighters, causing terminal damage. Shuttles, Bats, and Boems were lost. And the men inside. The survivors continued on. The Bats flipped their fighters end for end and fired off more missiles at the shuttles and Boems. Racing away from the Schlinal vessels now, away from enemy rockets and fighters, the Bats adjusted course for an eventual rendezvous with *Orion* and *Capricorn*—at the end of an eighty-seven-minute orbit of Tamkailo. Their batteries would not have enough power to kill their current speed and allow them to boost directly back to their ships. The Boems and the shuttles they were escorting—and the debris from those that had been destroyed—continued on their way to an earlier rendezvous, a landing on the northern section of Tamkailo's northern continent. There were fewer shuttles and Boems than before. The wrecks would, mostly, burn up in the atmosphere, a man-made meteor shower.

Kleffer Dacik had moved his command post as close to the front as he could reasonably get—too close, to the minds of his staff and the headquarters security detachment. The general did abandon his APC. That would have been too inviting a target to offer to Heggie gunners. The vehicle was more than a kilometer behind the MLR, the main line of resistance, behind a large rock outcropping that might shield it from enemy attention. Dacik had gone forward on foot from there, to less than three hundred meters from the front. He found a decent vantage and watched the battle with power binoculars. He couldn't see the entire line. Whatever fighting was going on at either end of the line, near the sea, was out of sight. But he could see enough. He scanned constantly, sometimes jumping to look toward a spectacular explosion, or in response to something heard over the radio.

"We're running out of time," he told his staff when he received word from CIC that the Schlinal fleet had launched shuttles. "They've got enough boats coming down to hold four thousand men."

"Intercepts?" Colonel Ruman asked.

"On the way," Major Olsen said. He had been on link to CIC constantly. "But the Bats won't get all of them." *They never do,* he thought. "The best we can hope for is a fifty-percent kill on the way down. Worst case, maybe ninety percent get through."

"And we'd better be ready to see something a lot closer to ninety than fifty percent land," Dacik said. "It looks as if they're heading directly for this peninsula. Unless they make a big change in course once they're in air. Ru, get the Wasps ready to go. Any that are up now, pull them down for fresh batteries and full racks. Then get them up to intercept as high as they can.''

''Already in the works, General,'' Ruman said. ''The first flight should pick up Heggies at twenty thousand meters. We'll keep hitting them as they come in.'' Those first Wasps to hit the Heggies would have trouble getting back down safely. The intercept point would be two hundred kilometers southwest of the peninsula. They would have to time the interception perfectly, and even then they would have little more than thirty seconds in which to do their damage and start back down for a landing on the peninsula with enough juice left in their batteries to see them softly on the ground.

''Look!'' Dacik shouted. The others around him turned to look where he was pointing—at a series of small explosions. ''Behind the Heggie lines. That's got to be Stossen's reccers.''

Dacik watched the evidence of fighting behind the MLR for a minute. Then, without discussing it with his staff first, he got on the link to the four regimental commanders whose men were pushing north. ''Hit them with everything you've got, right now. We've got the 13th's reccers in behind them. Hit them before they figure out what's going on.''

It took a couple of minutes before Dacik could see any new activity as a result of his order, but it came. Kane and Foss had been probing the Heggie line for an hour. Each had identified possible weak spots and had moved men into position to exploit them. The 5th and 8th hit those spots now, hard. The tempo of the battle increased all along the line. The Heggies who found themselves trapped between two Accord forces tried to fight their way clear. For most of them, that meant moving toward the nearest coast, either east or west, then heading north again.

The Schlinal commanders needed several minutes to even begin to restrain the exodus. But they did. There was no uncontrolled flight, no rout. Units withdrew in order, still fighting.

Dacik turned to look at his staff. He was grinning beneath his visor. "Let's get moving, gentlemen," he said. "The battle seems to be moving away from us."

Dem Nimz was finally getting low on ammunition for his test rifle. There had been no chance to get a new supply before this latest assignment. Down to his last three magazines, Dem held back, except for an occasional single shot when there was a clear target. The rifle continued to be wickedly effective. He loved it. But for now he made do with grenades as much as possible.

"We're doing something right," Fredo told him on a radio link. Fredo sounded uncharacteristically excited. "They're moving away from us as if they thought we're a full regiment."

"That's what they're supposed to think," Dem reminded him. "Just keep your heads down so they can't get a better count."

Dem grinned in the privacy of his helmet. Fredo was normally dour, even for a reccer, and his wound, a useless arm, had turned him almost mute. Until now. But Dem had noticed the same phenomenon that Fredo had. The Heggies were avoiding the reccers like a plague, even though they had been content to sit and face the remnants of four full regiments. It wasn't logical, but that was not unusual in the fog of battle. Perception was always more important than reality.

"Keep your heads down," Dem told the men with him. "We've stirred the pot enough. All we want to do now is keep them moving." He didn't let his enthusiasm carry him away. They were still just a handful of men in the middle of perhaps a hundred times as many of the enemy. A Schlinal platoon might stumble over one of the reccer patrols and wipe it out in seconds. Keeping down was a very smart choice.

Ten minutes later, Dem spotted the first Accord battle helmets coming up from the south. He needed a moment to get through to them over the radio—patched through

Colonel Stossen's headquarters links, through a similar link at the 8th's HQ, and to the men coming up the peninsula. It was safer to accept the delay than risk getting shot by mistake.

"Charley Company, 8th," a corporal said when he and Dem finally came face-to-face. "Fourth platoon, what's left of it." There were eight men with the corporal.

Dem identified himself and his unit. "I know what you mean," he added. "I've lost about eighty percent of my reccers."

"Colonel says we're to escort you lads back to your mates," the corporal said.

There was no humor in Dem's laugh. "Most times, I'd take exception to that. Not tonight. I've got my other patrols moving this way. They'll be here in a couple of minutes."

"Way I hear it, won't be much more than that before the Heggies drop another regiment or two on us from space," the corporal said, after telling his men to be on the watch for more reccers coming in.

"Helluva way to make a living, ain't it?" Dem said.

"This is living?"

"Where the hell are all the Heggies?" Wiz asked over the squad channel.

"They'll get to us soon enough," Sauv said. "Just stay alert."

But the first troops Echo Company of the 13th saw coming up from the south were Accord soldiers, their own reccers and a company from the 8th SAT.

"What the hell happened out there?" Baerclau asked Nimz when the reccers separated themselves from the 8th.

Dem shook his head. "I'm not sure. I *think* the Heggies just split and gave us the corridor down the middle of the peninsula. They broke to either side when we spooked 'em from behind. There's still a lot of 'em out there."

"Where are they? How many of them are left?" Van Stossen shot the questions at his intelligence officer. The

8th and 5th were moving down the center of the peninsula now, meeting only scattered resistance as they drew cordons around the two Schlinal concentrations.

"We don't know anything more now than we did an hour ago about the numbers of enemy forces on the peninsula," Bal Kenneck replied. "There might be a thousand Heggies on the loose, or three times that number. Not including the ones we sealed up under their base. What I'm getting from Olsen isn't helping at all. The Heggies pulled back from their prepared line and moved to either side. They're establishing new perimeters backed up against the sea on both east and west, hard semicircles."

"Trying to hold enough ground for the shuttles to land." Stossen didn't bother making it a question.

"They have to hold at least one LZ to have any chance at all," Teu Ingels said.

"Doesn't matter where on the peninsula they set down, they'll still be in range of the Havocs," Hank Norwich said. "Not just ours, the 8th's and 5th's as well. There's not enough room to get their shuttles out of range of our guns."

"Don't forget, the Heggies still have a few Novas on the ground," Bal said. "They might not have the range of the Havocs, but they can shoot far enough to hit any spot on the peninsula from those two pockets, and the Havocs are all out on the peninsula now."

"I know," Norwich admitted. He didn't like having his "dogs" bottled up so thoroughly. "But they haven't been doing much shooting lately. They have to be getting low on ammo since we're sitting on the only source of resupply they have."

"Getting low or saving what they have for when it'll do the most good," Kenneck said. "They know that help's on the way."

"It's just about here," Dezo Parks said. He had been on the radio for the last several minutes. "The high Wasp cap has just hit the lead shuttles. They've got Boems with them. We've got less than ten minutes before any that get through reach us."

CHAPTER 24

Battlefield intelligence is never 100 percent correct until after the fact, if then—except, perhaps, by accident. Observations and estimates made under the great stresses of mortal combat are remarkable if they come anywhere near the truth. The "fog of battle" is susceptible more to the laws of nonlinear dynamics—chaos—than to the logical plans laid down ahead of time. Sometimes the smallest incident, the tiniest "monkey wrench in the works" has more importance than position, strength of numbers, equipment, or leadership. A seemingly insignificant incident can snowball into overwhelming victory or crushing defeat. Of course, the "for want of a nail" syndrome has long been understood, if only vaguely.

Three Schlinal shuttles reported as destroyed by Orion's Bats survived, as did the troopers they were carrying. Two of those same shuttles were mistakenly reported destroyed by the Wasps of the 8th SAT. Schlinal shuttles *were* destroyed, both in space and lower, in Tamkailo's atmosphere, but not the seventeen claimed by Accord pilots. Later analysis would show that only nine shuttles were destroyed before landing. The rest, a total of twenty-one, reached the peninsula at the polar end of Tamkailo's northern continent—twenty-one shuttles carrying three thousand infantrymen and one battalion of armor. The Schlinal infantry shuttles carried considerably more men than their Accord counterparts. They were accompanied by eighteen surviving Boem S3s.

Those Boems went after Accord artillery first and infantry units only as an afterthought. The shuttles separated and came into both of the LZs that had been secured on the peninsula, moving low over the ocean through the last twenty kilometers of their run.

Not one of the shuttles was hit on the ground by Accord artillery or Vrerch rockets—until after they had all discharged their troops and equipment.

Sunrise was ninety minutes away.

Admiral Kitchener stood in the center of CIC on *Capricorn*. For a time the battle in space was suspended. The two fleets were moving away from each other now, on different orbital paths. The Bats had been recalled. On the other side, the Boem S3s had either been recalled or sent in with the landing shuttles. There were many Bats and Boems making their own orbits of Tamkailo, waiting for rendezvous on the far side.

Damage reports were still coming into CIC. Only one ship in the Accord fleet seemed to be a total—if temporary—loss, and even in that case most of the crew had managed to evacuate in shuttles and boost to the next ship in line. Even though the ship's drives had been seriously damaged, the vessel could be repaired, in time, if it could be towed back to a friendly shipyard. Three other ships had minor damage—hull punctures, some gastight compartments compromised. Repairs were already under way—and would be complete before the two fleets came within reach of each other again.

On balance, the Accord was the clear winner of the

engagement. Two Schlinal ships were apparently damaged beyond repair. No one had escaped from the ship that had broken in two. Only a single shuttle had made it away from the other seriously damaged Schlinal ship. There was a chance—a good chance, according to CIC estimates—that there were still considerable numbers of survivors on that ship.

"We'll have to face them at least once more," Kitchener said on a link to the captains of his ships. "Unless they pull out before our orbits intersect again." That was possible. The Schlinal navy had never shown much heart for space battles. Put the men ashore and get out. For that matter, the Accord had done the same often enough. And it had always looked to land troops on worlds where the Schlinal warlords did not maintain a fleet overhead. Kitchener shrugged. "We won't know about that for at least another thirty minutes."

Afghan and Basset batteries of the 13th had pushed hard down the center of the peninsula once the way opened up. They went past the few remaining Havocs of the 5th and past about half of the 8th's contingent. Their immediate assignment was to get back to the rest of the 13th and take up positions within the Schlinal base. Their support vans moved with them. The 13th's other two Havoc batteries were taking part in the action against the eastern Heggie landing zone. As soon as they finished there, Corgi and Dingo batteries were also supposed to head north as fast as their engines could carry them.

It was only a ten-kilometer trip from where the Havocs had been when they received the orders. At full speed, it would have taken them no more than ten minutes. The trip took rather longer in practice.

"We running on one engine?" Eustace demanded, looking at Simon across the barrel of the Fat Turtle's howitzer.

"Up yours" was Kilgore's response. Simon didn't even bother to look at Eustace. "We're doing what we can.

There are a half dozen Havocs in front of us. We can't climb over them.

Ponks growled deep in his throat.

"Besides, this way we're not the ones finding out if the Heggies left any mines along the way," Simon continued.

Eustace lost all interest in the conversation. He was busy trying to keep track of the piecemeal data coming in about the Heggie landings and everything else that was going on along the peninsula. In particular, he was trying to ease the nasty itch at the back of his neck that came from knowing that the enemy had Boems overhead again. A Havoc had no defense against air attack except to be somewhere else when it came. That was why the Havocs were racing for the Schlinal base at the end of the peninsula. Along the lanes separating the warehouses and other buildings they might find some cover from air attack, and they would have infantrymen around for support, men with Vrerch missiles to help keep the Boems away—or shoot them down if they did come close.

Joe Baerclau watched the Havocs and support vans roll past. The deep-throated roar of engines and the clanking of treads on rock were reassuring despite word that fresh Heggie troops had landed just a few kilometers away. The vehicles moved past the 13th's line and into the streets of the captured Schlinal base. Moving to the defensive, Joe thought. *Laagering up.*

"Anybody know what the hell's going on?" Mort asked.

Joe turned, shaking his head. "I sure don't," he admitted. Echo Company was on a half-and-half watch, one fire team from each squad manning the line facing south, the other resting or eating—or standing around worrying. Inactivity was draining Joe. The heat, too little sleep, and all of the fight that had already taken place—it was finally getting to him. It felt almost as if that exhaustion were a real, physical presence, a blanket trying to smother him.

"I'm going over to talk to the first sergeant," Joe said after a moment. Then he lowered his visor to tell Sauv and Low the same thing.

Echo's command post was some hundred meters west. Captain Keye and First Sergeant Walker had set up behind a jumble of the wreckage of three of the large umbrella-shaped "trees." The woody pulp of the fungi would certainly stop wire, perhaps even a slug fired from short range. When Joe arrived, Keye was sleeping, snoring softly, his head back on the trunk of one of the plants. Walker was sitting several meters away, his head hanging forward.

"Izzy?" Joe said softly.

The first sergeant lifted his head slowly. He raised a hand—half in greeting, half to tell Joe to wait. Walker got to his feet in what seemed to be slow motion. Once he was up, he gestured for Joe to follow him. They went several paces farther from the CP.

"Captain's about dead on his feet," Walker explained in a whisper. Both men had their visors up. "I guess I'm not in much better shape. Captain and me, we're too old for this crap. The heat is just too much."

"You got any idea what's going on?" Joe asked.

"Not much. I had a chat with Friz Duke about fifteen minutes ago." As a rule, the 13th's command sergeant major knew as much about what was going on as Colonel Stossen did, sometimes more. "All he knew for sure was that the Heggies have landed more men, on both sides of the peninsula. They brought more Boems in with them. Seems to be some new tanks as well."

"Any numbers?" Joe asked.

"Probably more than one regiment and less than two," Izzy said. "That's the best estimate CIC has. Plus whatever was left of the Heggies who were already out there." He gestured vaguely toward the south. Then he looked up. "I guess the Boems have already had to land for new batteries."

"We just gonna sit still and wait for them to come to us?"

"We're waiting to find that out now. Friz said that the colonel's been on link with the general and the other regimental commanders most of the last half hour trying to decide what to do."

"Sun's gonna be up soon." Joe turned to look east. There was, perhaps, the slightest hint of light on the horizon, out over the ocean . . . or, perhaps, it was all his imagination. "It's been a long night."

"It's been a long night," Izzy agreed, "and it's like to be a longer day." He shook his head. "We started out with five regiments when we landed. I doubt we could muster two full regiments now, putting everybody that's fit to move together. Heggies got at least that many to face us, what with the reinforcements, and the new guys will be fresh from just getting in."

"Day gets hot . . . men with no sleep." Joe shook his head violently. It was already hot—*still* hot—after more than ten hours of darkness, clear skies, and a moderate breeze. At the coolest time of the night, the temperature was still near 34 degrees. And it would start getting hotter as soon as the sun came above the horizon. Men who hadn't had much, or any, sleep would find it almost impossible to function at anything vaguely approaching normal. The few hours sleep that the 13th had had the day before—only the day before?—hadn't been enough to make up for what they had lost. And it had been followed by another dozen hours of work. And fear.

"Brass hats gotta know all that, Joe," Izzy said. "I were you, I'd have my guys ready to get moving on about ten seconds' notice. When they decide what we're gonna do, they'll probably want it done immediately."

"It never changes, does it?" Joe asked.

"What?"

"Hurry up and wait."

The two men looked at each other for a few seconds more, then Joe turned and started back toward his platoon. Izzy watched him for a moment, then went back to where he had been sitting before. *Even five minutes of* good *sleep,* he thought. *I'd sell my soul for five minutes.*

Even on the general's large mapboard, the situation didn't look anything but confused. Accord positions were marked in blue, the units labeled where possible. Known

Schlinal positions were marked in red. Suspected Schlinal positions were in a blinking pink. There were two primary concentrations of Heggies about halfway along the peninsula, anchored on either shore. But there were also several smaller groupings, scattered randomly almost from the 13th's line just south of the captured base to south of the line that the Heggies had been defending prior to the new landings. There might be other units that hadn't been spotted. And there were certainly Heggies below the base at the northern end of the peninsula—men who might, or might not, be trapped behind the metal doors that had been welded shut.

"The one thing we know for certain is that the Heggies can't retreat into the sea," Dacik said after staring at the chart in silence for several minutes.

"Only about half of the shuttles made it back off the ground," Major Olsen said. "That limits retreat upward for them as well."

"Our Havocs did a good job on the shuttles once they were on the ground," Colonel Ruman said. "Not to mention the Novas that were unloaded. The reports I've had suggest that half of the new tanks were knocked out before they could even think about shooting.

Dacik grunted. "Half? Figure maybe ten percent if our luck's running good. How many Wasps did we lose against the landings?"

Ruman hesitated before he said, "Three before the Heggies grounded, six more after they were down. Altogether, we're down to twenty-four Wasps that can still fly."

"Twenty-four out of the hundred eighteen we started with, plus more than two dozen spares that were pressed into service after the first go-around. That's more than eighty percent losses and we're not done yet. And some of our ground units have been hit just as hard. It's the worst pounding any Accord force has ever taken."

"Pilot losses aren't quite that extreme," Ruman said softly. "Bad enough, certainly. We've lost seventy-three pilots. A dozen who survived the loss of their planes will need extensive time in trauma tubes, even regeneration leaves. Some will need months before they're fit to get in a cockpit again.''

''I wish we had a few more spare Wasps, enough for the pilots who are still healthy enough to fly,'' Dacik said. *I also wish I had a couple of fresh regiments to send against the Heggies,* he thought. He closed his eyes for a moment.

''The two main Heggie enclaves are too close together for us to hit one and leave the second until afterward,'' Dacik said when he opened his eyes again. ''Novas in one can support the other side without any difficulty. Far as that goes, they've got infantry rockets that can reach as well.'' He sighed. ''That means we've pretty much got to go after both sections at once.''

''We've also got to keep them from pushing in toward the center of the peninsula and uniting,'' Napier Foss said over the radio. ''We let them get together and we'll have even bigger trouble.''

''I know,'' Dacik said. It was difficult to think straight. His mind wanted to shut down and get some sleep, with or without his cooperation. It wanted to abdicate responsibility for a time, if only for an hour or two.

Dispositions. The general stared at his mapboard again, trying to force a higher level of alertness. The 8th was in the center of the peninsula, linked to the 13th in the north, holding two-thirds of the perimeter against the Heggies along the west coast. The 97th had the rest of that and stretched east to where they met the 34th, which completed the line across the peninsula and hemmed in the southern half of the eastern Heggie foothold. The 5th, the regiment that had been hurt worst during the campaign on Tamkailo, had the rest of the eastern perimeter. They hadn't linked up with the 13th, though. They didn't have the men to extend their line north. Nowhere was the line around the Heggies as tight, as strong, as Dacik would have liked.

He lifted his visor long enough to rub vigorously at his eyes. They were burning from lack of sleep.

''We'll bring the 13th south to help the 5th and 34th,'' Dacik announced after he lowered his visor again. ''The

8th and 97th will have to do for themselves on the west, at least for a time. We may have to attack both concentrations at once, but we're going to put our emphasis on the eastern bloc of Heggies first. If we can get that under control, we'll try to siphon units over to the west as quickly as we can free them up.''

With the major decisions made, it took only a few more minutes to put together the details and timing.

Joe Baerclau had finally sat down and leaned back. He might not be able to sleep, but he did sort of drift in and out of a void that was almost sleep. He could hear sounds around him, but those did not intrude on his trancelike state. Since he hadn't noticed the time before he closed his eyes, he wasn't certain how much . . . rest he had managed before the call came from Izzy Walker.

"Mount 'em up Joe," the first sergeant said. "We're off to help the 5th on the east side. Echo will be third company from the rear on the move. Get your men in behind Delta as it forms up on the road." Alpha and Bravo were west of Echo on the line, as well as the remnant of the 13th's four recon platoons. "The reccers are staying behind," Walker continued. "Security for the Havocs and support people, and to cover anything that happens up this way."

Joe got the platoon up, then told the squad leaders and their assistants what was coming. "I don't know how long it's going to take to get into position, but unless something happens in one hell of a hurry, we're going to be fighting under the sun again," he added.

Under almost any circumstances, an infantryman preferred to fight at night, when darkness would give him some little measure of extra security. On Tamkailo, that preference bordered on obsession.

Rather to Joe's surprise, the 13th formed up and started moving quite rapidly. Less than ten minutes passed between the first sergeant's initial call and Echo's turn to move into line behind Delta Company. The column moved south for less than five hundred meters before it turned east toward the sea. On the march, there was another briefing for platoon leaders and platoon sergeants.

"We're going to try to roll the Heggies in from north to south," Captain Keye said. "The 5th and 34th will step up the pressure around the rest of the perimeter. We'll force the corner and tighten the noose around them."

"Everybody, check your weapons," Joe said on his platoon circuit after the captain's briefing. "I want fresh power packs and spools in all the zippers. RPGs and rockets in launchers, ready to go." *Let's get this over as fast as we can*, he thought. One way or the other. Joe was too tired to think in terms of victory or defeat. All that mattered was that the campaign should end, that they escape from Tamkailo's oppressive heat and heavy air.

The 5th SAT's recon platoons were holding down the north end of the line. The 5th only had twenty reccers left. They were to be the link between the 13th and the rest of the 5th.

The men of the 13th had a few minutes to rest after they moved into position for the attack. Fox, George, and Howard companies would be the first in. The rest of the 13th would follow, attempting to widen the front. Alpha and Bravo would go right to the seashore, trying to turn the semicircle of the Heggie perimeter into a complete circle—a noose that could be tightened until the Heggies could no longer breathe.

Only a relative calm fell over the peninsula. The fighting never really stopped. But there seemed to be a lull as the 13th moved into position for its attack. Thirty seconds, perhaps a minute. Then the comparative silence ended as the Havocs opened up against both pockets of Heggies.

Their first targets had to be the Nova tanks. On both sides of the peninsula, the Novas came under concentrated artillery fire. They returned that fire while they could, but the Novas had too little room to maneuver in to successfully evade the artillery for long. The Accord had too many eyes spotting for their Havocs, on the ground and above, Wasp pilots and spyeye satellites.

Less than three minutes after the start of the barrage, part of the Accord artillery was switched to infantry targets in the eastern pocket. As soon as the Heggie infantry came under attack, the 13th started advancing toward them.

The three companies that spearheaded the assault moved forward easily at first, the men hunched over and walking quickly while the artillery laid down a walking barrage in front of them. Only very scattered Heggie fire was directed at them in the first minutes. Most of the Schlinal soldiers were doing whatever they could to protect themselves from the lethal artillery fire, and from passes made by the Accord's remaining Wasps. Some stayed and died. Others got up and ran. *Some* of those survived.

As soon as the first wave was a hundred meters out, the next group of companies was up and moving.

Second platoon was near the western edge of the advance. Only the 1st platoon of Echo Company was farther west. On the other side of 1st platoon, the 5th's reccers started up from their positions as well, keeping the link between 5th and 13th.

Joe hesitated for a second before he crossed what had been the Heggie perimeter just a few minutes before. There was a line of bodies, and parts of bodies, left by the barrage that had moved ahead of the first companies of the 13th. Joe looked to both sides. He didn't see any Heggies still alive along the line—no wounded, just the dead, more than he had any thought of counting.

He stepped over the torso of one soldier. There was no sign of the man's legs, arms, or head in the immediate vicinity of the body. Of the parts strewn farther off, it would be difficult to guess which belonged to which body.

The sound of a man retching came over the platoon channel, then ended quickly. Joe looked to his left and saw someone lifting his visor and leaning over to puke. Joe wasn't certain who it was, and that bothered him more than the man's reaction. Someone in Low Gerrent's squad. But the man stopped for just the few seconds he absolutely needed. Then the faceplate came back down and the man hurried forward to regain his place in the line.

Echo had moved fifty meters beyond the original Heggie line and had started to move at an angle off to the right,

broadening the 13th's front, before they came under fire. A
spray of wire and slugs came from ahead and to the right.
The first Heggie troops had been trapped in a salient, a
bubble nearly closed off by the 13th's advance.

No one needed orders to drop to the ground and find
cover.

"You see where that came from?" Captain Keye asked
Joe over their private link.

"Just vaguely, sir," Joe replied. "I think we can get to
them."

"Just keep them busy," Keye said. "The 5th's reccers
are moving in. We're already starting to roll back that side
of the pocket."

"Roger." Joe switched to his platoon channel. "Make
'em keep their heads down but watch your fire. We've got
friendlies coming in behind them to do the work."

Although the ground sloped gently toward the sea, with
only very low irregularities—a soft, rolling sort of terrain,
like a very modest sea swell—the artillery barrage had left
plenty of craters. The artillery fire was no longer coming
in. The 8th and 97th needed all of the support they could
get from the big guns to keep their Heggies from breaking
out of the western pocket and moving across the peninsula
to unite with the other concentration.

Wiz Mackey and a man from second squad managed to
drop rocket-propelled grenades right on top of the Heggies
machine gun position. A few seconds later, men in Accord
camouflage ran forward and into the Heggie position. They
only needed a few seconds to complete the work there.

But as soon as Echo got up to resume their advance,
Heggies started firing all along the 13th's front—now five
companies wide. Wire and slug-throwing rifles, the 12mm
Schlinal machine guns, grenades, and rockets all came into
action at once.

Low Gerrent and the men on either side of him were
killed before they could get down. Several other men in
2nd platoon were wounded. Mort had a shoulder wound.
A burst of wire had nearly ripped the sleeve off of his shirt,
wire coming from so close that the net armor woven into

the cloth had no effect at all. Joe felt wire ricocheting off of his visor and helmet. The bits of wire hit and rebounded too quickly for him to see them, but the visor was scratched right in front of his eyes.

Joe rolled when he hit the ground, then slid backwards to get a little cover. Everyone who could move was doing the same, getting under whatever cover he could find—and dragging those who were hurt too badly to move on their own. Joe pulled Wiz back into a shell crater. Mackey had a serious chest wound. Joe put a bandage over it and told Al that he was needed quickly. "Sucking chest wound," Joe reported.

Al was already moving toward another wounded man. Bergon was the only medic left in the platoon—second squad's medic had been one of the men killed next to Low Gerrent—and there was too much for him to do alone.

"Mort, you'd better give Al a hand," Joe said. Everyone took first aid courses in the spaceborne assault teams, but Mort had had more training, and experience, than anyone in the platoon but Al.

"Yeah, I know," Mort said. The second squad medic's pouch was being passed along the line toward him.

Al took a second to look at the man he had been crawling toward, decided that his wound could wait, and diverted toward Joe and Wiz. Al did what he could.

"We've got to get him back to Doc Eddles, and soon," Al said. "I can't even get him stabilized with that wound."

"See if there's anybody else needs to be moved back," Joe said. "I'll line up the able bodies to guide them. On belts again." He switched channels. "Izzy, where's Doc Eddles set up? We've got at least one man needs him fast to survive."

"All the way back at the Heggie base," Walker replied. "We're gonna have to mount a convoy. We've all been hit hard. I think half of George Company's either dead or hurt bad enough to need trauma tubes."

"I've got at least four dead, including one of my two remaining squad leaders. Damn near everybody else has at least minor injuries."

"You?" Izzy asked.

"I'm okay. Just got my visor scratched."

"Hang on a second." When he came back on the link, Walker said, "Captain says we'll pull your platoon to escort the seriously wounded back to the medtechs and surgeons. Maybe 4th platoon as well if you need help. Call me back as soon as you're ready. We're going to gather all our seriously wounded at my position. You have my marker on your visor?"

Joe checked the overlay on his visor display. "I see you. About sixty meters from me."

"Captain and I are in a nice deep crater. Looks like three or four shells must have hit all at once. Room here for a full platoon."

"We'll start as soon as we've got the wounded in shape to travel," Joe promised. "I hope it's not too long."

The sun was just starting to show its upper rim over the eastern horizon . . . out over the peaceful ocean.

CHAPTER
25

At four separate points just south of the captured Schlinal base, there was movement where there should have been none. In gullies and under overhangs, what appeared to be sections of rock slid silently out of position as camouflaged doors opened. The more than fourteen hundred Schlinal troops who had been "trapped" underground had had plenty of time to reorganize. Their leaders had been in constant communication with the other Schlinal units that had been stationed at what the Accord called Site Charley and with the new arrivals.

Four exits, four columns of Schlinal infantry. Scouts dispatched before sunrise had reported that there were no Free-bies around any of the exits. The rest of the troops hurried out into the morning twilight. Each company, each platoon, had its assignment. The ranking Schlinal officer on Tamkailo, one of the new arrivals, had decided that speed of execution was the primary need now. Once the men from under the base were spotted, much of the advantage would be lost.

Three hundred men were sent north, back into the base. It was clear that aside from the artillery and various maintenance support units, there were virtually no troops protecting the base and its thousands of tonnes of munitions and other supplies. The Schlinal force desperately needed what was in those warehouses.

The rest of the Schlinal troops made their way south in their separate columns to attack the Freebies from behind. They would attempt to drive a wedge into the lines constraining both of their concentrations along the sides of the peninsula, attacking at the same time that the smaller detachment started to destroy the Accord artillery.

The seriously wounded were guided north, supported by their antigrav belts. Visible bleeding had been stopped. Broken bones had been immobilized as far as possible. Intravenous drips had been started on those who needed that level of maintenance. The twelve men of Joe's platoon who were still able to move on their own guided all of the more seriously wounded men from the company. Each man, including Joe, was responsible for two men moving on their belts. It was certainly easier than carrying the men, but it was still work, pushing mass forward, guiding the "packages" and making certain that they didn't get away.

Echo's 2nd platoon handled the wounded. Fourth platoon went along as armed escort. It was two kilometers from where the men had been wounded to the warehouse where the 13th's field hospital had been set up, slightly uphill most of the way.

"Just hang in there, Wiz," Joe Baerclau whispered. He had his helmet visor up so he wouldn't transmit, but he had been talking to the unconscious Mackey almost the entire distance, trying to keep him alive by willpower and words. It was clear even to Joe that Wiz was hanging on by only the most slender of threads.

"Another five minutes and we'll have you in a tube," Joe continued. The group had stayed close to the shore to this point, on ground that was relatively even. Now it was time to take a 45-degree turn to the left. Dieter Franzo, 4th platoon sergeant, was standing off to the side, marking the turn. He had a fire team with him, their guns covering the flank, looking inland.

Joe looked toward those men, then back to see how far behind him the column of men with wounded went. When he looked forward again, Dieter was down on his knees and waving frantically.

"Get those people moving, *double time*!" Franzo shouted over the company noncoms' channel. "Heggies, hundreds of 'em." He pointed west and south, then switched channels to report the movement to Captain Keye.

Joe got his platoon moving north at the nearest thing to a run they could manage with each able-bodied man guiding two limp casualties.

It was impossible to make the turn to the left now. Dieter and his men had gone flat, their guns trained on the Heggies they could see, about 150 meters away, too far for wire. Unless they were spotted, 4th platoon would hold their fire. A fight would endanger the wounded. Even if they weren't hit again, any delay in getting the most seriously hurt men to the medtechs and surgeons might be fatal.

Joe kept looking back over his shoulder. He didn't even have the small comfort of being able to point a rifle in the direction of the threat. He needed both hands to guide the two wounded men. His rifle was slung over his shoulder.

"I see at least a full company, headed straight south," Dieter whispered over the noncoms' link.

"You let the captain know yet?" Joe had to drag in a deep lungful of air. He was pressing too hard to talk and move at the same time with any comfort.

"I told him. Must be the Heggies we sealed up in the tunnels."

"Yeah," Joe said after a short hesitation. His thoughts hadn't yet traveled to the question of where these Heggies might have come from. "They *did* have bolt holes we didn't find."

"Didn't look too hard," Dieter said. "We just forgot about them."

Just after that, 2nd platoon moved behind a ridge that was high enough to hide them from the Heggies who were moving in the other direction. Dieter and his men moved down as well.

Now we're safe, Joe thought. The sudden feeling of relief was so great that he almost tripped over his own feet.

Dem Nimz would have liked to check every one of the welded doors himself, personally. They bothered him. The Heggies could have blown them by now, he thought. One door or all of them. It wouldn't take much in the way of explosives to knock down one of these doors. Bust out firing. Basic drill.

These Heggies haven't just lain down and played dead, he reminded himself. Maybe some of the Heggies at the other two bases had, but these guys had fought, even when they were retreating into the tunnels. They didn't mutiny. They didn't surrender. They retreated, but they kept fighting.

The 13th's recon detachment was still operating as four squads. Dem had taken his squad through three of the warehouses. He had inspected the welds on doors leading into the tunnel system. He had prowled around looking for additional entrances, concealed hatches perhaps, without finding any. He had even rigged up listening gear to try to hear any activity behind the welded doors. That too had yielded nothing, no sounds of people at all.

"They sure as hell haven't all asphyxiated themselves," he mumbled after listening at the second of the doors. "Even if the tunnel system was sealed with no oxygen getting in, they haven't been down there long enough for that." That was, of course, a wild guess. He had no idea how many people had gone down into the tunnels or how extensive the system might be. After checking one more warehouse, he was ready to give up on the welded doors.

"Let's get back out on the streets," he said.

The lanes between the buildings were far from empty.

There were Havocs parked just about anywhere that gave them an opening for their fire missions. The support vans for Havocs and Wasps were parked wherever they could find room, mostly in the northern half of the base. The crews had set up sentry positions linked by radio. Nervous mechanics patrolled, peering around corners and into buildings. The support crews weren't used to being left on their own. Generally, they remained in the center of defensive positions, with plenty of mudders to keep the enemy away from them. The first continuous and then intermittent firing of the 205mm howitzers reminded everyone that there was still fighting going on, no matter how peaceful it seemed within the base.

Despite his habitual distrust of radio communications, Dem spent a lot of time on the radio, in almost constant contact with the other reccer patrols. And even though he was normally more comfortable operating at night, in the dark, this was one day when Dem was relieved to see the sun moving above the horizon.

It was Heggies who might be hiding this time, he thought. The light was their enemy as well. Accord night-vision systems might provide nearly 70 percent of full daylight visibility, but he wanted that extra 30 percent.

Shortly after sunrise, Dem led his patrol to the east side of the base. "They're bringing in wounded. We'll meet them and escort them in."

Then he called to make contact. Joe Baerclau was on the other end.

"There are Heggies moving south from the base," Joe reported. "Company or more. The colonel's already been alerted."

"Where, exactly?" Dem asked.

Joe told him. "They must be the ones we sealed up," he added.

Dem hurried his patrol out to meet the column of wounded, and hurried the group along to the field hospital.

Although the hospital had been set up in one of the largest warehouses, it was already crowded. At sunrise, there were more than three hundred patients being treated or waiting for treatment. Most of the medical staff had been working without a break for most of the night, on top of several days of extremely long hours. The surgeons had performed more invasive operations than any of them could recall ever performing in a year. And the medtechs were having difficulty freeing up trauma tubes for new casualties. As soon as one patient was removed—often thirty minutes or more before he should have been—there was another casualty to be slid into place.

Two medtechs were pulled away from other work to do triage for the casualties that Joe Baerclau and his men brought in. The wounded were marked for surgery or trauma tubes. Tubes and operating tables had to be freed up. Several of the wounded, including Wiz, had to be placed on life-support systems to keep them going until a surgeon could get to them.

As soon as the wounded had been turned over, Dem took Joe aside.

"There had to be more than a company of Heggies locked up under here. More likely a couple of battalions."

"That's what I thought," Joe said. "Maybe 4th platoon just saw the tail end of the column. Not our problem now."

"Maybe." Nimz frowned.

"You think some of them might be closer?" Joe asked.

"I'm sure as hell going to find out. What kind of orders you have?"

"Just to get the wounded here."

"Nobody told you to drag ass back to the line afterward?" Dem asked.

Joe shook his head.

"Unless you get different orders, I'd suggest you keep your men here, around the hospital, for a while. I'll get my guys back looking outside."

Joe nodded slowly. "Sounds good to me. I'll talk to Dieter. Between the two of us we don't have one good platoon, but we'll do what we can." He would talk to Dieter *and* to Captain Keye. Joe had been a soldier too long to take it on himself to originate new orders, even at the suggestion of a reccer.

• • •

Basset Battery was on the move. "We've got to find a lane that gives us a good shot right down the center of the peninsula," Eustace had told the crew of the Fat Turtle. "New targets."

Captain Ritchie was in front of the Fat Turtle in Basset one. The rest of the battery trailed behind. Basset one turned a corner, left, aiming south again. The tail end of the howitzer had not quite disappeared from Eustace's view when it exploded, hit by at least one rocket from in front. Basset one stood on its tail and fell backward.

Eustace's first, fleeting, thought was *Cripes, that's the fourth Havoc the captain's had shot out from under him.* He was already shouting, "Stop! Trouble!" before his thoughts progressed to *It doesn't look like he'll make it out this time.* Basset one came to rest upside down. The turret was partially separated from the carriage, and it had been crushed, partly by the rocket blast and partly from having the rest of the Havoc sitting on top of it. Smoke was finding its way out from around the base of the turret, and through the bottom of the carriage.

"Basset one's been hit," Eustace reported over the battery channel. "Back off. There must be Heggies around the corner."

Simon was already turning the Fat Turtle enough to back out of line and off to the side. He didn't bother wasting time turning the gun around. The Havoc could travel as rapidly in reverse as it could forward.

"Why not bring the gun barrel down?" Simon asked. "We've got HE loaded. Anybody comes around that corner, we can give 'em a surprise."

"Why not?" Eustace said. "Karl, do it." The Havoc was definitely not designed for close-range, point-blank anti-personnel operations, but it didn't have anything else to use in defense.

The gun barrel came down as far as it would go, about 2 degrees above horizontal. A shell would have to be detonated in the air to do any good at close range. Even 50 meters away, it would be over the heads of infantrymen.

Eustace got busy on the radio with Major Norwich, the squadron commander. "We need some mudders here!" Ponks shouted when the major came on the line. "We've lost Basset one. There must be Heggies on the loose right inside this base."

"We can't get anyone to you now," Norwich replied. "You'll have to rely on the mudders already there."

"What mudders?" Eustace asked.

There was a long pause before Norwich said, "Our reccers and a platoon or two from several line companies. They were transporting wounded back to the field hospital. And the support crews. That's all there is until we sort the rest of this mess out."

"We're on our own," Eustace told his crew after switching away from the link of Major Norwich. "Us and whatever odds and ends happen to be around."

Basset one had been blown up right next to the field hospital. The explosion had echoed through the building and shook dust off of the ceiling and walls.

Joe Baerclau and Dieter Franzo had been talking, close to one of the hospital's two exits. Their men were gathered around them, right along the wall, trying to stay out of the way of the medical teams. That wasn't easy. Three times already surgeons or medtechs had yelled for them to get out from underfoot. The men with minor injuries had already been treated. Al Bergon had taken care of them after the more serious casualties had been handed over to the experts. Anyone who could still walk and use his hands was marked for duty.

The building shook. Dust fell. Baerclau and Franzo looked at the door next to them, then up at the ceiling, then at each other again.

Joe was the first to break for the door. "Second platoon!" shouted over his radio. At the same time, Dieter was collecting his men.

"How you want to work this?" Dieter asked. Joe was considerably senior to him as a platoon sergeant.

"We'll go left, you go right. When we see what's out

there, we'll figure out what to do next. Some of those Heggies must have come back.''

''Maybe a Nova shooting at our Havocs?'' Dieter suggested.

Joe shook his head. ''That was a rocket, not a tank round.'' He wasn't certain how he knew that—he had never particularly noticed a difference in those two types of blast—but he didn't have any doubt.

''Whenever you're ready,'' Dieter said.

''Mort, be careful,'' Joe said as Jaiffer moved into position to be first out of the door.

''That's why I go first,'' Mort said with a cold smile. ''Get out before they know what's coming.''

Joe checked his rifle, then pulled open the door. Mort jumped forward like a runner coming out of the blocks on a track. He didn't stop at the outer side of the thick stone wall but kept running, out into the lane. The stricken Havoc was only a few meters away. Mort dove for cover behind it. By that time, the rest of the men in the two platoons were also moving into position.

A squad of Heggies was coming down the lane, hugging the wall of the building across from the hospital. Joe stopped at the outer edge of the entryway and started shooting, getting his zipper into action as quickly as Mort did in the middle of the street. The rest of 2nd and 4th platoons were not much behind getting into action. Some of the men were shooting before they truly saw the enemy. They simply started firing as soon as they saw someone else shooting, aiming in the same general direction.

The Heggie patrol was slow to react—slow by no more than a fraction of a second—but that was all of the edge that the 13th's men needed. And there was very little cover for the Heggies. They might as easily have been standing against a wall for execution by firing squad.

The result was about the same.

Altogether, this firefight lasted less than twenty seconds. A dozen Heggies were down, dead or wounded. Joe moved away from the edge of the doorway, advancing slowly toward the Heggies, his zipper pointed at the men on the ground. He had gone only four steps when another group of Heggies started shooting from the next intersection, forty meters away.

Joe dropped to the ground as quickly as if someone had knocked his legs out from under him. A fraction of a second's warning had been enough. The first burst of enemy wire went over his head. Twenty Armanoc zippers answered immediately. Second platoon continued shooting. Dieter moved his men forward along both sides of the lane.

More shooting came from off to the left of the Heggies, and some of them got up, moving away from a threat that seemed closer than the two platoons of Freebies in the avenue.

Dem led his men into the fight. He had managed to get another ten magazines of cartridges for his rifle during his hours in the base. Several support vans were carrying them. He went through two magazines in a hurry now. There appeared to be a full company of Heggies trying to infiltrate the base. The sound of the Havoc explosion had drawn Dem like a magnet. His men had turned the corner from the next avenue and seen what was happening.

The new rifle continued to prove its worth. Dem kept a light finger on the trigger, firing two or three shot bursts, moving the gun from side to side, sweeping Heggies away with a facility that no zipper could match. He didn't even bother to go down low. Wire came his way, but Dem scarcely paid attention—other than to target the guns that were aimed his way. He felt impregnable. He felt stinging pricks against both arms, then against his legs. Wire hits: Dem registered that fact but hardly felt the wounds. Not until after he had emptied a second magazine did he bother to drop to the ground for cover.

When he had a full magazine in his rifle again, he tried to raise himself up to get a better angle of fire—and discovered that his legs would no longer support him.

He did not allow that to keep him from shooting. The rifle was still a new toy, his pride and joy. Dem smiled. Wire dinged off his helmet and bit into his left arm—again.

This time the arm went completely numb, useless. It still didn't matter. He could fire the rifle just as accurately with one hand.

His finger was still pulling the trigger up to the instant when he finally lost consciousness from the loss of blood.

Echo's 2nd and 4th platoons moved forward together. Twenty-five zippers kept firing into the Heggies at the southern edge of the base. Fire and maneuver: one platoon covered the other as it moved forward, then they reversed roles. When they reached the corners of the two buildings, they were within thirty meters of the largest concentration of Heggie infantrymen—who were also under fire from their left.

Three minutes more and the shooting stopped. A half dozen Heggies dropped their weapons and stood with their hands raised. Perhaps another twenty Heggies were wounded, unable to get up.

"Sauv, Mort, separate those men from their weapons," Joe said. Mort had taken over the second squad after Low's death. "Al, check our people first." Joe looked back the way they had come. There were a half dozen men from the two platoons down, though all were still moving enough to show that they were still alive.

Then Joe looked down along the edge of the building at the other group of men who had joined in the fight. Most of them were still in firing position, their guns trained steadily on the Heggies who had surrendered.

Joe walked over that way. Three of the Accord uniforms were down and motionless. When Joe saw the new rifle, he knew that one of the downed men was Dem Nimz. Reccers. Another of them had turned Dem over on his back and was working to stop the bleeding. Joe knelt next to them.

"How bad is it?" he asked. Nimz seemed to be covered in blood from his shoulders to the tops of his boots.

"Damn fool didn't even try to get down," the other reccer said. "Anyone else in the platoon did that, he'da knocked his legs out from under him." He gestured at Dem's legs. "Heggies did it for him. We've got to get him to the hospital. He's lost a lot of blood.''

''Here, I'll give you a hand.'' Joe slung his rifle and helped pick Nimz up. ''Hospital's just around the corner.''

More casualties were what the hospital needed least. Two reccers were dead. Nimz was the most seriously hurt of the wounded—from the recon patrol or from Echo's two platoons. There were three other men who needed treatment, but Al Bergon was able to handle those. The Heggie wounded would have to wait. They were carried up the lane near the entrance to the hospital and left under guard. The survivors of Nimz's patrol guarded them and provided what first aid they could.

Echo's two platoons started south again. Captain Keye wanted them back, as quickly as they could make it. The fighting farther down the peninsula was getting rough. The sounds of Havoc firing had resumed, a constant background noise, and the distant sounds of explosions as their shells reached their targets.

Mort was on point for 2nd platoon, even though his new position as squad leader should have moved him farther back. ''The point's my place,'' he had told Joe. ''I wouldn't feel comfortable anyplace else.''

The two platoons moved west, then turned south when they got to the shore, hoping to avoid any contact with Heggies until they rejoined the rest of Echo Company. There was not a single man in either platoon who did not hope—fervently—that the fighting would be over before they arrived. If Mort moved a little more slowly than he usually did on point, no one faulted him for it, not even his platoon sergeant.

Although the sun had been up for less than an hour, the morning was already stiflingly hot. The night breeze had disappeared, and there wasn't even a hint of shade on the beach.

When they passed the line of Heggie bodies left from the start of the attack, the two platoons moved back inland. Then Joe called Captain Keye. ''Where do we go from here?'' he asked after reporting their position. He could see the near end of the Accord line ahead, still perhaps two kilometers away.

Keye gave him instructions. ''Head southwest from where you're at. We should be the first unit you come across, right at the corner. We've turned them away from the shore on this side . . . mostly. Now we're trying to keep them from breaking through in the center and consolidating.''

The two platoons started moving on a compass heading. The ground sloped down toward the sea on their left and up toward the central ridge of the peninsula at their right. They were within five hundred meters of the rest of Echo Company when the Heggies sprung the ambush. The shooting came from the right, from higher ground. The Heggies were between sixty and eighty meters from the two platoons, close enough for wire to be fully effective. The initial bursts hit 4th platoon harder than 2nd, but both had men go down hit.

At first, Joe Baerclau wasn't even aware that he had been wounded again. His legs went out from under him and he fell, but he had just started to react to the ambush. His mind had already sent his body the command to drop. Before the impulse could reach his muscles, though, he was hit. A grenade went off fairly near and he could hear wire zipping past him. Some of the wire, he was vaguely aware, did not go past.

There was a little cover for the men of the two platoons once they went flat. They were pinned down, but the Heggies couldn't get at them without exposing themselves. For several minutes the groups exchanged desultory fire, neither side doing much additional damage.

That was all of the time that this group of Heggies had, though. Artillery rounds started dropping along the ridge where they were, five explosions just seconds apart. And the rest of Echo was responding to a call from help from Dieter Franzo, moving south, firing on the Heggies from the other side.

Joe Baerclau had lost interest in the fighting, though. He didn't feel any pain at all. He was conscious. His thoughts seemed to be coherent, but they weren't the proper thoughts. He needed nearly a minute to realize that he was looking up at the sky, that he was on his back rather than on his stomach. To remember where he was.

He blinked several times, slowly. The sounds of fighting were there, but they hardly impinged on his awareness. After a long delay, Joe finally realized that he had been wounded.

Pretty bad this time, I guess, he thought. Another very slow blink. There was no pain, anywhere. When he tried to move, he had difficulty, but still no pain. But he *could* move. He managed to turn over a little, partly onto his left shoulder, and he was able to lift his head. Eventually. He looked down along his body, as much of it as he could see, looking for blood—the evidence of his injuries.

His inspection went only as far as his thighs, though. For a very good reason. Both legs were gone above the knee.

CHAPTER
26

Echo Company's 2nd platoon walked away from the ambush as a single squad of nine men. Sauv was in command. Mort took the point again, for the few minutes that the platoon was moving in column order. But then the entire company moved into a skirmish line and turned south again. The company's 5th platoon made the trip back to the base with the seriously wounded this time—5th platoon with one addition.

The Heggie counterattack down the center of the peninsula had failed. The pocket on the east side was rapidly collapsing. Half of the 13th was moving across the neck of land to add their numbers to the fight on the west side.

Another two hours of combat saw an end to any unified resistance by the Schlinal troops on Tamkailo, but mopping up operations took most of the rest of the day.

Joe Baerclau managed to think that it was peculiar that he had not lost consciousness at any point, despite the shock and loss of blood. Al had been at his side before Joe was even fully aware of what had happened, tying tourniquets around the stumps of his legs and applying large medpatches over the open wounds, to stop the bleeding and prevent the destruction of more tissue. An analgesic patch over Joe's spine ensured that he would feel no pain.

Then there was the long haul back to the hospital for Joe and three other serious casualties. On belts. That proved to be a tricky business for the man guiding Joe. With both legs gone above the knee, the Bear was top heavy. The stabilizers had to work constantly to keep him vertical— which meant that he swayed back and forth quite a bit.

Al Bergon made the trip, the one healthy addition to 5th platoon. He took Joe in tow personally. He talked the entire way, but the words made no impression on Joe. The words went in and through without pausing long enough for him to bother really to *listen* to them. He was too busy looking at the sky, absorbed by that. Even thinking about his wounds—and the months that recovery, regeneration, and rehabilitation would take—was too much bother. The sky was *so* blue, without even a hint of a cloud anywhere in sight.

A peaceful sky.

Major General Kleffer Dacik walked back into the warehouse he had turned into his headquarters and took off his helmet. He simply let it drop to the floor. It was two hours past noon. There was no longer the slightest doubt about the outcome of the Tamkailo campaign. There were still some few Heggies fighting, but they could no longer hope to reverse the outcome. Then there were munitions and other supplies to destroy—or remove. Grunt work. Nothing would be left for the Heggies on Tamkailo except for empty buildings and the bodies of their dead.

"General, CIC says that the Heggie fleet is gone. They just made the jump to hyperspace," Jorgen Olsen reported. There had been two additional skirmishes between the fleets after the first battle, but the later clashes had been minor.

The only losses had been to Bats and Boem S3s.

Dacik sat heavily on a crate of uniforms. He stared at Olsen and, after a moment, nodded slowly. The general had just come from the field hospital. Seeing the carnage left to repair, and getting updated reports on the numbers of dead and wounded from his subordinate commanders, had taken too much from Dacik for him to feel even relief at this latest evidence that the battle for Tamkailo had been won.

The cost.

"Sir, Admiral Kitchener wants to know when you plan to start moving the men back up to the ships," Colonel Ruman said.

That caught enough of Dacik's attention for him to look up.

"He wants to start making plans for retrieval," Ruman added when the general didn't speak.

Dacik shook his head, a minimal gesture, then hauled in enough breath to talk. It required an unprecedented effort.

"I'm not sure yet. Certainly not before sunset for the bulk of the troops and equipment." He hesitated, then said, "Make arrangements to start moving the wounded up as soon as possible. They'll get better treatment aboard ship."

"Shuttles are already on their way down for the wounded, along with an extra surgical team. The field hospital's already been on to the admiral about that."

Dacik got to his feet again, moving as if he were three times his age. Movement *hurt*. "Tell the admiral that I'll get on to him as soon as I know what's going on. I'll try to start cycling units up by local sunset. The rest . . ." He made a vague gesture with both arms. "The rest depends on how long it takes us to account for the last of the enemy and destroy their supplies. With any luck at all, we'll be ready to lift everyone off by midnight."

Then the general walked away from his staff. Only Captain Lorenz, his aide, went with him, and Lorenz knew not to get too close to the general now unless invited. Dacik went to a corner and stood there staring at the intersection of two walls. It was several minutes before he turned halfway and gestured for Lorenz to come closer.

"Hof, there's only one thing that could possibly begin to make our losses here justifiable."

"Sir?" Lorenz prompted when the general went silent again.

"The thing that Mizatle and Hobarth kept harping on when they dumped this campaign in my lap. They said they thought that if we did a thorough job on Tamkailo, the Hegemony wouldn't be able to mount another offensive against us for a year or more, that it might well be enough to end the war between us."

"You think that'll happen, General?" Hof was genuinely curious about the answer to that question.

"I don't know." Dacik shook his head. "I *want* to believe that it will, but . . ."

There was absolutely no need for him to finish that thought.

EPILOGUE

There was never any formal cease-fire between the Accord of Free Worlds and the Schlinal Hegemony. There were no official diplomatic contacts of any sort. But as the result of a number of unofficial "non-meetings" a tacit understanding developed of the "You don't attack us and we won't attack you" variety.

No one in the Accord government counted on the understanding remaining understood one minute longer than the Hegemony thought they needed it.

Shortly after the return of the fleet from Tamkailo, Kleffer Dacik was awarded a cluster of medals, promoted to lieutenant general, and quietly transferred to a post at Headquarters, Accord Ministry of Defense. Although nothing was ever committed to writing, it was clearly understood that Dacik would never again be permitted to command troops in combat.

His victories were too expensive.